REFUGE

SHOCK POINT
BOOK 8

DC LAYTON
MIKE KRAUS

MUONIC
P R E S S

REFUGE
Shock Point Series
Book 8

By
DC Layton
Mike Kraus

© 2023 Muonic Press Inc
www.muonic.com

www.MikeKrausBooks.com
hello@mikeKrausBooks.com
www.facebook.com/MikeKrausBooks

CONTENTS

WANT MORE AWESOME BOOKS?

Find more fantastic tales right here at books.to/readmorepa.

***

If you're new to reading Mike Kraus, consider visiting his website at www.mikekrausbooks.com and signing up for his free newsletter. You'll receive several free books and a sample of his audiobooks, too, just for signing up, you can unsubscribe at any time and you will receive absolutely *no* spam.

***

Thank you for checking out Shock Point! This series was written as a collaboration between Mike Kraus and several individual authors listed below, the collection of which appears on the cover as D.C. Layton, and is the result of many months of hard work. We hope you enjoy it!

Kate Pickford
AM Scott
S.M. Schaefer
S.D. Clayton
Katy Hollway
Ann B Harrison
Judy Clothier

***

Special Thanks

Special thanks to my awesome beta team, without whom this book wouldn't be nearly as great.

Thank you!

SPECIAL THANKS

Special thanks to my awesome beta team, without whom this book wouldn't be nearly as great. Thank you!

BOOK ONE, SUMMARY:

Encircle Energy is celebrating the development of their revolutionary, non-toxic fracking formula by using it simultaneously in locations around the globe. Test sites include, but are not limited to: Australia, Las Vegas, Ohio, Arizona, and underwater off the coast of British Columbia.

In Las Vegas, Dr. Marina Goode, Encircle's Chief Scientist, oversees the launch of their new product. Her boss claims the credit, but knowing her formula will allow for cheaper, safer fracking, makes up for the slight. But when the demonstration turns into a fiery hell, killing reporters, politicians, and her coworkers, her boss wastes no time pinning the blame on her and imprisoning her in the company's penthouse, with a mandate to fix something she didn't break.

Encircle's headquarters are in danger of collapse, so Dr. Goode and security consultant, Blake Watson, escape and take refuge in an abandoned prison, where Marina hopes to build a lab and find a way to stem the unending fires, before the world swallows itself whole. Their plans are scuppered when they discover the prison has already been claimed by a hardened criminal.

Reporter Nora Bennani plans to blow the lid off of Encircle Energy's corrupt practices. She has proof that Encircle has bribed safety officials, gotten workers killed, and worse, there are credible rumors of slave labor.

When the undersea fracking births a volcano beneath their cruise ship, Nora escapes, but her family dies. Determined to get revenge, Nora will stop at nothing to bring the head of the parent company down.

She travels across the country, piecing together a dynamite story about Encircle Energy and its parent company, Martinez Corporation, but is met with organized resistance. While she's trying to find Martinez's imprisoned workers, none other than Michael Martinez orders that she be neutralized.

In Ohio, sculptor Evelyn Parker is content with her secluded life. Medication keeps her anxiety at bay, and her estranged husband's prolonged absences allow her breathing room. When everything around her explodes, Evelyn is sure remaining in her house is the only way to stay safe, but she's forced out of her comfort zone when her friend and neighbor, Floyd Beck, is critically injured by falling debris. Making matters worse, her husband, Jack, shows up, her medication runs out along with the electricity, and the boys next door turn out to be more than brats—they're murderers.

Evelyn begs Jack to go to Colorado with her, to find her daughter, Sandy. Jack forbids it, imprisoning her in her own home. It isn't until Evelyn has to face down the thieving neighbors that she finds her spine and decides to head out for Colorado, with or without Jack.

Meanwhile, Michael Martinez, the head of Encircle Energy's parent company, will not go down with the ship like his father did. No, he'll not only survive, he'll command this new world. And if he can take out Nora Bennani, the reporter who left his father to die along the way, he'll be one happy billionaire. He orders Nora's execution and, just to keep things lively, charges one of his goons to chase Jen McCreedy off the land his granddaddy once owned. After all, he needs a place that's way inland, to hole up until the tectonic plates get a grip and stop rattling civilization. Chaos brings opportunity.

BOOK TWO, SUMMARY:

Feisty and independent, widowed rancher, Cat Murphy, reigns over her desert estate with grit and grace. She's scratched and clawed her way up to build a state of the art horse facility and the cattle operation of her dreams. But when the nearby Encircle fracking rigs blow up, her idyllic world is blown sky high and all hell breaks loose.

The cartel have a people-smuggling ring that runs through Cat's land. Cat fights back, driving them from her land and is critically injured, only to find them ransacking her neighbor's ranch. With little more than a rope and some gasoline, Cat once again bests the invaders, but her beloved horse falters and splinters her leg, evacuees from a nearby city try to rob her, while the fracking fires are growing ever closer. Cat's injury renders her lame, but she presses herself at every turn, blunting the pain with whisky, until finally her injuries require surgical intervention.

Meanwhile, in northern Arizona, Jen McCreedy lives a hermit-like life, just the way she likes it. She raises chicken, grows a garden, and interacts with the nearby town folk as little as possible, preferring the company of her dogs. She gets caught in an earthquake-driven landslide returning from town, but it turns out she's not the only victim.

A child, Robin, is orphaned in front of her eyes, and the choice to rescue her a terrifying responsibility. Despite the little girl's pleading, she must turn her over to the authorities if any can be found in the madness.

The problem is, the authorities have their hands full. The area is cut off from all outside assistance and Michael Martinez's henchman, Charlie Billings, has been tasked with driving Jen from her land so that his pal can hunker down on her farm. He starts his offensive by insisting that Jen has to allow the townsfolk to camp out on her land "until the dust settles." Jen can't find a way to fend them all off, so she reluctantly allows her pasture to be turned into a campground for the displaced villagers.

Legal immigrant Alma Garcia was torn from her parents, and put to work on Encircle Energy's manufacturing lines, along with her younger sister and brother. Her mother charged Alma with keeping them safe, and she has, by keeping her head down and shoulder to the wheel. But when they're suddenly moved in the middle of the night and split apart, Alma must find new strength and rescue Emelia and Matias, and then find her parents, crossing a vast empty country she doesn't know, all while surviving earthquakes, the waterless desert and more people determined to take advantage of them. But she must succeed, or betray her mother's trust and break her father's heart.

BOOK THREE, SUMMARY:

Unable to find a laboratory in the shattered remains of Las Vegas, Dr. Marina Goode and security consultant Blake Watson find themselves at a prison, but they're not alone. Beset by trials, Marina and Blake fight off criminals, rogue soldiers, and their former allies.

Blake calls in a favor and hitches a ride to Northern Arizona University, where Marina and a resident biologist finally crack the mystery of the corrupted fracking solution.

Sculptor Evelyn Parker has lost her home and life's work to the treacherous Lewis twins. When her husband, Jack, is kidnapped by those murdering scumbags, she and her neighbor Floyd Beck join forces with Floyd's sister's militia to fight for Jack's life.

Firefighter Kit Walsh, on a wildland fire in the middle of nowhere, Idaho, has had enough—the earthquakes are causing trees to fall, and the increasing ash isn't from a fire. He's not obeying orders, or staying on the line, until he makes sure his wife is safe. When he finds out their Tacoma home is under a lava and mudflow, he leaves the wildfire fight, determined to find Taylor—even if it costs him his life.

Michael Martinez, CEO of Encircle Energy's parent company, is on a mission to rescue his only living sister. If you're in his way, you're as good as dead.

BOOK FOUR, SUMMARY:

Saddled with the local townsfolk who despise and revile her, Jen McCreedy must find a way to organize and feed them. Food and tempers are running short, and her greatest detractors—the wily and conniving Charlie Billings among them—are only good at making trouble. Despite her instincts to run and hide, Jen must step up and lead, or lose everything.

Reunited with Taylor, his wife, firefighter Kit Walsh travels south, through ash-darkened and earthquake-riven land, to find his only living relative—the aunt who took him in when his mother went to Jail. Tensions between Kit and Taylor mount as Kit entertains ideas that his best friend, Sean, might have eyes for Taylor.

Alma Garcia and her siblings—Emelia and Matias—find refuge in the deserted house where they were once held prisoner. Her victory is cut short when their vicious captor, Eric, returns. Alma fights to protect her sister and brother from Eric's deadly assault, but it's Matias and a cast iron frying pan that save the day.

In southern Arizona, Catherine "Cat" Murphy's ranch is on unsteady ground. Her former foreman and sometime-friend, Tom, has broken her trust by amputating her leg and he's madder than a hornet about her not-so-secret drinking. With the world exploding around them and the people-smugglers still in play, Cat and Tom have to team up to survive.

Nora Bennani has found some of the workers enslaved by Encircle Energy only to discover that Encircle also stole their children and used them as bargaining chips to keep the workers in line. No one dares break free for fear their children will die. With nothing left to lose, Nora sets out to find the workers' kids.

BOOK FIVE, SUMMARY:

Alma Garcia knows nothing about the dangers of crossing the desert or life in the wild. Her little brother, bitten by a snake, needs urgent medical treatment but there are only miles of wasteland all around them. She meets the leader of a large family and begs for direction to the nearest hospital, but they only want what she has. The family commandeers her van to take their dying father back to their farm where their mother gives birth, their father deteriorates and dies, and their grandparents make it clear that Alma and her kind are not welcome. Alma sneaks into the night and disappears, her only goal, to reach her parents.

Evelyn Parker is on a mission to reach Boulder, Colorado, where she hopes to find her estranged daughter, Sandy. But the journey is beset by setbacks. Not only is the earth conspiring against them, her almost-ex-husband, Jack, undermines her at every turn, while the Lewis twins attack their position, killing some of their band. After burying their dead, Evelyn, Jack, neighbor Floyd and his sister, Dana, hit the road again. Evelyn insists they pick up a young hitchhiker, April, who, in a twist no one saw coming, is also on the run from the Lewis brothers.

Eugenia "Jen" McCreedy must find a way to organize and feed the evacuees from the nearby town, Jackrabbit Bluff. Food and tempers are running short, and her greatest detractors are only good at making trouble. Despite her instincts to run and hide, Jen must step up and lead, or lose everything.

Jen, Doc, and Doc's son Aaron agree that it's time to take Robin into the city, to find her kin, but the city's in freefall and they hightail it back to Harmony Ranch, where Charlie Billings has attempted a coup. With the help of Stone, the friendly neighbor Jen didn't know she needed, Charlie's run off her land, leaving them to pick up the pieces.

Kit Walsh, his wife, and their best friend, Sean, travel south, through ash-darkened and earthquake-riven land, to northern Arizona. While scrounging for supplies, they stumble into a town that's being run by people claiming to be Kaibab Tribe, but Kit and Sean work out that the so-called tribe are nothing but a bunch of bikers, masquerading as Indians. The 'tribal' leader offers supplies in exchange for work, but Taylor counsels the men to be as deliberately clumsy as possible, with an eye to escape. The firefighters rig a building for collapse and Kit charges the bikers, providing the ultimate distraction, so that Sean and Taylor can run for their lives.

Still reeling from the loss of her leg, Cat Murphy and her new-found clan must protect the ranch—and each other—from those who would steal their supplies. Tom leaves the homestead in search of a lost pickup. The rain is fierce and the rivers and runoffs are rising. What should have been a two-hour trip turns into a three-day absence. Cat sets out to find Tom and pulls him, half drowned, from the raging flood. Cat and Tom agree that from now on, they'll stick together, come hell or high water.

Having razed his Vegas home to the ground, and murdered his former servant, Taj, Michael Martinez plots his next move. His assistant, Lisa, shows Michael all of Nora Bennani's videos, making

Nora, not just Public Enemy Number One, but a 'She Devil' in his book.

Though the cell towers are down, there are still SAT phones and HAM radios in play and they stumble on a video from Dr. Marina Goode, Encircle Energy's Chief Scientist, who's camped out at a University, claiming she has a microorganism that will stop the ground from quaking.

Michael plans a trip to Harmony Ranch, which he's tasked his lackey, Charlie Billings, with securing. Once the ranch is his, he'll have a secure base from which to deal with all these troublesome women.

BOOK SIX, SUMMARY:

Alma Garcia flees her friend Simeon's home when she overhears his grandparents saying she and her siblings aren't welcome. The trio stumble on an abandoned town and are helping themselves to supplies—food, water, and bicycles—when the local heavies roll by. The Garcia children are chased out of town, forced to abandon their van, and hike down to the river with their new bicycles to avoid detection.

The river's treacherous waters take Emelia under and her leg is injured in the rescue. Alma decides to hunt for medical supplies, but is spotted by Harmony Ranch's very own Doc Boleski. He insists the children can stay at Harmony Ranch while Em recuperates.

Nora Bennani—along with former Martinez workers Dunia and Faris—pairs up with local Native American Indian, Kaya, in their ongoing search for the Martinez factory-worker children. Nora receives a satellite call from fellow reporter David Miller, who claims Nora's former boss, Harvey Cosbie, has told him where to find the children. Nora and her friends take temporary refuge at Harmony Ranch before pressing on to Thompson Springs where Miller says the children are being warehoused.

Jen McCreedy and the doc juggle the demands of Harmony

Ranch with the dire medical needs of the newest arrivals, a couple who speak some English, more Spanish, and what sounds like Arabic. The husband, who insists his name is Juan, won't talk about the wife's injuries, terrified of something neither Jen nor the doc can identify.

Kevin, a Jackrabbit Bluff local, invites Jen to go on a scavenger hunt with him and his children. They've been harvesting plants from local gardens that have been abandoned. At the sound of gunfire, they flee back to the ranch and arrive in time to see Juan and his wife being gunned down as they flee Jen's property. Juan's dying wish is that his wife 'never stops looking for our beautiful children.'

Sculptor Evelyn Parker crosses the exploding heartland of America—while battling withdrawal from her anti-anxiety meds—in a race to get to her daughter's place in Golden, Colorado before the murderous Lewis gang does. She convinces her neighbor and fellow traveler, Floyd, and his warrior-sister, Dana that they should pick up April, a hitchhiker who claims she's also being hounded by the Lewis gang.

April is, by turns, charming and conniving, eventually poisoning her hosts in a bid to escape. She's recaptured and drinks contaminated ditchwater. As her health deteriorates, April confesses that she's in cahoots with Nathan Lewis and plans to help him gain access to Sandy. April faulters and dies. Evelyn grieves April's betrayal and her senseless passing but presses on, finally kicking her bully of a husband, Jack Parker, out of her life once they reach Golden, only to have her daughter Sandy shut her door in her face.

Kit Walsh, his wife Taylor, and their friend Sean escape the biker gang in Kanab with the help of the local Kaibab Band of Paiute Indians. The Band leaders make it clear the trio are welcome for a meal and no more so the three friends press on to Kit's aunt's place. Their journey is beset by trials, until finally the threesome survive a wildfire where Kit's hands are badly burned.

Harmony Ranch's Dr. Carlton Boleski, who's tending to Emelia Garcia's wounds, sends Alma to collect his medical bag from the sick room, where Alma is stunned to find her mother, pale and wan and grieving the death of her husband, the man who insisted his name was Juan.

The Garcia children are reunited with their mother, who tells Alma just how proud she is of all her hard work, only minutes before she dies. Once again, Alma and her little brother and sister are alone in a dangerous, friendless world.

Michael Martinez is headed for Harmony Ranch, which his granddaddy gifted to Jen McCreedy rather than seeing it fall back into the hands of the Indians. He and his crew take a detour to one of the Martinez factory-camps, in hopes of picking up some of the human assets that have remained there. The roads are covered in rock fall and the extra hands will make light of the work.

The work camp is a disaster, the assets lice-ridden and starving. Michael has to convince them to strip the dead of their clothes, so that they're not traveling with his convoy buck naked.

His sister, Helen—who's already proven a pain in the rear—rebels when she sees the work conditions and sides with the workers.

The convoy presses on through the earthquake-racked land, Helen bleating, his assistant Lisa proving more and more reliable, and his men ready for action.

They come upon a small, well-stocked town and take the children hostage until the townsfolk give up all the stocks and supplies Michael wants.

When Michael finally reaches the outskirts of Harmony Ranch, he discovers his man, Charlie Billings, hasn't secured the property, but has been lying about his progress. He shoots Charlie dead, to prove a point: Obey or die.

Harmony Ranch is within reach and Michael intends to take it.

BOOK SEVEN, SUMMARY:

Michael Martinez and his heavily-armed crew arrive outside Jackrabbit Bluff, but a massive rockfall blocks their progress. Michael approaches Harmony Ranch on foot, spots Alma Garcia—though he doesn't know who she is by name, only that she's one of his child-assets—which presents him with a unique conundrum. If the adult-assets in his convoy realize there are Martinez-camp child-assets at Harmony Ranch they're going to riot.

Helen continues to champion the rights of the adult-assets he collected from the camp. Furious, Michael convinces Helen to leave the convoy and head back to their Aunt's place near Sedona, where she can create her own workers paradise.' She agrees and leaves Michael, assets in tow, killing two birds with one stone.

Michael turns back to the matter at hand: taking Harmony Ranch back from Jen McCreedy. His crew sets to work, moving the rocks that have buried the road by hand, but the slide shifts during a quake burying one of Michael's men and slowing their progress. They rescue their comrade, but Michael can't wait for the road to be cleared. He and a small troupe sneak down to Harmony Ranch on foot. He creeps up on Jen McCreedy and overhears her telling the doc that his father, Martinez Sr., fathered another son.

Michael spots Nora Bennani and hatches a plan to infiltrate Harmony Ranch without his army. He convinces his head of security, Roger Campbell, to punch him in the face to further compound his disguise then he and Lisa approach Harmony's main gate, claiming they've been robbed and need safe haven.

The duo are taken in, Michael's wounds dressed, while Lisa befriends everyone in sight. Their intelligence gathering is a success. They come to find out they've just missed Nora, who left Harmony Ranch in search of his missing child-assets. Michael and Lisa leave the Ranch and return to his heavily armed crew, the other side of Jackrabbit Bluff.

Evelyn Parker hides outside her daughter Sandy's house in Golden, Colorado until Nathan Lewis and his gang attack. After a fierce battle, Nathan flees. Evelyn doesn't know if he's injured, dead, or on the war path.

Sandy's boyfriend, Dev, claims to have access to an underground sanctuary, built by his father, deep under Apache Mountain. He invites Evelyn's crew to act as their security detail as they travel toward their safe haven.

Sandy insists that they're close enough to Flagstaff to collect Dr. Marina Goode, her friend and mentor. Dr. Goode has been working on a solution to the global fracking problem. When they arrive at Marina's laboratory, it's clear something has gone very wrong. The good doctor waves from a window, warning Sandy not to approach the building—the solution she's been working on has been contaminated and rather than spread the contagion further, Dr. Goode blows her lab up, with her inside.

Evelyn lets slip that she had an uncle, who disappeared from their lives when she was just a kid. Sandy's furious that she's been denied access to her extended family and demands that they track down this long-lost uncle. Evelyn takes them to her uncle's last known residence, where they're reunited with none other than Thomas Callahan, cowboy and Rancho Seco supervisor.

Evelyn and Sandy try to convince Uncle Tom and his boss/friend Cat Murphy to come with them to the underground city at Apache Mountain, but Cat's not willing to leave her beloved ranch.

Evelyn, Floyd, Dana, Sandy and Dev press on only to be attacked again by Nathan Lewis just as they reach their final destination. Evelyn is badly wounded, but Dana ends Nathan Lewis' life, right before she dies.

Battered and bruised, Evelyn, Floyd, Sandy and Dev must prepare for an influx of people, and design rules to keep all of them safe; deciding who stays in the safety of the underground haven and who's to be cast out into the encroaching nuclear winter.

Nora, Dunia, and Kaya are reunited with the stolen Martinez children—to tears and elation –but the return to Harmony Ranch is fraught with challenges. They come upon an armed, hostile road-block and come under fire—whether it's the Hutchison militia or some other thugs doesn't matter—Nora has to keep the children safe. She sends them back toward Harmony Ranch with Dunia, while she provides a decoy.

Kit, Taylor, and Sean survive a wildfire where Kit's hands are badly burned. They make it across the Navajo Bridges at Marble Canyon, but at the last moment, Sean's load of supplies prevents him from escaping, and he falls to his death. Taylor and Kit barely reach Kit's aunt's place, Harmony Ranch, desolate and heartbroken, but immediately make themselves useful by helping to prepare the ranch for an attack by outsiders.

Kit's aunt, Jen McCreedy welcomes him back with open arms. She's been waiting for him all this time, but she's a strange bird who blows hot and cold and he's not entirely sure what to make of her. She's holding something back, but he doesn't know what and doesn't know how to ask.

Emilia Garcia takes a shine to Kit and follows him about the ranch as he hunts, tracks, and creates booby traps. There are signs that Harmony Ranch has been infiltrated, but Kit's never able to catch an invader red handed. Kit stays on high alert, ready for the coming invasion.

Michael Martinez haunts the outskirts of Harmony Ranch, certain that Nora Bennani will return. When she does, he doesn't hesitate, stabbing her in the back and piercing her heart, thereby ridding himself of his greatest enemy.

Which leaves only one challenge: Michael vows to haunt the woods around Harmony Ranch, picking off the inhabitants one by one, until he circles his way to the prize: Jen McCreedy, the woman who claims his daddy was more than a cad, Martinez Sr. was, at least according to the McCreedy witch, Kit Walsh's father.

CHAPTER ONE

Alma Garcia. Harmony Ranch, Arizona

A gasping scream pierced Alma's fitful sleep. She bolted upright and rubbed her eyes. All the noises from the ranch—snoring, barking, chopping, hollering—drifted through the tent's thin walls, but the sobbing came from close by. She unzipped her compartment, the melodic rip of the teeth on the tight nylon of the inner tent loud in the early morning. Crawling to the other side of their temporary home, the ground sheet crackled under her hands and knees.

"Mati?" His unzipped door hung limp. She pushed the flap aside and climbed in. His air bed hardened under her weight and lifted him. "It's alright." He sat up and clung to her. "It was only a dream." She stroked his head, smoothing his hair. They had given him a buzz cut at the prison house, but it had grown out over the weeks of traveling and she preferred it longer. Their mother's rosary, slung around his neck, pushed against her ribcage. Matias never took it off.

His sobs faded. "It's not fair. We came all this way, looking for them, hoping, praying, believing we'd see them. And then Mama dies and Papa's gone. I hate it. I hate all of it."

Alma kissed the top of his head. "Me too." It wasn't a lie, but it

1

tasted like one in her mouth, because it wasn't a strong enough description. Words didn't do justice to the riot in her heart. Mama and Papa should've been the ones waking early to comfort him. Papa would have known how to chase the night terrors out of their dreams and Mama would have set up a fire, making something wonderful from the feast's leftovers. Kit's birthday had been a kind of time out, a moment of not-being-in-charge, a second when she could pretend she was a teenager, rather than the one in charge. If they'd stayed together—if that awful man hadn't ripped her parents away from them—her childhood might not be in tatters. Mati pulled away, but she clung a little longer, composing her face to hide her bitterness. He didn't need to know that she cursed the skies and wished each day away.

The campsite was stirring, accompanied by the incessant rumble of Mister H's thunderous snoring. Even camped on the edge of the displaced community, she couldn't escape the wheezing throat rattle that shook his tent. Matias settled down and Alma crawled back out. Emelia's compartment was open, and her bed empty.

Alma flopped back on her skinny airbed. They'd argued the night before—Em wanted to stay at the party, tell tales around the fire— but Alma had insisted they return to their tent and keep themselves to themselves. It was all good and well for everyone to pretend like it wasn't the end of the world, but Jen and the doc were already evicting newcomers and while she had no love for the too-smiling Sarah and her creepy husband, Blake, the fact that Jen was willing to send them back into the wild, after Blake had been beaten bloody, told her what she needed to know about her host's *real* intentions.

Emelia had stormed off, calling Alma some fairly colorful names. She'd probably run to her new bestie, the firefighter hero. Kit had infinitely more patience than Alma. If Emelia was that upset, perhaps Taylor let her stay with them, but it would have been nice if someone had checked with her first.

She hid her face in the crook of her elbow, shielding it from the encroaching day. There was nothing to look forward to. Only chores, followed by more chores, accompanied by the galling long faces of the women who were "so sorry to hear about your mother." She wanted to run screaming from their pity and hide in the fluttering shade of the trees.

Footsteps thudded on the hard ground and swished through the grass to the side of the tent. A guy-line twanged, the fiberglass poles curved, and the fabric shook. Condensation dripped from the low domed ceiling, splashing onto the plastic ground sheet. She had half a mind to scold Mati. It was his job to collect water. All water. Even the morning dew. She caught herself, mid-thought. How ugly she'd become. How petty. She took a long, measured breath and tried to conjure up her papa's face. He'd have taken her aside and told her a story. Maybe the one about the rabbit that had been so loved-up that it had lost an eye and gotten all threadbare. She could almost—not quite, but very nearly—hear his voice. She pushed on the memory, willing him back into the space he'd filled, but there was only silence. Then again, perhaps that was his gift to her? A moment of hallowed aloneness before her responsibilities kicked in?

"Ow!" Emelia's voice punctured her hard-won peace.

Alma rolled over on her airbed, her back to the door. Feigning sleep might mean she could avoid yet another argument she didn't have the energy for.

Emelia ripped the flap open, shaking the whole tent. Not even Matias would sleep through that racket.

"Alma." Emelia tugged on Alma's foot. "Alma?" Her voice was breathy, almost panting.

"Em?" Matias hadn't gone back to sleep.

Alma propped herself up. Emelia stood in the small communal square of the tent, casting a shadow on the thin nylon wall between them.

"Go back to sleep, Mati." Emelia's feet scuffed the ground sheet and her shadow moved toward Matias' sleep pod.

Alma pushed aside the dangling door. Emelia crouched by Matias' sleeping bag and tightened her jean jacket around herself. "If you wanted him to stay asleep, you should've been quieter sneaking in."

Emelia turned. Her wild hair, riddled with twigs and pine needles, framed her face. Her eyes were red and swollen, cheeks smeared with inexpertly applied war paint. Her lower lip trembled. She opened her jacket. Deep red stains blotted the front of her top. Blood.

Alma scrambled to her. "Are you hurt? What's bleeding?"

Emelia collapsed to the floor, her body quaking with sobs. "She's dead."

Alma ran her fingers over Emelia's face. "Who's dead?" No cuts, but the smears were a mixture of blood and earth. She checked her sister's arms and hands. Emelia's palms were coated with dried blood. "Are you hurt?" She lifted the edge of her shirt. Emelia pushed it down and swayed. "Don't you dare faint on me, Emelia Garcia." She lifted her sister's chin. "Look at me. Em! Me! Not your blouse!" *Not the blood. Look away from the blood.* "Who's dead?"

"Nora." Emelia's reply was weak, but she fixed her gaze on Alma.

"What?" That made no sense. Nora had left to find the other children enslaved by Martinez Corporation. She couldn't be dead.

"It's not my bl..." Emelia shook her head. "Nora's. I'm not hurt, but the blood..." Emelia blinked slowly and wobbled.

"What in the world? Em?" She shifted gears, taking charge and shucking her pouty wish to be a child. "Let's get you cleaned up. Mati, pass me the pot." She pointed to their water ration. His mouth fell open. "It's going to be okay. Stop worrying." She couldn't bear to see the crease between his eyes deepening. He was a kid, for crying out loud; he wasn't supposed to be in a state of constant anxiety.

"She said Nora was dead." He shuffled back. "But she's the one covered in blood."

Matias was right. But it didn't mean what he thought it meant. Emelia couldn't. She wouldn't... No matter what had happened, Emelia would never harm another soul. She was the most law-abiding citizen on the planet! She'd made survival harder—refusing to take what the three of them so obviously needed—in order to stay on the side of right. But other people might not see it that way. They didn't know Em the way she did. They'd see the blood, put two and two together, and get five; just like Mati had done! Alma needed to tidy up the mess and protect her sister. She needed to protect them all.

Emelia grabbed hold of Alma's wrist. Her fingers were icy cold.

"She's dead." She looked down at her blood-soaked clothes and swayed.

Alma lifted Emelia's face. "I'm sorry, I really am." She kissed her cheek. "You're going to be alright. Don't think about it." That would only make her think about it more. Alma bit her lip. "Think about pink elephants."

"Pink elephants?" Emelia gave a weak smile through chattering teeth and opened her eyes.

"Yeah, on motorbikes performing jumps through flaming hoops." It wasn't as good as one of Papa's stories, but she didn't have much practice. Alma patted the spot next to her. Matias put the bottle and the pot down. "You sit next to her and hold her up. Can you do that?"

"Wait." He rushed to his pod, pulled out his rabbit and then did exactly as she asked, his stuffed toy on his lap.

Emelia leaned her full weight against her little brother, the two of them sagging like a couple of battered tent poles. "Em, I'm going to clean you up and you're going to tell Matias all about those pink elephants." Emelia opened her mouth, but only a sob escaped.

Matias stroked Emelia's face. "There once was a rabbit, a special rabbit." Papa always started his stories that way. The gaping hole he left made Alma's heart ache. "He was fed up with being at home, so he went on an adventure. He'd heard about the amazing pink elephants that rode motorbikes." Emelia smiled, and her sob cracked into a laugh.

Alma poured a little water in the pot, dampened the facecloth and rubbed it on their bar of soap, then wiped the marks from Emelia's face, taking care that the grit didn't scratch her skin. Emelia didn't flinch, she was focused on Matias, who had taken to acting out his story with his rabbit. Alma pulled off Emelia's baggy denim jacket. Blood edged the cuffs and splashed up the front. She'd worn it everywhere since Kit had given it to her. Too small for him, it was too big for Em, but that meant nothing to her little sister who was near-on besotted with the firefighter. She'd want that jacket back, just as soon as the bloodstains had been scrubbed out.

Mati rattled on, the rabbit's adventures getting more and more elaborate, which gave Alma time to think things through. The adults at Harmony Ranch had talked candidly—almost boasting—about how they forced a man named Charlie and his friends to leave only days before Alma had arrived. They let Blake and Sarah stay long enough for the doc to pack his nose with gauze, and they'd made a big show of inviting them to Kit's birthday feast, but they were clear that they weren't going to be allowed to stay at the Ranch. A girl covered in blood would be judged and found guilty immediately, especially an immigrant. No one would believe or trust three kids who'd managed to travel so far alone. Kids with accents, kids who'd killed before. Alma camped on the edge of the community because she felt the hard, suspicious glares of the residents like knives to her soul.

Alma scrubbed Emelia's hands, careful to pare the grit and grime from under her nails. *So much blood.* Warm, running water would have made it all so much easier, but that luxury was a thing of the past.

The last ribbons of dirt swirled in the pot, the water pink as sin and twice as damning. All she was doing was moving filth from one spot to another. "Almost done. Mati, can you wait in your room while Em changes, please?" Matias scurried away with his rabbit. "I've got to pull your shirt over your head. Just close your eyes and hold your breath." Alma pulled the stiffened shirt off, balled it up and tucked it under her sleeping bag. Blood had soaked through to Emelia's chest. "Just a bit more cleaning. You are ok." Alma wiped it away and dried her off. "All done." She put an almost-clean blouse in Emelia's hands. "Here you go."

Emelia opened her eyes and hurriedly covered herself up. "Thank you." She pinched the fabric of her black leggings, peeling them off and leaving them on the ground in a human-shaped heap, as if someone had evaporated out of them. "Those have *stuff* on them too." She pulled her knees up to her chest and her feet away from the garment.

Stuff. Emelia couldn't even say the word. Alma picked up the leggings, crusty with Nora's life, and added them to the bloodstained pile. She threw the towel over them, hiding them from Emelia's view. The dressing across the wound on Emelia's leg was intact, though the edges of the sticky tape holding the pad over the cut were smudged deep red.

Emelia wriggled into a torn, bloodless pair of pants and fished twigs out of her hair. "I'm sorry I didn't come back last night. There was too much... I couldn't... and then I fainted."

"Slowly." Alma passed Emelia an oatcake from her ration box.

She took it and nibbled the slightly burned rim. "He killed her. I was down by the little stream. She was by those old, falling-down buildings that Kit and Taylor are working on. She was talking to him. Nora, not Taylor. Nora was talking to him." She took another bite, swallowing more than oats. Alma held her breath, wanting to know what had happened, but dreading it at the same time. "Well, shouting. Then she calmed down and turned her back on him." A tear spilled down her cheek, but Em did nothing to wipe it away. "She walked away, Alma. So calm. Almost like she was daring him to..." The tears came in earnest. "I wanted to say something, but I was frozen. She was walking and he was stalking and he didn't say a thing. He raised his blade high above his head and stabbed her. In the back. Like a coward."

Alma leaned in closer and lowered her voice, stroking her sister's trembling hand. "Who stabbed her?"

"Blake."

Wait, what? "The one with the broken nose? The one who just left the ranch?"

"Yes, but..." Em shook. "Alma..."

Alma chafed her sister's hands between her own, but it did nothing to calm either of them.

"I don't think Blake is Blake." Em's voice shook.

The knot in Alma's stomach tightened.

"They were arguing about 'the children' and 'slave labor.' That's us, right?"

Alma's hand moved to the spot on her head where she'd bashed it, falling in the factory.

"Blake is Michael, but with a beard."

The ice in Alma's veins was replaced by molten lava, then ice again. She could see his eyes, crawling over her, taking her in. "Michael Martinez? Are you sure?"

Emelia pulled another twig from her hair and snapped it in two. "I'm ninety-nine percent sure, Alma. It was him."

Alma had handed the rucksack with the passports of the missing children to Nora; the one woman doing all she could to reunite families that were torn apart. She'd given Nora the evidence proving Martinez's crimes. She'd put Nora in danger. He'd found her and murdered her because of it. "He came here for her." Alma shivered. "For Nora." He'd been in their midst, walked among them, harmed no one. It was all about Nora Bennani.

"Nora told everyone it was his fault." Emelia rubbed her eyes, momentarily childlike. "She was the one that filmed the wave and the boat. Kit said she'd been brave and told the world that Encircle Energy and Martinez Corporation was to blame. I didn't understand what he meant, but I guess, telling the truth put her in danger. He killed her for telling the truth, Alma."

Alma balled her fists. "Coward. She was worth a billion of him. She was doing all she could to repair what he destroyed."

"I tried to help her, but she was gurgling blood. There was so much, I couldn't stop it. I blacked out and when I woke up, she was dead." Emelia's sobs shook her body. "If I was a boy, I would've been alright. I'd be able to handle it. I could've saved her."

"Stop it." Alma cupped Emelia's face in her hands. "You've been through hell and got back to us. Don't you go wishing you were someone or something else."

Matias scuttled out from his pod and snuggled up to Emelia. "We should tell someone there's a dangerous man."

Alma frowned at him. "Why? He's done what he came here for. He'll be long gone." She stood as tall as the domed tent would allow. "We're not telling anyone." She hurried into her compartment, took off her sleeping clothes and pulled on a pair of her old pants and a donated T-shirt with a faded flower print. Both were dark and would help her hide.

"What?" Emelia got to her feet.

Alma stepped out and crossed her arms over her thundering heart. "If we tell them about Nora, who is going to believe us?"

Emelia pointed to each of them. "Er... We're children. Why wouldn't they believe us?"

Alma bit her lip and swallowed hard. "Because we've done it before." Emelia had a blank, questioning expression. "Eric. We killed him. Even if we aren't guilty of Nora's murder, they'll throw us out because of what we did to him. We are..." Alma grabbed her hoodie and corrected herself. "Well, I am, capable of it. I've already murdered a man. If everything was right in the world, they should punish me one way or another for what I did."

"He was a bad man, Alma." Matias pulled on her sleeve. "Where are you going?"

Emelia put her hands on her hips. She lowered her voice to barely a whisper. "They don't need to know about that."

"You'll lie to them, will you?"

"Yes." Emelia flushed red.

Alma shook her head. "You wouldn't. I know you."

"I'm not going to tell them about Eric." Emelia crossed her heart. "I promise. That's got nothing to do with them. We should tell them about Nora though."

"No. We're foreigners and they don't need an excuse to kick us out. You know they send people away." She shuddered. *What if they hadn't sent Blake/Michael away? Would he have recognized her? Had he, already?* The bile rose, almost as fast as the tears, and she bent and grabbed the tent's zipper.

"Where are you going?"

"I'm going to hide Nora's body." Alma turned. "If they can't find her, they won't ask questions and you won't need to lie. We'll be able to stay here, where it's safe."

CHAPTER TWO

Catherine "Cat" Murphy. Arivaca, Arizona

Her home shuddered, the ornate iron chandelier above the table swaying back and forth, crystals jangling, rainbow fractals flashing across the floor. Cat Murphy and Tom Callahan sat at her kitchen table, unspeaking. Except to cover their mug with one hand or the other, neither Cat nor Tom moved. The two stared out the picture windows, the morning light indiscernible from that of the midafternoon sun. The wilted desert had never been so desolate and lifeless.

Sitting across the table from one another, knees touching, they both gazed toward Old Mexico. She savored her rich, dark coffee as he sipped his tea. Fresh cream had become a luxury she'd decided to forgo, the children needed the nutrients far more than she did.

"Cat..." Tom put his thick, calloused hand over her equally weathered but smaller one. "I think it's time."

Time? It was hard to believe that it had been mere days since the Jordans had attacked their home. The invaders had killed Dan. But, in the end, only one member of the Jordan family had survived—Grady. Remorseful, he'd been quick to surrender.

Days later, another group of would-be marauders attempted to take over the headquarters while Tom's niece and her people were at the ranch. That group of scavengers had been easily dissuaded, but Dana had caught a bullet during the process. Over the past few weeks, with Cat's world upended and the struggle over life and death, the concept of time itself had changed.

The strange, orange skies above and the intermittent shuddering ground below had become commonplace. Instead of diminishing and returning to the steady earth and the vibrant blue Arizona sky of her memories, the tremors had become more frequent, and the sky had grown darker. The birds no longer sang, the creatures of the desert had all but disappeared, the cattle were weakening, and only six horses remained.

The words of Tom's great-niece reverberated inside her head, "*Indications of impending catastrophic volcanic activity... nuclear winter events ... acid rain... extinction events... worldwide starvation.*"

Swallowing, she nodded, unable to force words past the lump in her throat. The ranch was dying. Tom was right, it was time.

Hot tears spilled down her face. Another casualty of the apocalypse, her stoicism had perished somewhere between her beloved mare, Hazel's, fatal step and the burial of Dan Miller. No longer able to control her grief, she covered her face and sobbed.

"Oh, honey." Tom stood, turning her chair to face him. He lowered himself to his knees and she threw her arms around his neck. Wrapping his arms around her waist, he engulfed her, burying his face in her long, dark hair. "I know, darlin'. Believe me, I know."

Cat lifted her chin off his shoulder, keeping her damp cheek close to his leathery neck. "This isn't the same, Tom. You lost your place..." She let the rest hang in the air, unwilling to voice what might land as an accusation.

"You're right. I drank my place away. But that was a lifetime ago and, in any event, isn't the point. " He pulled back and took her by the shoulders, his pain-filled eyes piercing her to the bone. "You did all you could. There was nothing you could do to save yours."

She stuttered and blubbered, but she couldn't argue with him.

They were both right. No matter the reasons, losing the ranch wasn't just losing property. It wasn't just losing land, buildings, and livestock. It was the loss of a historical, living entity—an ancient family member that had endured generations. Rancho Seco had told countless stories of the past, had held all the gleaming potential of the future, and she was dying an ugly, inescapable death.

Tom rocked back onto his haunches, put a hand on the seat of his chair, and stood. "We lost half our water reserves when that bunch of yahoos shot up Dana and the headquarters' water tanks. And what's left has to be filtered before we can use it for anything. We don't have the resources to do that for our little tribe, let alone the livestock and greenhouses." His knees cracked as he stretched himself to full height. "Even the plants and animals don't like this light. The hens aren't reliable, the cow is barely giving enough milk, several of the horses look pretty puny..."

"I just can't wrap my brain around leaving Rancho Seco." Cat wiped her eyes. "What would we even take with us? How do you pack your life up for... for forever?"

"I don't know. It sounds like they've got the essentials figured out at that bunker." Putting his hands on his hips, Tom arched his back, stretching. "We'll probably need to pack pretty light. Luckily, I ain't got much left."

"Clothes, food and water for the trip, weapons and ammo, something to barter with along the way?" Her brain raced and bounced from logic to sentiment, ideas fluttering in and out of her mind. "I don't know, Tom. Can't we make it work here?"

"Well, we probably could... for a while. But, I think we oughta get there before it's too late." He gazed out the window, rubbing his chin. "And, if Evelyn's daughter is right, things are only gonna get worse —rapidly."

The screen door slammed and Jim Miller sauntered in carrying a milk pail. "Mornin', Ms. Murphy, Mr. Callahan."

Cat conjured up a smile. "Good morning."

"Mornin', Jim." Tom sat back down, his words overlapping hers.

The leggy cowboy set the bucket on the counter and stepped into the pantry. Emerging with a gallon glass jar, a funnel, and a flour sack cloth, he placed them next to the pail. He stacked the funnel in the jar, laid the cloth in the funnel, then poured the milk through his filtration system. Metering it as he went, he kept his attention on the stream of milk. "313's giving half the milk she did two weeks ago."

"Yeah." Tom knocked on the table twice. "We were just talking about that."

"I didn't mean to be eavesdropping, but I did overhear a sliver of what you two were saying." Jim finished pouring the milk, set his filtering apparatus in the sink, then screwed the lid on the half full jar. "'Strella and I have been talking about what Sandy said, too."

Tom and Cat exchanged a knowing look. He cleared his throat. "What are your thoughts, son?"

Jim strode over to the refrigerator, opened the door, and slid the jar of milk in behind the nearly empty jar of yesterday's milk. "She doesn't want to leave."

"Rancho Seco is dying, Jim..." Cat's voice cracked and trailed off.

The young man poured himself a cup of coffee. "That may be so, but we're relatively safe here, strategically speaking. We've already fought off several attacks. She doesn't want to take the children out into the unknown."

"Valid point." Tom raised his bushy eyebrows at Cat. "What are *your* thoughts, son?"

"Well, Ruby needs to stay with 'Strella..." Jim ambled closer to the couple, then leaned back against the island. "And I don't want to leave her."

"You don't want to leave Ruby? Or Estrella?" Cat tipped up her coffee cup, draining the last sip.

The young man studied his boots. "Both. I couldn't leave 'Strella to fend for herself." Jim looked up, his face set. "And, I need to keep my sisters together."

"You're a good man." Cat fidgeted with her empty mug. "But, how will you survive? It feels like everything around us is dying."

"I've been thinking about it, and I'm not sure what we'll do for greens, but we should be able to scrounge up enough hay and grain to keep some chickens and a couple of cattle alive."

Tom rose and skirted around the island, crouching down next to the range. "What about water?" Pots and pans banged together.

Jim didn't speak until the clanging stopped. "It's still monsoon season. If you'd let us stay on the place, I'm thinking we can jury rig a catchment system off the barn and machine shed roofs. And, I can weld good enough to repair the tank."

"Pardon my language, but that sounds like a hell of a gamble." Tom carried an empty stockpot and the coffee pot to the sink. Setting the coffee pot down on the counter, he put the stockpot in the basin and turned on the water. "Not to mention, a lot of work."

"I know, sir, but 'Strella's dug in pretty good and I've decided that I'm gonna do whatever I must to keep what's left of my family together."

While the stockpot filled, Tom leaned over Cat's shoulder and refilled her coffee cup. "I don't feel right about leaving you kids behind."

Cat twisted toward Tom. "They're not kids." She turned back to the young man. "I understand. This place is your home now, Jim. And, Tom, it's only a hundred miles away, they could always come to the bunker later."

"There might not be a later, Cat." Tom placed the stockpot on the stovetop, covered it with a glass lid, and cranked the knob to high. "They're locking the place down." He opened an upper cupboard, the building shook again. A cannister fell out, spilling oatmeal on the counter. "Damn it."

"We're gonna batten everything down and ride it out here." Jim hustled to get the broom and dustpan. "If your niece and her friends are wrong, you'll have Rancho Seco to return to." He swept the oatmeal into the dustpan.

"Make sure that gets put in with the chicken scraps, Jim." With his big mitt, Tom brushed the oatmeal from the counter back into its container. "It sounds like you've made up your minds."

"Yessir." The young man opened the cabinet under the sink and dumped the oats into a bowl where they saved any inedible food for the chickens.

"It isn't my place to tell you what to do..." Tom shook the oat cannister over the boiling pot, then added raisins and brown sugar. "So I won't. But, I will tell you this. We're sure gonna miss you young'uns." He picked up a wooden spoon and stirred the concoction.

"Miss us?" Lil had entered the room while Cat was focused on Tom. "Where are we going?" She ran over to her big brother, her only brother.

"We're not going anywhere, Lil." Jim took his sister under his arm and squeezed her.

Tom continued stirring the breakfast. "Ms. Murphy and I are going to that bunker Evelyn and her friends told us about."

"What? No!" The freckled little redhead stomped her foot. "We need to stay together."

Cat shifted in her seat. "As much as we would love that, it just isn't practical. We're afraid the trip would just be too hard on the littlest ones."

"Then why are you going? Why are you leaving us?"

Not wanting to scare the child with terms like 'nuclear winter,' Cat chose her words with care. "If we leave, your resources will go further."

"That doesn't make sense." Lillie pulled away from Jim. "Mr. Callahan *is* a resource."

"True, sweetie." Cat reached for the girl. "But, I'm not. I'm a drain, a burden. I know it's a shock, but Tom and I are going to try to leave as soon as we can get packed up."

Stepping into Cat's hug, Lillie wrapped her spindly arms around her neck. "Ms. Murphy, we *need* you." The child sobbed, her crushing embrace forcing the air out of her.

She waited for a moment then pried the little arms free. Brushing the carroty hair from Lillie's damp, red face, Cat pressed her lips together. "Baby Ruby needs *you*."

"They're right, Sis, we need you." Jim hunkered down next to his sister and took her by the shoulder. "Ruby can't make the trip, you see?"

"I guess." Lillie backed away from Cat.

"Breakfast anyone?" Tom pulled a stack of bowls from the cupboard and set them on the counter next to the stove. "I'm afraid it's just oatmeal. No eggs today." He retrieved the jar of day old milk from the refrigerator. Filling two bowls, he put a little milk in one and went to sit back by Cat. He gave the one with the milk to her.

She smiled. "Thank you."

"Why don't you go let 'Strella know that breakfast is ready?" Jim tousled Lillie's head. "Try not to wake the little ones, k?"

"Duh!" The girl was already gone, the screen door cracking shut behind her.

"I know you feel like you need to help us get everything taken care of before you leave, Mr. Callahan. But there'll always be another thing to do." The young man stood with his hands on his hips. He'd matured more in the past month than anyone should have to. "I think it's best if you just go. Rip off that bandage."

Chewing his breakfast, Tom grunted. "Mhmm."

"I got faith, Mr. C." The cowboy clapped his hand on the older man's shoulder. "Either we'll survive, or we won't, but we'll do it together. You gotta go be with *your* family."

Tom reached across his chest and patted Jim's hand. "I admire your grit, son."

"Yes, Jim." Cat wasn't a hundred percent convinced that it was time to abandon her home, a tiny part of her was still holding out. But she didn't want to be the reason that Tom stayed behind, he'd given up enough for her already. "We should go as soon as possible, Tom."

He stroked his mustache. "I'd sure like a sign."

The building trembled and the cracking sound of splintering earth filled the room. A new fissure in the southern landscape materialized, one of Cat's favorite old saguaros teetering on the edge of the crevasse. Another tremor rumbled beneath, and the cactus fell, swallowed by the chasm.

"So..." Wanting to avoid death by impalement, Cat pulled herself up and moved out from under the chandelier as it pitched back and forth above the table. With the aid of her crutch, she hobbled out of harm's way. "How do you interpret that, Tom?"

Tom jumped up and hurried to her side. "That was definitely something, but I don't rightly know—"

His words were interrupted by a thunderous rapping. In unison, everyone swiveled their heads from one end of the building to the other. Someone was pounding on the door leading to the barn.

CHAPTER THREE

Kit Walsh. Harmony Ranch, Arizona

Just after sunrise, Kit joined Taylor, Doc, Aaron, and Faris at Aunt Jen's breakfast table. Jaya served them carefully measured portions of beans and rice, along with some scrambled egg. Kit ate slowly, trying to make it last. The memory of his birthday party—with the rich, roasted game and endless helpings of canned fruit—only made him hungrier. That sort of luxurious gorging wasn't going to be a regular occurrence. On the contrary, it was going to be the lone exception to a frugal, belt-tightening way of life.

The party spirit, which had given him so much hope for Harmony Ranch's chances at survival, flickered and died when they posted the mandatory work schedule.

Some of the townsfolk had voluntarily stepped up, working hard since they arrived, like Alma, who had taken on the hail-damaged vegetable garden. Kit worried about her and her siblings, but wasn't sure how far to push the young woman. In her culture, she was old enough to be married and have children of her own; caring for siblings was expected. Perhaps that would be the norm in their new reality. Or maybe teenagers would learn to take abstinence seriously. Kit hoped for the latter, but didn't believe it.

Thuds sounded from the front door. "Where's Jen? We want to talk to Jen."

Kit stomped to the door and yanked it open, revealing about half the ranch's residents. The biggest complainers were right up front, of course. "What do you want?"

"Who do you think you are, telling us what to do?" Debra Williams, Jackrabbit Bluff's star gossip monger according to Doc, poked Kit in the chest. "You can take your chore board and shove it!" She waved at the blackboard he and Taylor had set up.

"Oh really?" Taylor ducked under his arm and wagged her finger in front of Debra's nose. The woman backed up a step. "Who do you think you are to sit around and do nothing while we work our fingers to the bone? Why should we feed you? We don't owe you anything. Not one darn thing." Taylor kept walking, moving Debra off the porch.

"You're eating, we get to eat!" Debra raised both arms dramatically, then crossed them over her chest.

Mirroring the woman's pose, Kit crossed his arms but leaned forward. "Why? Is the food in this house yours? Did you give any to Jen when you got here? Or did you hoard it all, and take from her when yours ran out?"

Debra scowled, but looked away.

Kit glared at each man and woman gathered around Jen's front porch. Especially the belligerent. More joined, probably attracted by the raised voices. "Look, you want to stay here, then you need to help. If you won't work, you need to leave. In case you didn't notice, we're in a world of hurt. We have armed people to the north, dwindling food supplies, no electricity, and limited water. Winter is coming. We're all working and watching, or we're all going to starve to death, got it?"

Mr. H, a morbidly obese older man who snored like a freight train and complained about the lack of food constantly, held up a hand. "Some of us can't do much physically. Gardening is impossible, and walking to a watch spot is equally so."

Taylor narrowed her eyes. "You can use a hoe on weeds. Move slowly and carefully. That way, you don't take out the plants with the weeds. Alma can show you what to do."

"And you can carve trap triggers with the rest of us in the evenings, instead of sitting in your pretty trailer and complaining." Jaya pointed at Faris, who held up his trigger and carving knife. "My husband got shot in the shoulder, but he still works."

Kit held up his hand. "Stop. We're done with the whining. You've all been assigned tasks according to your abilities. Some of you will have to dig deep and find new strength. But guess what? If you don't, you won't survive the coming winter. Unlike all of you, I care about Jen herself, not just her land. I care about the woman who was bullied into letting you come here. Bullied by the criminals you backed up." It was Kit's turn to point an accusing finger. "Now that I'm here, I'm going to be backing her play."

His aunt was tucked inside the door, listening to every word. She'd gone out of her way to make him feel welcome—stockpiling gifts for him, for all those years—the least he could do was share the burden of leadership. "I'm just going to go ahead and say it: I'm in charge now, whether or not you like it, and you can do your part or leave. I'm pretty sure those armed people at the old campground," Kit jabbed his finger at the north, "won't welcome you. They'll probably steal everything you've got. If you're lucky, they'll leave you the clothes on your back. If you want to take your chances with the refugee centers in Flagstaff or Phoenix, good luck and goodbye. But you might want to remember what Nora, Dunia, and Jaya told us about Flagstaff and Hutchinson Security. Some of you won't do so well in the hands of those thugs. Do any of you think those guys will let you sit around and do nothing? Not likely. No matter where you go, the easy days are over. Freeloaders aren't welcome anywhere. Work or leave, those are your choices. One more protest and you're on your way. Don't let the gate hit you on the way out."

Doc stepped forward. "I believe gardening is an excellent activity for you, Mr. H. I've been suggesting that sort of mild activity to you for years." He scanned the group. "Remember, whatever medications you're on will run out soon. We tried to get more and got robbed.

Me, Jen, Robin and Aaron almost didn't make it back here alive. If you want drugs, you'll have to go to Flagstaff and get them yourselves. Physical activity, meditation, and a few natural remedies are the only real cures we have left. So start working."

Kit cut off the remaining grumbling with a sweep of his hand. "Enough. We posted your assignments on the front porch. If you want to trade among yourselves, change the board. Don't ask me or Taylor or Doc to change anything, because we have more important things to do. Don't just erase your name, or write someone else's in. It won't work. We know who and what was assigned. If it doesn't get done, we'll come looking for you and you won't be eating tonight." Most of the people seemed resigned, but a few remained sullen or angry.

"And if you're leaving, please let me know." Taylor glared. "And no, you can't take any of our food, water, or other supplies with you. You can take what you brought, nothing more. Stealing will not be tolerated. We'll run you out of here with nothing. Is that understood?"

Kit smiled at his beautiful wife. Her spine of steel combined with her survival knowledge made him an incredibly lucky man. The crowd broke up, most looking at the posted list, a few retreating to their RVs, including Mr. and Mrs. H. They'd have to make an example of those two tonight. No work, no food.

"Those two will be a problem." Aaron thrust his chin toward the couple climbing into their trailer.

"No work, no food." Taylor turned to the house, echoing Kit's thoughts. "And speaking of work, you and I need to dig some latrines."

Aaron sighed. "Yay. Well, better than sewage everywhere."

"We don't need waterborne disease spreading. We'll have enough as it is." Doc hefted his bag. "I'm off on my rounds. Don't do too much, Kit. Be careful with those hands." He bent, leaning to call down the hallway.

Jen waved him back inside the house. "You didn't need to do that, but thank you. They're so..." She hunted for the word, but didn't find it.

"Demanding? Draining? Entitled?" He followed her to the front room, picking up errant pieces of wrapping paper. "Oh!" He bent and retrieved a crushed fire truck. "What the heck?"

She took the toy from him. "There were a lot of people coming and going yesterday. I guess they weren't looking where they were going." She rested it on the mantel with his other treasures. "So, what's my job, Mr. Bossman?"

They laughed, an easy, familiar sound that he'd missed without knowing he was missing anything.

"The livestock need you. Blake and Sarah's account of the robbers has me on edge. They're going to need food and what's better than a free goat?"

Ladybug hovered in the living room doorway, waiting on Jen's instruction. She clicked her tongue a couple of times and the dog took off running.

"I don't know what you've signed Robin up for, but I want her with me, if that's okay?" She fiddled with the edge of her cuff, pulling loose threads free. "No one's seen Kevin for a couple of days and I'm nervous."

"Kevin?" Kit had been introduced to so many Harmony Ranch residents, he couldn't keep them all straight in his head.

"I don't know if you met him? He was helping me and Doc organize things, but he's just vanished." She snapped her fingers. "Without a trace."

"It's a big property, could he be—?"

"Probably! Yep! He's a go-getter. He probably went to fix something further out on the Ranch! He's been training his kids to forage. I bet that's where he's gone!" She forced a smile and looped her arm through his in a gesture so wholly surprising he found himself wrapping his aunt in a bear hug. "What's that for?" She beamed as he let her go.

"For not giving up on your people. Not giving up on me. Not giving up on Robin. For taking me in when..." Did he want to dig all that stuff up about his mom, when they were having *such* a warm moment? "For taking her in. I can see she's bonded to you, big time!"

The color rose in her cheeks but she merely nodded and pushed him toward the door. "I'll change the work roster, so she's with me."

Robin was already on the porch, whittling, but when she saw Jen she put her supplies aside and ran to the woman, peppering her with questions. "What are we doing? Where are we going? Is Ladybug coming, too? What are the goats eating?"

Jen turned and waved, her smile only half as bright as it had been.

Dunia waited until his aunt rounded the barn and stepped in front of Kit. "I'm worried about Nora. She should have been back a long time ago."

Kit shrugged. There were too many people unaccounted for and no way of knowing which way they'd gone or who they'd run into in the surrounding woods. "Not much we can do. We don't have the firepower to go up against those people. We'll be lucky if they leave us alone; I'm not starting a fight we can't win. I'm sorry." It was a tough truth; they didn't have what it took to wage war. They were going to have to hunker down and protect what was theirs. He turned to Taylor. "I'm going to look at the traps." He searched the tents pitched beyond the RVs and yurts. "I thought Emelia was joining me, but I guess not."

Taylor's head tilted and her lips twisted. "I don't like sending you out there alone." Her brows rose, she whistled, and a few seconds later, Smoke trotted to her. "Take Smoke. He's smart. If something happens, he'll come back and get us." They both knew Ladybug wouldn't leave Jen's side.

Kit kissed Taylor quickly, hefting his fire pack and putting the binoculars around his neck. "I'll be fine. I won't go far, but sure, Smoke will be good company. Come on, Smoke." He filled his water bottles and headed out across the back pasture, the big white dog roaming around him.

Dunia was right; Nora should have been back already. If she had been with them last night when they designed the chore board, Kit was fairly certain she would have anticipated the complaints and come up with a much better speech. She'd never shirked or stopped. She kept trying to tell the world what happened. And when it became clear the world couldn't afford to care why it happened, she moved on, hunting for the smallest, youngest victims, missing kids most Americans cared nothing about. And then there was this Kevin chap his aunt was worried about. He sounded like another of the genuinely good guys. Even so, if either of them had been injured or captured, he had no one to send searching for them.

At the pasture gate, Smoke rose, putting his front paws on the gate, sniffing at the latch, then licking it.

"Impatient, are we?" Kit reached for the lever and stopped. Rusty red smeared the latch. Smoke had found blood. Kit sucked in a breath and swallowed hard, surveying the surrounding area and peering into the woods on the other side of the gate. A rapidly drying red drop stood out against the dull dirt and rock. He opened the gate, scanning side to side, and followed Smoke. The gate clanged closed, making him jump, then chuckle at his ridiculous overreaction.

Smoke put his nose to the ground, stopping at a rusty red drop, then trotting ahead to the next one, straight along the trail to the bunkhouses. The distance between drops increased, as if the injured person had been running, then slowed for the gate. Or from exhaustion.

Kit trailed Smoke, but he wasn't sure it was the best idea he'd ever had. Maybe he should go back, get reinforcements. If one of their people had cut themselves, he'd feel stupid. But, if it had been a simple injury, that person would have gone to Doc and Kit would have seen them before he came out here, all by himself. No, turning around was the smart thing to do.

"Smoke, come on." Kit turned back, jogging to the ranch house with the dog on his heels. At the ranch, Doc's office was deserted, and the kitchen was too. Kit trotted through the encampment, asking about injuries while he looked for Doc. But no one had been out to the bunkhouses that morning, nor did anyone report an injury. He finally found Doc chatting with the front gate guards. "Doc, you seen any wounded today? Bleeding?"

"No, just the usual aches and pains. Why?" His brows rose.

"I found blood smeared on the back gate latch, and a blood trail."

Bill Richards, a retired oil executive, twirled a piece of dry grass. "Maybe someone got a grouse and didn't want to share."

Roger Wentworth, a local ski bum, chuckled. "Sounds like something Mr. H would do."

"Except he couldn't waddle that far." Bill chewed on the stalk.

Kit frowned. While he agreed with Roger's assessment, he didn't want to put down anyone for a physical disability. "I kind of doubt it was a grouse. Seemed like a lot of blood for a bird."

Doc shook his head. "Blood spreads out a lot more than you think. A little blood looks like a lot."

Kit snorted. "Trust me, Doc, I know that." He'd seen a lot of carnage during his time with Tacoma Fire. Probably far more than a small town doctor. And even with the awful domestic disputes, vehicle crashes, fires, and industrial accidents, he'd give a lot to be back in those simpler times. Back when survival meant jumping out of the way of a speeding car rather than trying to feed fifty people over a winter. Even a relatively easy Arizona winter. The weight of all that responsibility made his shoulders and his spirits sag.

Maybe they should join Sandy, Evelyn, and Dev at the Apache complex. Those people at least had a plan, scientists, and real supplies. He and Taylor had hopes and dreams, but those didn't feed anyone. He couldn't leave, not after what his aunt had done for him. She wouldn't ever leave Harmony Ranch and go underground, even though she knew, just as well as he did, that there were going to be more and more refugees seeking shelter, more and more opportunities to say no and make potential enemies. Sending Blake and Sarah away had been the right decision, but that didn't make it easy. But that was their life for the foreseeable future; dwindling supplies and more calls on their resources.

"I forgot you were a big city firefighter." Doc's words shook Kit from his musings. "Are you going to trace the blood trail?" Doc pointed at the gravel drive.

Kit grimaced. "I think I'd better. If we've got a problem, it's better to know early."

"I'll tell Taylor." Doc waved and walked away toward the orchard.

Kit jogged back through the pasture again, sweating as the sun rose, Smoke on his heels. After they passed through the gate, the dog bounded ahead, trotting from blood drop to drop. At each of Taylor's marking flags, Kit left the main trail and checked the traps. A couple had sprung; the triggers were broken or pulled out. The remains of something small and furry waved from the top of one tree; whatever had sprung the trap provided a meal for some other predator. Kit looked up— in the distance, birds circled the sky. A bird of prey could have ripped a rabbit free. Or maybe Arizona had small tree climbing predators like martins and fishers. *And the humans who are circling the camp. Don't underestimate them!* Whatever it was had taken their catch, their hard work had fed something or someone else and that was a big problem.

Kit reset the traps, gingerly tying new triggers to the ropes attached to the tops of the sapling trees. Then, he threaded the trigger rope around an S-shaped piece of steel about two feet from the trigger. Clamping the steel S between his armpit and his chest, Kit pulled the rope to the right spot, placing the trigger, then gradually letting the trigger rope go. Once in place, he wiggled the steel S loose. Taking a stick from the brush, he maneuvered the foot trap loop into place on the game trail, trying to leave as little of his scent behind as possible.

Without Em's clever little fingers helping, it took him two or three tries to get the trigger and trap in place, even with the help of the steel S. Some of the more complex traps he couldn't reset by himself. He marked those with a second piece of plastic tagging. Taylor or someone else could come out with him later to fix them.

As he trod down the trail, he contemplated all the changes they'd gone through. A few weeks ago, he and Taylor were happily working in Tacoma, Washington, trying to figure out their next steps in a simple, easy life. Now they battled for survival. A few days ago, they'd protected Emelia from the reality of what these traps were for, but with the decrease in their food supplies and the knowledge that heavily armed people lived just to the north of them, none of them could remain ignorant. Even the youngest children had to be told they couldn't go beyond the main ranch area and why. Kit hated the idea of crushing their innocence, but they lived in a dangerous world. A world where earthquakes were so common, no one even noticed. A world where the sun dimmed more every day, the ash and smoke in the sky thicker. A world where water burned. So far, that contamination hadn't made it to Harmony Ranch, but it might. Their relatively clear skies were a simple accident of the motion of the wind currents around the surrounding mountains and wouldn't last.

Being crushed by a falling tree during a forest fire would have been easier for him, but Taylor needed him. Better yet, she still wanted him! Kit huffed a laugh. He couldn't even be mad about his best friend wanting his wife. Not when the guy had died saving her. He still woke in the night, shaking, as the canyon swallowed Sean again and again, hands slipping, arms flailing and a simple 'I love you' on his lips. Truly, the stuff of nightmares.

Smoke's cold nose bumped his hand and he jumped. Smoke was right—they had work to do, and he should pay attention. They still didn't know what had bled or why. It didn't seem likely that Blake would be bleeding again, but it wasn't beyond the realm of possibility. Smoke followed the blood trail, patiently waiting for Kit while he checked and reset traps.

Finally, they neared the end of the track. Smoke, twenty feet in front of him, reached the clearing around the bunkhouses. He'd been nose down the entire way, occasionally looking up and around.

At the edge of the clearing, Smoke stood with his body taut, neck stretched, lips curling to show his teeth and a low growl rumbling from him.

Kit sidled to the edge of the track and crept forward.

CHAPTER FOUR

Alma Garcia. Harmony Ranch, Arizona

Alma squared her shoulders, praying for courage and a strong back. She'd never buried anyone before. Eric had been entombed in their prison house after Mati thwacked him with a frying pan and all the bodies they'd passed on the road—dead in their cars, clawing for freedom or splayed on the tarmac—had stayed where they fell. Nora was different. A hero deserved a hero's send off, even if it was a secret, private, hidden thing.

Emelia stuffed her feet into her shoes. "We're coming with you. We'll help."

Alma held the zipped door shut. "You two are staying here."

"But you shouldn't do it alone."

"You can't come with me, you'll faint again." She was being cruel and rubbing Emelia's face in her weakness, but it was to protect her. Given how she'd responded to Nora's murder, Alma didn't want her anywhere near the dead body. "When you collect breakfast, grab my portion too, but don't talk to anyone." She ducked out of their tent. Emelia followed her out, but Alma grabbed her and motioned for her to go back in. She lowered her voice. "Listen to me carefully. Wait inside until it is time to collect food." She pushed her sister's shoulder, forcing her back in. "And I don't want you talking to anyone."

"Taylor is at the house this morning and I'm helping Kit this afternoon."

"You can say hello, but nothing else. We want to stay at the ranch? You mustn't tell her anything." Alma zipped her brother and Emelia inside.

Emelia and Matias' mutinous whispering was only a muffled hiss. She'd have to deal with Emelia's attitude later. She could complain all she liked to Matias, especially if it meant she didn't blab to Taylor or Kit. And if she got it out of her system before Alma got back, all the better. There was no time to argue with her.

Leaving them to their conversation, she hurried past the gate at the back of the barn. A loud yawn and zip on a yurt buzzed. She dashed out of sight and crouched behind the tall cover of the flowering weeds. She skirted the sturdy fence around the main yard and crept through the depleted rows of Jen's vegetable garden. Once she was sure she'd evaded the yawner, she surveyed the garden.

Shiny objects perched high on canes shook in the breeze, flashing reflected shards of morning light down on her. She'd retrieved and remounted the miniature bird scarers after the hailstorm tore them down, although many were too damaged to use. The ice pellets had shredded leaves and torn plants from their climbing frames, so the little growth left needed protection from pests. She'd propped the plants up and trimmed the worst of the damage. Jen hadn't said much, she never did, but perhaps impressed with her effort, instructed her to keep digging. A larger garden would mean more fresh food, and she would make sure they were still around to enjoy it.

Although the strange, hazy morning sun warmed the night's chill, it wasn't the reason the sweat ran down her spine. Every little chirping insect, hungry chicken, and distant farm bleat resounded in her head a hundred times louder and a thousand times more threatening. She searched for the murderer behind each new noise, and jumped at shadows. Mr. Martinez was probably miles away. *Say it until you believe it. He got what he came here for and now he's gone!* She pulled her hood up and crouched behind the garden trellises until her heartbeat settled. Then she grabbed the shovel she'd left by the patch of turned soil and jogged away from the garden.

The yellowed grass pricked her ankles and crackled under her hurried footsteps. The quicker route across the field would take her past the big camper van and the yurts owned by the refugees from the local town. She gave them a wide berth taking the longer route instead. Crouching low in the hope she wouldn't be spotted, she sped across the open ground.

An easy-to-climb double railed fence bordered the far edge of Harmony Ranch. The land north afforded a rich view over the tops of the pines and through cleared gaps. The space beyond the fence hadn't become a forest, but the tree line was advancing. Younger and smaller saplings spread over the gentle slope, slowly taking back what might have once been part of the ranch's spread. She followed the fence to the northeast corner. The tall grasses grew tangled with dried thorns and briars that caught at her clothes and scratched her bare arms.

The tents were distant enough for her not to crouch any more, but with the community stirring and going about their business, she didn't dare stand upright. She was so grateful that Emelia had made it back to the tent before the community woke. Her blood-soaked sister would've been in dire trouble if anyone had spotted her. *But maybe they had. What then?* She hadn't asked about the route Emelia used to return to the tent. She could only *hope* that no one had seen her. But even if she'd lucked out on that front, there was Michael Martinez to consider. The hairs on her arms stood up. *Say it again: He's gone. He's gone. He's gone.* The more she said it, the less she felt it. He could be lying in wait, watching, waiting. She prayed that he wouldn't come after Emelia next. She'd told her sister that he'd be 'long gone,' but she wasn't convinced. Bottom line, if he was still around, she had to stop him.

She hiked until she reached the abandoned buildings, keeping her mind busy with notes about trees and snares and piles of scat. When the first hut came into view, she ducked behind a trunk, her heart in her throat and her mind empty of everything but Michael Martinez.

The eyes were the same. The beard was new and the nose was weird, but his eyes were his dead, glassy eyes. Why didn't I notice?

Rust had pitted holes into the sheet metal roofs and crept along the jagged edges. Yellow lichen grew in the crevices between the rocks, giving the walls a sallow and unloved sheen. A stream gurgled nearby, and birds scuttled along the branches spreading over the dumpy houses. She stepped closer and they sounded an alarm call, flapping into the air, then returning to their perches. One bird jumped to a lower branch, its beady gaze jerking from her to the flock above and then to the ground. The caw of crows, the beating of wings, and a scuffle came from the other side of the wall.

Her pulse pounded in her ears and she gripped the shovel tighter. She crept as close to the wall as the weeds would allow, drawing on the solid strength of wood and stone to protect her back. More squawking sent prickles down her spine, and she leaned around the corner.

Nora's body lay in a patch of flattened dry grass beside the open bunk house. Her limbs weren't splayed as if she'd fallen, but neatly straightened. If it hadn't been for the puddle of blackened blood and the vicious birds, she might have been sleeping. Alma took a step toward her. The crows hopped back but didn't leave her body.

"Shoo. Leave her alone!" Alma waved her arms, forcing them away.

A few patches of blood stained the front of Nora's clothes, but the majority had seeped into the ground surrounding her with more on her right side than the left. Alma gasped. Emelia had probably rolled Nora onto her back to try and save her. With so much blood, it must've taken Em an immense effort to stay conscious as long as she had.

Alma stepped near Nora's left side and placed two fingers to Nora's neck. No heart beat beneath her clammy skin and no breath rose in her chest. Any residual hope that her sister had been wrong was shattered. Nora had once suggested that the old buildings might be suitable for housing the people she'd rescued. No one had rescued her.

If Alma dug a grave anywhere near the potential homes, someone could find the body too easily. The ground would be softer next to the depleted stream flowing nearby, but since they couldn't use the main Harmony Ranch well, she couldn't risk polluting what little water was available. If they were to stay for another season, that stream would swell and become the river that the steep banks suggested it could be. Her body wouldn't stay hidden. However, the earth near the trees beyond the ranch's fence would give plenty of cover.

She backed away from the body, dropped the shovel to the other side of the fence, and clambered over after it, pushing through the thickets of small pines to a clearing. The dry ground beneath her feet was springy. Soft brown pine needles covered the ground, muffling her footsteps. She pushed beyond some twiggy plants growing in the shade of the larger pines, creating a second screen from the ranch.

Alma used the edge of the shovel to sweep away the loose needles, piling them to cover the mound once she'd hidden Nora away. She thrust the shovel into the hard ground but barely sank the blade an inch into the dirt. Lifting the tiny amount of earth, she stabbed the shovel harder. Standing on the shovel's rim, she wriggled the blade deeper into the ground. Again and again she attacked the dirt, until she hit a root. There was no way she could break through living wood. She moved further from the tree and started again, willing herself not to cry.

She shucked her hoodie. Even without any interfering roots, the dig was a challenge. She stood on the shovel over and over again, but the hole barely seemed to get any deeper. It took an age and a half to even mark out a square big enough for a body.

Her shirt stuck to her back, gross and gritty. Her hair clung to her slick neck and blisters formed on her palms, but she pushed through until she'd made a hole that reached her knee. It was pathetically shallow—nothing like the deep graves she'd seen on TV—but it would have to do.

Leaving the shovel propped up against the tree, she dragged herself to the fence and climbed over. The birds had gathered at Nora's body again. She rushed forward and they flapped away noisily, protesting the disturbance.

She cringed and stepped onto the grass, tacky with Nora's blood. The crows had pecked at her face and hideous clumps of exposed flesh scarred her cheeks and eyes. Alma bent and put her hands under Nora's shoulders. Slippery, thick blood coated her fingers. She swallowed hard, gripped the fabric and tried to lift. Nora wasn't a large woman, but Alma couldn't grab anything tight enough. She scrubbed her hands on the grass, getting the slickness down a notch, and gripped Nora's wrists. Leaning back, she pulled. Nora's shoulders lifted slightly from the ground and her head fell back, her blood matted hair swept the grass but she managed to drag the body a couple of paces.

Alma's arm muscles burned. Digging a shallow grave had been hard work, but dragging a body was twice as hard. She shuffled a couple of steps, stopped to rest, and began again. Nora's clothes caught on stray plants, flattening them, the route from dump site to grave a clear (if wiggly) line. The trail of evidence—broken stalks and heel grooves—was like an arrow pointing to Nora's final resting place.

She heaved again, stumbled back and bumped into the fence. The wire twanged and Alma winced. She turned and slumped against the post. Her arms were screaming, her legs trembled, and Nora's blood and dirt smeared her clothes. She climbed over the fence, stood on the second rail, leaned down and gripped Nora's wrists, but she didn't have the upper body strength to lift Nora's corpse.

The cawing crows shuffled along the branches, their beady eyes focused on Nora. They took off from the branches with a clatter of flapping. Alma crouched. A snuffling came from behind the group of buildings, and then a bark.

She turned and ran over the exposed ground toward the trees and the grave. She ducked behind a thick tree trunk, and peered around the edge.

Smoke, the big white dog, barked again and lifted his muzzle. He'd caught her scent. She stank of sweat. Alma was grateful that the fence was still intact; the dog couldn't reach her. A rumbling growl drifted toward her. He backed away from Nora's body.

Kit appeared from behind the buildings, strolling through the long weeds, binoculars swinging from his neck. The dog barked again, and Kit ran toward Nora. Bending over her body, he touched her face and neck, then scanned his surroundings. The dog sat on his haunches and howled. Kit muttered something Alma couldn't make out and patted Smoke on his head.

He traced the route of broken weeds back to the spot where Alma had found Nora, dabbed at the pool of dark earth, and wiped his hands in the grass.

Returning to the fence, he climbed up on the lowest rail, leaning his weight against the upper rails, lifting his binoculars. She hid against the rough bark of the trunk, listening for his approach. The trees weren't thick enough to conceal her if she ran toward the ranch, but if she ran a straight path deeper into the woods, the trees might give her enough cover. The dog whined and barked once more, but it was distant. She stole a glance back to Nora. Kit and Smoke were gone.

Alma checked farther up the fence, to the left and right, through the trees and toward the stream. She listened hard. She was alone again. Emelia raved about Kit, and from what she said he was a man who did the right thing, the honorable thing; go to Jen, to the community, and tell them of Nora's terrible and violent death. He would protect the whole, warn them of a murderer in their midst and get them worked up to throw Alma and her family out, just like when she was tiny.

Alma ran to the hole she'd dug and grabbed her hoodie. Sweat trickled down her spine, but blood darkened her shirt. She pulled it over her head. She leaped over the shallow grave and sprinted; dashing to get back to her tent before Kit reported anything amiss.

CHAPTER FIVE

Catherine "Cat" Murphy. Arivaca, Arizona

Cat's heart vaulted into her throat, adrenaline coursing through her veins. Her Glock was six feet away, sitting on the side table next to her favorite chair. Being one-legged meant the pistol was almost useless anyway. Balancing her crutch and wielding her weapon was next to impossible.

Striding to the barn door, Tom pulled a handgun from his shoulder holster and racked a cartridge into the chamber. Jim did the same. Gun drawn, Tom pointed the young man toward the left side of the doorframe and cracked open the door.

She grabbed her crutch and floundered to the table. Retrieving her sidearm, she leaned against the back of the couch and waited.

"How can I help—Oh, it's you, Mr. Jordan." Tom lowered his pistol and swung the door open. "You look like hell. Come in."

Cat questioned Tom's easy admittance of the neighbor. Until she saw him. The man was almost unrecognizable. Gaunt, unshaven, and pale, their neighbor had aged twenty years in the past few days since his family's failed coup. "I am so sorry, Mr. Callahan." Grady Jordan staggered into the apartment carrying several egg cartons. He took off his sweat-stained trucker's cap and nodded in Cat's direction. "Ms. Murphy."

"Here, have a seat, Mr. Jordan." Glaring at him, Jim pulled a stool out from the island.

The neighbor threw his hat down by the door, then set the cartons on the counter. "I brought you all some eggs." His mouth turned down at the corners, he climbed onto the barstool. "They're getting scarce."

Stagnant, whiskey-infused sweat oozed out of the man's pores and mingled with the smell of musty, soiled clothing. Cat took a step backward and wobbled. Tom caught her, and, holding her by the elbow, escorted her over to her chair.

"Coffee, sir?" Jim pushed a coffee cup toward Grady and filled it with steaming coffee.

"Thank you, son." He wrapped his hands around the mug. "We—uh, I mean, I ran out of coffee about three days ago."

"Thanks for the eggs, Mr. Jordan." Jim took the eggs and put them in the refrigerator. "Our hens have all but quit laying."

"Yeah, I've been saving up for a few days...this weather is hard on every living thing." The haggard man looked up from his coffee. "You have refrigeration?"

"Yeah, we jury-rigged up a fairly decent solar system pretty early on." Jim filled a bowl with oatmeal and set it next to Grady's coffee cup. "Have some breakfast. It's just porridge with a little brown sugar, but it'll stick to your ribs."

"Thanks." Grady took a tentative bite, then another, bigger bite. "This is great." He shoveled in the boiled oats as though he hadn't eaten in some time.

Tom plunked down in the chair next to Cat and propped a foot next to hers. She scrunched up her nose and threw a questioning look at him, grateful to be upwind from the hungover—or perhaps still inebriated—neighbor.

Grady set his spoon down. "I don't mean to be sticking my nose in other people's business, but you all need better fortifications." He tapped a finger on the counter. "I could have just walked right in here, you know?"

36

"That's true." Tom grimaced, shaking his head. "I didn't hear your vehicle pull in."

"Oh. Well, I wasn't sure how welcoming you'd be—given our last interaction—so I parked out by the gate and walked in." Grady started to get up. "That reminds me, there's some stuff in my UTV that might look pretty attractive to a person with sticky fingers. I need to go get it."

"Stay." Cat sympathized with the pathetic shell of a man. "One of us can go get it."

"I got it, Ms. Murphy." Jim jogged out the door, grabbing his cowboy hat along the way.

Grady stopped midway between sitting and standing, hunched over, shoulders drooping. "Why are you all being so nice to me?"

Tom's eyes darted from Grady to Cat and back. "You look like a fella who could use a little niceness."

"Maybe I do, Mr. Murphy, but I sure as hell don't deserve it." He slammed his hand down on the counter, rattling the spoon in the empty cereal bowl. "I should've died with the first explosion. I've done nothin' but ill since then."

"Now, Grady, don't say that." Tom sat upright in the armchair, striking both boots on the concrete, the report of his leather soles echoing. "You helped my niece, Evelyn, find this place, I'm mighty grateful for that." He made his way over to Grady and put a hand on his shoulder. "You say that you didn't mean to kill young Dan, and if that's true, I'll not hold it against you. I can't speak for anyone else, but I know first-hand what it's like to kill a young man in battle. You were doing what you thought you needed to do to survive. We can't undo what's done."

Lillie bopped into the room. "Where's Jim running off to?" She started toward Cat but soon froze in her tracks. "What is *he* doing here?" Her nostrils flared, her sweet face reddened and drew pinched. "What are *you* doing here?"

"I brought some supplies that I thought you might need. Your brother went to go collect them." The barstool creaked as he rose. "And..." He shuffled over to Lillie, dropped to his knees, and bowed his head. "I know I don't deserve it, but I came to beg your forgive-

DC LAYTON & MIKE KRAUS

ness. I am so profoundly sorry." He opened his hand, and in his greasy palm lay something small and gray. "I want you to have this."

"I'm afraid I'm not ready to forgive you, *sir*." Lillie bit her lip and stared at the trinket in his hand. "You killed my Danny."

"And you can't have any idea how regretful I am about that, but I do understand." He continued to hold out his offering. "This was my mama's necklace. It's a hand engraved sterling silver mariposa lily..." His eyes glazed over for a moment. "They were her favorite wild-flowers."

"My daddy loved those, too." She took the piece in her thumb and index finger. She turned the dangling bauble in her hand. "That's where my name came from, you know? Lillie Jane."

"Please, keep it." The broken man locked eyes with the feisty little girl. "And know that I'm not going to give up until I've earned your forgiveness."

Lillie gulped. "Okay." She put it in her shirt pocket, then backed away. The child went into the kitchen and dished herself a bowl of oats, then went to sit at the table. Staring out the window, she took a small bite of hot cereal.

Grady clambered to his feet, then turned to face Cat. "Now, about those fortifications. I'd like to help."

She slid her hand in her pocket, comforting herself with the prox-imity of her revolver. "What did you have in mind, Mr. Jordan?" Whether it was his drunkenness, his tragic devolution, or something else, the man made Cat uncomfortable.

"I'm pretty handy, I can help build shutters for the barn windows. And, I learned a little bit about field fortifications when I was in Iraq." Slumping, he stalked across the room and stood with his hand on the door handle. "I brought a few things that I thought you could use. I'll—" The whine of a small engine interrupted the conversation, becoming clearer as he opened the barn door. "I'll be right back."

Tom returned to the sitting area, where he sat perched on the ottoman next to Cat's foot. "Hon?" He rotated in his seat and put his hand out, palm up.

Unsure of what he wanted, Cat hesitated, leaving his gesture unanswered. She cocked her head. "Yes?"

He moved to the edge of his seat, leaned toward her, and put his hand on her knee. "I think this is it."

"It's what?" She frowned, afraid she knew what he meant.

"The sign."

The sign, just what she thought. "So. Does this mean we should stay or go?"

"Honestly?" He leaned back in his chair and scratched his head. "I'm not sure."

Jim came through the door carrying a large cardboard box. "It's a surveillance system. And, a nice one at that." He sat it on the floor near Lillie and the two dove in, pulling out electronic gadgets and inspecting them.

"Didn't have much use for it at my place." Grady followed, holding something behind his back. "Nothin' worth stealing there." He lumbered over to the seating area where he stopped near the ottoman that Tom and Cat shared. "Ms. Murphy?" Producing the item from behind his back, he held out a unique contraption made of metal, plastic, and straps. "Pardon my boldness, but I built this for you."

Tom sprung to his feet. "Is that a prosthesis?" He took the apparatus from Grady. "Oh, that's genius." Kneeling next to Cat, he held out a sort of modified crutch. "It's a knee walker, see? Your shin goes in that perpendicular cradle there. These straps hold it attached to your leg."

"I'm not sure how well it'll work." The neighbor flushed. "It might need a bigger base."

"Why would you do this for me?" Cat twisted in her seat to get a better look at the gift.

"Amends. Sitting alone in that house over there I've had a lot of time on my hands. A lot of time to think." Grady kneaded his blistered and wounded hands. "Every time I close my eyes, I keep seeing that boy, jerking, when my bullet ripped through him. His blood is on my hands." He ran his arm under his nose, then shoved his hands in his pockets. "The guilt is tearing me apart. And, like I said, I need to make amends." The neighbor stared at the young girl with her back to him, facing the window.

Lil snorted in her cereal. "Amends?" She didn't take her eyes off the vista of sinkholes and crevasses where Old Mexico used to be. "Some things can't be fixed."

"How'd you come up with this idea?" Tom's eyes softened and the ends of his mustache turned up.

The ghost of a smile formed on Grady's face and he addressed the aging cowman. "Well, I figured Ms. Murphy was getting sick of that crutch. I know how raw that'll make a person's armpit." He peered down at Cat. "Then I remembered when my mom had her knee replaced, she had a rolling knee walker. It was good for inside, but didn't work worth a darn outside. And, I knew you were an outside kinda gal. So, I modified an old crutch we had sitting around. I just shortened it, turned the armrest ninety degrees to cushion the front of your thigh, and added the cradle for your lower leg. Oh, and added the leather straps to go around your calf and thigh."

Tom fiddled with Grady's peace offering, gauging it next to her good leg, pushing buttons and adjusting the lengths of the different supports. He leaned it against the ottoman and stood towering over Cat, arms outstretched. She took his hand and pulled herself up.

"I'm not sure about this, Tom." Cat put her hand on his shoulder and jockeyed into position. "I think you could make it a notch shorter."

"Here." Tom handed her the crude old crutch he'd made. Once she was standing steady, he shortened the leg one click. Kneeling, he slid the new prosthesis under her suspended footless shin. He buckled the straps around her upper and lower leg, then stood with his hands on his hips. "You're strapped in. Ready?"

"Ready." The brace was a little short, so she leaned into the cradle, lowering the rubber tip to the floor. It was steadier than she'd expected it to be. "This is awkward. Take my crutch?"

Grady cringed. "Why don't you hang on to that and just try putting a little of your weight on my contraption?"

"Too late." She shoved the crutch toward Grady and stood, wobbling, feeling more independent than she had in a very long time. "This is pretty nifty."

Wide-eyed, Tom stepped closer to Cat, his hands set to catch her if she fell. "Your wound has just finally closed, don't overdo it, Cat."

She took one cautious step. "Fine. It needs a little tweaking anyway." Taking another step, she stopped, tottering. "It's just a quarter of an inch or so too short. It would be great if it could be adjusted in smaller increments. And I think a more substantial base might be good, but I don't want it any heavier than it already is." She pointed at Grady, then turned her hand and beckoned to him with her index finger.

The man plodded over and stood in front of Cat, his eyes downcast. "Yes?"

"Thank you." She extended her hand, offering to shake his. Just as Grady took his hand in hers, the room rumbled and the floor juddered. Cat pitched forward and he caught her in an unexpected embrace. His stubble scraped across her cheek, the stench of his unwashed body triggering flashbacks of her father. Cat pushed the memories, and the man who was holding her, away. "I love it."

He stood and stumbled backward, catching himself before falling onto the couch. He examined his shoes. "Gee, Ms. Murphy. It was the least I could do." Straightening his wrinkled shirt, he dragged his hand through his hair and tucked a curl behind his ear. "The cradle angle is adjustable."

"Thank you, son." Tom reached for Grady's hand. The two men shook and Tom clapped him on the back.

"I just wish I could do more, sir. Oh..." Grady paled. Forcing his hand into the pocket of his grimy jeans, he shoved a fist out to Tom. "Here." The older man opened his hand under Grady's and the neighbor dropped four valve stem cores into his palm. "I took these to flatten the tires on your truck. I'm sorry."

"Oh, I already forgave you." Tom set the cores on the island. "I'm just thankful you had the foresight to remove them rather than slash the tires."

"Enough is getting destroyed without my help, I figure we've got to salvage everything we can." The rain began to patter on the tin roof and Grady glanced out the window. "There's a monsoon rolling in. I best be on my way." He skulked toward the barn, picking up his cap from the floor under the coatrack.

"Maybe you should stay here and wait it out." Jim moved between the neighbor and the exit.

"Aww, you don't want me hanging around here." He inclined his head in Lillie's direction. "Especially her."

"I said I hadn't forgiven you, not that I wanted you dead." The rain pelted the windows, echoing inside the apartment and Lillie raised her voice. "We can't let you go out in the storm, our parents wouldn't allow it."

"It's settled. You're staying." Jim cupped his hand over his mouth and spoke in a stage whisper, "You do not want to argue with that little redheaded she-devil."

Lillie ran over and pinched her brother's arm. "I heard that."

"Ouch! See?" Jim raised his eyebrows and waggled them at his little sister. His face darkened. "Man, I wish we had a catchment system set up."

"Why are you worried about that? You've got tens of thousands of gallons of water right across the lot." Grady stared out the window that faced the ranch's two enormous water tanks painted with the words "RANCHO" on one and "SECO" on the other.

"We *did*." Lillie's tone was defiant, almost accusatory.

Cat repositioned herself in her chair. "After you left, some jack-asses shot one of the tanks full of holes. We lost half of our storage."

Grady pointed to the east. "You know there's a guzzler a few miles that direction, don't you?"

Tom pulled his readers from the chest pocket of his shirt. "I guess I do remember something about that. The feds put it in a few years ago to store water for wildlife in the event of a drought." He brushed some lint from the leg of his pants. "But I don't know exactly where it is. Anyway, it has to be contaminated by now."

"It wasn't last time I checked, and I believe it's at least five thousand gallons." Grady's face grew serious. "I can show you where it is, I sealed it off."

"You'd do that?" Cat furrowed her brow. "That would sure ease my mind."

"Sure. You all need it a hell of a lot more than I do." Grady twisted the cap in his hands. "Everything I cared about is gone."

"Jim? Why don't you and Grady go check the machine shed and see if you can find whatever he needs to get Ms. Murphy's new leg brace dialed in?" Tom returned to his chair next to Cat. "The boss lady and I need to have a visit."

"Sure thing, Mr. Callahan." The young cowboy strolled past Grady. "Let's go, Mr. Jordan." He picked up the valve stem cores from the island. "We can get those tires aired up, too."

"Oh. Okay." The neighbor stammered and then fell in step with Jim.

The cowboy side-eyed Grady. "Nice job on that knee walking thing."

"Think you can incorporate one of my boots in the base?" Cat half joked.

"We'll give it a shot." Jim grabbed a boot from the ones lined up next to the door.

Tom pointed at Cat's favorite boots. "The blue topped ones, son. With the spurs."

The young man traded out the boots and jingled out the door. It had just closed behind Lillie's brother and the man who had killed her other brother when the redhead jumped up from her seat at the table. She trounced over and stood in front of Tom and Cat, her hands on her hips, her face unsmiling. "You know we have to invite him to live here, right?"

CHAPTER SIX

Kit Walsh. Harmony Ranch, Arizona

Kit crept forward, staying near the trees at the edge of the trail to the bunkhouses. Smoke, his big body outstretched, watched the clearing, sniffing and growling low. He barked once, then charged, the crows launching into the air in a demented swirl of black. He stopped, sniffing the ground where the murder of crows had gathered, and stalked forward.

Kit followed Smoke, the crows circling around him, cawing wildly, some landing on the bunkhouses, staring down with their beady black eyes. A pool of blood soaked the pine straw and dirt where the dog had stopped. The rapidly browning mass of blood had cracked as it dried and the cracks were relatively deep. The ground was oddly disturbed, as though something large—from the amount of blood, a large animal or a human—had been dragged, then someone tried to cover the track with pine straw and weeds. A mountain lion would drag a kill away and cover it, but it wouldn't cover the trail.

Smoke barked again and sniffed, padding along the drag trace, stopping and growling every ten feet. Kit followed, surveying the surrounding area. The dog could be so occupied by the carcass that he would miss a person hiding nearby. The flattened path streaked with blood continued past the bunkhouses. Peering around the ends of the building, no one waited to jump him. Despite the lack of attackers, he didn't feel the least bit foolish about his caution.

The body lay half propped against the fence. His first instinct was that it was Kevin, the guy his aunt said was a go getter. But the closer he got, the less that seemed possible. *No, definitely a woman.* The frame, the clothes, the small hands... they all pointed to the corpse being that of... He hoped it wouldn't be Nora. The shreds of flesh hanging from her savaged face made her unrecognizable, but the clothing and hair positively identified her as Nora Bennani. Kit closed his eyes, slumping against the nearest tree; what a horrible end for someone who'd done so much for others. From the amount of blood at the bunkhouses, she was killed there, then pulled to this spot. Worse, her killer (or killers, plural) could still be around.

He checked his surroundings again, but nothing moved. His guard still up, he retraced his steps. Nora's body had remained where she was killed long enough to almost bleed out; the pool of blood and her picked-over flesh proved that. Also, she wasn't a big person; anyone who was strong enough to kill her could have picked her up and carried her away while her clothes soaked up the blood, so there wouldn't be much of a trail to cover. He pulled her body away from the fence and checked her for wounds—a clean cut, probably from a knife, a few inches long. Peeling her sticky, drenched clothing away from the back of her neck, Kit confirmed his guess—someone had stabbed her in the back; someone who knew how to pierce the heart and kill quickly.

He laid her on the ground. Taylor and the others needed to know immediately—they had a killer in the area. If only they had working radios! He could try a smoke signal, but it would probably be lost in the hazy air. He'd simply have to take her body back to the ranch.

Smoke sat, lifted his head and howled. Kit bowed his head, joining Smoke in his mourning. He could afford the few seconds to pay tribute to a brave woman, one killed trying to do the right thing for everyone else. When Smoke's howl faded, Kit scruffed his head. "Yeah, I agree, Smoke. Good boy." The dog's tail wagged slowly, brushing the ground, and he nosed Kit's hand until he was rewarded with an ear scritch.

"Nothing doing but getting it done, Smoke. This isn't going to be pretty, but the people need to see what we're up against."

Grasping Nora's bloody wrists, he grimaced. His hands were better, but not fully healed. That was only one of several challenges. Her blood-soaked clothes would mean washing his, no trivial task without running water or electricity. He crouched, pulled, and put his shoulder into Nora's belly, flopping her upper body over his back, and grasped her clammy, bloody legs. Grunting, he lifted her dead weight and started back to the Ranch.

Smoke trotted circles around him, but didn't range far. Kit trusted the dog to let him know if anyone was near, which wasn't a foolproof surveillance technique, but between the effort of carrying Nora and ignoring the pain in his damaged hands, it was all he could do.

As Kit performed his grim task, he tried to make sense of the murder scene. Someone had killed Nora and left her body. Then, hours later, someone—else? maybe?—dragged her away from the kill zone. A person, not an animal. If the killer had returned, he'd have carried Nora the same way Kit was—a firefighter's lift. So, whoever had dragged her away wasn't strong enough to carry her. A young man or woman, or someone elderly. But hiding a body when the killer didn't bother was strange. The killer was sending a message—he or she could kill one of theirs whenever he wanted to and there was nothing they could do. Perhaps the person or persons trying to hide the body was trying to prevent the killer from making their point, keeping the ranch in the dark.

Everyone at the ranch needed to know about the threat on their doorstep. They had to set watches and more traps at the corners of the ranch, and insist everyone work in pairs or groups if they were leaving the base area.

If only Nora had returned with Dunia and the children. Maybe if he'd been able to spare a few people to go look for her, she'd still be alive. Of course, if everyone had pitched in to help like they were supposed to, there would have been people working on those bunkhouses. Nora would have found them, and she might have lived.

He crossed the back pasture and entered the main animal barn, leaving Nora's body inside a stall where it couldn't be disturbed by any animals. Smoke laid down outside the stall. Kit rubbed his head. "Good boy."

Removing his shirt, Kit grimaced at the rusty red staining the bright yellow. The reminder would never wash away, and maybe it was better that it stayed. With one look, the ranch's residents would know they had killers nearby. He jogged back to the house, his brain going a mile a minute.

Taylor dropped a box piled high with pears on the kitchen table. "If we cut them thin, we can dry them, right?"

Jaya picked up a pear, sniffing it. "Yes. These are a little green."

"They were disappearing and birds were flocking, so we had to get them now, or we wouldn't get any at all." Aaron pointed at the door. "These people just don't seem to get that we're in trouble."

Kit stepped forward. "We're in bigger trouble than you know." Taylor, Jaya, Faris and Aaron turned to him. He knew his news would upset everyone, but ripping a bandage off fast was usually best. "I'm sorry, but I just found Nora Bennani's body at the north bunkhouses. Someone stabbed her in the back, right through the heart, probably yesterday. Much later, maybe early this morning, someone much weaker tried to drag her body away. So, we've definitely got an enemy or several out there, and whoever killed her isn't the person who tried to drag the body away. And it wasn't an animal." Kit described the scene and told them where he'd left her body. Jaya cried on Faris' good shoulder.

Taylor squeezed her eyes shut for a moment. "Poor Nora. She did so much for so many, and she gets killed for it."

"The question is, who killed her and why?" He decided, in that same breath, not to mention that Kevin was possibly missing. He didn't know the guy and no one but his aunt had mentioned the fact that he'd gone AWOL. They were all upset enough as it was. And, in any case, the missing go-getter might turn up at any minute.

Kit unclenched his fists and put an arm around Taylor. She laid her head on his chest and wrapped her arm around his waist. Some maniac could come here, killing Taylor like he'd killed Nora. He had to protect her. "No one here had any reason to kill her. She rescued a bunch of kids, then acted as a decoy to let those kids get back here. So, that probably means someone at the campground followed and killed her. They left her at the bunkhouses, probably as a message to us. 'We can kill you any time we want to.' We need to make sure everyone understands they can't go *anywhere* alone, and the kids all need to stay here, around the house. I don't think it's safe for Dunia to leave yet, either."

Taylor nodded. "I don't want to scare any of the kids, so I'll go talk to all the adults individually. The disbelievers and shirkers I'll take to the barn. It's gruesome, but for some people, seeing is the only way they believe."

Kit was so lucky to have her. "I hate to ask you to go through that, but we've kind of established I'm the enforcer, you're the survival expert."

Taylor blew a raspberry. "Some expert. But yes, I think some of these people respond to me better than you." She squeezed his waist again, then pulled away. "I'll get started. We'll need another big meeting soon."

"Yeah, and we've got to find a way to charge batteries." Kit picked his fire radio off the table. "It would be so much safer if we had a way to talk to our distant watches, rather than relying on fire or flashing signal mirrors, or whatever else we can come up with. The enemy can see most of those things."

"We need to create more traps, too." Jaya handed them all tiny servings of rice and beans. "We need more food."

Taylor turned back, accepting the dish. "We need more of those big falls up on the ridges to the west and south of us. I think those hills are steep enough that we could take out a lot of people if they attack us."

Traps were a good idea, especially if they could keep the watchers

48

safe, too. "Since Nora was killed at the bunkhouses, maybe we should make some of those into traps. A couple are basically unusable. So, watchers could sit on top of one of the good ones, then if someone is coming, they'd get down, and lead anyone pursuing them through a trapped house. We'd cut beams so the watchers could pull a rope when they got out, collapsing the whole bunkhouse on whoever's inside."

"Great idea, Kit. Just like you and…" Taylor swallowed hard. "Like you and Sean did in that town, only planned, rather than on the fly with a chainsaw."

Kit stepped toward Taylor to comfort her. They both missed Sean so much. The front door opened and Dunia pushed past Taylor, standing between them. "There is a steep hill between us and the campground, too. We could set traps there."

Taylor grabbed Dunia's shoulders, turning her to the back door. "Come with me. I have bad news." Dunia swore under her breath and followed Taylor outside.

Faris lifted a bundle of sticks to the table. He'd taken the news of Nora's death hard, but like everyone who'd seen war, he swallowed whatever feelings got in the way of getting stuff done. "We made triggers. I come with you and set traps?" He pointed at his injured shoulder, then at Kit's hands. "Two makes one?"

Kit chuckled. "The two of us make one person? That's about right. We'll take a saw and go to those bunkhouses in the southwest. We can trap those first, because they're useless. Then we'll go to the ridge lines and build log rollers, and from there, we can scope out the hill near the campground."

They filled water bottles, gathered rope, string, and tools from the collection in the tool shed, and walked through the orchard. Several of the children watched the chickens scratch, making sure they stayed in the orchard, while one adult watched the kids. Kit nodded at the young man, but kept moving.

Jen was nowhere to be seen. He was hit with a rush of anguish. She couldn't have gone missing. That would be too, too cruel. He sent up a prayer. *I've just found her. Don't take her from me.* He shook off the low grade panic. His aunt was a sensible woman, who knew the land. She'd be with the livestock or the gardeners, showing Robin the ropes. He had a lot to do, and only a half a day to do it in. He couldn't lose it to worry. *Keep her safe. Please.* They trudged on, half an eye on the people he passed, half on the job ahead.

When they reached the south bunkhouses, Faris shook his head. "These bad."

"Yes. But that's good for us. If we can draw people in here, then we can easily collapse them." Kit put his forearms against a rock and mortar wall and pushed—solid. He peered in, then stomped on the floor. The planks creaked and cracked, but held. The roof sagged in the middle, the long pole at the roof's peak drooping, each of the rafters crossing below the ridgepole sagging too. "We find some poles, prop the rafters up, then saw small wedges from the tops of the center rafters and the ridgepole." He put his damaged hands together, to show Faris what he meant. "We saw the wedges two-thirds of the way through. Then, we saw straight from the bottom, almost but not quite up to the wedge, leaving a tiny bit of wood in place. Next, we attach rope to the top of the wedges, and route the ropes through a loop on the top of the roof. When you yank on the rope, it pulls the top wedges up and out. That will let the beams collapse, like yanking a keystone from an arch."

Faris nodded. "Yes, I understand. We work." Faris was a hard worker and took direction like a pro. Between the two of them, they rigged two of the bunkhouses, sawing partially through some of the floor planks as they left. They threaded the pull ropes across tree branches, Kit clearing each branch of needles, sap and twigs to let the ropes move smoothly. The ropes converged at a group of boulders about forty feet from the bunkhouses.

"I wish we could test these, but we'll just have to hope." Kit surveyed the steep hill to the north of them, recognizing the path he and Taylor had explored earlier about three hundred yards away. Nearer to their location, another animal path headed up through the rocks, so he and Faris climbed. Halfway up the hill, Kit stopped and pulled his boot back. A footprint, smaller than his by far. Smaller than Taylor's, too. "See that? Someone's been here recently." Kit put his foot next to the print.

"Small. Child?" Faris' head turned and twisted.

"Maybe. Let's go. Watch for people." Kit led the rest of the way up, finding more small prints, along with a few larger boot prints, about the same size as his. Toward the top, the ground became rocky, and the prints faded away. They climbed, circling rocks, and ended on a rocky platform overlooking the ranch and the campground to the north. The ground was heavily scuffed. "People have been here, for sure."

Faris brought his arm up, as though he was shooting. "Good place to hunt."

Kit agreed. "I wish we could leave someone up here all the time, but we don't have enough people or guns. We can have whoever's watching the south bunkhouses keep an eye on this place, but any signal will warn an enemy up here that they've been spotted. We've got to find a way to charge the batteries for the radios." He led the way along the top of the hill to the log he and Taylor had already set as a trap, showing Faris what they'd done.

They walked on, trying to stay hidden from anyone watching below. Kit was grateful he'd left his blood-stained shirt behind, because the bright yellow would shine like a beacon. Fifty yards later, Kit found another fallen tree. "Not as good, because it fell at an angle. It won't hold as many rocks." Like the other, roots still clung to the earth, but the top of the tree was down the hill from the root ball. It was further down the slope, too, where they'd be exposed as they worked on it. "Let's go on, find a better one." Eventually, they found three trees stacked high in a tangled mess about a quarter of the way down the precipitous slope. "Perfect. We can stake them in place, cut the roots loose, then stack more rocks and logs behind them. We can do some work now, behind the trunks, then finish early tomorrow morning or late tonight, when no one can see us."

After scanning the campground and the area north of the ranch for movement, or the flash of binoculars, he and Faris skittered down the loose shale to the trees. Faris sawed through the roots holding the bottom tree on the uphill side, while Kit ducked around the ends of the tree to place some of the larger trigger sticks the team had carved, bringing the strings attached to the triggers around behind the tree, but not all the way up the hill.

"Done." Faris wiped sweat from his brow.

"Good job. We'll finish tonight or tomorrow." Kit scanned the campground with his binoculars, then swept back to the ranch, ending just north of the northeast bunkhouses. "Shoot. Smoke!"

CHAPTER SEVEN

Alma Garcia. Harmony Ranch, Arizona

The blood under Alma's nails was dark enough to be dirt from the garden. She'd dug it out from her thumb before realizing what it was while Jen called the meeting to order. She hadn't managed to clean herself up fully before the community was told to gather. With only enough time to wash her hands—and not very thoroughly, as it turned out—she hadn't changed her clothes. Thankfully, her hoodie covered her stained shirt and Matias had wiped away a smear of Nora's blood from her cheek prior to Taylor interrupting with the invitation.

A sheet covered Nora's body on the ground in front of the barn. The community circled, staring with disbelief and shaking their heads. As Kit told them about the scene he'd found, gasps and curses flew. Jen didn't speak as she scanned the faces in the yard, her fists clenched. Alma kept Emelia, and Matias as far from Kit and his aunt as possible, but Jen's peaceful ranch had been defiled. Alma understood that kind of pain. Jaya cried and spoke about how Nora had rescued them and delivered them to the ranch, tears rolling down her cheeks.

"We won't accept violence in our community," Jen's voice quavered. "We will find her killer, and bring them to justice." The words sent a shiver over Alma's body. She pulled the hoodie down, ensuring her shirt was hidden. Matias clenched her hand tighter.

Emelia pulled Alma further back from the crowd and put her lips to Alma's ear. "Can't we just tell them?"

Alma turned sharply. "No." Her command, though barely whisper, made Emelia's lower lip tremble but Mama had said she was proud of the way Alma had kept her siblings safe. She'd do whatever was needed to protect them.

The gathering shifted, splitting into families and groups of friends. None of them asked Alma's family to join them. They were alone. She was right to cover up what she knew. No one would believe them. Alma tugged Matias and Emelia away. She hurried her family back toward the tent, following Mister H and his wife, Sharon, through the orchard.

"It sounded like they thought it was someone here that stabbed that poor woman." Sharon's voice was hushed.

Mister H pulled his wife closer, his arm around her waist. "I thought that too, hon."

She leaned her head on his shoulder. "I'm scared."

Alma winced. Adults shouldn't be scared of anything; they should be in control.

Sharon lifted her face to Mister H. "But what about that crowd in the old campground to the north? Could it be one of them? Charlie went there, didn't he? Do you think he came back and got Nora instead of Jen because Nora was alone?"

Alma walked faster, still holding Matias' hand tight. She hadn't heard of any crowd and didn't know anything about Charlie's personality, but if they thought him capable of killing, she didn't want to. That meant the ranch fortifications weren't just a precaution.

"All the more reason to not go out by yourself. You stick close by no matter what Jen and her lot tell us to do." His grip must have tightened because Sharon staggered a little closer to him. "I don't want them to pick you off. If anyone wants to mess with you, they'll have to go through me first." Mister H led Sharon away through the gate. It banged shut behind them.

An outsider had proven the defenses were so weak anyone could and had wandered in. Michael Martinez wasn't just anyone though. Maybe he was part of the crowd Sharon was so concerned about. He might have killed her and returned to the north to rejoin his people. He wasn't alone! "Em, has Kit said anything to you about the people outside the ranch?" Alma turned. Emelia was dragging her feet and glancing back at the huddled family groups.

Matias pried his hand from Alma's. "He saw a big group north of the ranch the day he arrived. But he said they wouldn't come here."

"Why not?" Alma wasn't asking him; she was asking herself. Why wouldn't the big hotshot who had taken her parents, enslaved her siblings, and changed the world come after her? If he'd recognized her, he almost certainly would!

Matias plucked an apple from one of the trees in the orchard and polished it on his t-shirt. "Kit says they'd go to the town. There's nothing here worth taking."

Alma frowned at him. "Were those his exact words?" She took the apple from him, checked no one had seen him stealing rations, and tucked it into her pocket.

"No. Robin told me." Matias pushed open the orchard gate and it squealed. "She said she'd heard Jen and Kit talking about them being like a small army so there wasn't anything here for them. They'd need proper supplies."

"But Kit and Taylor are making traps, aren't they? I thought that they were trying to make the ranch safer."

Matias shrugged. "I don't know what they are doing. You'll need to ask Em." He stepped onto the low bar and swung on the gate. "I like Robin, but she talks a lot."

Alma swept a hand over his hair. He'd found Robin, or she'd found him. Alma didn't really know which came first, but Robin was orphaned too and they'd discovered each other in their grief. While she weeded the vegetable garden, they played a game with colored stones and grasses. Their giggles lightened Alma's heart.

She continued to the tent, letting Emelia fall behind. No one had bothered to tell her what was going on in the real world. She was not a child. The existence of a small army shouldn't've have been hidden from her. She was the head of her family, responsible for her sister and brother. She shouldn't be kept in the dark simply because of her age. If they wouldn't tell her what was going on, she'd find out for herself, but the mess had to be cleared up first.

Ripping open the tent zipper, she scurried in. Matias and Emelia followed. Alma hurriedly changed and added her blood-stained shirt to the pile she'd taken from Emelia and bundled all the clothes into the canvas bag. "They can't find us with this."

Emelia's hands shook and her eyes were wide. "You said that about Nora, but you didn't stop them finding her." She grabbed her thick hair in her fists and pulled it, screwing up her face.

"Please, stop doing that!" Alma wrapped Emelia in a tight hug. Her sister's arms trembled under her grip.

"We've got to tell." Emelia's voice was muffled against Alma's shoulder.

"No!" How could she get her sister to understand that they couldn't risk being kicked out?

Emelia buried her face deeper. "Kit will believe us."

Alma rubbed Emelia's back, more to calm her thoughts than to comfort her sister. "Kit found the body and the first thing he did was to tell everyone. We can't trust any of them."

"I trust him."

Alma drew away and pried Emelia's hands open, releasing her curls. Alma held Em's shoulders. "Did he tell you about the people north of the ranch?"

Emelia shook her head. "Not really."

"What are you making when you work with Kit in the afternoons?"

"I don't know. He tells me what to do since his hands are so badly hurt." She fiddled with the hem of her shirt. "They might be traps or something. Some of them are for food."

"Is he making fortifications?" Alma put the word in quotes since Kit had offered Emelia that much a few days earlier.

"That's all he said." Em tried to pull away.

Alma's grip tightened. "We can't tell them anything. Mama would want us to stay. We should do what she wanted." The lie flowed from her lips easily. Emelia would obey Mama. "They won't let us stay if they find out we knew about Nora. This place is our best chance at surviving."

The stiffness in Emelia's shoulders eased and Alma dared to let her go. Alma couldn't work out when all the familiar fight had disappeared, but Emelia's slumped shoulders and downcast face told her she shouldn't expect a challenge. It frightened Alma that her boisterous, opinionated little sister was a shell of her former self.

Alma picked up the canvas bag and stuffed a lighter into her pocket. "I didn't have enough time to hide the body properly before. But this I can do." She jerked the bag. "Once this is gone, you'll be safe." She kissed Em's cheek. "I promise. Wait here." Emelia dropped to her air mattress and curled up facing away. "Mati. Stay with her."

Matias sat and pulled out the book on simple mechanics Jen had lent to him with a bemused smile. It wasn't a children's book, but Matias seemed more than content with the highly illustrated manual he'd found on her shelf. "Don't be too long." His fingers tightened around the book.

"What is it Mati? What's the matter?"

His lower lip trembled. "Will that Michael come back for Em? If he is with the people outside the camp, he could."

Alma shook her head. "He didn't know Em was there when he killed Nora. She'll be fine. I'll keep you both safe."

"But he's not sorry for what he did to Nora or to us or to America. He's not trying to make it better at all. He's a very bad man."

Matias put everything together in a simple way that made complete sense. Michael Martinez wasn't trying to undo what he'd been a part of. If watching the world, not just America, fall apart had no effect on his morals, nothing would change him. Alma slung the strap over her shoulder. "He is a bad man, you're right, but I'm not going to let him hurt you. I promise."

She left the tent zipper open and pushed the bag to her hip. Removing their link to Nora's death would be simple if she could find a spot to burn the clothes. Since she'd already dug a pit outside the fence, it was as good a place as any.

She followed the fence of the back pasture toward the tree line and stream, then squeezed through the open gate. Jen had kept the animals nearer the property after the hailstorm and—now that Alma knew about the external threat—it made far more sense that she didn't let them roam free. The adults had stayed busy with secret tasks around the ranch, popping into the house every so often, speaking to Taylor and Kit in hushed voices. Everything was slotting into place. Perhaps the ranch wasn't as safe as Doc had made it out to be. Alma rushed to the shadow of the tall pines, checking behind her.

She hurried over protruding roots, tripping and slipping on the soft pine needles. The crows had left, but Nora's blood stained the earth and dried grasses a brownish red. Bloodied footprints crossed to the far fence and through the spot where she'd left Nora propped against the fencepost. All the prints were considerably bigger than her own. She hadn't even checked if she or Emelia had left evidence behind before she'd fled. No one could check DNA or match hair strands in her broken world, but it didn't stop her from shivering. The ghost of Nora lingered everywhere. There were bound to be traces of her, or Em, too.

Alma slowed long enough to listen for pursuit. She was alone. She sped past the murder scene, climbed over the fence and ran to the trees.

The pit was undisturbed, and the shovel was still propped against the tree where she left it. She threw the canvas bag down and yanked out the clothes. Her shirt stank of sweat and the blood mixed with earth in crusty patches. She balled Emelia's sweatpants, shirt and jacket on top of hers. There was more blood than she remembered. It was a miracle Em made it back to the tent unseen. If Michael Martinez had seen Em, she would've been dead too.

Alma flicked the lighter. The flame licked the edge of the fabric and hungrily spread over the sweatpants forcing her to stumble back. Bright orange flames shot up but without the friendly crackle of wood, the unnerving, quiet whisper was out of place. Everything was out of place.

Fire crept up the sleeve of Emelia's prized denim jacket. Back at the tent, Emelia huddled, her spirit crushed by what she'd witnessed. Michael Martinez would pay. He'd pay big time for making Em watch his hideous actions, making her a part of his crimes.

The fire dripped from the sweatpants and caught at Emelia's shirt. The fabric blackened and the flames tinged blue when they crept over the print. Alma crouched at the base of the tree, heat shimmering near the wilting leaves. The nearest twig caught alight and she jumped up. Grabbing the shovel, she whacked the tiny spark to the ground and stamped on it.

Only an idiot would light a fire so close to a tree. The branches above were too high to catch, but plenty of other plants were nearby and with everything so dry, it was too great a risk to let it burn uncontrolled. Most of the clothes were already indistinguishable, too charred to pick out any motif on the fabric. She filled the shovel from one of the piles she'd made earlier and threw it over the failing flames at the edges, allowing the center of the fire to burn on. Musk scented smoke drifted through at the dirt in long lazy plumes, then the fire spat and sparked. The mound of pine needles she'd mistakenly fed it with caught alight. She hissed and backed away. Dark smoke welled up, the black plume rising straight up in the air without a breeze to carry it away. Alma coughed, reached for the soil pile and shoveled earth over the unexpected bonfire. The smoke billowed above her like a mushroom, giving her a temporary break from the choking cloud. She chucked more soil into the hole, her eyes stinging and tears streaming down her cheeks. Another plume swirled, gathering over the partially filled in grave and wafting upwards on the hot air.

She pulled back, her stomach lurching. The smoke rose like a signal for all to see. She tossed the last of the soil over the flames. The black bitter smoke tickled the back of her throat and made her retch. She scooped one last mound of earth over the smoldering fragments, a single thin wisp curling in the air. She grabbed the shovel and ran for the fence, but not the gate.

She threw the shovel over the wire, coughing violently. If anyone had seen the smoke they would run straight to the site, so her best bet was to take a long, circuitous route, avoiding the camp and main yard. She sped to the stream's steep bank and staggered down, slipping on the mud. Her feet squelched in the dregs of the river and she stepped over the trickle of water.

She gulped a lungful and coughed enough to make her eyes water. Swiping the tears away and wiping her mouth, she jogged to the overhanging trees. Their broad leaves and spindly branches swept low to the ground. She pushed them aside with the handle of the shovel and a soot-grayed hand. "Oh, no!" She lifted her hoodie and wiped her cheek. A dark streak stained the material. It would be no use walking into camp covered in soot and claiming nothing had happened.

She kept to the cover of the trees and followed the stream along the edge of the back pasture. Pulling up her hood, she sank deeper into the shadows, dashing from one tree to the next, keeping her charcoal-plastered face out of sight. The stream ran to the far corner of the back pasture and through a wild garden. She approached the water several times, but she didn't have any cover which meant she'd be easy to spot. The dribble of water ran across her end of the summer pasture with the fence and the large, terrifying cattle. She skirted the boundary and past the far corner, then sprinted across the cracked asphalt road, and back into the trees. Following the stream she climbed a gentle rise. The water dribbled over the rocks in an unimpressive waterfall.

She scrambled up the gentle incline, her sneakers slipping on the smoothed wet stones. Loose pebbles scuttled over each other, and she ducked behind the larger rocks that formed a ridge. She leaned on a large boulder shaded from the sky by twiggy branches, her manic heart drumming hard against her ribs. Water pooled in a shallow natural basin no bigger than a baby bath, rippling where the water trickled in. She pulled her hoodie off, kneeled, and plunged her hands into the pleasantly cool water. It was deeper than she thought, reaching halfway up her forearms. Ripping leaves from the bough above, she scrubbed her palms and the clear water clouded. She shook the droplets from her fingers, tightened her ponytail, twisting her hair and wrapping it around, tucking it into a bun. She splashed her face, the air momentarily shocked out of her by the chill. Then, pulling more leaves from the tree, she scrubbed her cheeks, forehead and eyes. Her skin tingled from her fierce attack.

She stripped off her shirt, sweatpants and shoes, then climbed into the pool. She washed, scooping and pouring the water down her chest and back. She scrubbed the dark patches on her knees and grime between her toes. At last she felt clean.

She shivered, stepped out, and swiped the water from her skin. Sitting on the rock, she lifted herself up and stretched her neck. She rooted around in her hoodie pocket and pulled out the confiscated apple Matias had picked. She hadn't had time to eat her breakfast rations.

Alma crunched, the juicy fruit cleansing her mouth from the foul smoke and scratching her sore throat. But she'd done it. She'd made the ranch safe for them again. He couldn't know Emelia had seen him. If he had, her sister wouldn't have made it back to their tent. He wouldn't have hesitated to kill a witness. He didn't have a single, real human emotion. He'd stolen her parents' lives and enslaved her and her siblings. He was, as Matias had said, a bad man. The worst. He'd set the world shaking and exploding and stooped low enough to take the life of someone doing good. He didn't deserve to get away with it and live.

She threw the stripped apple core to the ground. It bounced and lodged itself between the rocks. "You won't grow if you're stuck there." She crept over and shoved it through the gap, then grabbed her shirt and slipped it on. "We're stuck with Martinez. How will anything be normal again if he is in the world? All he does is destroy everything good." Alma bowed her head and reached for her sweatpants. It was wrong, she shouldn't even consider it, but it was like the pink elephants she'd told Emelia to think about; she couldn't shake the dream of a world without him.

She slipped on her shoes and grabbed the shovel, then scrambled across and up the rocks. She'd come down a different path. The trees were beautiful from a distance, but up close, their leaves where pitted from the hailstorm and their roots exposed from the recent earthquake. The hillside seemed untouched and peaceful, but things had changed.

A large rock, almost as wide as she was tall jutted out of the hillside. She gripped a branch of a gnarled old tree growing out over the slab and tested the ground for stability. It was solid. She took a couple of steps over the gentle slope pushed the foliage away and breathed in the splendor of her new home. Admittedly, it was bedraggled but it had potential, and plenty of it. Emelia had Kit and Taylor who adored her, and the dogs to keep her entertained. Matias loved the machinery and was finding his voice with Robin by his side. She only needed to prove that she was trustworthy enough to be treated as an adult before she could settle and find out if it really was safe with the crowd to the north of the ranch and Michael Martinez on the loose.

She adjusted her grip on the shovel. Safety was what mattered. They would be safer if *he* was gone. Mama had been proud of her choices. Unforgivable though it might be, she would do it if she was given the chance. He had to die.

CHAPTER EIGHT

Catherine "Cat" Murphy. Arivaca, Arizona

The monsoonal rain had come and gone with the abruptness of an unexpected guest. A bespectacled Tom sat in the armchair next to Cat, mulling over a clipboard, rolling a number two pencil in his fingers. "My personal stuff is packed and ready to go." He made a check mark on the paper and slid the pencil in between his teeth.

"Lillie and I have packed a big duffle bag of clothes, toiletries, and a few small mementos. Most of my favorite things were dirty, so we washed a load of laundry." Cat picked up a pair of readers on the side table between her chair and Tom's. "I'm so thankful for that solar/generator setup that you and the boys put together. Could you imagine having to cook and do laundry without electricity right now?"

He took the pencil out of his mouth and scratched something on the list. "I can. I've been washing my stuff by hand and hanging it out over the fence to dry." He glanced over at the kitchen. "Okay, so Sandy said something about lab-grown meat."

"Blech." Cat stuck her finger to her tongue and faux gagged. "I'd like to take some chickens and a few cattle. Even if we can't keep them underground, maybe we'll have access to come and go for a while."

"I was hoping we could travel a little lighter than that. As in, throw what you've got packed in a pickup and maybe get there before nightfall." He turned to face her, his eyes narrowing. "Things around here aren't getting any better, and in a hurry. If we're going to go, Cat, we need to get gone."

"I know. Something's on the horizon, I can feel it in the air." Her heart sank, her body humming with a primal sense of urgency. "I just wish the others would reconsider and come with us."

"We've all made our choices, honey." Tom reached across the table and enveloped her fingers under his. "I'm afraid the time for wishing and talking is over." His grip tensed for a moment, then he released his hold, patting the back of her hand as he withdrew his touch.

She shook away the foreboding heaviness and refocused her energy on the business at hand, a tactic she'd learned the hard way, over many years as a rancher. In this tough country, making decisions based on emotions could be costly, and the price was often paid in lives. More than once she'd had to weigh the life of a single animal over the lives of many, and the lives of humans over the lives of animals. "I just hate to travel empty handed. If we take some live-stock, maybe we can use them to barter?"

Fiddling with his mustache, he blinked his steely eyes. "Cat, even though the livestock *are* the most abundant and marketable assets we have at hand, we'd be taking resources from the kids. We won't need them... and they'll just slow us down."

Her heart pounded at the reality of leaving behind everything she'd ever worked for, everything she'd built. "What about horses?"

"Same, hon. They wouldn't contribute to the bunker, they'd just consume." His head swiveled to the picture windows. "I know how much you love them, but the kids can make good use of them here. I reckon this is another sacrifice we're going to have to make."

"You're probably right." Through the great windows, the black outlines of several horses dotted the decimated vista. She inhaled, knowing she'd most likely never smell the salty, pungent smell of their scent again. "Taking them would probably be selfish." But to never ride again was a terrible blow. "Chickens? We wouldn't need a trailer for them." As the words left her mouth, she saw Tom's face darken. The hair stood up on the back of her neck as an uncomfortable warmth spread across her cheeks.

"Dammit, Catherine. Taking *any* livestock is just impractical." Rubbing the back of his neck, he touched a finger to his mouth before he continued, metering out his words. "It would require a lot more work to pull together before we could hit the road. We'd have to get the trailer ready, the animals loaded, food and water gathered. Pulling a trailer will limit where we can go and how fast we can get there." He scribbled some figures on the page. "If we left in the next hour, we could be to the bunker tonight—before nightfall."

Cat sat in silence, waiting for him to say something else, knowing that the next thing she said would be crucial. She chewed on the inside of her cheek and contemplated her options.

Tom's neck stiffened. "For crying out loud, woman, we're burning daylight."

"*Woman?*" Cat's ribcage tightening, her heartbeat pounded in her ears. Instead of backing down, she pushed further. "I don't think we need to worry about feed or water for the cattle. The bunker's not that far away." Her mind started to race as she computed figures out loud, her voice shaking. "Even at twenty-five miles per hour, we should be able to make it to the bunker in four hours—eight hours worst case scenario. These desert cattle can go six, maybe seven days without water, and a hell of a lot longer without feed." Realistically, all the animals should be able to go at least a day without any food or water without much discomfort, but the idea of depriving them even a little still made her sick to her stomach. "We'd be on the road less than half a day. This is totally feasible. I'm not being impractical."

"Yeah, Cat. It's doable." Tom looked up from his notepad, his eyes narrow and flinty. "But just because you *can* do something, doesn't mean that you *should.*"

His rationale wasn't flawed. Even if she was torqued at him, Cat knew better than to let her emotions supersede her logic. She balled her hands, flexed her fingers, and forced down her feelings. Cracking her knuckles, she acknowledged his wisdom. "Valid points." She peeked over at his paper, surprised at his precise penmanship. "What's that?"

"It's a list of all the things we'd need to—responsibly—do in order to do what you want to do. Bare minimum." He didn't look up from his cyphering, but his tone softened. "Say we took a dozen cattle and a dozen chickens. We'd need something to contain the chickens, a tote of grain mix, at least thirty gallons of potable water, an emergency vet kit, a stock trailer, extra spare tires, additional fuel..." Looking over his readers at Cat, Tom tapped his pencil on the table. "...and I'm sure I've forgotten more than one thing."

Before she could say anything, he turned away. Some hopeful anticipation seeped from her body, replaced by an aching near her tailbone. She twisted in her chair, a twinge of pain running through her stump. "Well, just us humans are going to need five or ten gallons of drinking water and some emergency rations. Let's just ask Estrella to pack up whatever she thinks is best?" Cat rubbed her thigh above the amputation, kneading her tender muscles. "She'll be pragmatic. Don't you think?"

"Hmm?" Tom stopped scrutinizing the window, unclenched his jaw, and exhaled through his nose. "Yeah. Good idea."

"Fine." She took the notepad from his hands, slapping it on the table. "Now. About Grady. Do you think he and Estrella can co-exist?"

Tom leaned back, pulled his readers off and folded the glasses. Closing his eyes, he rested his elbow on the side table and rubbed both his temples with one hand. "Are we done arguing about the livestock?"

"Yes." She lowered her chin and attempted to smile. "For now."

"Fine." He opened his eyes and studied Cat. "Okay, I've talked to Estrella. She sees the practicality of having Mr. Jordan around."

"I hope he understands that she only killed his brother out of necessity. Banding together is the only way we're all going to survive this." She wrung her hands. "Without us here, they're going to need each other."

"Oh, they'll come to an understanding—or he'll just wither up and die. Men are funny that way." Tom grabbed the arms of his chair and pulled himself to his feet. "Even if there are hard feelings, he might warm up to her after he eats her cooking. As shy as he is, and as much as he likes tinkering around in the shop, he'll probably spend most of his time outside anyway."

"I'm uneasy about it all, but—if your great niece is right—we're running out of time." She studied her hands and frowned. "Much as I hate it, since we can't convince them to go with us, we've just got to trust that they'll be able to make the right decisions and pray that they're able to take care of themselves." A shadow crossed her lap. The handsome old cowboy standing next to the picture window, gazing off into the distance. "Tom?"

"Yeah?" He turned and strode to her.

Cat looked down again. "I sure hope she's wrong."

He crouched in front of her, resting his hand on her injured leg. "Me, too, honey. Me, too."

She let her hands settle on his shoulders. "Do you think we should put off leaving until tomorrow?" Maybe he'd reconsider the livestock debate and wake up on the same page as her.

He reached across his chest and touched the tips of his left fingers to the tips of hers. "We've got a break in the weather right now. I think we need to get on the road as soon as possible, before another storm rolls in, or another big earthquake hits, or whatever other hell breaks loose."

"Are you sure?" Now that they'd made their choice, she didn't want to stick around for all the feelings. "Won't we be traveling in the dark?"

"Maybe, but..." He stood, his knees cracking and popping. "It's going to be dangerous either way—in the daylight or in the dark, Cat." Stretching, he braced his lower back with his hands. "If we don't go soon, we might not have the option of going at all."

The door creaked and Jim and Grady entered. Shedding their coats, they stamped the mud from their feet. "We've got the tires fixed on the truck." Jim hung his hat on a hook. "And, Mr. Jordan made a few upgrades to your knee walker, Ms. Murphy."

The grubby farmer removed his boots, then shuffled over to Cat carrying the apparatus. He knelt, propping the leg against her side table, then back peddled a few steps.

"Thank you." The neighbor had figured out a way to fine-tune the height adjustment on her leg *and* made a foot using one of her favorite boots. "Nice job, Grady. I think I'll call her 'Leg 2.0'.... Or maybe 'Peggy.'" The tension broke as the men let out groans and chuckles.

"You're welcome, Ms. Murphy." Grady set his hat on the floor.

She examined the gadget further. "Is that a hinge on the cradle?"

"Yeah." Grady trudged closer to Cat and crouched by her chair. "I've made the cradle hinge so that you can put your weight on your knee. Or..." He pulled a pin on the support, dropping the cradle from horizontal to vertical. "...you can swing it down and have more of a traditional wooden leg. If I had a little more time, I could probably get it fitted better—it'd be more comfortable. Maybe make a socket out of paper mâché..." He set down the leg and rose to his feet. "What you really need is a good fiberglass guy."

Tom ambled over next to Grady. "This is good, Grady, really good. Brilliant." He patted the man on the back, then hunkered down to inspect the updated brace.

"Mr. Callahan? Ms. Murphy?" Jim approached the group and stood on the carpet in his stocking feet. "Grady, err, Mr. Jordan and I talked about it and we'd like to send some provisions with you."

Tom twisted his neck to face the boy. "That's great son, we could really use some extra food and water, just in case." He smiled, then returned to studying the leg.

Jim stepped closer to Cat. "I was thinking that you'd want to contribute to the bunker, and I hate for you to leave without anything to barter with. We were thinking maybe you could take a few cattle and some chickens?"

Cat bared her teeth, sucking air through them, but didn't say a word. Tom was looking at her, and his jaw was set.

"I'd sure like to keep the truck, Ms. Murphy." Jim stroked his chin and stared at the ceiling. "I've been thinking about it and I'm hoping to figure out a way to use it to haul water from that guzzler." He tugged on his chin, his eyes darting back and forth. "Would it be okay if I went with you and brought the truck home?"

"That's a thought, but I don't think it's a good idea for you to leave your family right now—for any amount of time. Every time we separate, something goes haywire." Cat waved the idea away. "No, you stay here."

Tom placed a half-chewed toothpick in his mouth. "And keep the livestock, you've got young 'uns to worry about."

Cat reconsidered their earlier conversation. "Now, Tom, I..."

Tom interrupted her. "Plus, the ranch is getting dangerously low on diesel. This is going to be a one-way trip. We've got to figure something else out."

"I don't mean to be butting in, but I could probably drive you." Grady stood, wringing his hat in his hand. "I still have a pickup and horse trailer. How far are we talking?"

"It's about fifty miles past Sahuarita, so probably over two hundred miles round trip." Tom bent down, picked up the brace and turned it in his hands. He kneeled next to Cat, then lifted her calf and held it up, pushing the footstool over several inches.

"I'm not sure you can even get to Sahuarita. The freeway between Nogales and Tucson is jammed with rigs." Grady gazed out the south facing windows. "Can you get there any other way?"

Tom bent Cat's knee and she scooted forward, letting him fit her leg in the cradle. He slid his hand between the chair cushion and her leg, buckling the strap around her thigh. "I s'pose we could go through Old Mexico, but that route wasn't the safest before things went to hell. I expect it'll be worse now." Strapping her calf in, he stood up and offered his hands to Cat. "And..." He cringed. "... we'd have to go through Nogales."

"I've always hated Nogales—even on a good day. I don't want to go that direction. How'd Evelyn's crew get here?" Setting her foot on the floor, Cat laid her wrists in Tom's hands and grabbed his fore-arms. "I'm ready."

He pulled her up to stand on the brace, then held her steady. Reaching for the crutch, he slid it under Cat's arm. "I think you should practice with this until you get the hang of your new toy."

Grady loomed next to the couch. "They were driving in the barrow pit when I saw them."

"So, it'll be off-road if we go that way." Cat used the crutch and the brace to take a small step. "But it can be done." She glanced up at Tom towering next to her and took another step.

"With a pickup. I'm not sure about a trailer." Grady swiveled, tracking Tom and Cat as she plodded around the room. "Again, I know this isn't any of my business. But where are you going, anyway?"

Tom growled, leaning close to Cat's ear. "*With a pickup.*"

"That's something we wanted to talk to you about, Grady." Cat ignored Tom, stopping next to the neighbor. "Tom and I are going to stay with his niece and family, but we'd like to invite you to stay here, with Jim, Estrella, and the children."

"I, er." He pulled back, his eyes shifting from Tom to Cat to Jim and back again. "What did Lillie say?"

"It was her idea." Tom slipped an arm around Cat's waist. "She's off making up a room for you right now."

"The little firecracker went around and pitched it to everyone else." Jim sidled over to stand next to Grady. "It's unanimous."

Grady picked at the frayed edge of his filthy trucker's cap. "Oh, now, I don't know."

"Mr. Jordan." Tom stopped walking and didn't speak again until the man looked at him. "You'd be doing us a huge favor. I've been torn about leaving, but I need to go and I'd feel much more comfortable about it if I knew you were here—fellow veteran, and a jack of all trades."

"I need to sit now." Cat circled back to the dining room table. "Plus..." She sat down and pointed at the barn entrance. "Nobody goes against Lil."

The young girl emerged in the doorway and bounced into the room. "Nobody goes against me, what?"

"They say you want me to stay here." Grady mumbled, his head bowed. "Are you sure about that?"

"Yup. It's the right thing to do. You need a family..." Straight backed, Lillie stepped closer to Grady. "Besides, you said you weren't going to give up until you'd earned your forgiveness. You can't do that if you're not here."

Grady kept looking at his shoes. "I don't deserve a family."

"We don't always get what we deserve." Lillie stepped closer, her chin set. "Or deserve what we get." Everyone sat in silence for a moment, then she spun around and walked over to her brother. She reached up and grabbed the front of his shirt, twisting her little fist and pulling him down to her level. "Jim, convince him."

"Yes, Fire Lil." He glared at his sister, then put his hand over hers and disentangled her slender fingers. "Mr. Jordan." Jim pushed the girl away, grinning. "Why don't you and me go over to your place and gather your things, then you can take Mr. Callahan and Ms. Murphy to the bunker? When you come home, come to this home. We'll do a trial run."

Tom unstrapped and removed Cat's artificial limb. "I think that's a great idea, son." Lifting her legs, he pushed the ottoman up against her chair.

"Okay, that's settled. What do you think you can spare, Jim?" Cat rested her throbbing legs on the ottoman.

His back to Jim, Tom hunkered between the boy and Cat. Scowling, he shook his head.

The young man blushed. "Gosh, Ms. Murphy, I don't know... this is your place."

"Nope, it's yours now." She paused, searching the side table. "I wish I had some keys handy, something I could give you to demonstrate how very serious I am. Oh, well." She gritted her teeth. "Now talk to me."

"Yes, ma'am." The cowboy thought for a short time. "We can surely spare a dozen head of heavy heifers, that way you'll get some calves after you get there and settled in without the hassle of hauling babies." He glanced over Cat's shoulder. "Oh, and maybe a couple dozen chickens?"

"We've got a couple of totes of corn, oats, and barley back at our—I mean, *my* farm." Grady blinked rapidly, looking away. He cleared his throat and addressed Jim. "Chicken pellets, alfalfa, other feed, too. None of our livestock survived. Let me know what you want to take with you and we'll load it in the trailer. We can bring the rest over here when I get back."

"Catherine." Tom grimaced and grasped her by the wrist. "I thought we'd already discussed this."

"Thank you, Mr. Jordan." Cat pried Tom's fingers from her arm, plucking his notepad from the side table and thrusting it toward Grady. "Here's a list of the things we'll need. Now, you two get going. I want to be on the road by sundown."

Tom slapped his thigh and sprang to his feet. "You're the boss, Ms. Murphy. Let's go boys!" He led the young men to the coatrack.

The three men geared up. Tom stood on the threshold, holding the door open as the two other men hurried off into the late afternoon. He turned to face Cat, his gravelly voice venomous. "That was one snakey move, Catherine. I thought we were past this." He shoved his Stetson onto his head. "That kind of garbage don't fly in a partnership. You might want to think long and hard about coming with me."

As the door slammed shut, the bile of regret churned in Cat's bowels. She'd gone too far, and she didn't know if there was any way back.

CHAPTER NINE

Evelyn Parker. Anil Kumar Sanctuary, Arizona

Evelyn dragged the blanket over her face, wishing away the pain in her shoulder and hip to no avail. She'd soon need the meds Dr. Fulknier had given her, despite her reluctance to depend on them. Addiction and withdrawal were terrible—she was in no hurry to hallucinate snakes again.

Soft footsteps padded across the floor, ceramic clinked on the bedside table, and Evelyn pushed the cover away. A heavy, white stoneware mug rested on the nightstand, steam rising and wafting the scent of rich, dark, liquid energy to her. Floyd sat on the edge of the bed, tucking into a bowl of oats.

Evelyn attempted sitting up, then sighed and waved him toward her. "A little help for your new roommate, please?"

It was their first morning together in their shared apartment. Floyd had moved her from the infirmary the night before. He set down his bowl, and lifted her, stacking pillows behind her, and passing her the weighty coffee cup. "You still feel up to the council meeting today, Ev?"

She yawned, and half-stretched, careful of her injuries. "Yes. I know Dev wants to discuss Alec's behavior the other day." She savored the strong coffee, letting the steam dampen her face.

"You already told him how you feel. He'll understand if you want to skip it." He went back to work on the oatmeal, cupping the small bowl in one hand.

"I don't want to miss the first meeting, and I'm tired of lying in bed. Dr. Fulknier said I shouldn't be sedentary."

"I know. I just worry you'll over-do it." He rubbed her leg through the blanket. While she'd been confined to the infirmary, Floyd had settled them into one of the furnished one-bedroom apartments. With her left arm in a sling, there was little she could do to help, and she was happy to let Floyd handle it. She hadn't been so well-cared for since she was a child.

She finished her coffee, and he helped her from bed and to the bathroom. He washed the dishes while she brushed her teeth, then helped her dress. "Don't forget that." She pointed to the knife he'd given her back at the beginning of the disaster. She'd barely gone a minute without wearing it, and it had become of good luck talisman. He lifted her pant leg and strapped it around her calf. "We ought to get going."

They left their apartment at the end of the hallway on the fourth floor and walked to the elevator, taking it up to the first-floor conference room. Dev and Sandy waited at the oval conference table, Dev tapping a pen against the clipboard that lay in front of him. He stood when they entered. "Welcome back, Evelyn. It's good to see you up and around. I hope you're not in much pain."

"Not too bad." In fact, the ache in her shoulder was severe. Simply drawing a breath sent a hot jolt through her, but she hated lying in bed while other people were working. Dev, Professor Benson and Floyd had established contact with the Boulder School of Mines. More students, teachers, and families were on their way to the bunker, and Dev had provided lists of items people should bring with them. There was talk—excited talk—of continuing Dr. Goode's work. Sandy had even gone as far as whispering the word "cure" when she thought Evelyn wasn't listening. Whatever the reason for her daughter's uptick in energy, Evelyn was grateful; determined to do whatever was necessary to create a laboratory. They had a lot of work to do around the facility to prepare for those science-type arrivals.

Dev closed the door, and returned to the table, fingers steepled under his chin. "Thank you all for agreeing to sit on the council, and for meeting today. There's a lot to do, and hopefully, we'll have more people here to help soon. In the meantime, I'd like to discuss Alec."

Evelyn jolted back to the present. So much for hope! There were problems they had to solve below ground before they could hope to solve those above.

Dev consulted the clipboard. "On his first day here, Alec showed signs of agitation and used inappropriate language. I asked him if he was unwell, and he denied it, as did Professor Benson. Floyd, you searched his room for any signs he might be a danger to himself or others."

"His room was clean. No pills, no pill bottles. Nothing amiss." Floyd shrugged. "Which doesn't prove anything one way or another."

"Have there been any more outbursts?" Dev angled his chair toward Sandy.

She crossed one leg over the other. She wasn't wearing the engagement ring Dev had shown to Evelyn. "None that I've seen."

"That still doesn't prove he's okay." Dev pursed his lips.

Evelyn rested her hands on the table's cool surface. "We should give him the benefit of the doubt. He's a kid. Imagine how traumatized you'd be if you were a teenager, your parents were dead, and the world seemed like it was ending."

"I suppose that's true. But we're all traumatized, aren't we? The road trip was traumatic in itself." Dev leaned back, crossing his arms.

Evelyn laced her fingers. "Back when the explosions started, I had medication withdrawal pretty bad. Hallucinations, muscle cramps, headaches, paranoia."

Dev widened his eyes. "Do you mind sharing the nature of your illness?"

Evelyn looked down at her laced fingers, clutching her trembling hands. "Psychological. I suffer from severe anxiety and I ran out of Paxil. I can't imagine what would have become of me if I'd been alone."

"I appreciate your candor, Evelyn. What are your symptoms now?"

"I mean, the world's so crazy I barely notice my own anxiety." She laughed, the echo loud in the confined room, and her face warmed from embarrassment. "I'm fine. Some of the things that used to trigger me—going out in crowded places—I don't have to do anymore. You might want to ask Floyd. He took care of me."

Floyd started. "Well, she had some rough moments, but she made it through okay." Evelyn regretted putting him on the spot. It couldn't have been easy trying to manage her when she was hallucinating and half out of her mind. "She was never aggressive or abusive like Alec was with Sandy."

Dev pointed his pen. "What about you, Sandy? His aggression was focused on you. Will you feel safe if he remains here?"

Sandy pushed her hair behind her ears. "It's not the first time someone's raised their voice at me. Probably not the last. I say we give him another chance. We need biochemists." She flashed a smile at Dev.

Yep, she believes they can solve the fracking problem! Amazing! My daughter, the hero!

The door rattled and opened. Alec poked his head into the room. "Hey. Oh, sorry. I didn't know there was a meeting in progress." He pressed a palm to his chest and fluttered his eyelashes. "Are you talking about me?" He grinned and burst into laughter. "Just kidding. Sorry to interrupt." He turned to leave but stopped. "Oh, sorry about the other day, Sandy." He stepped out, easing the door closed.

Dev leaned forward. "See what I mean? What was with the theatrics? He's a very strange fellow."

Evelyn waved a hand toward the door. Sandy'd said that they needed biochemists. So Alec was a bit strange; if Sandy wanted him, they needed to keep him around. "He's *joking*, Dev." She cocked an eyebrow. "Maybe you feel guilty because we *were* talking about him."

"Perhaps that's true, but we're talking about him for good reason, given his outburst the other day." Dev tilted his head. "Floyd, what do you think?"

"I don't know, Dev. I made deliveries for years. I went inside peoples' homes. You can't imagine the things I've encountered. Is he high-strung? Sure. Is he dangerous?" Floyd shrugged. "Impossible to say."

Dev sighed, lifting his hands. "All right then, he stays. But I want to know immediately if any behavioral issues arise. Let's take a look at the outstanding projects." He tapped his pen against his worklist. He discussed the intercom system with Floyd and the power grid with Sandy—but made no mention of their science project—before finally addressing Evelyn. "You have limited mobility. I want you to stay as busy as you want, but also take care of your health."

"I will, Dev." She touched her sling. "And thank you for taking that into consideration."

He nodded. "The food systems all need preparation. The fish tanks need filling with water, as do the hydroponic planters. It's fairly light work and can be spread over a few days."

"Sounds perfect." Pain knifed through her shoulder, but having a purpose, helping others, gave her a contentment that lightened the agony. "With your permission, I'd like to look around the art studio, check out the supplies. Floyd said there are some kids coming soon. I could teach art classes."

Dev grinned. "Wonderful, Evelyn. Tell me if you need anything."

The meeting wrapped up a few minutes later, everyone leaving the conference room and heading off to their assignments.

Evelyn's stomach growled. She nudged Floyd. "I'm going back to the apartment for a nibble, and I'll get started afterward."

Floyd turned to her. "Want me to go with you and make you something?"

"No, thanks." She pulled him toward her for a kiss. "I'm going to take a pain pill, so there might be a nap in my future."

"That's a fine idea. I'll see you later." He hurried to catch up to Dev, disappearing down the hallway.

Evelyn rode the elevator back to the apartment, humming as she entered. She loved the spareness of the place, the basic, model-home furnishings Dev's father had chosen when he was planning to sell the apartments: a simple couch, chair and coffee table in the living room, a queen-sized bed with nightstands on either side. No useless tchotchkes collecting dust. She entered the small kitchen, palmed one ibuprofen and a codeine pill, following it with some water and a granola bar. The morning hadn't been eventful, but fatigue set in. She went to the bedroom and lay down on the bed. She'd nap for a couple hours, then start work in the agricultural area.

She lifted an old windup clock Floyd had found in one of the bunker's storage rooms and set it for noon. She closed her eyes, the clock ticking nearby. Somewhere deep within the bunker, water trickled. Day and night it flowed; Floyd suggested it was the underground stream. Between that, and the ticking, she drifted off.

Something woodsy scented the room, warm and pleasant like a campsite. The scent entered her dreams, carrying memories of summer nights and s'mores. She inhaled. A cough erupted from the back of her throat, jarring her awake. The aroma turned acrid, leaving a bitter coating on her tongue. The windup clock read 12:15.

A high-pitched wail pierced the air, jolting her with adrenaline. Her ears buzzed with each repetition of the alarm. A metallic voice sounded. "This is not a drill. Evacuate to the nearest safety zone. This is not a drill. Evacuate ..." The warning repeated over and over.

The Anil Kumar Sanctuary was on fire.

Evelyn trembled, her heart banging in her chest. The bitter smell of burning rubber seared her nostrils and throat. The metallic voice on the emergency alert system repeated while a light strobed on and off. She groaned, rolling onto her right side, and pushed to sit on the edge of the bed. Easing off the bed, her feet landed on the frigid floor. Her heart pounded in time with the flashing emergency light.

The room spun around her, her head swirling, an effect of the drugs she'd taken. Despite her vertigo, she rose, hanging on to the bed, and slid a foot forward. Edging along the wall, she jumped when a banging sounded from the front door. "Coming!"

She opened it and Alec stepped into the room, his splotchy skin flaring bright red. "Evelyn." His pupils were enormous, with the thinnest sliver of green irises circling them.

She stepped toward him, shouting over the alarm and recorded announcement. "Are you all right, Alec?"

"I'm fine." He brushed bangs off his pink forehead. "There's an electrical fire. Floyd sent me to make sure you're okay while they put it out."

Typical Floyd, doing the most dangerous thing and taking care of others. "Where's the safety zone?"

"Outside, off the entrance tunnel." He pointed vaguely. "We'll have to take the stairs. Can you manage?"

Fortunately, the apartment was on the fourth floor, and they only needed to climb to the first. "I don't have a choice, do I?"

"No, you don't." Alec put his left arm under her right to support her weight. "Lean on me as much as you need to."

Evelyn let him support her, leaning against him as he walked her out of the apartment and into the hallway toward the elevator. Next to the elevator, he put the back of his hand against the door marked Stairs. "It's cool to the touch. Let's go." He opened the door and helped her through, letting it slam behind them. Emergency lights illuminated the stairwell.

They climbed ten corrugated metal stairs to a landing, each one an effort. At the landing, they turned left and climbed ten more steps. "What happened?"

"Don't know yet. But there's nothing like an emergency to make you realize how unprepared you are for one."

"We've been racing to catch up to a situation that can't be caught." Evelyn gasped for air, struggling to talk and climb at the same time.

"I got off to a bad start here." He slowed to her pace. "That day in the conference room, what I said to Sandy. Now Dev wants me gone."

Evelyn stopped on a step, squeezing his forearm. "Oh, I don't think so. Dev's very understanding."

"Sure, he seems like it, but I disrespected his girlfriend. He's gunning for me now. Just a matter of time before I'm out."

"You're wrong." She stopped on the landing. "Between you and me, Alec, we just discussed it, and we all want you here. Sandy advocated for you more than anyone."

"That's right, you'd know, being the mother of the bride and all." His tone held an edge of sarcasm. He was hard to read, laughing one minute, and arch the next. He might be serious; he might be mocking her. She couldn't keep up.

She patted his hand. "Actually, I doubt the bride thing is going to happen for Sandy."

"Oh, I predict you're right." He grinned, widening his eyes and juddering his head like a cartoon villain.

Dev was right; Alec was an unusual fellow, theatrical and over the top. But it was more than that. Sweat beaded over his top lip, his pupils were enormous. She forced a grin in return, trying to bring moisture to her mouth, her tongue thick and panicky. "I don't know what you're thinking, Alec, but I promise you, you're wanted here. You're a scientist—"

He brayed with laughter. "I might be a scientist, but I'm not wanted. But whatever. I'm used to being the outsider. I mean, great idea, Dad, to send me to college at fifteen. What could possibly go wrong?" He rolled his eyes high up in his sockets.

"That must've been difficult. I had a similar experience, going from being home-schooled to public school. I didn't have the right clothes or anything else." She squeezed his shoulder. "On the bright side, you must be incredibly smart to have gotten such early admission."

He laid a palm against his heart. "I am. I can promise you, I'm smarter than Dev and Sandy *and* Professor Benson. I could solve this fracking, fire-water puzzle with my hands tied behind my back. I've been on the forefront of so many Mines projects. We can create something out of nothing, did you know that?"

Evelyn's radar was on high alert. Alec wasn't making a whole lot of sense.

He dropped his head, wringing his hands. "The funny thing is, they all treat me like I'm stupid."

"Oh, sweetie, I'm sure that's not true. Sandy told me how smart you are. The youngest person ever admitted to School of Mines. She made a point of telling Dev what an asset you were!"

He stomped his foot on the metal landing, the clang echoing through the stairwell. "I'm still in that terrible little room from my first night here."

Evelyn started. Yep, there was something off about Alec, and she was the very last to see it. Whatever it was manifested itself in a more aggressive way than her anxiety had. She clung to his forearms and looked into his eyes, hoping to calm him. "I'm sure that's not personal, Alec. Dev's been busy with so many things."

He loomed over her, backing her toward a wall. "You've got a room, and you're not a scientist. I'm a biochemist! I'm going to be creating food. Can you do that?" He threw his arms wide.

Evelyn shrank back. "I can't, Alec. I'm sure Dev realizes that you're vital to our future, and your room will reflect that. And if he doesn't, I'll talk to him to make sure he does."

"You remind me of my mom, the way she always took my side." He pulled her against him, squeezing her tighter and tighter.

White stars specked in front of her as daggers shot through her wounded shoulder. She couldn't breathe but she didn't dare break away. "I am on your side, Alec. All we have now is each other."

He pushed her to arm's length, his fingers jabbing her shoulder. "Yes, you're right. We need to form an alliance. You and me. I need to know you're with me."

The pain was nauseating. "I'm with *everyone*, Alec. It's more important than ever that people support each other. Alex, please. My shoulder."

He let go of her shoulders, instead gripping her arms and shaking her. "You can't be with them, *and* with me. You have to choose."

Below them, a door banged open. "Evelyn?" Floyd's voice echoed upward through the stairwell. Evelyn took in a breath to yell.

Alec clapped his hand over her mouth, pushing her against the wall and shaking his head. "Not a word."

"Ev?" The door slammed. His boot clomped on the bottom landing, followed by dragging across the concrete, and a gasping moan. Floyd was hurt. Evelyn struggled against Alec, desperate to break free.

His hand bit into her cheeks, pressing her head into the hard concrete, covering her mouth. He turned slightly, pulling a handgun from the back of his jeans. "Your boyfriend's tougher than he looks. I put a bullet in him already. Maybe the second time's the charm."

The boot clanged up a metal stair, Floyd wheezing with the effort. Each step brought him closer to Alec, and certain death. Her gut rolled, queasiness weakening her legs. She let them collapse, sinking toward the floor.

"Stop it. Get up, damn it." Alec squeezed her face, her teeth tearing into her cheeks, and blood filling her mouth.

Sweat covered the back of her neck, the pain so deep her stomach rolled. She forced herself down, her dead weight taking him to the landing with her.

"Evelyn?" The top of Floyd's head appeared, his dark hair mussed. She wouldn't let him die the way she'd let Dana die.

She bit into Alec's palm, sawing her teeth back and forth, yanking her face from his grip and spewing blood. "Floyd, get down!"

Alec screeched, his bloodied hand shaking. Floyd ducked as Alec lifted his pistol. Evelyn yanked up her pant leg, struggling to free Floyd's big knife. Alec steadied his gun and fired. The gunshot echoed like a bomb, her eardrums aching like they'd been jabbed with ice picks.

The knife came free of the sheath. Evelyn drew it back and plunged it into Alec's belly. He shrieked, convulsing backward, his scream blending with the wail of the emergency alarm. He dropped his gun, clutching at his gut. Evelyn released the knife handle, grabbed his pistol, and pulled the trigger. He fell back against the wall, a smile spreading across his face. She scooted closer, the muzzle inches from his chest, and fired again. His smile fell away, his body sagged. She crawled over the landing. "Floyd."

He lay crumpled on the stairs, his blood staining the metal.

CHAPTER TEN

Alma Garcia. Harmony Ranch, Arizona

The tent fabric flapped, and Alma rubbed her eyes. Stretching her body, weary from the lack of sleep, she climbed out of her compartment. She staggered back, startled by Emelia sitting cross-legged on the floor. Alma hadn't heard her moving about.

Emelia tilted her head to one side and rested it in her hand. Dark lines sagged under her eyes. She yawned. "Good. You're up."

"What's going on?" Alma crawled into the central space and grabbed a sneaker from the brown grass by the zipped door.

"I couldn't sleep." Emelia passed Alma her other shoe. "We need to talk to Kit."

Alma slowly inserted her foot. "Why?"

"He can help us if he knows what happened to Nora."

Alma leaned back and stretched out her legs. Her stomach rumbled. "We don't need any help. I've already sorted it..." She was going to say she'd sorted it all out, but Martinez was still at large.

Emelia uncrossed her legs and kneeled in front of Alma, almost begging. "I can't keep this secret."

"You can't trust them." The thoughts the churned through her mind were like a broken record: the three of them were foreigners, outsiders. No one would believe them. But she could keep Em and Mati from that pain a little while longer.

Matias' zipper rattled up. "Can't trust who?"

"Kit, Taylor, Doc, Jen." Alma counted them off on her fingers. "They don't tell us anything important."

Matias grabbed his mechanics book. "I've got something really important I want to show Jen. Can we go and see her today?"

"No. We're staying out of sight. I'll get the food box and you two can stay here."

"But I don't want to stay here." Matias opened his book and flicked to a page with cogs and belts. "I think we can make a machine that will get the motors working again. Jen will love that. I know it."

"Please, Alma." Emelia's shoulders drooped. "I trust him."

"You can't." Alma got to her feet. "I'll prove it to you." She thrust her hands into her pockets. "I'll ask Kit about the crowd outside the ranch. He'll deny it and you'll see you can't trust him. Or any of them."

Emelia already had her shoes on and crawled to unzip the door. "He's not like that."

Matias shoved his sneakers on, gripped the book under his arm, and followed Emelia. They were far too eager to trust. They always had been. The months on the road—and all they'd overcome—had taught them nothing. Alma eased down the zip and turned. Emelia and Matias were already halfway to the gate at the rear of the barn.

Alma hurried up to Emelia. "Stay quiet until I've said my piece."

Emelia nodded, her expression bright and hopeful. Alma's growling stomach clenched. She shouldn't have agreed to talk to Kit, giving the firefighter a chance to prove her wrong.

Chickens scratched at the ground in the main yard, and Smoke rested near the gate. He raised his head but stayed at his post. Their feet clattered up the front porch and past the neat boxes of rationed food. Taylor sat in the chair on the porch. She looked as tired as Alma felt.

"Your box is at the end." Taylor cupped her mouth. "I popped a raisin cookie for each of you in there, too. I found a handful of dried fruit in Jen's Christmas cake ingredients at the very back of her pantry. Don't tell anyone!"

Emelia put her hand on the door handle. "Is Kit in there?"

Taylor jumped up. "He's busy, but you can help later."

Emelia frowned and Alma raised her eyebrows, trying hard not to smirk at the obvious secrecy. She straightened her face and stepped in front of Emelia. "There's something we want to talk to him about."

The door opened, and Kit stepped out. "Good. I was hoping you would talk to me."

"What are you doing in there?" Alma leaned around him, but he shut the door behind himself.

Kit wrapped his arm around Taylor's waist. "Em must have told you we're making the ranch a bit safer." His stare sent a shiver over Alma, making the hairs stand up on her arms. "I'm listening."

"I've got a great plan, too." Matias rested his book on the porch rail. "Come and see." He opened his book, tugging Taylor's arm and pulling both her and Kit closer.

Kit turned toward Mati. "What's this?" He flipped the cover over and then laid it back. "Where did you get this from?"

"Jen." Matias pointed to the biggest drawing. "I think we can use my bike or Alma's bike to get the motor on the water pump working." He circled his finger at the edge of the illustration. "I don't understand this bit." He jabbed at the picture of the cams and belts. "But I think I saw some things like these in the barn the other day."

"A pedal powered engine!" Taylor wrapped her arms around Matias and ruffled his hair. "That's a motor. We'll check Jen's tool shed. There might be something in there we can use. You are so clever, Mati. We might even be able to modify the generator engine to take to pedal power too."

Alma leaned in. "It will work?"

Emelia folded her arms. "See, Taylor and Kit are our friends. They think we have important things to say."

Alma glared at Emelia and caught Kit giving Emelia a sideways smile. "Thanks, Squirt!" His smile faded, and he tugged at Emelia's shirt. "Where's your jacket?" The question was for Emelia, but he frowned slightly at Alma.

Emelia unfolded her arms and sagged a little. Alma put her hand over Emelia's. "It needed washing, and she doesn't need it in this heat." The jean jacket was nothing but a charred mess of ash at the bottom of the grave. Alma needed to draw Kit's attention away. "You were saying something about making the ranch safer. Why?"

Kit ran a hand through his hair. "Well, we don't want any more unexplained deaths."

"I thought we were safe here."

Taylor nudged Kit. "And we're keeping it that way." She winked at him. "We don't want a repeat of Blake's situation. He got beaten by strangers, but it was close by. We can't take any chances."

Alma waited for Taylor to say more, but she returned to the drawing from the book. "How are you keeping it safe? Can we see? Can't we help?"

Kit shook his head. "There're too many bits all over the place in there. It's best not to get them jumbled."

She wanted to stamp her foot, but she wasn't a kid and didn't want to give them more excuses to treat her like one. "Em's seen it. Why can't I? Is it to protect us from people outside the ranch?"

"What people?" Taylor stepped away from Matias and took Kit's hand.

Alma snorted and faced Emelia. "See!"

Emelia pushed her to one side. "We heard there were people outside the ranch. Bad people like Charlie." She blanched. "Are they coming to get us, like that Mart—"

Alma's heart thrummed. She grabbed Emelia's hand and she spun round. "Is it safe here or not? Don't lie to us." Her voice drowned out Emelia's. She heard Emelia say Martinez man, but Kit and Taylor were focused on her.

Taylor narrowed her eyes. "Who told you about the people?"

Alma reached for the front door handle. "So, there is a problem? And you didn't want us to know about it?"

Kit stepped in front of the door. "It's not that we didn't want you to know. It's just that we didn't want to frighten you."

Matias slammed his book shut. "Should we be frightened?"

Taylor cupped his cheek. "We're not saying that at all. The thing is, the ranch is a safe place, so others might want to take it. There was some guy called Charlie from the local town who thought he could take the ranch from Jen. We think he might not be too far away. We've got to protect what we have and look out for each other." Taylor clamped Matias in a sideways hug. "We've got all sorts of plans to stop him or anyone else from taking the ranch and we're doing our best to keep you and the ranch safe."

"But he won't be the last to come for the place, will he?" Emelia's hand shook. "Anyone who can see what we have—food, chickens—is going to want to take it from us."

Alma squeezed her sister's fingers. "Let us help. Don't leave us out of this."

Kit stepped away from Taylor and gripped Alma's elbow with his bandaged hand. "Alma, can I have a word?" He steered her down the porch steps and a short distance from the house. "Scaring them isn't helping."

"Me?" She glanced over his shoulder. Emelia watched them both. "You're the ones leaving us out of all the preparations."

His grip tightened. "If you get involved, you could get hurt."

"I'm old enough to help." She pulled her arm from his grasp. "We built circuit boards and worked for Martinez in an Encircle factory. We are capable. You know that, right?" He frowned at her. She shouldn't have mentioned either. "We should be allowed to protect ourselves."

He took her closer to the chicken pen. "If you get hurt, Em and Mati will be without family. Who will protect them then?" She flinched. "They don't want that. You don't want that. They need you."

She stood up straight and stared at Smoke guarding the gate. "I can't keep them safe if you keep telling me lies. I know there is a threat, and I know you are preparing for it. Who are they?"

He lowered his voice and he furrowed his forehead. "Why did you mention Michael Martinez? Em said something about him, too." She didn't look at him. "You know something about him."

"He's destroyed the world and Nora didn't like him very much."

Kit didn't need to know more. Not about Michael Martinez and most certainly not about Eric.

"True. She brought the families he split up back together." Kit leaned against the tree and dug the toe of his boot into the soil. "I'm sorry she couldn't do anything for yours."

Alma pulled a twig from the tree and splintered it between her fingers. "If it's dangerous here. I have to get Emelia and Matias out."

"No one is going anywhere. We tried to send someone into town to scavenge a few things from the hotel yesterday and they came back saying that the road out was blocked and guarded. They reported seeing a man that looked like Michael Martinez."

Alma held still, trying not to react to the news that Martinez might still be in range. *If he is, the unforgiveable task becomes a necessity.*

Kit studied her, his face gentle even though his eyes never left hers. "If you'd gotten here just a few days earlier, you could've gone with a group heading for some bunkers in the Huachuca Mountains. Aunt Jen told me they were talking about some extreme weather coming and it would be the safest place in the world. I'm not convinced going underground is so safe with all the quakes, but there was so much ash up north, it will mess with the weather for sure." He tapped the soil from his boot. "That's got to be about 350 miles away. You wouldn't make it alone."

Kit underestimated her. Alma remembered the scientist on the van's radio after they had escaped the prison house. He talked about the freakish weather and global cooling. "But the quakes are getting better and they will stop. They won't keep rumbling." She turned back to the gate. Smoke lay still, undisturbed. "Did they say where the bunkers were?"

Kit stepped in front of her. "I don't know the details. You can't leave."

He just couldn't help himself from treating her like a child. Angry tears rolled down her cheeks. "You can't stop me."

He stepped back and raised his hands. "Please stay. You could be picked off like Nora. It's a dangerous world out there."

"And you think I don't know that? You have no idea what I did to get Em and Mati here." She balled her fists.

"Emelia's told me a few things." He reached for her, but she didn't need any of his stupid sideways hugs and flinched away.

She scowled at him. "Well, if you want her to help you out with your bendy tree traps and whatever it is you are making inside Jen's house, you'll need to reconsider how I'm involved. If not, we're leaving. She's not coming back until you tell me what's going on."

Kit put his heavy hand to her shoulder. "I'm not stopping you from leaving, but the people blocking the road will. Believe me, I want your family to be safe and I'm doing all I can to make the ranch safer for all of us."

She'd heard about the local town, Jackrabbit Bluff, and the ski resort being destroyed by a landslide, but knew nothing about where Michael and his crew might be. "You don't think we have a chance against the outsiders, do you?"

"Of course we have a chance. Taylor knows all sorts of tricks that will help us. We know that one day they'll come and we're getting ready." He laughed without any joy reaching his eyes. "No one messes with my wife or Aunt Jen and gets away with it."

Alma swiped her cheek, determined to drive her point home. "You can't leave us out. Let me fight, too."

Kit shook his head. "You're not listening to me. You have a more important job. Em and Mati need you. And—like I said—you need to stop frightening them."

He wanted her to pretend everything would be fine. With the number of traps Emelia had said they'd already set it was clear that Kit and Taylor were preparing for an attack. He was pushing her away. She brushed his hand from her shoulder. If she was going to be barred from the fight and from the preparation, the most important job she faced was to get Emelia and Matias somewhere safe. She marched back to the house, grabbed the box and Matias' book. "We're going."

Emelia reached for the front door. "Since I'm already here, I can help Kit this morning."

"Not today, Squirt." Kit bounded up the porch steps. "I want your sister to keep you away from the perimeter. That's it. Can you do that for me?"

Kit's insinuation—that she couldn't fight or wouldn't be useful—caught her squarely in the chest and it stung. She stomped down the steps with Emelia and Matias following closely, rushed down the side of the house, and rounded the barn.

Emelia grabbed her arm. "Hey!"

Alma rounded on her. "Your friend thinks I'm useless."

"Are you sure he said that?" Em tilted her head.

Matias pulled the book from Alma's hand. "Kit and Taylor are kind. They don't say nasty things."

"Well, he said he wished we'd arrived earlier so could go to some bunker that's supposed to be safer."

Matias pulled out his raisin cookie from the box. "Or we could go back to Simeon. His farm was nice. We could go there."

"Don't be ridiculous, Mati. If our friends are in danger, we need to help them." Emelia pulled on Alma's sleeve. "Let's go back and tell them we can help defend the ranch again."

"You don't get it, Em." Alma's eyes filled with tears and she blinked them away. "They don't want us here."

"But Kit's my friend."

"A friend who has lied to you about the people outside the ranch and not even told you what you are helping him to make. No one wants us here." She felt like a broken record, but no amount of repeating herself seemed to get through to her sister.

Tears glistened in Emelia's eyes, and she turned away.

Alma stopped in the barn's shadow. Her brother had a point; they *had* been safe at Simeon's farm. Safer than they were with Michael Martinez massing an army outside the ranch. "We'd have to sneak away and travel all the way back to him."

"Or use the radios Kit brought with him." Matias pointed at the house.

"There's a radio in there?" Alma had all Simeon's contact details memorized.

"Yes, but they have no power." Emelia pushed open the gate, kicking the dead grass.

Matias offered Alma his book. "We just need to get them charged up again. Taylor said that my bike idea might get the generator going."

"Then we stay until we can contact Simeon. Em, you'll still help Kit and find out all you can about what is going on. Hopefully, we'll get away before Martinez comes back for more of us."

CHAPTER ELEVEN

Catherine "Cat" Murphy. En Route to Amil Kumar Sanctuary

Cat sat upright in the backseat of her neighbor's four door pickup, waiting for Tom and the other two men working in the corral nearby. Several hours had passed since their heated argument and he still hadn't spoken to her. As he loaded up the livestock and their things, his loyal dog Belle circling his feet, she could've assumed that she'd won, but she knew better. He may have acquiesced, but she'd broken his trust and she didn't know if she could fix it. If only she could go back in time.

Silent shadows grew tall as the alkali dust sifted through the elongated beams of the dimming evening light. Sitting on the sidelines chafed her, but after all the damage she'd done to her body—and to her relationship with Tom—it was all that she could do. Three weeks ago, she would've been right out there helping, taking the lead. But, then again, three weeks ago she wouldn't even have considered abandoning her ranch.

Cattle chuffed, a young man's voice murmured low, and the pickup swayed. Hooves pounded and the livestock trailer tailgate banged shut, the whole outfit juddering. Moments later a noisy hinge groaned open, several heavy thuds rocked the vehicle, chickens clucked, and metal scraped against metal.

"Trailer's loaded." Jim's voice was deep, his tone all business. In the horrors of the fracking aftermath, the young man had matured far faster than Cat would've liked. She prayed that it hadn't hardened him as well. However, if she had to leave her little clan—and her beloved Rancho Seco—at least she was leaving them in capable hands. "We've added a few extras, another spare tire, and thirty-five gallons of potable water. Anything else I can get you, Mr. Callahan?"

"Sounds like you've got everything more than covered, Jim." Tom stepped through the corral gate closest to Cat, swinging it shut and latching it behind him. "Thank you."

Savoring the last echoes of her final bittersweet Rancho Seco sunset, Cat swallowed the lump in her throat, rubbing her aching leg. Her eyes welled and she blinked the tears away. The coarse saddle blanket seat cover irritated the delicate skin on the back of her arms. She shuddered and craned her neck toward the bed of the pickup. "Tom, would you mind grabbing me a long-sleeved shirt?"

The lanky cowman approached the back of the pickup and shuffled through their small accumulation of supplies. A plastic tub clattered and clicked. "One of mine okay?" He appeared next to her, a blue chambray shirt in his hand.

"Sure." Cat braved a weak smile. "Thanks."

Tom clasped her shoulder. "Lean forward, let me help you."

As he lifted her thick mane of hair, his rough-hewn fingers grazed her neck. A soft, warm breeze washed over her, sending a shiver down her spine. She leaned forward, shrugging into his oversized shirt, rolling up the sleeves. Breathing in the fresh, starchy scent, she put her hand over his. It was a shame that it had taken a catastrophe for her to notice the sweet soul cloaked in the rugged foreman standing next to her. She shuddered, praying that she hadn't driven him too far away. "Tom?"

"Yes, Catherine?" His tone was curt, but not harsh. Maybe there was a chance.

The neighbor materialized behind Tom, unspeaking. She released her grip on his hand and lifted her chin. "Mr. Jordan."

"I heard your house burnt down, Mr. Callahan." Grady held out a stack of clothing. "I'd like you to have these. They were my brother's."

Tom took the bundle. "Why, that's mighty thoughtful of you, son."

"Thought you might be able to use these, too." He produced a pair of handmade, underslung cowboy boots. "They're Van Zants, top of the line, practically brand new." Grady's eyes glistened in the fading daylight, and he turned away. "Made by Andy himself. Glenn waited almost two years for 'em.

Tom shook his head and stepped back. "Oh, I couldn't."

"Well, they don't fit me." Grady thrust them toward Tom. "No use hanging on to 'em for sentimentality's sake."

"Take the boots Mr. C." Lillie marched up to stand next to the neighbor, Estrella and her little ones following. The thin redheaded child crossed her arms, her chin jutting forward. "You've got to hit the road."

His head bowed, Tom stepped away from Cat and reached for the boots. Lillie sprang forward, wrapping her wiry arms around Tom's great frame and burying her face in his chest. Everyone stood unmoving as the shaking girl sobbed and the big man held her. Time slowed to a crawl, his generous hand smoothing her long red locks. She pressed her palms into his torso and shoved back. She sniffled, her lips quivering. "Now, get the heck out of here!"

"You're right, Lil, it's time." Tom smiled at her, his eyes downturned. "I'm going to miss you, ya little firecracker."

Jim stepped forward, putting one arm around his sister, his other arm outstretched. "Thank you for everything, Mr. C."

The two men shook hands. Tom pulled the young man close and clapped him on the back, then stepped back next to Cat. "Son." He inclined his head. "Are you sure you won't come?"

"No, sir." Jim glanced down at Lillie, then over at Estrella. She and the small children hung in the background. Ruby in her arms, her youngest son strapped to her back, she held her older son's hand and he held Lucia's. "We're staying."

The little Miller girl ran to the pickup, climbed up on the running boards, and hugged Cat. "Goodbye."

"Oh, LJ, this isn't goodbye." Jim put his hands around her waist and helped the child down. "It's see ya later. We're gonna take good care of Rancho Seco for them." He leaned in and embraced Cat. "She'll be here for you when you're ready to come home."

"Okay." Cat nodded to Tom. "See ya later."

Tom stepped between them and closed the pickup door. He ambled over to Estrella, addressed her, then patted her shoulder. He rubbed Gabriel's back, kissed Ruby on the top of the head, tousled Lucia's hair, then hunkered down to shake Joaquin's little hand.

Grady got into the pickup and started the engine, the headlights shining upon Cat's cherished barn. Except for a few bullet holes, it was as strong and as beautiful as it had been the day everything exploded. She was leaving her garrison.

The last of the color faded from the sky, the atmosphere graying. Tom strode across the high beams and opened the front door. "Is it okay if Belle rides in the cab, Mr. Jordan?"

"Aw, sure." He patted the seat next to him. "Load up, girl." The dog jumped into the front seat and Grady stroked her ears.

The earth rumbled and the vehicle jounced. Lucia screamed and one of the infants wailed. "To the barn!" Jim herded the children toward the building. "Safe travels!"

Tom braced himself, his fist white knuckled as he clamped the door. The ground quieted and Tom unclenched his jaw. "Mr. Jordan. Mind if I sit in the back with Ms. Murphy?"

Grady's shoulders, and his grip on the steering wheel, relaxed. "No problem."

Shutting the front door, he opened the back and climbed into the seat next to Cat. "Home, James."

"Huh?" Grady put his arm across the back of the passenger seat and raised his eyebrows at Tom.

Tom chuckled. "Never mind." He slid closer to Cat, placing his hand over hers.

Cat's mouth went dry and she opened her mouth to speak, but— for possibly the first time in her life—she was speechless. The neighbor put the pickup into gear, they rolled through the massive entryway, and away from Cat's headquarters. She turned her palm over and grasped the back of Tom's thick hand. Kneading it she kept her eyes on the road ahead and didn't look back.

A maze of large rocks, chasms, and sinkholes had taken the place of what used to be a fifty mile per hour gravel road. Fifteen minutes down the road, Cat laid her head on Tom's shoulder. "Tom?"

He reached across his body and cupped the back of her head. "Yes?"

She sat upright and turned to face him square on. Clearing her throat, she blinked, and a hot tear rolled down her cheek. "I'm so sorry. I..."

"Stop right there, Cat." He brushed away the tear. "I forgive you. What's done is done. Let's just move forward."

She threw her arms around his neck, his embrace encircling her. Tears flowing, she burrowed into his chest.

He rubbed her shoulders and crooned in her ear. "It's okay. Everything is going to be okay."

"I love you," she whispered into his shirt.

His voice was husky, his breath hot against her hair. "Ditto, kiddo."

Moments passed and her tears ebbed. She wiped her eyes and focused on the road ahead. The landscape hadn't gotten any more forgiving. "Tom?" She gathered her composure, pushing away from his chest, but continued to cling to his bicep. "I think you need to move. It makes more sense for you to sit up front. Watch for hazards."

"You sure, hon?" His eyes searched her face.

Cat nodded, afraid her voice would betray her. She didn't want to let Tom go, she wanted him right next to her. Three feet away was too far, but she was a pragmatist. Danger was around every corner, nothing looked familiar.

Tom reached up and tapped the driver on the shoulder. "Better stop the rig for a sec, Grady." The vehicle ground to a stop and Tom squeezed her leg before he opened the door. She held onto his hand until the very last moment. Metal creaked and the cab light shone for a second, then he closed the door, and got in the front seat. Cat scooted over to sit behind him, leaning on the door.

With Tom as lookout, Grady picked his way through the minefield of crevasses and jagged rocks. From the backseat, Cat scoured the path and tried to ignore the dash gauges, longing to see the speedometer creep over twenty miles per hour. The digital clock caught her eye. 11:47. They skirted around a heap of dirt and cacti, their headlamps illuminating the wreckage of a twenty-foot-tall cow skull. The tourist attraction that once graced the frontage of the Longhorn Grill had split into two almost symmetrical halves. They'd made it to Amado.

"Dangit." Cat's heart sank. "I knew we weren't traveling very fast, but I can't believe we've only covered sixteen miles."

"Everything's gotten worse since the last time I was here." Grady stopped the pickup and turned off the engine. The restaurant's ruins glowed orange, small embers drifting into the starry sky. One massive horn balanced over an enormous smoldering sinkhole. The other horn lay across the remains of the highway. "You wanna turn back?"

"No." Cat leaned forward, reaching over the bench seat to pet Belle. "We've made it this far. We'll go until we can't go any further. Right?" She rubbed Tom's arm.

"I'm with her." The corners of his mustache turned up and he gave her a slow wink. "Hell or highwater."

"Okay, then." Grady opened his door, leaving it open, the cab light piercing the darkness. "I'll be right back."

Tom twisted in his seat to face her. "Cat, this is only gonna get more difficult. Are you sure about this? We could go home."

"That place isn't my home anymore. It's just wood and nails, brush and thorns." Butterflies filled her stomach and she gulped, her heart racing. "You're my home and our family is at the end of this road."

Grady grabbed the steering wheel and pulled himself into the driver's seat. "Everything seems to be holding up." He started the pickup. "I found a way around the Longhorn, too."

Tom turned to face forward. "Onward, then."

"Hold on. It might get a little western." The pickup crept

forward, and Cat braced herself. Grady eased the rig around the edge of the sinkhole.

The scent of burning rubber wafted into the vehicle and Cat tensed. "You're getting a little too close for my—" Her sentence was interrupted by a resounding clatter and crash. The back end of the trailer thunked, dropping violently. "Gun it, Grady!"

The driver stomped on the accelerator and Tom lunged for the transfer case lever, jerking the truck into four-wheel drive. Like a machine gun, dirt and gravel peppered the undercarriage of the pickup and trailer. Dust and ash swirled around them as the vehicle gained purchase and lurched forward. Cat was tossed around the backseat, banging her head against the window as they careened through the brush, over rocks, and through a small draw.

Tom swiveled in his seat. "You doing alright back...." A loose, heavy-duty crescent wrench bounced from the dashboard knocking off his cowboy hat, striking him in the forehead. Cat grabbed for the wrench, missed and half fell off the seat, hanging on to the back of the front seat with a death grip as they bounced and bumped.

When the terrain flattened out, the driver let the pickup roll to a stop. He sat, staring straight ahead, with a death grip on the wheel.

Cat pulled her body back into the seat. "Tom! Are you okay? Your face is covered in blood."

"Oh, sure." He wiped the back of his hand across his brow. "Whatever that was just grazed me."

Grady flipped on the overhead light, inspecting Tom's injury. "You've got a pretty good gash, there, Mr. Callahan." He reached under the seat and produced a roll of blue shop towels. "Here."

"Face wounds bleed like heck, but it'll be fine." Tearing off several pieces of the thick, absorbent fabric, Tom folded them into a square and pressed it to his temple. "Everybody else okay?"

"Yeah." Grady and Cat answered in unison.

"Okay." Tom pulled his hat down, tucking the makeshift bandage up under the band. "I'm gonna give the rig a once over, check on the cows." He jumped out of the pickup.

"I'll go with you." Grady followed, slamming the door behind him.

Cat sat in the dark, wondering why she'd lied to Tom. The base of her neck tingled, her head swam and throbbed as she mentally suppressed the nausea. She knew the feeling. It was whiplash, and it had messed with her capacity to make good decisions.

Tom opened the door across the seat from Cat. "Hey, hon. I've got good news and I've got bad news. The bad news is, we've got two flats. The good news, Jim planned ahead for that." He picked up the pillow from the floorboard. "You look exhausted. This is gonna take a little while. Why don't you try to take a nap or something while we get 'er taken care of?"

"Okay." Cat yawned and rubbed her eyes, already having trouble keeping them open. "Sorry I can't help." He left and she propped the pillow against the door, shifting it under her head. She drifted off to sleep, waking for a moment when the overhead light blinked on, then off. The doors slammed and the pickup rumbled to life, then she floated back to her dreamless slumber.

The pop of a firecracker followed by the sound of shattering glass jolted her back to consciousness. The pickup was bumping through the brush, headed straight for an ancient saguaro. She clambered to sit upright. A crisp breeze swept through her hair, and, ahead, the desert was illuminated by the dawning sun.

"Get down!" Tom ducked, fiddling with something in his lap.

Dazed and confused, Cat searched the horizon. "Where are we?"

"I said, get down, Cat!" Tom leaned over the seat, cupped the back of her head, and pulled her toward him. "On the floorboard! Now!"

The pickup shuddered to a stop as gunshots rang out from the front seat. Cat covered her head and closed her eyes as a volley of bullets rained down on their vehicle. After what seemed like an eternity, the world fell silent. She waited—praying that the shooting was finished—then she felt something warm dripping onto her face and opened her eyes. A horrifying amount of thick, dark blood seeped through the crack in the back of the seat, oozing into a puddle on the floor.

"Tom!" She scrambled, screaming herself hoarse, unable to escape the growing pool of sticky liquid.

CHAPTER TWELVE

Kit Walsh. Harmony Ranch, Arizona

Out of breath from running from the rocks to the southwest back to the ranch, Kit rammed the front gate, opening it with his body, rather than his hands. "Fire! Fire near the north bunkhouses. Tell Taylor. Grab shovels so we can put it out. One of you go, now!" He forced the words between gasps, then turned to Faris. "You stay here. Help guard the gate."

"Yes. Go." Faris closed the gate behind them.

Kit ran down the drive to the house, legs burning. He'd gotten out of shape; a mile run should be easy. Taylor tore out of the house, the door banging. "Fire at the north bunkhouses?"

"Yes. Smoke." He forced his aching legs to the animal barn and grabbed a shovel. "The water there's nothing more than a trickle right now. We'll need to dig it out."

Taylor grabbed his arm. "You can't dig, not with your hands."

"Shoot. You're right." He dropped the tool, examining his stinging palms, the left still wrapped, the right scarred and tender.

Dunia, Jaya and Aaron ran in. Dunia picked up the shovel. "You tell us what to do, yes?"

"Yes. Grab another shovel and a stiff rake, or a hoe." He led the group out of the barn and to the back pasture, searching the sky for the trail of smoke. He pointed. "There, you see? Just a single trail."

"Kit, you're the expert, but that looks like a campfire or a chimney to me." Taylor shaded her eyes with a hand. "Could someone have started a fire in one of the bunkhouse stoves?"

"Maybe." Taylor was right; he might be overreacting, but his nerves were raw. Finding Nora's body, but *not* finding any trace of Kevin or catching sight of Jen had him cycling fast, imagining the worst. Taylor didn't need to know any of that; not yet. "Hazard of being a firefighter, I guess. I still want to check it out."

"I am more worried it is a person we don't know." Dunia patted her gun. "I'll go with you."

"Good idea." Taylor grasped the back of his neck and pulled him down, kissing him quickly. "I'll stay here and keep organizing the ranch residents. We'll talk about next steps when you get back. Stay safe."

"Love you." Kit returned her kiss with compounding interest, because he'd learned not to take anything for granted, then set off through the back pasture. Dunia had no trouble keeping up with him, and they reached the north bunkhouses quickly. As they neared the clearing, they slowed, going to opposite sides of the trail. Nothing moved except the trees in a light breeze. If there was a fire, at least the wind wasn't whipping it into a frenzy. They split at the bunkhouses, peering between them, then rejoined on the far side and continued to the gate. "Nothing."

Dunia nodded and opened the gate. Kit followed her through, waiting for her to close it. She pointed at the ground; the pine straw was scuffed. Dunia followed the trail, so Kit watched their surroundings for movement or anything out of place. Before too long, they found the source of the fire—a too-shallow fire pit, the remaining ashes smoldering.

Dunia pointed at the ground again. "Tracks go back to the ranch." She handed him the shovel, and followed the tracks.

Kit gingerly stirred the ashes, looking for clues, but there wasn't much left. A clinking of metal on metal drew him down to a crouch.

He dragged the remains to the edge, then teased the ashes apart, searching for the source of the sound. A second clink, and he carefully pulled the item to the edge of the cut soil. Drawing his bandanna from his pocket, he picked up the relatively heavy mess, careful to shield his hands from further damage. Dunia returned and crouched next to him. He brushed it off, finding blackened metal, the compass points warped from the heat, the feathers gone, the state of Arizona intact. "This is from the jacket we gave to Emelia. Why would anyone burn it?"

"I tell you, the child Alma is crazy." Dunia twirled a finger near her ear.

He frowned. "I don't think so. Alma is scared and scared for her family. Weren't you scared that you'd be kicked out of the country? That's why you stayed at the Martinez factory, right?"

Dunia nodded slowly. "That is true. We could have overthrown the guards, but we all knew staying in the US is hard. And they had our passports."

"Alma gave that stack of children's passports to Nora, who gave them to Jaya. So, we know she escaped with her siblings, and got away with all the documents at that factory. We don't know what she had to do to make that happen or what she did on the way here. She was probably in some really dangerous situations. So, she's even more scared. And she's desperately looking for safety, someplace she can stay, and make sure Emelia and Matias are safe. She won't talk to us, as if everyone is her enemy, and no one will ever help her. She's disappeared a lot over the last day or so, too, and her siblings just shrug when we ask where she is. Both of them are pretty easy to read, and I think they're hiding something. This morning, they wanted to tell me something, and Alma kept distracting me. She talked more to me this morning than she ever has." Kit looked back along the trail to the bunkhouses. "Plus, someone tried to drag Nora's body away, someone without the strength to carry her. What if Alma found Nora and got blood on her clothes? Would she believe that we'd think she murdered Nora?" Kit scoffed, unable to believe his own words. "It's ridiculous to think she could kill Nora; especially a stab in the back.

That took strength and callousness. That's not Alma. But it's pure Alma to think the worst of everyone."

Dunia nodded. "It is Emelia's jacket, yes? Alma would do anything for her sister and brother. The Martinez factories were bad; the guards would have threatened her sister and brother, and told her the police would throw her out of the country. They would make up anything to make the children behave, and she is young enough to believe all their lies, because some of them were truth. If Emelia found Nora and got her jacket bloody, perhaps Alma tried to hide it."

"That would explain why Nora's body was left resting against the fence. Alma wouldn't have the strength to carry Nora. Even she and Emelia together would have to drag Nora." Kit shook his head. "That poor kid, so sure everyone is out to get her. We've got to protect all of them from what's really out there."

Dunia took the shovel from him, digging deeper in the fire pit, turning the soil to put out the smoldering remains of the fire. "You know those people will try to take this place, probably soon. They have many guns, military equipment. Too many people who will need food. Not the kind to farm. They will try to make us work for them." She leaned on her shovel. "I will not be a slave again. I will fight."

Kit put the back of his good hand against the dirt. Cold. "Good job with the fire." He rose, leading the way back to the ranch. "You're right. I'm sure they'll attack us soon. Not that we have much, but it's more than they have now. I agree with you, though; I'm never working at gunpoint again. I'd like to pack up and move, but I know Aunt Jen would never voluntarily leave." Which was how he knew she was somewhere on the ranch. Absent foul play, Jen McCreedy would *not* leave Harmony.

Dunia worked the back pasture gate. "You know she's still having headaches."

Kit stopped. She hadn't said a word about any pain. Not to him, anyway. "Are they—" He didn't want to finish the sentence. 'Serious?' 'Life threatening?' "Is she taking anything? Has doc given her painkillers?"

Dunia shrugged. "I watch and wonder. She touches the place

where she banged her head on the rock, but doesn't say. I wanted you to know, in case she falls."

The worry that ate at Kit started back up again, lining his stomach with acid. Her disappearance might not be related to Nora's murder or Kevin's disappearance; she might have fallen, concussed, and failed to get up. *No. If that happened, Robin would come running. She's fine, she's fine, she's fine. She's busy!* He'd only just gotten his Aunt Stickler back and she'd turned out to be nothing of the kind. He couldn't lose her again. "Thanks for the heads up. Appreciate it."

Dunia nodded. "We all look out for each other."

They trekked in silence, each lost in their own thoughts, Kit finally returning to the fact that they were surrounded by hostile forces. He had to face the fact that his Aunt Jen might have been taken which had all kinds of implications. "If what you're saying is right, those people won't let us leave. They'll want us working for them. We'll have to fight. The problem is, I'm not a military guy, I'm a firefighter. Taylor knows a little about a lot of survival, but fighting isn't her thing either. Either way, we're going to need a lot of luck to survive."

They strode back to the ranch. About halfway back, a commotion in the trees drew their attention. Kit pulled up his binoculars, but the trees were too thick. He and Dunia skulked into the thicket about twenty feet from each other.

"Yah! Go!" Dunia's voice was loud, so Kit pushed through the trees to her, making as much noise as possible. When he reached her, a thick red tail disappeared into the trees; perhaps a fox. Dunia inspected their catch, a small deer hanging from one of the spring tree traps. "Not too much damage. These bony lower legs can go to the dogs, anyway." She pulled a knife.

Kit put up a hand. "Wait, we don't want to attract predators. We'll butcher it at the ranch. There's a spot my Aunt uses." They pulled the deer down, and Kit hefted it over his shoulder, holding the back legs with his good hand, but it stung by the time they got back to the ranch. Another shirt to wash, and he needed a shower. Neither of those was likely.

Back at the ranch, he handed the deer off to a resident with hunting experience and showed him where to process the carcass. Then he washed his hands and face in the washbasin, and rebandaged his left hand before entering the house. He flexed his fingers; he was using them too much and was going to tear the tender skin if he wasn't careful. But disasters didn't wait for human healing. Inside, Dunia and Jaya were chatting in a foreign language; from the motions, they were talking about how to butcher the deer.

Taylor and Stone—the giant who manned the main gate—sat at the table with the map of the ranch. "Kit, you're back." Taylor rose and hugged him. "Woah! You don't smell so good."

"Deer." Kit shrugged. "Did Dunia tell you what we found?"

Taylor led him to the table. "Yes." Her mouth pinched. "At some point, we'll have to confront Alma, but I don't want to send her running. She deserves the safety of the ranch."

"I understand you need someone with some military experience. I did a couple of tours in Iraq, so I know a little about base defense. Unfortunately, I don't know much about defending someplace that's so open, unless we can fill a whole lot of sandbags really fast." Stone chuckled.

Kit sat down. "I don't think there's too many sandbags around here, and I don't think we can build a log fence around this place either." Not in the time they had left, anyway. "I'm worried that—"

All eyes turned to face him.

He gulped down his doubts. It was time. "I haven't seen my Aunt Jen for—"

"Oh!" Taylor smacked her leg then clutched her hand to her chest. "I was so worried! She's with the goats. We just had a nice, long chat about the benefits of goats' milk!"

Kit returned Taylor's smile. She was such a ray of sunshine. They hadn't been at Harmony Ranch more than a couple of days and already she was making friends with his aunt.

"That it?" Stone hadn't joined Taylor's laugh. "Because there are a couple of people I haven't seen."

The smiles around the table fell away, one after the other.

"Kevin, our Ops Manager, has been missing since the Garcia woman's funeral."

Kit didn't know who the Garcia woman was, but he had heard whispers of Alma's mother being buried, right before he and Taylor arrived, so he had a rough timeline in his head. "He's been gone days?"

Stone nodded. "His wife raised the alarm, but we figured he'd be back. So, we waited..."

The silence that hung over the kitchen was spooky-bad, rather than contemplative. They all knew there were bad men out there, and now the evidence of just how bad they were was starting to amass.

"What do we do?" Taylor threaded her fingers through Kit's.

"Keep working to secure the Ranch?" Kit shrugged. There wasn't much more they could do.

"Right." Stone met Kit's gaze, stony and resolute. "Deal with the things we can, put the rest in the hand of God."

"Amen." Taylor lifted Kit's hand and kissed it. "We do our best. So? What does that mean? Practically? In the here and now?"

Kit loved how well his wife turned into the wind, how she navigated, how practical she was. If it had been possible to fall anymore in love with her, he'd have done so, there and then, but he was already head over heels in love, admiration, and awe.

"Here's what I know..." Stone pointed at the hills above the ranch to the west, on the other side of Highway 77. "After you went off to find the fire, I went up here to see if I could tell how big it was. I saw little smoke, but a lot of activity at that campground. With all the trees, it was hard to tell exactly what the outside forces were doing, but it looked like they were loading up vehicles, and they have military vehicles, like Humvees. People stood in ranks, too, like someone was giving a briefing to troops or inspecting weapons or something. So, we don't have time to build a fence or anything else. What we can do is use what we have. I know you were building traps and log rollers to take people out, and that's a good first step."

Taylor raised her hand. "Why would they bother with Harmony Ranch? Anyone looking at us knows we've got nothing."

Kit shook his head. "We have people. Some aren't much use, but in today's world? Someone's going to use everyone else. Especially someone used to being in charge, not doing manual labor themselves."

Stone pointed at Kit. "Exactly. I'm a live free or die guy. So, we use the people we have to protect the ranch. I know we've got some hunters; we put a couple of them up on top of the barn. We'll have to build a little perch up there, give them some protection, but it shouldn't be too hard. That's a good watch spot too; from up there, someone could see small signal fires, and watch for signal mirror flashes during the day. Since the solar arrays are toast, the generators are a good shelter for shooters. The main house is suitable too, since it's got rock walls, but the other sheds and all those RVs? Bullets will go right through those. We can make the animal barn a little safer by stacking the remaining hay against the walls, but rifle bullets will penetrate."

Dunia hovered over them. "We can cut extra escape holes in the walls; leaving just enough to leave the surface material in place, but if someone needs to get out, they pull the hay bales and punch the siding out."

"That's the problem with the house; not enough escape routes." Taylor pointed at the door. "Windows leave you exposed too much while you're climbing out."

Kit remembered the report from the bunkhouse repair group. "I think there are some extra metal roofing panels. We could add those to the interior of the house and the barn, make it a bit more bullet resistant."

"For offense, we can put shooters up on the hills with the log roll traps, too." Stone slid his finger over the map. "Just like the special forces guys, a shooter and spotter together. The spotter can trigger the traps and protect the shooter, while the shooter takes out the leadership." Stone's brows wrinkled. "And that's who you need to target—leaders. It's gonna be harder to spot them without uniforms. Make sure whoever's going up there is willing to kill. Not everyone can do that if they're not being shot at themselves."

"Yeah." Taylor shuddered. "That's not me. I've seen enough death already."

"You can't be up there." Stone turned to Taylor. "You have to be here, making sure the non-combatants stay safe or get away." He pointed at Kit. "You have to be here, too, leading our forces. We'll have to set up a way to signal people."

"Or find a way to power the radios." Taylor tapped the useless Forest Service radios sitting on the table. "Matias had some ideas on that." She pushed her chair away. "Actually, I promised to help him, so you three, figure it out." She left.

"How's a little kid going to do that?" Stone's brows wrinkled.

"He is smarter than his age," Jaya called from the kitchen. "If anyone can do it, he can and he enjoys it."

Kit shrugged. He knew nothing about any of those kids—except Emelia, who'd latched onto him—but they all deserved to be children, rather than miniature adults. They deserved to thrive rather than merely survive. He, Stone and Dunia went over the lists of ranch residents, assigning them to guard duty and specific positions during an attack.

Dunia pointed at the south bunkhouses. "I don't know rifles, but I know pistols. I'll run the trap lines to collapse the trap and shoot anyone who escapes. I will stay free."

"Amen, sister." Stone snapped a finger gun at her. "I'll take one of the high shooter spots if someone will give me a hunting rifle. My AR-15 isn't a sniper rifle. Or I'll be a spotter. Once we've done all we can with precision shooting, I'll lead the cliff squad down and take the rest out."

Kit held back a shudder. He'd spent his life saving others; now he had to kill to survive. There had to be a better way, but with the dog-eat-dog world they were in, he didn't know what or how. From everything he'd heard, Martinez wasn't someone who'd accept anything but a full surrender, and they couldn't do that. Not to Alma, Em, and Matias or any of the other children living on the ranch. Or the rest of them, either. Mr. H and Sandra wouldn't survive long and even if they were a pain, they still deserved to live. "I'll need your help. Or maybe I should be up on the top of that hill with you."

"That would be the ideal place to direct our forces from." Stone huffed. "Such as they are." He leaned toward Kit. "I got to tell you, I don't like our chances. There's too much firepower at that campground, too many people with training."

"Yeah. I know." They had to make the ranch a tougher place to invade.

Stone stood up. "Let's make this place a harder target. There are some simple things we can do with what we've got. For example, we've got plenty of cars with no fuel and no one living in them, so let's block the road."

Kit joined Stone at the door. "Great idea. We can get a bunch of people to push them into place."

"Yes." Stone walked up the drive. "And someone can gather vines or bushes with stickers, and put them on the gates, making it more difficult to rush in. Poor man's concertina wire."

Kit stopped when they reached the center of the camp. "Hey, ranch hands! Listen up."

Heads popped out of RVs and tents. "Anyone who's not on duty right now or nightshift, come help us. We're going to move some things around. If you've got vehicles without gas that you're not living in, bring the keys. If you have gloves, bring those, too."

Within a few minutes, twelve people gathered around them. "So, we're going to make it harder for anyone to break in here by putting up some roadblocks. Since the driveway is downhill from here, it shouldn't be too hard to push vehicles across the road. Once they're in place, we'll block the tires with rocks or logs, and pile logs near the vehicles, so no one can just drive around. We'll break into two groups of six. We want cars on the front drive, outside the pasture gates, the orchard gate, and outside the gate by the barn. Leave enough space for a person to walk, or ride a bike, but no more than that."

A woman named Cindy raised her hand. "What if my brother shows up?"

Stone scoffed. "There's no fuel. If someone has fuel, they stole it or they've been hoarding it for no good reasons. No one we want here is going to show up with a vehicle now."

Kit bumped Stone's shoulder. "They can leave the vehicle outside the ranch. If it's an RV, we'll move stuff again. Anyone who can't push vehicles, grab a set of clippers or trimmers, and go find brush with stickers or cactus, or any bits and pieces of extra barbed wire you can find. Put it on the fences around the main house. Leave room for us to reach the latches on the inside. If anyone else has good ideas for slowing down invaders, now's the time to share. Let's go." Stacking vehicles to fortify their perimeter wasn't just a good idea, it was great. It gave him a chance to roam wide and see his Aunt Jen, even if it was only for a minute. He wanted to see her for himself, tell her that he was grateful. He gulped. Tell her that he loved her.

"Kit!" A voice bellowed. "Come to the gate, quick!"

CHAPTER THIRTEEN

Alma Garcia. Harmony Ranch, Arizona

Alma deposited Mati's bike behind the chicken feed shed and hurried Matias away from the hens. Em jogged away from them without a backward glance. Emelia knocked at the ranch house door and Kit welcomed her in with a smile. He waved at Alma, evidently fooled into believing she agreed with him.

Alma left Matias with Taylor looking for items to build his pedal powered engine. She retrieved her bike and wheeled it to the gate. Smoke got to his feet, sniffed at her, and swished his tail. A hefty padlock secured the latch on the main gate, and barbed wire ran along the top rail. A man walked away from her along the fence line, a rifle on his back, stopping every ten feet to scan outside the ranch with binoculars. Doc had walked them straight in when they'd arrived; she hadn't counted on having problems leaving the ranch. She jogged her bike over to the orchard, ducked through the trees and small, squeaky gate, then over to the fence.

The top rail of the fence had vicious prickly branches tied to it. Pulling the dull gardening knife from her pocket, she cut away the string, making a gap next to the second post wide enough to squeeze past. She leaned over and pulled the bike to the other side. She'd add more thorns when she got back. She tucked the knife safely back in her pocket. The trees encroached on the boundary and the bike wheel caught on fallen branches. She dragged it over the uneven ground and through the tangle of growth, emerging onto Harmony Ranch Road a few feet from the main entrance. She tripped and the wheel yanked a wire strung between two trees. Deep in the main yard, a string of cans rattled.

Smoke wagged his tail and barked. Alma rushed away, keeping to the line of trees at the side of the road and circling the newly installed log-and-car barrier. At the top of the long drive, she considered the broken bike. Riding it with bad brakes would be stupid. She stood on the pedal with one foot, treating it like a scooter, and freewheeled it down the gradual slope, scuffing the ground with her other foot to slow her speed, but not enough to stop the wind blowing across her face. The rich scent of pines and the chatter of birds accompanied her away from the stifling ranch. Kit might think of her as a child, but she was old enough to protect those she loved. She'd heard that Michael and his crew were at a campsite to the north.

The road was much shorter than she remembered, but then, she'd been climbing it with an injured Emelia before. The trees thinned, and the road opened to the highway. Kit's supposed guard was nowhere to be seen. Alma pushed her bike out onto the main road. Harmony Ranch was without power and there were places where the land slipped and trees toppled, but having been sheltered from the wider devastation for a few days, stepping back into the real world with its riven tarmac and damaged landscape caught her off balance.

She mounted her bike and headed north, back up the deserted highway. The chain clicked, and the bike bumped over the rough surface, thudding in the silence of the open space. Without Matias and Emelia nearby, it was strangely exposing. Her pulse quickened, and her pedaling slowed.

A low and raucous laugh drifted along the highway. She stopped and checked behind her for anyone following. She jumped off her bike and bounced it down the ditch next to the road on the far side from the ranch, then slipped into the edge of the forest. A second laugh roared, and a crack bounced off the trees and in a hollow echo. The voices were coming from the highway ahead. She rested her bike against the vast splayed roots of a fallen tree. Sheltered from view of the road, she crept alongside it toward the voices.

The trees were sparser than the giants surrounding the ranch and Alma bent low. Each footstep disturbed fragile twigs and spindly branches while the tall grass and weeds waved signals when she brushed past. She retreated deeper into the refuge of the shadows and softer ground, keeping the brighter patch of the roadside near enough to not get lost.

She climbed the slope, following the direction of the voices. Strong sentinel trees held back a flood of rich dark soil, several boulders and broken branches blocking her path. Torn trees and shifted earth scarred the hillside farther up. Choosing not to get closer to the road where she might get spotted, she scrambled to get higher over the landslide. The soft earth crumbled under her feet and cascaded with a hiss.

The voices stopped their chatter, and she stood still. Rolling stones clattered against the logs and she ducked. There was nothing to hide behind and her movement only sent another trickle of soil down the unstable slope.

The laugh rose again. Alma gripped her chest and skidded down the far side of the embankment. She dug her fingers into the loose soil and scraped her palms over sharp rocks, but she stopped herself from rolling down the slope. Her footprints left an obvious trail. She panted and brushed the dirt from her hands and backside.

Light filtered through the tree line ahead. She pulled out her knife, crouched, and edged closer. A weed ridden track cut through an avenue of mature trees. Branches, recently sawed with withered leaves, were discarded trackside and provided cover. Alma inched nearer.

The highway peeked through the tall trees at the end of the track, but the access down the track was blocked. One man with a black rifle strapped to his back puffed on a cigarette and passed it to a man wearing a baseball cap. He sat high on the hood of a sand colored vehicle that looked built to tackle anything. The wheels were enormous, with the tinted windows and roof squashed out of proportion for a normal truck. A large open metal box was fixed to the roof, with a cluster of spotlights at the front corners. The man laughed his laugh and leaned back, throwing his shadowed face into the light.

The hairs on Alma's neck rose and her mouth went dry, the knife nearly slipped from her fingers. She pinched herself and felt the sting. *How in the world?*

Eric, regaled in a tatty military style jacket and pants, wasn't rotting in the prison house, but perched on the army vehicle outside her ranch. Her safe haven. A long, dark gash ran down his cheek and into his uneven beard stubble. His eye was bruised and his exposed left forearm heavily bandaged. A short-barreled gun sat comfortably on his lap.

Alma shook her head and stepped back, gripping the handle of the knife tightly. He couldn't have gotten through the bars on the window. She'd locked the door and secured it by pushing the furniture against it. He should be dead.

The other man turned toward the trees. With a shock of recognition, his name came to her: Mason! He wore a faded black t-shirt and camo pants, his tan jacket nowhere to be seen. His unkempt hair was slicked back and greasy. "But seriously, do you really think that slide is safe?" The two guards from the prison house were working together again.

"It hasn't shifted, today." Eric drew deeply on the cigarette, the end glowing orange. "And it's nothing when you've lived through a house falling on you."

"Dude. I *literally* got caught in a landslide. And lived. I know what I'm talking about."

Eric laughed, the sound a sickening reminder of the times he'd leered and jeered at them, back in the factory. "That was one sick rescue op, brother. I thought you were gone, for sure. But that Lisa chick did right by you."

Alma didn't know who Lisa was or what this rescue op was, but everything coming out of Eric's mouth was a kind of evil-miracle. *How? How, how, how had he made it out of the house?*

"You might be indestructible, but you'd still be stuck if the boss hadn't called me." Mason's taunt was almost as bad as his friend's, but he'd never shown her the same callous disregard so while his voice grated, it didn't make her nauseous, the way Eric's did.

Eric flicked the ash at Mason. "I knew where to meet the boss. The fact you chauffeured me was an added bonus." He leaned against the vehicle's windshield and closed his eyes. "I'd have made it to the meeting even if you hadn't shown up. A couple of dirty kids stealing my stuff wouldn't have stopped me." Eric's sneer sent shivers up and down her spine, pricking her arms with chillybumps. "Besides, you couldn't show up without me. I vouched for you, dude."

Mason stuck his middle finger up, insulting his buddy. "You're lucky you just got a black eye and not the same treatment as Charlie."

"He should've done what the boss wanted." Eric opened one eye. "When this all kicked off, he was up against a single old hag. No wonder the boss dealt with him. Even you could've taken her on." Mason laughed, and Eric joined. "Still, it won't be long before the place is his, now we're in position."

"Rocket launcher versus old woman..." Mason scratched his head. "I know which one I'd bet on."

"I'm starving." Eric put the gun to one side and stood up on the hood. "When's the shift change? No one will save us anything. Those guys will eat all the good stuff before we get back." He lifted his cap and ran a hand over his glistening, sweaty head, looking farther up the track. Alma ducked lower behind the sawed-off branches and parted a couple of the leaves obscuring her view, her heart in her throat.

"Good stuff?" Mason puffed. "That's what that sweet ranch is for. Beef steak. I can taste it now."

Eric plonked down to the military vehicle hood, lay back, and pulled his cap over his face. "Wake me up if anything happens."

Mason popped open the cab door, pulled the gun from his back and climbed in. He rested the barrel on the open window and mimed shooting consecutive shots toward the highway.

Alma backed away, sneaking into the shade of overhanging trees. Wincing at every minute crackle underfoot, she withdrew, her pounding heart drumming hard against her ribs. The pine-filled air clogged her lungs and sent her mind racing. She jogged away, her hands trembling, the knife in her stinging palm dull and useless compared to their arsenal.

The rough track led up the steep hill and into the forest. She reached the top, and turned to parallel the highway far below. Many snapped and sheared off branches littered her way. On the slope below her, another landslide had cleared a section wider than Jen's main yard, and twice as long, with trees felled in the chaos, taking out smaller growth so that they tottered like unsteady toddlers. The mound of earth spilled over the highway, with rocks and trees part buried in the compacted soil covered in multiple tire imprints.

With Eric and Mason far behind, and only the empty forest at her back, she stole into the open at the top of the hill, then sank flat to the ground.

From the highway, a gravel road led to a large parking lot, with a narrow structure with a pointed roof at the far side. Three SUVs and another army-type vehicle were parked facing the road in a long line. Big dark green tents, with ropes tied to stakes, were set up under the trees at the far edge. Two box trucks sat at the far end of the gravel parking lot. Two of the four pickups had long fifth-wheel trailers attached to them. A luxurious RV took the prime spot on a concrete pad under a stunning tree with wide, shady branches. Armed men dotted the site. They sat at picnic benches chatting and stood around the tables cleaning gear. One man wiped down the barrel of a rifle and rested it on a low stand. Another pulled a radio from his belt and placed it next to the lined-up guns of various shapes and sizes filling the table. They were readying themselves for a war.

Charlie might've been thrown off the ranch, but the group must have grown since then because Jen would never have pushed such a well-armed force from her property. Alma shivered. Her heart beat so hard that her body quivered with each thud. She'd only seen a handful of weapons on the ranch. The residents were normal, everyday people, the townsfolk of a sleepy vacation spot away from the hustle and violence of the cities, sheltered at Harmony. The most they'd ever shot was probably a warning into the air to frighten a raccoon. The contrast with the armed militia outside the gates was stark.

"God, please save us." Her whispered prayer gave her a moment to steady herself. She scanned the crowd. Some wore the same army-style clothes as Eric and Mason, while others were in ripped jeans and stained plaid shirts. A couple sat together in shorts and flip-flops.

The RV door swung open, bashing against the wall with a bang and two women stepped out. The shorter, older one, with wild brown hair to rival Emelia's, pulled the other behind her. They both looked as if they'd stepped out of a hiking magazine, but the younger, taller woman's outfit didn't hang past her hands and fabric didn't bunch at her feet. It fit her well even if it wasn't designed for someone in her early twenties. Alma couldn't place where she'd seen her face. There was no reason she should know her, but she was familiar. Long hair tumbled down the young woman's back and caught in the breeze, but her scowl at the shorter woman cancelled all signs of beauty. She cradled her hand and pushed the older woman away.

A man, who'd been picking something from his teeth, sauntered over from the nearby bench. Alma flattened to the dirt. He spoke to the wild-haired one, then grabbed the younger woman's injured wrist. She screamed, her high pitch silencing the general muttering around the camp and making everyone turn toward her. He forced her back into the RV, slamming the door behind her. The older woman's head hardly reached the man's shoulder. But despite her appearance, she had power. She snapped something, and he slunk back to his bench, turned his back, and hung his head.

Two men stepped out from behind one of the box trucks parked on the other side of the site. Both were in heavy, dark gear. The one with flushed cheeks lifted the binoculars from around his neck. The light glinted off the glass and Alma scrambled back down the earth mound. She crouched and ran back to the trees, weaving through the trunks and tripping over roots. No alarm call sounded behind her. She skimmed the edge of the forest and arrived back at Eric's post.

A radio beeped, and Alma's footsteps faltered. Mason jumped and the barrel of his rifle clattered against the window frame. She stood stock still and waited for her former jailor to capture her.

Eric lifted his cap and pulled the radio from his hip. "South 89 Station. Over."

"I'm coming in. Get out of the way. Over."

Eric slid from the hood and clambered into the cab. The engine roared and Eric reversed the vehicle in a wide arc into the undergrowth at the edge of the road nearest to Alma. She stepped back and ran to the soft earth of the landslide. Launching herself over the loose dirt sputtering down the bank, she sprinted away. Rocks and dirt slid, but the engine would cover any noise she made. She pushed through the trees at the bottom of the hill, away from the men. Panting, she turned, expecting the trees and ground behind her to be churned up by the massive wheels. There was nothing. She slowed, sliding through the trees, orienting herself by keeping the highway to her right side.

The splintered asphalt flickered through the screening branches. The huge fallen tree guided her back to her bike. She grabbed it, bursting from the shelter of the upturned roots. It wasn't too late. She could get Emelia and Matias off the ranch and away. The small army wanted the cattle and buildings; a few children wouldn't interest them as long as Eric didn't lay eyes on her. Her bags were still packed and Mattias could easily attach the trolley to her bike. If they were extra sneaky, they could gather enough food and water for a couple of days. It wasn't as if those on the ranch were going to need any of it when they came face to face with a rocket launcher, guns, and miniature tanks.

An engine hummed, and another of the giant, mottled sand colored vehicles bumped over the broken surface toward her. She dove backward into the small trees, leaving her bike to tumble into the ditch. The windows were down, an elbow leaning out. The buzz-cut brown hair and the handsome face of Michael Martinez drifted by. He'd shaved, so there was no mistaking who he was. His looks might charm others, but something stronger and more poisonous churned inside Alma. The knife was in her hand. He'd taken everything from her and he had to pay. As it turned out, she hadn't murdered Eric—or left him to die—but she knew she had it in her. The monstrous vehicle sped off and turned onto the track to the armed camp.

Alma stood. Her hand was steady, and she wasn't going to run.

CHAPTER FOURTEEN

Catherine "Cat" Murphy. En Route to The Bunker

"Tom?" Horrified, Cat trembled. Covered in blood, the congealing plasma tacky on her hands, she hid on the floorboard. Her heart thudding in her throat, she waited for the attackers to come, or for Tom to answer, but there was only the creaking and thumping of cattle shifting in the trailer.

"Grady?" Her voice shook. No one answered. A rooster crowed, and several chickens squawked, settling into a gentle hum of clucks and cackles. Quaking, she gagged.

A beam of sunlight blinded her and she covered her eyes with a sticky hand, smearing blood across her forehead. Fighting to breathe, she guarded her throbbing ribs as she pulled herself to her knees and peered over the back of the pickup seat. Grady was slouched over the steering wheel, his neck bent at an unnatural angle, the left half of his skull missing. Bits of flesh mottled the open passenger door, a pair of blue jean clad legs unmoving on the ground. She retched, her core convulsing, but there was nothing inside to vomit. Her being was hollow, empty. "Tom!"

Cat's door flung open, and she dropped to the floorboard,

searching for her pistol. Her heart in her throat, she scrambled, slipping and floundering in the bloody mess.

"Cat, stop! They're gone." Tom's deep, calming voice washed over her like a sedative and she collapsed into a blubbering heap. Pulling her from the floor, embracing her as he turned her to him, he set her on the edge of the bench seat. He pushed her away, patting her down, his eyes searching her body. "Are you hit?"

The adrenaline drained from her body, numbness flooding from her head to her toes. She slumped, sinking into his solid chest. Pushing her face into the pearl snaps of his heaving shirt, a dull ache shot across her tender cheek bone. Consoled by the beating of his heart, rapid as it was, she ignored the discomfort and pressed in closer. A golf ball sized lump formed in her throat and she embraced the silence, unready and unwilling to speak.

"Honey! Are you okay?" He pushed her to arm's length, his face ashen. "Cat?" Tom shook her. "Cat!"

Her vision went blurry, and her jaw tightened. She swallowed hard. "Yeah. Yeah, I think so." She tugged at the hem of her tee. The blood-soaked fabric made a sucking sound as she pulled the shirt away from her body. "This must be..." Cat swallowed and turned toward Grady. "... his."

Tom put his hand against her cheek, turning her face away. Wrapping her arms around her shivering body, she pointed to Tom's equally sodden left arm, her teeth chattering. "Are—are you injured?"

"Oh, that. Aw, that's just a scratch." Tom drew her in, crushing her against his chest.

She melted into him and surrendered. Resting, she let his comforting presence warm her from the inside out. The quivering subsided. "Who was that?"

"I don't know." He held her head against his ribcage, his heartbeat slow and even.

She looked up at him. His blue eyes were fixed on the horizon. Cat swiveled in her seat. There were no houses or vehicles in sight. "Where did they come from?

"I don't know, honey, but I do know where they went." Tom tapped the butt of the pistol in his shoulder holster. "Those fellas got a one-way ticket to Hell, courtesy of Samuel Colt." He, pivoted, still surveying the countryside. "But, who knows who else is out there. We should get on our way before another welcome party shows up."

Cat scrunched up her face. "This looks like the middle of nowhere. Where are we?"

"Somewhere between Green Valley and Sonoita." Tom glanced up at Grady's lifeless body sprawled against the dash. "So pretty much the middle of nowhere." He stepped away from her. "Sit tight."

Tom leaned over the bed of the pickup and extracted a shovel. Stalking around the back of the trailer, he disappeared. A fly landed on Cat's arm, soon several were buzzing inside the cab of the pickup. Annoyed, she shooed them away.

Five minutes later Tom returned with a determined look on his face. He refilled Cat's water bottle, then moved past her and opened the driver's door. "I'm sorry, Grady." Bending at the knees, he placed the dead man's arm over his shoulder and raised up, holding him in a fireman's carry. Chin set, he strode by Cat without looking at her. "I'll be back soon, hon." Belle—who'd been as quiet as a mouse, even when the bullets were flying—followed on his heels.

Cat twisted and turned, searching for her leg. The floor of the pickup was littered with everything that had been on top of, or shoved up underneath, the seats. Candy wrappers, crushed beer cans, random tools, and leaking oil jugs were strewn about.

She peered over the back of the front seat. A dusty bottle, half full of amber liquid, sat on a pile of debris. The label worn away from rolling back and forth over miles of backcountry roads, but she still recognized the shape. Her entire body achy and bruised, the whiskey beckoned to her. The toe of her boot peeked out from under the heap and as she was scooting toward it, Tom reappeared. Her pulse quickened and her face grew warm, her cheeks tingling. "That was quick."

"I found a small sinkhole out in the mesquite there. I just put him in the hollow and filled it in." He tossed the shovel in the back, returning to her side. "Not ideal, but better than leaving him out for the buzzards. How you doing?"

She gulped water from her bottle. "Thirsty." Avoiding his eyes, she wiped the stray droplets from her upper lip.

"Me, too. Kinda lost my appetite, though." He clapped a large hand on the seat in front of Cat, grimacing at the grisly chaos in the front seat. "We better get moving. Which direction?"

"What do you mean, which direction?" Confused, Cat looked for an alternative route than the one they were on.

Tom straightened up, his thigh pressing into hers. "I'm saying, do you want to continue forward, or do you want to go back to the ranch? We can do whatever you want, we're about halfway."

"Going back isn't really an option. is it? I mean, it can't get much worse, right?" Cat's words still hung in the air as a growling, gurgling sound came from the front of the pickup.

Muscles in his jaw flexing, he dropped to hunker on his heels. He craned his neck to focus on the ground under the pickup. "Oh, for crying out loud."

She leaned over and lifted the sweaty cowboy hat off Tom's head, his silvery hair damp. "Please tell me it's not the radiator."

"If it isn't, someone else left quite a ration of antifreeze behind." He rose, brushed off his jeans, and stalked to the front where he opened the hood, looked inside, then slammed it shut. "The radiator core looks like Swiss cheese."

"Can't fix that."

"Nope." He pressed his lips together, turning them white. Pushing his hat back, he scratched his head. "The rig's leaking oil, and diesel, too. She's dead in the water."

Cat's heart plummeted, her throat growing thick. "Oh, no."

Tom circled around the back of the stock trailer. The screech of metal pierced the air; he'd opened the trailer gate. The outfit shook, a few moments passing before the gate slammed shut and the pickup shuddered. Soon Tom made his way around to the passenger side. He opened the front door, debris spilling out. "What the?!" Jumping back, the whiskey bottle thudded as it bounced out the door. Tom bent over, then stood there for a moment, rolling the bottle against his palm. He lifted it by the neck, swinging it. "Wanna swig?"

She hesitated. "Nope." Even though she wanted it, Cat clenched her jaw and shook her head.

"Good." He tossed the bottle over his shoulder, and it landed with a crash of glass. Leaning back into the cab, he emerged with Cat's leg.

Her shirt had begun to stiffen from the bloodbath. "Um, can you get me something else to wear?"

"Sure." He returned to her side carrying a black T-shirt. After handing it to her, he turned away.

She tugged at the bloody shirt, but it was glued to her body. In her weakened state, she was ready to pitch decorum out the window. This wasn't the place to waste her energy. "I'm gonna need a hand here, I can't get this off."

"Alrighty." He turned, looking her up and down. "Wanna try and go over your head?"

"Gross. Just cut it off." She pulled the hem away from her stomach.

He flipped open his pocketknife. "You got it." Prying the material from her body, he zipped the knife blade up from the hem, between her breasts, and to the collar in seconds. "Good thing I just sharpened this thing." He took the knife and held it between his teeth, then peeled the shirt away from her shoulders.

She shrugged out of the garment. "My bra is soaked too." Reaching behind her back, she undid the clasps, whipping it off as he attempted to spin around. Instead, he tipped his hat low, covering his eyes. Sliding the new tee over her head, she shook out her hair. "Awesome, there's blood in my hair again. I want a shower." She combed her fingers through her long mane, grinning at his modesty. "You can look now."

She plaited her hair while he rolled up the leg of her jeans. "Don't worry, Catherine. We'll figure something out. It's only fifty miles."

Fifty miles. Vomit rose in her throat. "Tom?" The stock trailer jounced, the animals in the back moving and shifting. "Are the cattle okay?"

"Most of them are." His eyes dulled. "One broke a leg in the commotion, and another caught a bullet. I put them down." He manipulated her prothesis and her leg, lining them up.

A pronounced line of darkening blood was smeared across his flank where he'd wiped something sharp—his pocketknife. He must've cut their throats. Her heart sunk. For him, and for her mama cows. She held her leg out straight, rubbing the stump. "What are we going to do with the ones who made it? With the chickens?"

"I'm not sure we *can* do anything with them, Catherine. We might just need to set 'em loose." He cocked his head to one side, then the other. "Where's your wrap?"

She pointed at a pile of ace bandage that had migrated under the seat during their off-road experience. "We can't just leave them here to fend for themselves, Tom."

"I understand the sentiment, honey, but right now it might be all we can do to keep ourselves alive." He wrapped her leg. "Too tight?"

"Nope." Cat bowed her head. The animals were her responsibility, she'd brought them along. They wouldn't be in this mess if she hadn't manipulated and forced the situation.

"Well, we're gonna need another vehicle, or at the very least, some horses." He slid her leg into the contraption.

"Strap me in this way." She swung the cradle vertically.

He fastened the straps. "You sure you're healed up enough?" He unpinned the hinge, swinging her leg down.

Steadying herself, she put her hand on his shoulder. "No, but I want to be."

He handed her the handcrafted crutch. "Try that out?"

Putting most of her weight on the crutch, she took a tentative step, then another. She walked in a small circle. The pain was acute and she pressed her lips together, biting back the tears. She couldn't let Tom see how close she was to buckling. With each step the contraption was carrying more of the burden. She forced herself to sound hopeful. "Not too bad."

"Looking good. I'm gonna hike up to the top of that mesa and try to get my bearings." He lifted his chin in the direction of a small flat-topped hill a few hundred feet away. "That sound like a plan?"

"Yeah, but I'm not too keen on splitting up." She stopped, leaning against the bed of the pickup.

"Oh, we're sticking together, doll." Tom retrieved her shoulder holster from the vehicle, holding it open for her to shrug into. "I'll keep you in sight, and I'll stay in whistle distance." He squeezed her shoulders and moved to stand in front of Cat.

"Me, too." She winked. "Wanna help me back into the rig?"

"Sure thing." Tom lifted her by the hips and placed her back on the seat. Grabbing the shotgun from the front seat, he laid it across her lap and threw a rifle over his shoulder. "Rest up while I'm gone, we can't have you wearing yourself out." He leaned down and gave Cat a peck on the cheek. "Come on, Belle."

Tom strode across the desert, disappearing into a mahogany thicket, his dog at his heels. Cat kept an eagle eye on the base of the table while waiting for him to emerge, but he didn't reappear. As the time ticked by, her anxiety grew. She scanned the hillside and the flat, her eyes straining. The vastness of the country and the thick vegetation causing her eyes to grow weary, and her heartbeat to skyrocket. Soon thirty minutes had passed, and Cat had convinced herself that Tom was dead or seriously injured. He should've at least made it to the bottom of the hill. "He's okay. He's okay. He's okay." She repeated the mantra over and over, trying to assure herself that he was fine.

The pickup door swung open, and Cat jumped, her stomach flying into her throat. She tipped over, then scrambled to prop herself up. Fumbling, she jockeyed the scattergun to her shoulder and swung the barrel toward the intruder. "Tom! Where the hell did you come from?" She lowered the shotgun.

"Oh, I walked back down the draw, it was easier going. Overshot the pickup and had to circle back." He seemed oblivious to her distress. "I've got good news and bad news." He dug through the mess on the floor and held up a beat-up old map. "The good news is I know where we are." Spreading the map out on the seat, he tapped a spot on the crumpled paper. "Helvetia is just over the hill. Remember Andy Van Zant's old cow camp? He used to keep a hand and a few head of horses there year-round."

"And the bad news?" Her voice trembled as she fought to regain her composure.

He studied the filthy, torn paper. "I've got to leave you again while I go check it out."

Cat's body went rigid. "Oh, that's not happening, buddy. You disappeared for the majority of your little hike up the hill and I about lost my mind. The experience was not restful. We're sticking together." She slid out of her seat, bracing herself against the pickup. "How far is it?"

"Hon, you can't walk that far." Tom dropped the map and met her at the corner of the vehicle. "It's just a bad idea for so many reasons."

"How... Far... Is... It?" She set her chin and made herself as tall as possible, leaning into his chest.

"A half mile or so?" He stepped back. "But it's rough country."

Cat pushed past him. "The road goes there, doesn't it?"

"Yeah, but that doubles the distance." Tom scurried around the pickup, slamming doors, finally catching up with her. "Dammit, Cat. You're gonna kill yourself."

"Tom, we don't have any other options." She stopped, her ire dwindling. "We—and the livestock—are sitting ducks right here, you know it."

He harumphed, snorting like an irritated horse. "Fine." Slinging the rifle over his shoulder, Tom strode out in front of her, then slowed to walk beside her.

It didn't take many steps before the adrenaline from the ambush wore off and the pain returned. She was getting used to it. Instead of focusing on the pain, she counted her steps—one, two, three... one hundred. She did the math, estimating a hundred of her baby steps was about seventy or eighty yards. With 1,760 yards in a mile, it figured out to around 2,500 steps. They were 1/25th of the way there. Forcing the dread and fear down, she carried on. She'd take it in small chunks, a hundred steps at a time.

Two hundred steps. The road had gone from a nice gravel lane to a rutted, fractured, obstacle course lined with saguaro, barrel cacti, jumping cholla, and prickly pear. Her armpit chafed and her stump ached, already throbbing.

Three hundred steps. Trudging along the uneven ground, Cat twisted her ankle, catching herself before she fell. A short, insignificant zap of pain shot up her leg.

Tom stopped, looking her up and down. She continued walking and he walked next to her, backward, his eyes narrowed.

"I'm fine." She lied, and the pain faded almost as quickly as it had come.

Four hundred steps. Regret reared its ugly head. Her steps slowed as the incline increased, her legs burning. Cat questioned her decision, then persuaded herself that there was no other option. Her stump had begun to swell, the straps growing tighter and tighter. She urged herself to the top of the hill, stopping to rest when the terrain flattened.

Tom grinned at her, concern in his eyes. "How you doin'?"

Her chest heaving, she didn't answer. Taking a deep breath, she raised her eyebrows and forced a weak smile.

"That good, huh?" He eased closer, taking her crutch, and drawing her under his arm. "You ain't foolin' nobody." Tom pointed at a nearby boulder. "Wanna sit down for a spell?"

She leaned into him, shaking her head. "No." If she sat down, she had a pretty strong feeling that she wouldn't get back up. "Let's go."

Taking her crutch back, she took thirty-two steps across the top of the hill, her thighs quivering. Her legs were no longer burning, they were numb—and turning to jelly. The knoll dropped off and halfway through her 433rd step, she knew she'd made a mistake. Her amputated leg failed. She hyperextended her knee, and her boot disappeared. Her other leg crumpled beneath her, sending her tumbling down the hill. Bouncing off rocks and skidding through the dirt, Cat thrust her hands down. Every kind of cactus known to Arizona lined the side of the road, she tucked her legs in an attempt to dodge the thorny beasts.

"Cat! Cat! Oh, dang, Cat!" When she came to a stop, Tom was standing over her. He hunkered down, his eyes searching her body. "Are you okay?"

The fall had knocked the air out of her lungs and the wind out of her sails. "Ugh!"

"What?" He leaned closer, running his hands over her body.

"I said, UGH!" She pushed herself up on her elbows. "Is my leg okay?"

"I can't see through your pants, but I imagine it's pretty bruised. He waved at a prickly pear inches from Cat's face, a cholla dangling above. "I don't know how you managed to avoid getting turned into a pin cushion."

"No, my other leg." She pointed to her homemade prosthetic, struggling to sit.

Tom stepped behind her, putting his hand under her arms. "Oh, that one. Can't tell." He pulled her away from the cacti, lifting her to a sitting position. "How's that noggin?"

"Oh, my skull's fine." She rubbed the back of her head and coughed, dust falling in a cloud around her face.

"I guess it's a good thing God made it several inches thick." He circled around to her foot, crouching to push up the jeans on one leg, then the other. "Whelp, your body actually survived that tumble pretty well, but I'm afraid your new leg is busted."

CHAPTER FIFTEEN

Alma Garcia. Harmony Ranch, Arizona

Alma sat on the dusty ground of the barn drawing patterns in the dirt while Taylor removed the battery pack from a battered cordless drill. Her brain was stuck on a loop: Michael Martinez, it said. Michael Martinez is out there and he's coming for you.

Matias measured and marked lengths of recycled lumber to construct a stand for his partially mutilated bike. They'd already removed the back tire and fitted a loose rubber belt around the spoked wheel. Matias willingly gave up his bike to create the machine, but it left her family trapped on the ranch when they could be miles away from the madness of Michael Martinez's small army at the campsite north of the ranch.

Emelia's wounded leg was probably recovered enough for them to cycle away from the threat. Alma could have reversed Matias' offer of his bike and they would've been on their way. But Mama's grave was still fresh and Alma's lie about staying to fulfill Mama's wishes wouldn't die so easily. Emelia might see leaving as a betrayal. Alma scratched at the pattern she'd drawn. She was torn. On the one hand, Eric made her blood run cold and sent her brain skittering to escape, but once she'd spotted Martinez, she knew she had to stay and finish the business between them.

Kit and Emelia were out there, somewhere, laying medieval traps against Martinez's gun-toting thugs. Sweat slicked her hands. Cords and bent saplings, rocks and traps would be futile against the line of weapons at his camp.

Alma picked up a stalk of straw and folded it in her fingers. Smoke's deep bark and Alma's shouting brought the gate guards running to the entrance, but it wouldn't be quick enough if she'd been Eric, Mason, or Martinez. Any of the crew from the campsite could easily take down the weak defense guarding the ranch. She trembled at how easy it was to enter the ranch. She had no choice but to tell someone what she'd seen. Harmony Ranch belonged to Jen, and it would be right to speak to her about it, but Alma had barely spoken to the woman, so she waited for Kit. Emelia trusted him.

Emelia's laugh, all innocent and with no concern, preceded her. She skipped around the corner and stopped in her tracks. Alma stood up and brushed the dust from her pants. Emelia's carefree smile faded, and she lowered her gaze to the ground. Alma wasn't welcome.

Kit followed behind. He pulled a large rucksack from his shoulder with his good hand. He dropped it to the floor, strode over to Taylor, and kissed her cheek. "That's coming along nicely."

"Kit, can I talk to you please?" Alma couldn't hide the tremble in her voice. He nodded, and she left the barn, heading for the darker side of the house. "You told me not to scare Em and Mati. Well, I'm not going to do that, but you should know about the men at the campsite."

"Alma?" Kit turned his back to the barn and murmured. "What did you do?"

"I went to see what we're up against." Alma pulled her ponytail tighter, and Kit frowned. "You wouldn't tell me anything. What do you expect me to do? Em and Mati are my responsibility."

His brows raised. "You could've gotten hurt."

Alma couldn't deny it. She could've gotten more than just hurt.

"There isn't a guard on the road near the Harmony Ranch driveway, but there is one on the track to the campsite."

"Alma! I thought you were smarter than that."

She couldn't deny that assessment either, but at least she could share what she'd seen. "They've got so many guns. And radios. There are these army car truck things and loads of men down there." She stared at her feet. "I know some of them."

"Wait." Kit took a step closer to her and bent toward her. "You know them?"

"Guards from the house where *Encircle Energy* kept us."

Kit rubbed a hand over his face. His bandage was stained with sap. "Aunt Jen said that Charlie went there."

"I don't know who Charlie is, but a man called Eric is there with his buddy Mason. They..." Alma took a steadying breath. "They used to beat us. They aren't frightened to hurt people. I thought Eric was dead. He should be dead." She swallowed. "They said they had a rocket launcher."

Kit was silent for far too long, then he put his hand on her shoulder. "You should've stayed on the ranch."

"Are you going to take this seriously or not? Did you know this stuff already?"

Kit shook his head. "Alma, we have military veterans helping us. We are taking it seriously. We'll protect everyone."

"Have I at least helped you?"

Kit turned Alma to face him, putting his bandaged hand on her other shoulder so that he held her in his weak grip. "Yes, but—I need you to listen to me—it wasn't worth the risk. Is there anything else?"

Alma picked out the laughter lines around Kit's kind eyes. "Michael Martinez is there. I saw him. Well, I saw him driving to the campsite."

"Martinez of Martinez Corporation? You're sure?" Alma nodded and he let go of her shoulders but kept his gaze on hers. "Nora's death makes more sense now."

Alma's pulse quickened. "Did Em—?"

"Did Em, what?" Kit's kind eyes narrowed.

132

She had to find a reason for her question that wouldn't give her away. "Did Em help you build more traps?"

He frowned. "Yes. She was quiet today." He steered her back toward the barn. "Thank you for telling me what you saw, but you need to stay close to your family. They need you more than you know. Especially Em. She's been too grim since I found Nora's body."

"I can help you protect the ranch. Please, let me. Eric said that the old woman wouldn't stand a chance and that Charlie should've done a better job. I think he was talking about Jen."

Kit scowled at the ground, then met her gaze again. "It sounds like Martinez has been trying to get Harmony Ranch from Jen for longer than we realized."

"Definitely. They're coming for us. Some men were cleaning guns, but others were waiting in lines. I don't think it will be long. I don't know why they're waiting."

Kit stepped toward the barn. "I'll tell Taylor and get our defenses ready."

He turned to go, once again excluding her from the planning, and it felt like he'd dropped her from a great height. "You're not going to let me help, are you?"

He turned back, shaking his head. It was either sadness or more likely pity etched on his face, Alma couldn't be certain which, but she spun and ran before he had a chance to drop whatever patronizing garbage he was working up to, bursting around the corner of the house. How dare he treat her like a kid! She unhooked the gate and yanked it open, the squeal an echo of her frustration. A hand gripped her wrist from behind.

A woman wearing a dark green hooded jacket pressed her slender forefinger to her lips. "I'm not going to hurt you."

Alma stumbled backward through the open gate. Her heart raced, but she kept her voice low. "You! I saw you at the camp."

Long wavy hair fluttered at the edge of the woman's hood. Her shadowed face was olive and flawless. Her dark brown eyes widened. The woman's outfit was unmarked and clean. At the startlingly close quarters, the baggy clothes didn't fit her as well as Alma had thought.

But she wasn't dirty, like Alma. She'd been sitting in their luxury RV, not out working.

Alma backed away. The woman glanced behind her and pushed a step closer. "Chill! I'm not going to hurt you. I just want to talk."

"How did you get here? Where are the others?" The older woman and the large man that forced the green jacket woman back in the camper weren't behind her, and the orchard seemed quiet.

"Geez, girl! They've underestimated you, haven't they?"

"I don't know what you mean." Alma took another step back.

"You understand the danger better than half the goons guarding this place." Her rolling eyes made it clear she didn't think much of their defenses. "I heard you talking to that hulk of a guy. You made it to the camp, and back, didn't you?"

Alma frowned at the woman. She wasn't telling her anything.

The woman lowered her hood. "I'm Helen." She held out her left hand, the other she held close to her chest. It was covered in a bulky bandage not unlike the one wrapped around Kit's burned hand. Alma fumbled and shook it. "Helen Martinez."

Alma withdrew as if Helen's hand were on fire and snorted. "You're not welcome here."

"You can't choose your family." She laughed, though it was a humorless sound. "And, in my case, they actively didn't choose me. I'm an outcast. An outsider."

She'd been in the photo from the news report the night the van blew up and the newspaper from the town house doorstep. Helen was Michael Martinez's sister. "Why are you here?"

Helen shrugged. "I heard my brother's name, that's why I listened in. You should be grateful."

Alma snorted, yanking her hand free of Helen's grip. "No one is grateful for your brother or for any of your family. You ruined everything."

Helen raised her hands. "Not me. You don't get to put any of that trash on me. I'm not in the business. Never have been and never will be. That's why I'm here." She took a step back from Alma. "I don't want brother dear to do even more harm. I'm not going to let him 'ruin everything,' as you say. You've got to be prepared, but then you know that already, because you've seen what he has down there."

"We're making the ranch secure." She raised her chin, mimicking Em's bravery.

A smile caught at the corners of Helen's mouth. "*They're* making the ranch secure. Am I right?"

Alma's irritation made her bite down on her lip. Helen wasn't even part of the community but she'd discovered Alma's sore spot immediately.

Helen put her hand in her jacket pocket and pulled out a small pistol, holding it by the barrel. "I want you to have this."

"What? Why?"

"I like you. You're feisty." Helen stroked her thumb over the gun's grip. "You need to protect yourself even if the grown-ups around here don't think you're old enough to do squat." She grabbed Alma's hand, pulling it toward her. "You've got family, right? Protect them. You've got to get them out of here. Michael has everything planned to kick off tomorrow. Get them out now. Go anywhere but here." Helen shook her head. "They'll be watching the road. Find some other path or back trail out of here." Helen pointed between the branches of the apple trees to the high slab of rock jutting out of the hillside on the other side of the highway. "If you can't get out, make sure no one up there can see you." Alma had watched the ranch from the same rock perch. "He's a horrible specimen of a human being, but his aim is perfect. Too many kids have suffered already. Don't let him catch you. Get out." She put the gun into Alma's palm and pushed it away.

Alma curled her fingers around the grip, revealing the Martinez Corporation logo embossed on the top part of the gun. Helen was barely an adult herself and she'd offered Alma everything within five minutes; trust, responsibility, and a weapon. She'd invited her into the grown-up world without a filter. Alma caressed the weapon and put her finger to the trigger.

"No!" Helen put her hand over Alma's then stepped back. "There's no safety and I've already loaded the chamber. There's also a round in the magazine. Don't point and squeeze unless you want someone to die. The Ruger LCP might be small, but it's no toy. The trigger pull is long and heavy and there's still a snappy recoil."

Alma had never touched a gun in her life. "I don't know how to use it."

"Seriously?" Helen took back her gun. "Stand strong. Dominant foot forward." She adopted a stance, ran a finger over the barrel, and winced. Gripping it in one hand, she lifted it then curled her injured hand over her other. "Line up the sights and squeeze the trigger. Don't jerk it." She placed it back in Alma's hand. "Use the grips on top and pull back to get the ammo in the chamber. Got it?"

"I guess. But why? Why give it to me?"

Helen lifted her bandaged hand. "I can't shoot and every gun will count. It's the only thing I can do to level the playing field. I can't get you out of here. I probably can't even get myself out of here. I tried, but it all fell apart. Long story. Very boring. But the one thing I can do, is give you a chance to survive."

"You've seen us and them. You don't think we have much hope, do you?"

Helen shrugged. "I hope you do."

"This is Jen's home." Alma pointed back toward the house. "This is everyone's home. They'll fight to keep it. Have you told Jen about them coming?"

Helen shook her head and shrugged. "I found you first." She pulled up her hood. "I need to go. When Michael finds out I left, he'll be in a bad mood. Things don't end well when he's in a bad mood. If I run, I can draw away some of his men and help you out." She paused. "I didn't catch your name."

"Alma." She could give Helen that much in return for the gun.

"Well, Alma. Good luck. God speed. Let the stars align and all that jazz." Her smile was one of those terrible not-happy smiles that so many grown-ups wore. "I hope you stay alive long enough to get out of here."

"You've given me a better chance." Alma lifted the pistol. "Thanks." She was grateful someone had finally treated her like the adult she was.

Helen jogged through the trees, then turned, continuing to the east side of Harmony Ranch. Alma hurried along the path, emerging from the orchard at the opposite end.

A distant gray line in the hillside of trees marked the rocky ledge; the outpost Helen had told Alma to avoid. The next day Michael Martinez would be there, picking them off one by one with his on point aim. She placed the pistol in her pocket. Its reassuring weight dragged at the fabric. He'd only be picking people off if he was still alive.

CHAPTER SIXTEEN

Catherine "Cat" Murphy. En Route to The Bunker

"Busted? Dang it." Tears welled up in her eyes. "My leg's busted." She shook her head, avoiding Tom's gaze. "Of course, it's busted... by the infamous Catherine Maureen Murphy and her hard-headedness of colossal proportions." Halfway down the hill, she sat in the dirt, sniffling, and trying not to cry. "I'm sorry, Tom."

"Hey, hey, hey..." He took her by the chin, turning her face to his. Belle nuzzled her way up under Cat's arm. "These things happen. Maybe we can fix it when we get back to the pickup."

As he kissed her on the forehead, the ground shook. A great cracking sound rang out, followed by the increasing rush of running water. No, not water, it couldn't be. It was something else.

Tom's eyes grew, his crow's feet diminishing. "Cat..." Pivoting on his heel, he threw off his rifle and glanced back at her. "Climb on."

A small rock bounced past her. "Huh?" She recoiled.

"Piggyback. Now." He tapped on his shoulder. "It's either that, or I throw you over my shoulder."

Cat shook her head. "The heck you—"

Whipping around, he swept her off the desert floor and slung her over his back. "There's an avalanche on our tail!"

Before she could catch her breath, Tom sprinted down the hill. "Hang on, darlin'!"

Her chin bounced against his spine, her teeth rattling. Dust roiled around them, pebbles and debris pelting her face. Her knee slammed against the pistol in Tom's holster, her broken prosthetic flopping against his chest. Blinded by the onslaught of rocks and powdery dust, she squeezed her burning eyes shut. She inhaled, wheezed, and choked. Her body wracked with spasms, she clung to Tom and prayed for the assault to end.

The earth's roar dulled, and Tom's gait decelerated to a canter. As the jouncing eased, she pulled her tee shirt over her nose. Taking a deep breath, she wiped her eyes.

He slowed and stopped in his tracks, his ribs heaving against her cheek. "Sorry 'bout that." Crouching, he set her down and stood hunched over, his hands on his knees. He filled his lungs and coughed, a hacking, barking cough. Standing tall, he cleared his throat. "Now, you want to climb on my back, or should we continue travelling like we have been?" He turned away from her. "We gotta keep moving."

"Ugh." She pressed her aching chest to his back, wrapping her arms around his neck. "Fine."

Tom stood, reaching behind his back with both arms and, adjusting her holster, lifted her by the hips, a little groan escaping his mouth. He cupped her thighs and squeezed. "You good?"

Her ribs stung, but a tingle ran up her spine and—transcending the turmoil and anguish—a sparkling airiness filled her lungs. She sighed and laid her face against his back. Even after all her poor decisions, stubbornness, and just general selfishness, he still cared about her. "Yeah."

He set off walking. An eerie silence hung in the hazy air, not a chitter or hum to be heard. The animals were quiet. Or gone. Tom's denim jeans rustled with his rhythmic stride, Belle's paws padding alongside him, and Cat's eyes grew heavy. After several moments passed, he stopped abruptly, jolting her back to reality.

"Dang. This place is nuked, too." He twisted, surveying the landscape.

The weight returned to Cat's chest. The countryside was a charcoal wasteland where the skeletons of several ancient saguaros still smoldered in the distance. A vast network of fissures gaped open, branching out in fits and starts like disconnected veins. "All except for that." She pointed to a blue plastic trough and the remains of a weathered windmill.

"Huh?" Tom turned, stopping as he faced the waterhole. "That. Is. Fantastic." He took off toward the ruins, his pace accelerating.

"Whoa, there, cowboy." Cat's voice jumped and dove as she bounced along on his back. "Isn't that the wrong way? Don't waste your energy."

"Yup." Dissuaded, Tom continued tramping toward the only evidence of humanity visible for miles.

His gait grew choppier, his long legs covering distance quickly. The inside of her thighs chafed against his hips and she squeezed tighter. Biting her lip, she held her tongue. She was wasting *her* energy. Besides, her mouth had gotten her in too much trouble lately.

Soon they reached the waterhole. He backed up to the oval trough, bending his knees until the back of Cat's thighs touched the lip of the plastic tub. "Sit here." Prying her fingers loose, he turned to steady her on the thin ledge. "You okay?"

She gripped the edge with both hands and pushed her foot into the ground. "Yup." The trough was dry and from her precarious perch she wasn't sure if that was a good or a bad thing. At the sight of the crusty basin and the rusty faucet Cat's tongue thickened. She'd forgotten to pack any water.

Tom loped over to the windmill, orbited it several times, then grabbed an upright and pulled. The structure creaked and he yanked. Nothing moved. Muttering something, Tom picked up a stray piece of galvanized pipe. He positioned his feet shoulder width apart, twisted at the waist, and swung, connecting with the angle iron structure. Over and over he swung, the sounds of his clanging barrage deafening Cat.

Shaking, Belle pushed in close to Cat's leg. "What the heck, Tom?"

Finally, he stopped, flinging the piece of pipe off into the burned area. "I thought we could scrounge some materials to build a travois, but the bolts are all rusted together and I got no confounded tools."

Her pistol digging into the side of her leg, Cat twisted on the lip of the trough. Orange tinged water seeped out of the rusty faucet, the droplets calling to Cat's wooden tongue. "Do you have a lighter?"

Tom produced a lighter from the left pocket of his shirt and handed it to her. "What for?"

"This." She flicked it under the spigot, a tiny teal flame bursting, the vapors floating up into the atmosphere. Dropping the lighter in her lap, she frowned. She pried her tongue from the roof of her mouth, making a slight clucking sound. "Just checking."

"Not a good sign." Tom paced around the trough, his little blue merle dog at his heels. Undoing a middle snap on his shirt, Tom produced a bottle of water. "You thirsty?"

"Oh, thank you." Taking the bottle from him, she twisted off the cap and took a small sip. She relished the warm, damp liquid then put the lid back on. Thankful he anticipated her thirst, she extended it back to him.

"Keep it." Tom shook his head. "Drink a little more." He patted his stomach. "That one's yours. Got my own right here."

"Thanks." Cat took another sip then set the bottle between her knees. "Heads up." Twisting, she tossed the lighter toward him, losing her balance in the process. She flipped backward, landing in the trough, knocking the air from her lungs and dropping the water bottle. Floundering, she sputtered curse words under her breath. She scrambled to salvage the precious liquid, her ineffectual leg twisting at an unnatural angle. Slipping on the plastic floor, she shoved the bottle further away. It spun across the trough and she pushed herself up onto her elbows, a shadow falling over her legs.

"Girl." Tom smiled down at her, his hand outstretched. "You are a genius."

"Huh?" She took his hand and he pulled her into a sitting position, the last of the water dribbling out onto the blue plastic. Her heart sunk. "Genius? I think the word that you're looking for is 'klutz.' I wasted all my water."

"Nope." Tom picked up Belle and set her in the trough. The dog wiggled over to the small puddle and lapped it up. "See? Not wasted." He dug a pocketknife out of his jeans' pocket. "We're gonna make a sled out of that trough." Unfolding it, he held onto the blade and offered her the handle. "You're not really using the south end of that pantleg there, are you?"

She raised an eyebrow, taking the knife. "Not really."

"Cut it off." Standing over her with his hands on his hips, his eyes danced as she cut the pantleg off. "Okay, now lay the leg out flat and cut one inch strips as far as the seam. Don't cut through the side seam." He circled the trough as she worked.

She followed his directions, thankful for the sharp knife. "Done."

"Alright. Hand it here?" At the bottom of the pantleg he positioned his knife next to the uncut seam, slicing from the bottom seam up to the first cut. Leaning over, he laid it flat on the floor of the trough and gave the knife back to Cat. "Now can you work in spirals up the leg? It ought to make a long strip of rope."

Cutting the fabric as he'd instructed, she produced a continuous piece of fabric at least thirty feet long. "Now what?"

"I'll take that." He indicated the cordage. "And, the knife, too."

She gave him the two items and sat waiting in the trough. Belle licked the bottom of the trough as Tom set to work.

Cutting a small eight-inch piece from the end, he split the chunk into three strips and tucked them into his left shirt pocket. He then cut the remaining denim into three equal length pieces, laid down the knife, and stacked the tips of the fabric together. Pinching the end, he handed it to her. "Hold that part?"

She took the fabric. As she held the end, he wrapped one of the smaller pieces around the stack, cinching it down next to her fingers. She held tension and he plaited the rope into a braid, finishing it by tightening another of the smaller pieces of fabric around the end.

He laid the rope across the edge of the trough and climbed in with Cat. Kneeling, he straddled her leg and removed the final strip of denim from his pocket. "You wanna take that broken thing off?"

Since her tumble down the hill, the leg had been nothing but awkward deadweight. She'd put it out of her mind, but it had been chafing her stump, rubbing the delicate skin raw. "Oh, yes, please."

He lifted her thigh and unbuckled the damaged apparatus, setting it on the floor between her and the dog. Gentle with her bandaged stump, he pulled the crude hem of her jeans around the exposed end and used the last strip to tie the opening closed. "Too tight?"

Cat scootched around, testing the fit. "It's okay."

"Good." Tom patted her leg and ruffled the dog's mane. Rocking back onto his heels, he retrieved his pocketknife, then stabbed it into the hard plastic of the floor. Near the wall of the trough, he sawed along the edge, sweat running off his brow. It had taken several minutes to cover less than a foot.

"Tom?" Cat lifted his cowboy hat from his head.

He looked up at her. "Huh?"

"Um, we're kind of running out of daylight." She pointed at the sun hanging low in the sky, the muddled tangerine orb floating just over Rancho Seco.

"We are." He stopped cutting and took a drink from his water bottle, offering it to her.

She shook her head, embarrassed and unwilling to rob him of the hydration. He was the one sweating it all out. Especially since it was her bonehead move with the lighter that cost them the water.

The lighter. "Where's the lighter?"

"In my pocket." Tom sat up, his head swiveling. "Why?"

Pointing to the unburnt remains of a lone brush stub, Cat became animated. "Think we can make a fire out of that?"

"Yes." Tom hopped out of the trough and ran to the stump.

"Bring some of it over here." She combed her fingers through Belle's pelt.

He stood over it, straining and tugging at the vegetation. Using his pocketknife, he shaved and whittled at the base, gathering a pile of kindling.

"I think that'll do." Cat beckoned to Tom. She scooted her back up tight against the head wall of the oval trough. Pointing to the foot of the trough, she pulled her knees to her chest, and handed Tom two handfuls of Belle's hair. "Build it there?"

He pursed his bushy eyebrows, then made a small pile with the fuel and lit it. "We're going to melt the edges off?"

"Not exactly, cowboy." She handed Tom the pocketknife. Drawing the prosthetic leg toward herself, she pulled the bulky contraption across her lap. "Work smarter, not harder. Warm the blade."

Holding the blade in the flame, he smiled at her. "Darlin', you really are a genius." Tom heated the knife, moving from the fire to the spot he'd earlier quit sawing. Using the blackened blade, he worked back and forth melting through the trough floor while the small fire eroded the end.

Cat sneezed, the fumes of burning hair and melting plastic caustic in her nose.

Tom stopped cutting and lifted Belle out of the trough. "Sorry, Belle."

Covering his mouth with a handkerchief, he went back to work. Soon most of the sides were separated from the floor. He slit the wall up either side of Cat's torso, creating a backrest, then hoisted the walls of the trough away. Maneuvering the makeshift sled, he lifted the far end, positioning the hard plastic over the smoldering fire. After it warmed, he bent the floor rounding the foot upward toward her toes. Once it was shaped, he rewarmed his blade and cut two holes near the front. Threading the denim rope evenly through the two holes, he removed his leather belt and tied the ends of the cordage to the belt. "You gals ready?"

"It's behind that little knob?" Cat pointed to a slight rise not a mile across the flat.

"Sure is." Tom slipped the belt around his waist, fastened his buckle, his faithful Belle dancing circles in front of his elongate shadow. "And, I'm fairly certain this trail leads directly to the cabin."

"Okay." Cat nodded and pushed the palms of her hands against the trough floor, bracing herself. The line between the man and the sled tightened and after a slight tug, the trio set out.

With its upturned front end, the sled met little resistance. The well-worn path was devoid of rocks and Tom covered ground in long, determined strides. Cat leaned against the back wall of the sled, balancing herself and swaying with the rhythm of his steps. After traveling several hundred yards, they came to a stop.

Hands on his hips, Tom stood on the threshold of a severe crevasse. The fissure was deep, but not wide. It tore through the two-track road, snaking around the base of the small knoll they'd spoken of earlier. "Looks like it's piggyback time again." He removed his belt and dropped it on the ground. Turning, he stepped toward the sled, reaching for Cat's hand.

She let him pull her into a standing position, hopping into his arms. "We're close right, Tom?"

"Yup. Just across this draw and around this hill." He slid his hands around her waist. "We're going to perch you on the edge, here. Then I'm going to scoot this sled up next to you." Tom lowered Cat to sit on the brink, small chunks of the ledge breaking off and skittering down into the break. Moving the sled near Cat, he eased over the cutbank. "I'll take the sled across and be right back for you." He wrapped his beefy hands around the end of the sled and lifted it out of sight. Belle ran back and forth along the bank, sending little avalanches down into the crevice. "Stay, with Cat, girl."

The dog returned to Cat's side, sitting on her haunches. Moments after she'd lost sight of Tom, an unearthly cry drifted down from the ridge above. Belle's ears swiveled, a low growl emanating from her core. "Canine coyotes?" Unholstering her pistol, Cat stroked the back of the dog's neck. "Or human ones, Miss Belle?"

The fiery sun had all but set. A chill wind rode in on the desert air, carrying the whispers of high-pitched giggling. From across the fissure, a loud, heavily accented voice interrupted the eerie murmuring. "*Manos arriba, gringo.*"

Tom's steady voice was low and husky. "Come on, man, you don't wanna do this."

"Those are some pretty fancy boots you have there, *vaquero*." The voice drew closer. "They look pretty pricey for an ol' *caballero* like you. Maybe you give them to me and I don't kill you?"

CHAPTER SEVENTEEN

Alma Garcia. Harmony Ranch, Arizona

Matias burst into the tent. The light from the wind-up flashlight offered a weak yellow glow. His cheeks were rosy and a sheen of sweat covered his forehead. He beamed.

"It's working?" Alma left the tarpaulin she'd been packing in her bag.

Matias nodded. "We had it charging up the batteries on Kit's fire radios. And before that, Nora's phone."

"It's no use charging a phone. There's no signal." Eric's stolen phone was tossed in the corner of her sleeping pod somewhere.

"She had a special satellite one. It's still working." His eyes were wide and excited.

"What?" Alma abandoned the bag and shoved her feet into her sneakers. Her heart thundered.

"Taylor used it to ring a reporter. Probably a friend of Nora's."

Emelia poked her head out from her sleeping compartment. "And are more people coming to help us?"

"I don't know." Matias slumped to the groundsheet.

Alma pushed aside the tent flap. "Where's the phone now?"

"It was on the bench in the barn. I can show you."

"No, stay here." Alma pointed to the half-empty bag. "I want you to pack up everything we have."

Emelia crawled out of her pod. "Stop. Tell us what's going on!"

Alma stepped out of the tent. The moonlight cast a wide but weak glow through the clouds. A few adults were moving around like misty ghosts and a child cried. The whoosh of the heavy plastic yurt doors and muffled conversations drifted in the night air. The ground-sheet crackled, the green glow through the fabric extinguished and Emelia rushed out, forcing her foot into the laced-up sneaker with Matias close behind.

"Get over yourself, Alma. We're coming with you." Emelia grabbed Alma's hand and dropped the flashlight into it.

Emelia's jutting chin was unmistakable. Alma shrugged. "Fine."

They half jogged to the gate near the back of the barn. Hiding in the shadowed light and being mere children, they were easily ignored. Alma rounded the barn and walked through the tall, open door. She wound the flashlight and switched it on. "Where is it, Mati?"

Matias pushed past her and his bike on the stand. The machine was a thing of beauty made out of junk. What wasn't beautiful was her bike, with the back tire removed. "Mati, what did you do to my bike?"

He turned to face her, his lower lip trembling. "My bike is too small for the adults, and me and Robin can't pedal very long. We needed a bigger bike and yours is broken anyway."

Alma clamped her lips shut to keep from yelling at him. She hadn't explained that they needed the bikes to leave, because—per Kit's instructions—she hadn't wanted to worry them. "Where is the phone?"

He shrugged. "They must have taken it into the house. It's valuable, maybe?"

"Can I try?" Alma turned. Emelia was standing by the bike with her hand on the handlebars.

"Sure. Robin already had a go." Matias' face glowed with what Alma considered pride, as it should. He had created something worthwhile. If the community got through the next day, if by some miracle Michael and his crew were overthrown, they would all benefit from it. "We were trying to charge a car battery earlier, but it takes a lot of pedaling. It's still wired up. Taylor was called into the house and told me I should go to bed."

Alma went back to the barn door. A dull, flickering glow filtered through the back window of the house, silhouetting a pot full of cooking utensils sitting on the windowsill. "Is Kit in there too?"

"Yes. And Doc plus a few others."

She turned her back on the meeting they'd barred her from. Emelia climbed on the bike. "Mind your leg."

Emelia's feet touched the ground, even with the bike on the stand. "My leg's fine." She put her feet on the pedals and turned the wheel. "It's like cycling uphill."

"It's not that bad. Taylor said we could raise the saddle a bit to make it easier."

Alma stepped out of the barn and sat on an upturned bucket. She bowed her head. There might not be a chance to raise the saddle. "Look God, please keep Mati and Em safe. If I don't make it through, please help them." She rose and tiptoed to the house, peeking in the kitchen window. The clunky-looking phone sat on the windowsill, a thick antenna poking up from the top. Alma snatched it from the sill. The phone was heavier and much thicker than Eric's phone. It was similar to the old cell phone the factory guard team used at the house that sat mostly unused on the kitchen counter.

Alma's fingers shook, but she trotted behind the barn, away from everyone. She pressed the red button and the set vibrated in her hand. The screen flickered to life and a message stating it was searching for satellites flashed. The phone tinkled a tune and the screen said it registered with a network. Since the cell towers weren't working, it must have meant that it had connected to some satellite way above the clouds.

She dialed Simeon's number and punched the green button. Long seconds passed, then the phone on the other end rang twice.

"Hello?" A man's voice answered.

"Simeon?" Her heart rose in her throat.

"Alma? Is that you?"

She grinned. "Yes. Are you alright? How's the baby?"

"The baby is doing great, but things aren't good. A storm ripped up our crops and the solar farm we were siphoning electricity from got badly damaged. We've seen fires every night for the last three nights. I think there's something wrong with the water too." His voice wasn't the calm she remembered. "You found your parents?"

"Yes. No." It was an awful truth to have to tell. "Not exactly. They both died."

"I'm so sorry, Alma." His voice dripped concern.

"Our paths crossed outside Flagstaff and I got to say goodbye to Mama." She turned to the laughter in the barn. "It's a small mercy, at least."

"Are you calling to say you're coming back? Although I want you here, it isn't safe. Don't come back."

Alma's heart sank. Simeon's lovely family ranch being unsafe felt like a low blow.

"I want to see you, though." There was something about Simeon that warmed her, made her feel safe, gave her hope. The world had turned so grim since they'd made it to the Land of the Free, but he was a beacon of hope. "Is it safe there? Where you are?"

She didn't have time to explain about Eric or Michael or the fact that a war was coming to Harmony Ranch. "No? Not really." She leaned up against the side of the house, wishing she could have shown Simeon her *real* home, back in Egypt, before the ugliness there drove them away.

"I wish this was over." He'd dropped his voice to a whisper. "It's all so... hard now. Like, nowhere's safe... There are days I wish I could crawl into a cave and hibernate until the world rights itself."

Alma's pulse quickened, the thoughts tumbling over each other in quick succession. "I know of a safe place." She'd held the glimmer of hope lightly for fear that it would be extinguished, but it was quickly becoming the only light on her ever-darkening horizon. "A woman came to the ranch and told us that there are some underground bunkers in the Huachuca Mountains, near Sierra Vista. Does that mean anything to you?"

"If she thinks going underground is the best thing when the quakes are still rumbling, she's not thinking straight."

Even if her chances were slim, his family might still make it. "It's not the quakes we need to worry about because they'll stop. Haven't you noticed they're slowing down now? What we need to worry about is the weather. It's going to turn. You must have already felt it. There have been volcanoes and fires all over the place. A firefighter friend..." She cringed at the term. Kit was far from being a friend. He thought her nothing more than a waste of space. "... said that the ash in the north is so bad that entire cities are buried and the forests are burning out of control. You've got to get to the bunkers because they will protect you and your family from the cold that could destroy everything." Alma glanced at the flickering light from the main house kitchen window. "Do you know the place, Simeon?"

"I know of the Huachuca Mountains, but they are probably ten miles wide and about 20 miles long. I'm not exaggerating. We did a trip before Martha was born and even though they probably seemed a lot bigger when I was a kid, they're huge. That's a lot of mountain to cover to find a bunker." He laughed. "I mean, if they are military, they won't be making it easy."

"You've got to go there." Her voice shook, and she swallowed back the panic burning her throat. "They'll let in families. Please Simeon."

"Are you alright?" His tone—gentle, non-invasive, beaming with genuine care—broke something inside her.

She turned her face to the wall, her throat burning with unshed tears and unspoken truths. She hadn't been alright for months. Everything had escalated since the exploding van and she stood on the precipice she couldn't escape. Saving her family from the coming army relied on pulling the trigger of the tiny pistol. It was so small a weapon against the monster who destroyed her world, but it had to be enough. If she failed, her family wouldn't make it out alive, but she could save his. The phone trembled in her hand. "I will be when you promise to go."

"I promise to take them. Are you there now?" His voice remained steady, low and soothing.

The knot in her throat eased as she made the final decision. "I'm staying at a place north of Flagstaff for now, but we'll be leaving Harmony Ranch. It's not very harmonious."

"I can pick you up and we can all go together."

"No. Don't come here." She restrained the yell. "And you need to avoid the cities and towns. People are going crazy and there are too many idiots trying to take over."

"Alma, you're not okay, are you? Please, let me help you."

She scrubbed the tears away, a shout bursting out of her. "Go to the mountains and find the bunkers, Simeon." She jabbed the off button and the screen light died. She didn't have the willpower to offer him a goodbye without begging him to rescue her and putting his life at risk.

The curtain behind her twitched, and Taylor peered out into the darkness. Matias and Emelia burst out of the barn and rushed to Alma. Matias patted her clenched hand around the lifeless satellite phone.

"Is everything ok?" Emelia put her arm around Alma's shoulders. "We heard you shouting."

She'd shout as much as she liked. "Mati, did you say the radios were charged up?"

"Yeah. But Kit couldn't pick up the bad guys' radios."

Alma took his hand in hers and turned toward the house. The pistol in her pocket knocked against her leg with every step. It was an odd and uncomfortable sensation. It should make her feel safer, but ever since she'd taken the weapon from Martinez's sister, she felt like a target had been painted on her back. Everything quivered inside, making her queasy.

Now that she'd made the decision to leave, everything was more urgent, more necessary. Even her footsteps on the solid wooden steps going up the porch at the front of Jen's house banged with more finality. Emelia rushed ahead of her and opened the door.

Only Taylor and Kit sat at the kitchen table. A large map showing the ranch, road and surrounding forest was rolled out and held down in the corners by a chipped plate, cutlery, and two boxy black objects. Red crosses and colored circles marked the boundary line.

"Alma, Em, Mati."

Alma tutted. Kit had no right to shorten his name. "What was the meeting about?" It was harsher than she'd wanted, but Kit straightened up. Emelia sat herself next to Kit at the kitchen table and scowled. Mati pulled out the chair next to her and joined them.

"We were organizing the last jobs." Taylor leaned on the table and the edge of the map.

Alma adjusted her weight to her other leg. "And we're not good enough for that?"

Kit shook his head. "Far from it. Taylor and Mati did an amazing thing with that bike. Their pedal machine got us some power. Not much admittedly, but enough to charge the bricks." He picked up a slightly battered radio with a couple of dials on top, a keypad and a green screen. The corner of the map curled. The phone was large even in his big hand. "I mean the Forest Service radios. But more importantly, we've been able to charge the sat phone Nora left behind. Mati said you have a friend you could call and a place you could go to be safe."

Alma crossed her arms and stood in the doorway, hiding the satellite phone. "It's a bit late for that, don't you think?" She unfolded her arms and took a step forward, putting the big phone on the table. "I've called him and told him about the bunkers. It's not safe on his farm anymore. If he can get there, he'll be alright at least. Who did you call? Have you got reinforcements to back us up?"

Kit shook his head. "Aunt Jen doesn't know who's left alive. There's no one to call. She's been alone for a long time." For a big man, and a firefighter at that, Alma didn't expect so much sadness in his voice.

"I know you think I'm a useless child, but I have an idea to help with the fight. It involves your radios."

Kit leaned back. "You aren't a useless child, Alma." He ran a hand over his forehead. "You've endured more than most of the adults on this ranch and you are taking care of your family better than most of us."

"We only wanted to protect you." Taylor's chair squealed across the floor. She walked over to Alma and took hold of her hands.

"You're too young to be a mother, but you took on the responsibility willingly and did a wonderful job. You don't need any more pressure added to your load."

Simeon's kindness, Taylor's touch, Kit's exasperation, Emelia's piercing gaze, and Matias' wide smile made her eyes sting with tears again. All this time she had it wrong. Strangers and family cared about her. She kept her mouth shut and her eyes trained on the map, hoping they'd all look away and let her feel whatever it was that was welling up inside her, threatening to burst her banks.

Kit circled the buildings on the map on the southwest side of the ranch, too close to Martinez's rock perch overlooking the ranch. "We're booby-trapping these buildings, but I like the idea of using a radio to draw people in." Kit picked up his flashlight and headed for the door. "Let's go." He turned to Alma. "Are you coming?"

CHAPTER EIGHTEEN

Catherine "Cat" Murphy. En Route to The Bunker

On the edge of nightfall, two shadowy figures appeared in the bottom of the fissure. One a head taller than the other, the shorter man walked a step behind. "You can pry them from my cold, dead hands, you sawed off little son of a—"

Cat racked a shell into the chamber of her pistol. The desolate country had been still moments ago, where the heck had this guy come from?

Hackles raised, Belle's muscles tensed. Cat grabbed the scruff of the dog's neck, twisting her fingers in Belle's long hair. "Stay."

"Watch eeet, *el gigante*." The two were almost underfoot when the smaller man nudged Tom, causing him to stumble. "I said, '*manos arriba*.'"

Tom stopped in his tracks, turning to the other man. "For goodness sake, Van Zant, tone it down." The grin in his voice echoed across the expanse. "Cat's armed. You'll get us both shot."

Stepping from behind Tom, Andy Van Zant's silhouette emerged. Even in the near darkness, Cat recognized the bespeckled bootmaker's signature hat. It had an eight inch, rounded crown with three creases—a small one in the front and two "reach and grab" dents on the side. He tipped his head back and laughed. The brim was upturned, mirroring his wide grin. "Why, Ms. Catherine Murphy!" He'd dropped the exaggerated accent; his tone was jovial. "You wouldn't shoot little lol' me, would ya?" The last two words dropped, a hint of gravity weighing them down.

Cat leaned back and slipped her pistol into her holster, laughing at herself. "You scared the heck out of me, Andy."

Climbing up the cutbank, Tom leaned over the ledge. The dog whimpered and whined, dancing along the rim. "Come here, Belle." She shot to him, and he scooped her into his arms. He twisted, lowered her into the draw, and she bounded onto the ground. Positioning himself between Cat's legs, he gripped her by the hips. "Your turn. I'll pack you over to the other side."

She put her hands on his shoulders, rolling her eyes. "Ugh. I am so sick of being an actual, bona fide burden." Groaning, she scooted toward him. Her whining was answered by a mournful howl in the distance, soon echoed by another. The hair stood up on the back of her neck. "What the heck was that?"

"I have a pretty good idea." Andy crouched down and took Belle's face in his hands. He reached up under her ears, scratching, and addressed the dog. "But you're not gonna believe it."

"Try me." Tom lifted Cat from her perch on the hard ground, pulling her toward him. "I think it'll be best if you kind of slide off the edge and I'll piggyback you. It's only about seven feet down." He turned his back to her, backing into the hillside.

As Cat worked her way onto Tom's back, Andy rapped a can of smokeless tobacco against the palm of his hand. Reminiscent of the quintessential western movie star—and larger than life—the wiry man nipped a pinch of chew, wiggling it in between his lower gums and bottom lip. "Hyenas."

"Huh?" Cat froze, a giggle working its way up into her mouth. She choked back the chuckle. "What?" The thought of hyenas running wild on the Sonoran Desert was preposterous.

"I saw a pride of lions take down—and believe me, I know this is ridiculous..." Andy ran his tongue over his teeth and spit on the ground, his voice as serious as Cat had ever heard from the old rogue. "...a zebra yesterday."

Tom coughed and cleared his throat. "Lions? A zebra?" He gestured for Cat to climb on his back. "You been smoking some of that goofy tobacco you found out by the coyote trail?"

"Naw, man." The pocket-sized John Wayne chuckled. "They must've escaped from Reid Park or something." His voice dropped. "I've been hearing crazy laughter and cackling too." As if on cue, a distant chatter of tittering sniggers punctuated his statement.

"That makes me wanna move a little faster." Tom patted Cat on the thigh. "Let's get out of the open."

Her heart thumping harder in her chest, Cat wrapped her arms around Tom's neck and nodded even though he couldn't see her actions. Her head spun. The world was upside down.

"Yeah, I watch those nature channels." The slim cowboy strode ahead into the inky twilight. "Hyenas ain't no joke."

Cat buried her head in Tom's back. He took a step down, then stalked across the draw.

Covering the distance in what felt like fifteen or twenty steps, he slowed. "Hang on, darlin'. This side's a little steeper, I kinda gotta claw my way up here."

"Hold on a sec, Tom." Andy's voice echoed from above. "I'm gonna run and grab a rope, then I can help haul you two up out of that cut."

Cat leaned close to her partner's ear. "How long do you think he'll be?"

"Not long, I reckon." He backed away from the bank. Leaning his chest forward, he reached around and boosted Cat's thighs above his waist. Whoops and cackles reverberated off the walls of the newly formed canyon. The strange animal noises grew louder, and Tom moved his hand to his holster.

A rope cut through the air, thwacking against the cutbank. "I'm snubbed." Holding the other end of the line, Andy peeked over the edge. "Come on up!"

Tom sprung toward the bank, catching Cat off guard. She clung to him as he snatched the rope from the pungent dirt and scaled the wall. Cresting the brink, Tom crawled onto the flat ground. He stood, dropping the rope. Clapping his palms together, he brushed the dirt from his hands off on his jeans. "Thanks."

Andy made a grunting affirmative sound. Unwinding the rope from his torso, he coiled it into a set of loops as he walked toward a corner post in the nearby fence line.

Tom readjusted Cat's seat, then picked up the denim lead from the sled and followed the other man. In silence, the three followed the trail around the knoll. They gained elevation and several minutes later the angular outline of Van Zant's little adobe cottage grew visible against the starlit sky.

Stomping up the front porch steps, Andy opened the screen door, then a solid wood door. "Welcome to Helvetia." He held the door open for Cat and Tom.

"Dang, Andy, this place looks abandoned." Tom stepped into the shadowy room.

"That's the idea." He flicked a lighter and lit the thick wick of a glass oil lamp, illuminating a sparse all-purpose kitchen-dining-living room. Setting the globe back on the lamp, he pushed it to the center of a round mesquite dining table. Four chairs surrounded the table, and he hung his hat on the ear of the nearest one. "I got the livestock locked in the barn."

Opposite a tidy kitchenette, a small sitting area with an upholstered chair called out to Cat. She squeezed Tom's shoulder and pointed to the chair. He ambled over and backed up to the armchair, lowering himself and Cat. She let go, dropped into the cozy cushions, and waited as her aching muscles relaxed.

"What're you two doing out this way?" Andy puttered around the kitchen, opening cupboards, and setting several full mason jars on the counter. "Pardon me, Cat, but you look pretty rough."

"Oh, I know it." Closing her eyes, Cat rubbed her throbbing stump. "We're headed underground."

The big man crossed the room and shut the screen door in front of his dog, leaving her on the porch. "Go lay down, Belle." Facing out the main door, he leaned against the doorframe. "We've got some livestock in a disabled outfit not far from here. We're hoping to trade it for some transport." He turned and walked to the dining area. "I don't 'spose you can spare a rig? We've got about fifty miles to go."

"Along with the perforated vehicle, we've got a couple dozen chickens and ten cattle that would fit in real well around here." Propping her leg on a worn leather footstool, Cat examined the room. Finding a stack of books and a few periodicals on the end table next to her chair, Cat selected a back issue of Range magazine and flipped through it.

"Sorry, friends. The pickup's broke down and the stock truck is all I've got. That fuel guzzling deuce and a half is dang near outta fuel or else I'd just chauffeur you to your destination." The little man opened a jar, the seal popping. "Plus, you're better off traveling horseback around here right now. Get away from 83 and any other decent road. Those coyote sonsaguns have got roadblocks and booby traps everywhere."

Cat nodded, a grim smile stretching across her cheeks. "Yeah, I think we found one of those."

"Where you headed?" He dumped the contents of the jar into a pot and placed it on the stovetop. Turning the knob, he pushed a clicking button several times, and a blue flame erupted. "I've got a horse you could take."

"Close to Kartchner Caverns." Resting on his forearms, Tom leaned over the kitchen counter.

His eyes flicked from Cat's missing leg to their makeshift sled. "You plan on dragging her the rest of the way?"

She pictured bumping across the desert for fifty miles. "Ugh, no."

"Uh, I guess with one horse she could ride and I'd have to walk. We could pull our supplies in the sled. Your horse broke enough for that?"

"Oh, she's no bigger than a cricket bug, you two could ride double on Hercules. And I've drug thousands of calves behind him, he should be just fine." Andy opened another jar. "As the crow flies, that's less than 25 miles. Just the other side of Apache Peak." He dumped the jar into the pot with the other. Producing a wooden spoon, he stirred the concoction. "I'd be happy to take the chickens off your hands, and maybe a cow or two. To be honest, I don't have the water for the animals I do have."

Tom stood, pushing the heels of his hands into the small of his back. "Andy. You could come with us."

"Nope. I'm too much of a saddle tramp. I couldn't stand being cooped up like that." Van Zant disappeared through a door leading from the kitchen. A pop and a fizzing sound preceded his return. He extended a silver can to Tom. "I didn't figure you for the kind of guy that could, either. Beer?"

"Oh, no thanks, bud." He smiled in Cat's direction. "It's time to retire my spurs. I got family to take care of."

"Well, if this ship's sinking, I'm going down with it." He cantered into the sitting area and offered the beer to Cat, the faint hoppy smell wafting into her nostrils.

She waved him off. "Thanks, Andy, but I'll pass." Parched and salivating, she wanted nothing more than six or eight of those beers.

"I'm sorry can't offer you much *agua*, I'm damn near out." Returning to the kitchen, he poured two small jelly jars full of water. After handing them to Tom and Cat, he returned to his stove, stirring the food in the pot. He gestured to a pie safe near the dining room table. "Grab us some bowls, Mr. Callahan?" Pulling open a drawer, he rummaged about and produced three spoons. "You seen any good water on your travels?"

Something savory and garlic laden was brewing in the kitchen. Cat focused on that smell, turning her mind from the alcohol. "None."

"Hey, if you could get over to Rancho Seco, the Miller kids are there." Tom plunked three earthenware bowls on the counter. "They've got a way to purify water, and a line on some uncontaminated water."

Andy ladled food into the bowls. "Oh, I don't know. I wouldn't want to be a bother."

Tom picked up a bowl and a spoon, taking it over to Cat. "You'd actually be helping us out. They need someone around with a little experience. Grady Jordan was driving us to the bunker, and he was going to go back to help out the kids." His voice cracked and he swallowed, his Adam's apple bobbing. "But, he didn't make it through that ambush back there."

"Thank you, Mr. Van Zant." Cat took the bowl, breathing in the wonderful scent of a hearty stew full of vegetables, meat, and beans. "You could take a message to Jim for us, too. That way he won't come looking for Grady."

Andy tipped up his hat to reveal a shiny, bald, liver spotted head. "Hmmm. Well, my water ain't gonna last much longer." Pulling a handkerchief from his pants' pocket, he wiped his furrowed brow. Handing Tom a bowl, he picked up the last dish for himself and made his way to the table. Tom trailed behind.

The wiry man sat and twisted the lid from a plain, brown, glass bottle. Using the eyedropper attached to the lid, he dripped a few drops into his stew and he nudged the bottle toward Tom. "Hot sauce? I make it myself."

Tom raised one eyebrow, then followed suit. Taking a heaping spoonful of the meal into his mouth, he made a gurgling sound, sputtered and coughed. He swallowed and wiped the back of his sleeve across his mustache. "What the hell is in that unholy concoction? I can't feel my face."

"Satan's tears." The little man cracked a grin. "You like?"

"No, Van Zant, I don't. I'm starving, so I'm going to eat this, but I'm pretty sure it's ruined." Picking up the bottle, Tom waggled it at Cat. "Wanna try?"

"Uh-uh." She shoveled the food in. "This is amazing. What are these beans?"

"Tepary. Grew 'em myself." Andy flurried into the kitchen, bringing the pot with him when he returned. He stood over Cat, ladle in hand. "One of the few things that thrive around here. They're real high in protein and fiber, the ancient ones cultivated them. More?"

Cat hesitated. "Oh, I couldn't."

He moved forward and held the steaming ladle over her bowl. "You better tank up, they'll go to waste if we don't eat 'em...we've got no refrigeration."

"Okay." She acquiesced. "But we need to discuss our plans. How are we going to get to Kartchner? How are we going to take care of those livestock in the trailer?"

He set the pot on the table in front of Tom, then situated himself on the edge of a hand-hewn bar stool. "I've been ruminating on that." He ran his hand back and forth over his shiny pate. "Eat up, Tom."

"Don't mind if I do. Think I'll pass on the sauce this time, though." He refilled his bowl, then looked around the room. "Where's Rosie?"

"She's out in the barn with the livestock." Andy thumbed up the hill, then jumped up and grabbed his hat. "I'm going to run up and let her out for a bit before we turn in. Mind if I give Belle a little supper?"

"That'd be mighty kind of you, Andy." The screen door slammed shut before Tom had finished his sentence. For a moment, the room went silent except for the clinking of Tom's spoon against his bowl. Pushing his dish away, he leaned back in his chair. "I guess we're spending the night here, huh?"

"I hate leaving those animals in the trailer overnight, but they're probably safer there than anywhere else right now. The chickens have water, and the cows filled up before we left." Cat set the magazine aside. "I want to keep moving, but I'm exhausted. I can't believe that your eyes are still open."

"Barely." Tom got up from his chair and sauntered over to Cat, lowering himself to one knee in front of her. "I think you're right. We could both use a good rest, and there's nothing we can do about the livestock right now." He took her thigh between his hands, kneading her crampy muscles. "If Andy decides not to go stay with the kids, he'll go get those animals. At the very least, he'll turn them out and give 'em a fighting chance."

"Okay." Putting her hands on his shoulders, Cat gripped the sinewy strands. Working her way up his neck, she leaned in and pressed her cheek to his. The last two days' stubble pricked her weather beaten skin, but she squeezed harder, thankful for the moment of peace.

Tom tensed. "Did you hear that?"

"No, what—" A low growl grew from below the window behind Cat's chair. The hair rose on the back of her neck as hideous laughter —intertwined with the unmistakable snapping and snarling of a dog fight—permeated the night.

Tom burst to his feet and strode across the room, grabbing a shotgun from over the door. "Get your gun out." He swung the door open, staring her down. "Do *not* come out this door until I tell you it's safe. You hear me?"

The melee continued, and she nodded. Her heartbeat thundered in her throat.

Three booming gunshots exploded and Tom jerked the thick wooden door shut, the house shaking. A dog yipped and another three shots rang out.

CHAPTER NINETEEN

Alma Garcia. Harmony Ranch, Arizona

The forest crept past the south-western corner of Harmony Ranch's boundary fence. Trees, still young compared to the giants on the thickly wooded landslide-scarred peak to the south, cast gloomy shadows over the cluster of old bunkhouses. The scent of pine sap and dust tickled Alma's nose. She shivered, but she wasn't cold.

The four dilapidated houses had suffered from years of neglect. Debris from the trees gathered at the foundations, weeds and saplings warring for light and space. The porch to the front of the old building groaned under Kit's feet. Alma directed the beam of her flashlight to the weathered boards bouncing under his weight.

"We already sawed through the interior roof supports and ran lines out so someone can collapse them with a strong yank. Maybe we could engineer something to take out the porch support, too, once we've gotten them inside. If we can get the porch to collapse, it would slow them down even more." Kit turned to Taylor. "If we can get any of them inside."

"Sean would've loved doing this." Taylor rubbed Kit's arm. "Reckless was his middle name."

It only took Alma one wide step to cross the porch. "They'd easily jump it. Bringing the building down is better."

Moonlight filtered through clouds and the branches above. Alma shone her windup flashlight toward the bluff where the flat rock jutted out. Her weak beam only caught on nearby weeds and undergrowth. She tightened her ponytail for the hundredth time and grit her teeth. If she did her job, Martinez would be dead before his people reached the property.

Kit flicked the switch on his flashlight but Taylor instantly covered the powerful beam with her hand. "Let's not draw attention to ourselves."

Kit peered in through the grimy window. "We need to block them from entering the ranch and steer them this way. Then trap as many of them as possible even if it's just to get them out of the fight and even the numbers."

Taylor's frown deepened. "Your Aunt Jen wanted to talk to them."

Alma stepped closer to the door and twisted the rusty handle. "I don't think they have any intention of talking."

"I think you're right." Kit joined her. "Careful, the roof beams are already cut most of the way through."

Cobwebs shone like ghostly torn cloths hanging from the wooden ceiling. They fluttered in the breeze gusting through the open doorway and the holes in the rusty roof. Alma trained the flashlight beam up into the rafters. The aged wood was soft at its edges and fine dust clung to the cobwebs. She reached up, but was too short to touch the beam. "Is it rotten?"

Kit pushed a dusty cobweb back so Alma could see the string ready to pull the keystone they'd sawed away, collapsing the rafters and hopefully, the roof. "It was easy to cut, because it's beetle-infested. No wonder Aunt Jen hadn't used these buildings." Taylor took the flashlight from Kit. He put a hand on her arm. "Careful, babe. Stay near the walls. We trapped the floorboards."

She nodded and padded to the door on the far side. The floorboards creaked under her slight weight. "What's in here?" She pulled the door open, the hinges groaned at being disturbed and the door scraped over the floor, leaving a curved track in the dirt.

Alma crept after her into the room. Three sets of metal framed bunk beds were crammed into the space. Pungent mildew tickled her nose, and she sneezed.

Taylor pushed aside the mold-stained curtain over the tiny window. "We can use these bed frames, if we can get them out safely." She stepped carefully back to Kit. "How are we luring the enemy in here?"

Alma followed Taylor, careful to step on the same floorboards. "We use the children." Kit's eyes widened in horror. "I'm not saying we put children in here. But we let him think that, by using the radios. If we close that bedroom door, they won't know no one's in here." She turned back to Kit, grateful that he wasn't scowling anymore. "He collected children as hostages, and made them work. I think he'll keep doing it. He'll want children so he can control the adults. It's the way he works. We let the children talk on the radio and draw them in."

And that way, Em and Mati would be safe inside Jen's house, while she did her grim duty. She wouldn't fail.

Alma's fingers buzzed with energy. She slipped her free hand into her pocket. The pistol was almost warm from being close to her body. Martinez didn't care about anything or anyone. He'd hide behind his army and let them do all the work while he sat on top of a rock outside the ranch, picking his enemies off one by one. Her fingers twitched. But he wouldn't be alone for long.

"Then we'll make sure his people don't come out." Taylor nodded to Alma. "We can collapse the porch after they enter, trapping them, then bring the roof down."

Kit scratched his chin. "We can make getting to this part of the ranch relatively easy, but that means adding more traps between here and the main housing area, something we'd planned to do, but haven't had the time. But we don't want them to have an easy time if they don't fall for this trap."

After cutting partially through each porch support and stringing more lines, they walked back to the ranch house. Alma volunteered Emelia to be the voice to draw the men in. Her voice was childlike enough for them to be tempted. Taylor thought Robin and Mati could add something too, making the idea of scared children hiding more realistic.

Her back ached from moving usable furniture and dragging it out of the buildings so others could carry them back to the barn. She rubbed her palms, fingers sore from making knots in the rough cord for the porch traps, and her eyes stung from dust. Despite the discomfort, the warmth from both Kit and Taylor staggered her. Emelia was right; they were people she could trust. Matias was also right—they were never unkind. She rubbed her tight chest. They had included her in protecting and guarding the ranch, but she'd kept her plan secret. Perhaps it wasn't lying if she just didn't tell them. At least if it went badly, she no longer doubted Kit and Taylor's affection for her sister and brother. If something happened to her, they would never abandon Emelia or Matias.

The sun hadn't fully set when Alma crept into the main house and slithered into her sleeping bag next to Emelia. Taylor had insisted they move inside, "Where we can all protect each other." Her sister stirred only enough to let out a small snore and Matias was snuggled close, his rabbit tucked under his arm. They were all exhausted.

She turned over. The silver light from the night filtered through the thin curtain and shadowy shapes morphed into dangerous people from the camp to the north. She lay still, waiting for movement, and the shadow returned to the outline of a chair. She fidgeted and changed her position, desperately trying to please her screaming body and fall asleep. She couldn't get comfortable with all the scenarios running through her head like an out-of-control movie.

She sat up and pulled the pistol from under her pillow. Not daring to put her finger on the trigger, she held it out and tried to line up the notches, which must have been what Helen had called the sights. The room was too dim to pick out anything; the hated Martinez Corporation logo on the top of the gun wasn't visible. She turned to face the window and the silhouette of the pistol's barrel darkened against the filtered light. Her hands were relatively steady but the window handle she had roughly in her sights was stuttering all over the place.

"What are you doing?" Emelia's breath caught on Alma's cheek.

Alma almost dropped the pistol and turned. "Why have you got a gun?"

"Go back to sleep, Em." Alma's heart pounded.

"Don't baby me, Alma. Where did you get the gun from?"

"Keep your voice down." Alma tucked the pistol back under her pillow. Emelia didn't take her gaze from the weapon's hiding place. "It's so I can keep you safe."

"You've never fired a gun in your life." Emelia reached for Alma's pillow.

Alma batted her hand away. "Don't. It's dangerous." She laid back down, her head blocking Emelia from accessing the pistol. "It's very late. We should sleep."

"What did you plan with Kit and Taylor?" Emelia tried to sound authoritative, but her words slurred with exhaustion.

"Em. Go to sleep. I'll tell you in the morning." Alma rolled over, feeling the lump under her pillow. The pistol was so small, she wasn't sure if the bump was imaginary or real. She closed her eyes and pretended to sleep. Emelia's breathing slowed, and grunting snores faded, letting her thoughts go silent as well.

CHAPTER TWENTY

Kit Walsh. Harmony Ranch, Arizona

The sun washed the man's white flag pink—or perhaps it was bloodstained. A heavy dark beard concealed half his face; tactical-style sunglasses hid the rest. An Army green bullet-resistant vest hung across his chest, and a pistol sat in a holster strapped to the outside of his thigh.

Kit bellowed across the divide. "What do you want?"

"I've got an offer for you!" He waved the flag.

Since the man was armed, Kit was fairly certain the offer wasn't good. "Drop your weapons, and we'll let you come closer. Otherwise, you can keep yelling."

"Your man has me targeted." The enemy pointed to Kit's right; he risked a glance. Stone crouched behind the leaning light pole with his rifle aimed at the man. "My pistol won't do me much good."

"Slow and easy," Stone yelled.

The enemy guffawed. "Yeah." He drew the pistol, letting it dangle between his forefinger and thumb, and placed it on a rock. He put a large knife next to it, then strolled toward them, stopping about ten feet away. "You've got until noon tomorrow to organize your surrender. All weapons will be dropped right here, on this side of the gate, and you'll line up along the driveway on that side of the gate. Surrender or die."

Kit couldn't believe the arrogance of the man. "And what makes you so sure we'll die?"

"You missing anyone?"

Kit's blood ran cold.

"Yeah, thought so. You didn't even notice when we picked off one of your own."

Stone raised his weapon.

"Woah, there, cowboy. Don't be doing anything hasty."

Kit scanned the tree line. There were not-tree shapes, but he couldn't tell how many of those shapes were human and how many humans were packing heat.

"We've been watching you. You're a disorganized bunch of slackers and idiots. Can't even watch your borders. We've been slipping in and out of your ranch, and you didn't even know it." He shook his head. "Civilians."

Unfortunately, Kit believed the man; they were unprepared. Nora's death and Kevin's disappearance proved it. "And who exactly are we surrendering to?"

"You'll be surrendering to the new leader of the free world, Michael Martinez." His chin tilted up like he was proud to work for the slime ball.

Kit snorted. "The man who killed the world is going to lead it? Into what? Total annihilation? Right. Thanks, but no thanks. We're not surrendering to a man who thinks nothing of enslaving children. A guy who forces five-year-olds to work on assembly lines for sixteen hours a day. Nope. I'd rather die. But I'm not a dictator like Martinez. I'll ask my people and we'll let democracy rule."

The enemy didn't flinch at Kit's description. "Surrender or die. You've got until noon. Better be ready. Make sure you keep those kids safe, because we've got plans for them." He turned and walked away, picked up his weapons, and sauntered off.

"I want to kill that guy so bad." Stone kept his rifle up against his cheek, aimed at the enemy, moving sideways toward Kit.

Kit shrugged. "He's the messenger, just following orders. We're not descending to their level."

"Yeah." Stone dropped the rifle's muzzle to the ground. "It will probably get us killed, but I can't shoot a guy in the back in cold blood."

"You're doing the right thing." Kit turned to the gate guards. "Keep a real good watch. I don't expect them to wait until noon. I think they'll attack tonight."

"Yeah, they might." Stone put a hand out to Kit. "Give me your binoculars, please."

Kit handed them over. Stone swept the cliffs where they'd laid their traps. "Yeah, they've got people up there watching. We'll have to be sneaky to get up there. I wish we had some hand-to-hand special forces types who could take out those guys, but we don't. I can get our people in place tonight, but without some way to signal you, coordination will be tough."

Kit sniffed. "What coordination? When they make a move, trigger the traps and start shooting. The gunfire will tell us it's started, and we'll start shooting."

"Hey, Kit, I got an idea." Cindy, one of the less-than-helpful residents of the ranch, put a hand on his forearm. "Why don't we string a bunch more of those aluminum can tripwires around the outside of the ranch? We'll get some false positives from animals, but it's a warning."

"That's a great idea." Kit forced a smile for the woman. All it took was a genuine threat, and suddenly, she was helpful. "If I send you a couple of people, can you take care of that tonight?" He'd been trying to do that for the last week, but there hadn't been enough willing hands and he'd run out of time.

Stone shook his head. "Cindy, if your team puts them together, my team will string them up on this side. I'm not sleeping tonight, anyway." He snorted. "I'll sleep when I'm dead. Before I go, I'll help you take cans to the guards on the other sides of the ranch, Cindy, and you can run the wires over there."

"Thanks, Stone. I really appreciate you stepping up. Thanks again, Cindy." Kit turned back to the ranch. "Let me go tell Taylor what's going on. Stone, check in with me before you go out, please." Between the confrontation with Martinez's guy, the confrontation with Alma, and Aunt Jen's mystery headaches, fear churned his gut and exhaustion weighed his whole body. But Stone seemed energized by the coming conflict.

"Wilco." He strode off to the shed, Cindy following.

Kit continued down the drive into the heart of the RVs. Mr. H stepped out of his trailer. "Hey, Kit, I heard little Mati got a generator going. Can you use these?" Two small walkie-talkies sat on his palm with earpieces wired in. "They're FRS band."

Kit held out his hands, and Mr. H dropped the black plastic radios on his outstretched palms. "Yes. This is perfect. We needed a way to coordinate between us and the hills up there. Hey, Mr. H, can you and the missus do me another favor?"

"Sure, whatever you need." The man's head bobbled.

"We just got an ultimatum from the people at the campground at the north to surrender or die by noon tomorrow."

"What?" Mr. H stepped back, eyes wide.

"That's not the worst of it. That ultimatum came from Michael Martinez, you know, the guy who's family killed the world. You've heard what he did to Alma, Em, and Mati; we can only expect worse. So, I need you to take charge of everyone in the camp area who's not on duty already. Get water and food for a day into the barn and the house for all the non-fighters, and help Jaya and Faris get both structures ready. We need to be stealthy. They've got watchers on the hills. Don't let them see what we're doing. Also, send a couple of people to the vehicle barn to help Cindy make more alarms. Maybe people who can't move around easily. Can you do that for me?"

"Yeah." Mr. H's eyes narrowed and his mouth flattened. "Yes, I can. I will get us as ready as we possibly can. Because you're right. Working for that man just means dying a painful death." He squeezed Kit's arm. "I know I haven't been the strongest supporter, but you can count on me."

Kit smacked Mr. H's shoulder gently. "Thanks, man. I appreciate it. We're not going down, especially not without a fight. We'll make it." His heart lighter if not his body, Kit continued to the house.

The kitchen was the model of calm. His aunt was at the sink, chatting to Robin, the two of them laughing. Kit closed his eyes and breathed a sigh of relief. Even though Taylor had confirmed a Jen sighting, he'd needed to see his aunt with his own two eyes. And there she was, right where she ought to be, at the center of everything. He snuck up behind her and launched a side hug. "Glad you're okay!"

She blushed and went back to the dishes, but her grin was for him as well as Robin and that small gesture—nothing more than a smile—healed something inside him. The world might be teeming with bad guys, but his aunt had held a place in her heart, just for him.

Taylor and Doc were deep in conversation, his wife laughing and the doc grinning.

The emotional bomb he clutched to his chest was going to change all that. He longed to slide onto the chair beside his beautiful wife and watch her pulling people together and knitting them a future, but that was going to have to wait. War was coming to them and while they were outnumbered and outgunned, they had to stand together and face it down.

"I've got bad news." He told them about Martinez's so-called offer and their expressions morphed from sad to angry, with more than a little fear. "On the good side, we've got people watching the corners of the ranch already and we can get Alma and her siblings into the pantry quickly, luring at least some of the bad guys into that trap with the radios. Mr. H is stepping up and organizing the noncombatants. They're getting the barn ready, and they'll work with Jaya on the house when Faris relieves Dunia at the southern bunkhouses. And he gave me these." He held the FRS radios out to Taylor. "Can you charge them? With these, Stone can talk to us from his position in the hills."

Taylor took them. "Yeah, I can do that."

"Kit, I'll get Aaron to help Mr. H." Doc sighed. "He's been scouting the area for food sources, but that can wait."

Another name that meant little to Kit. There were so many people to track; he was glad of the doc's help corralling people.

"What do you want me to do, Christoph— Kit?" Jen's hand drifted to the bump on her head. She'd done a damned fine job of concealing her injury, but Dunia was right, his aunt was still in pain.

Doc turned to the back of the house, but spun back almost immediately. "I'm serious, Jen. There's nothing holding us here and, you know what, I believe we're facing nuclear winter." He held up his hand to quiet her. "We have no medicine, my dear. If your pain gets worse—"

She shushed him, brushed past Kit and took herself to the living room without another word.

The doc wasn't done. "If we survive the battle, and that's one big if, we should leave for the bunkers. It's not that far away; I know exactly where it is. Getting there might take some doing, but we can do it. Even if we make it through this, we're too exposed here. Someone else will try to take what we have."

Kit nodded. He needed to talk Aunt Jen around, though he didn't know where to begin. "I agree, Doc. There's nothing for us here." Nothing except heartache and more death, trying to defend the undefendable.

"I'll help get the house ready and get all the children bedded down in here. You and Taylor need to get some sleep. Just a couple of hours, so you're useful later tonight and tomorrow, okay?"

At Doc's words, Kit's muscles ached, his lids drooped, and his stomach rumbled, but there was one thing he needed to do before he let himself rest. He padded down the corridor and into the darkened front room, where his aunt sat, her head in her hands. "You okay?"

She straightened and it was only then that he saw Ladybug curled beside her on the couch. "He's been nagging me since daybreak. I just needed a time out."

"About leaving?" Kit eased himself into the overstuffed chair opposite her.

"Well, I guess he'll add that to his list of things I've got to do, now that you've put the idea in his head." It was the old Aunt Stickler, acerbic and biting and pointing the finger. "I—"

173

He waited, the silence stretching between them and filling the air with an energy he hadn't felt since he left her house all those years ago.

"So?" Again, she waited.

"So, what?" He could have sworn a tear snuck down her cheek. He knew she loved Harmony Ranch, but he hadn't prepared himself for the fact that she was *that* bonded to the place.

"Are you going to ask me? I know you want to. You have to have a million questions about her."

"Huh?" The conversation had taken a sudden left turn and he was well and truly lost.

"The papers. You have questions."

"Aunt Jen, I don't know what you're talking about."

"Your birth certificate."

The world spun a little slower. Kit didn't remember seeing a birth certificate. He'd always assumed his mother had it in whatever drug den she was bunking down in.

"I always meant to tell you." She reached for Ladybug, her hands twisting in the dog's fur. "But the moment never came and then you were gone and now that you've found it, I feel about as bad as a body can feel." That was a lot of words for his aunt and it cost her. She was panting. "It was left blank intentionally."

"Okay." He tried to think his way through a birth certificate, but his brain had turned into a heap of Jell-O and he couldn't find his way forward.

"Mr. Walsh was a good man. He gave you his name."

Kit shot to his feet. "Wait, what?"

"Your mother didn't want you to know."

The walls were closer and the ceiling pressed down on him. "Just tell me. All of it. From the beginning."

"From the beginning. Okay." Her hands moved over the dog's back, so fast the little beast squirmed and shook her off. "Your mother worked at 'the big house.' That's what she called it, 'The Big House.' She made good money, had good hours, and she liked the children in her care."

"She was a nanny?" The things he didn't know could fill a football stadium.

The story was as old as the hills. Master/servant, demand/relent, pregnancy/end of job. He knew, long before she got to the part about naming names, what was coming. The ringing in his ears blotted the actual words out when they came, but he could read her lips. "You're a Martinez, Christopher."

"How long have you known?"

His aunt let her head slump forward. "They deeded me this ranch to keep your mother quiet and far from prying eyes."

He couldn't listen to more. He stood, mumbled some excuse and stalked back to the kitchen. Everything looked just as it had, peaceful and welcoming, but nothing was what it seemed.

"Eat." Jaya led him to the table, and served him a big bowl of rice and meat.

"This is a lot." Despite his objection, Kit picked up his spoon and shoveled a huge scoop in his mouth, the flavors turned to nothing. *I am a Martinez.*

"You caught the deer. You deserve the biggest portion. Besides, you and Taylor work harder than anyone else. You both need more food."

Kit took another bite. "Thanks, Jaya. Make sure you eat, too." *I am a Martinez and my brother's bringing a war to my doorstep.*

She scraped the last bits into his bowl. "I did. I serve people the same amount they work."

"Well, Mr. H earned his ration." Kit scraped the last bits up and wiped his mouth on the back of his hand. "I think everyone will earn one today, if there's anything left."

"We have food for the battle." She scrubbed the big cook pot. "We knew this day would come and saved something special."

Well, that was good and bad. Kit rose from the table. "Thanks." His stomach full and his brain on fire he wandered toward the shed where Mati put the charging bike. He needed to put some space between himself and the truth. He needed another conversation with his Aunt Stickler, but he didn't know how to come at it. *Work first, talk later.*

The ranch resembled an upset beehive, people running round, carrying supplies, reinforcing structures, and hammering stuff. It was loud and chaotic, but Mr. H directed the people like a maestro with an orchestra. It wasn't stealthy, but maybe that wasn't such a bad thing. If Martinez's forces—*my brother's army*—thought they were fighting ridiculous civilians, maybe they'd be easier to fool. The food in Kit's stomach tossed. Or he'd set them up to be killed. Taylor came out before he could go in, so he caught her around the waist. "Hey, I know you're busy, but we both need some rest. We've got to be ready for anything and everything by midnight tonight." He didn't want to tell her the news. They'd just gotten over his Sean-jealousy. If she found out he was related to the enemy—*the man who brought down the world*—it could change everything. No, would! Who'd love a Martinez? No one!

"But..."

"But nothing. Everyone's working hard. We'll rest now and be ready when they all go to sleep." Kit pulled her by the hand to their tent. "Besides, there's something else I'd like to do before we fight a battle I don't know how to win."

Taylor cupped his cheek. "You've convinced me." She slid into their yurt, and he followed. Even if he died tonight, at least he'd die knowing Taylor loved him, and she'd know the same. He could be Kit Walsh for at least one more night.

CHAPTER TWENTY-ONE

Alma Garcia. Harmony Ranch, Arizona

Kit woke all three of them well before the morning light brightened the room. Alma huffed at the bustling of others around the house, setting themselves in position. The noise should've been enough to wake her, but she'd slept through the prep. She peered out the window; the moon was high in the sky, so it was late at night, not early morning after all.

Kit picked up their sleeping bags and led them to the bare pantry, where layers of old metal sheets lined the lower half of the wall facing the main yard. The tiny window above it would've looked out toward the gate if it hadn't been boarded over and the night left the room chilly. Alma dumped their things on the floor. With nothing to distract them, waiting would be painful.

He made their sleeping bags into a cozy spot, leaning their pillows against the wall. "We don't know when they will come for sure, we're just guessing it will be at sunrise. The trip line alarms will warn us when they are nearby. We'll send a signal, and someone outside will make a string of cans rattle right outside your window. Whisper into the radio like you are scared."

Kit handed her the handset. It was heavy and nothing like Eric's dead cell phone. It was about twice the size of the satellite phone. Brick, the term Kit had used, made sense. "I've fully charged the radios, put them on the right channel and hidden the other in the bunkhouse. We didn't write a script but all three of you should talk about being left alone and being scared. If there are noises, you could scream through your hands, like you're trying to be quiet, or gasp, and hush each other." He pointed to the radio. "Don't fiddle with any of the dials, just push and hold the big button on the side and hold it up to your mouth to talk." He pointed to the button with the raised dots. "We only need to fool them long enough to get them inside, but you'll have to keep talking until we tell you to stop. Make them believe you are hiding and scared."

Emelia prodded the talk button. "Or they tell us to shut up." Her voice shook. Emelia and Matias wouldn't need to pretend. They were pale and wide eyed.

Kit gave Em one of his patented side hugs. "I put a lock on this side of the door, which I want you to use if you hear strangers outside. Stay hidden in here. Do you hear me?" He looked at all of them, then focused on Alma. "I'll come for you if I can, but if you hear a bunch of strangers, then wait for a good time, then get out the little window, run and escape."

"The traps will work." Emelia's smile quivered, much like her voice. "You'll stop them."

Alma touched her pocket. The pistol felt somehow heavier. She'd stop their leader; that should stop all of them.

"You got that right. We'll stop them dead." Kit didn't keep eye contact and the ache in Alma's chest squeezed tighter. Even the adults weren't sure. "But, you know where the traps are and how they work if you need to run." Kit turned Em to face him. "If everything goes wrong, I want you to run and then hide."

"You're scaring me." Matias' forehead furrowed and his lower lip trembled.

Kit gripped Mati's shoulder, too. "I don't mean to, but I can't lie to you and tell you it will all turn out fine. We're going to do everything we can to protect you, but I can't promise we'll win. If you need to run, run fast and hide. Promise me."

Emelia grabbed Kit and pulled him into a hug. "You won't make promises, but you want us to." She hid her face in his jacket. "You do all you can, and we won't need to promise anything."

"Good enough." Kit pushed Emelia away, took the single step to the door, and turned. He lifted Alma's hand with his injured one and turned it over. He covered her hand with his and something small fell into her palm. He curled her fingers around it. "I'll see you soon." He closed the door softly, but it still landed like a death knell.

She couldn't think that way, or she'd never find the courage to go after Martinez. She opened her hand. A fire-blackened metal circular pin rested in her palm. She turned it over. The surface was buffed back to the original copper color with the state of Arizona embossed on the front of the sun symbol. She rubbed her thumb over the surface. The feathers had burned away in the grave pit fire, but it was the pin from Emelia's jean jacket.

Alma's heart pounded, and she shoved the evidence into her pocket. A tiny clink of metal against the pistol made her shiver. *Kit knows.* Her efforts to hide Emelia's involvement in Nora's death were all for nothing. He knew about it. He'd worked out a version of the truth and let Emelia help him set the traps anyway. He'd taken the time to care for Mati and herself. He really knew. He hadn't come after them and accused them of murder. They were safe in his hands. Alma turned away from the door, the lump in her throat reappearing as if it had never gone away.

Emelia slumped sideways and rested her chin on her knees, her arms wrapped around her shins. The thin gap between the boards over the window showed a moonlit sliver of the front yard. Smoke, the dog, was missing from his spot by the gate. Kit jogged by, Taylor joining him. They faded into the gloom.

"What's going on out there?" Matias' voice was small even in the tiny room.

"Nothing. Kit went to the gate. There's no one out there." She pulled the pantry door open and put the radio next to Emelia. Everyone, including Kit, would be too focused on their own tasks to check if she was doing hers. "When the cans rattle, start talking."

Emelia picked up the brick and stood. "Where are you going?"

"I need to do something."

"More important than taking care of us?" Emelia grabbed Alma's wrist.

"I *am* taking care of you." She stared into Emelia's eyes.

Emelia pulled Alma closer and whispered in her ear. "How can you do that, if you and the gun aren't here?"

"Let go of me, Em." Alma loosened Emelia's fingers. "You need to stay here and talk on the radio to trap as many of Martinez's men as possible. Eric is with them. He can't get away again. You are perfect for the job. If they are out of the way, I can deal with the big boss."

"No! How?" Emelia reached for her, her eyes wild. "Eric? Eric's here?"

Mati's face folded in on itself, his eyes going blank and the tremor on his lips falling to nothing. He was back to silent-Mati, who'd kept himself to himself for so, so long.

Alma had to tell them the score. Not to do so was pure hypocrisy. Holding things back from them—the way Kit and Taylor had held things back from her—was not the way she wanted them to remember her. "Give me your hands."

The three of them made a triangle, their breaths falling into a synchronized rhythm and she told them what she'd seen.

"Eric?" Em whispered his name. "Escaped?"

"I can't be sure of the facts, but from what I heard, the earthquake brought the house down and he escaped." She wasn't sure if the sweat was hers or Em's but their hands were on fire.

"And he came here?"

It did seem improbable, when she heard it out loud, but that didn't change the facts. "One of Michael's security guards brought him here."

Mati's hand shook in hers.

Em lifted Mati's hand to her cheek, kissing it gently. "It's going to be okay, baby brother. We're in this together. Alma's going to take care of us."

The tenderness caught Alma off guard. Her sister had been her biggest critic, finding fault with so many of her decisions, but she was as soft as she'd ever been.

"You can't do it." Em kissed Alma's hand in turn. "If you're thinking what I think you're thinking—with that gun burning a hole in your brain—you can't do it."

Alma shook her head. "I have to. Michael Martinez wants the ranch. We both know it won't end well if he's in charge. I'm not becoming one of his slaves again and neither are you or Matias."

Emelia threw her arms around Alma's neck. "Don't. Please. I can't do this by myself. I need you." Sobs shook her body held tight against Alma.

"If I don't go, this new world will never be safe for you or Mati."

"Let someone else do it. You don't know where he'll be."

Alma pictured the rock where she'd vowed to kill him. He was probably already there. She backed away. "I love you both more than you'll ever know. I'm so proud of you."

Mati rushed at her and hugged her tightly. "I love you too, Alma. Come back to us."

She kissed him on his head and pulled Emelia close. "You take care of each other. Family is everything."

Emelia's voice trembled. "Please, God, look after Alma. Amen."

"Amen." Mati whispered.

"And look after these two. Amen." Alma pulled away and closed the door behind her. She hurried through the kitchen, out the back door, and sprinted down the side of the barn. She ran out the gate into the back pasture, crossing the yellowed square grass patches where tents had once stood, through the pasture heading for the trees and the dried-up river and away from the battlefield.

CHAPTER TWENTY-TWO

Kit Walsh. Harmony Ranch, Arizona

In the dark of night, they gathered in the house, finalizing their plans by flickering candle light, the dawn not brightening the horizon yet. Children's soft snores kept their voices low.

His Aunt Jen held back, avoiding him, and he was glad of it. There was too much to say and not enough time to say it. *The talk* would have to wait until after the battle had been won.

Dunia racked her pistol, checking the chamber. "I'm off to the south bunkhouses. Good luck."

The radio sitting on the table next to him beeped. Taylor jolted and pushed the button on the small FRS radio. "Go, Top."

"Incoming, single rider ATV. Back door. Not obviously an enemy. Our guys have eyes on. Out."

"Now what?" Kit picked up the rifle Stone found for him. He wasn't comfortable with it, but it was better than the revolver for the coming battle. He trotted past his aunt—the two of them nodding a greeting and nothing more—out the door, past the barn, and into the space between the pastures. *Concentrate, Christopher. Don't think about THAT.* At the far end beyond the makeshift barrier of cars, a young man waited on an ATV, the interior lights on to show his face, hands on the wheel. One of the east side guards ran along the track behind the boy, rifle raised.

Kit didn't draw his gun or raise his rifle, but stopped about twenty feet from the man. "Who are you?"

"I'm Simeon. Is Alma here?" The young man was lanky, but with enough food, he'd probably bulk up over the next year or two. A rifle was clipped to the front rack on his ATV.

"How do you know Alma?" Shoot, he shouldn't have confirmed he knew the girl.

He smiled. "The three of them stayed with us for a few days. She helped out my mom a lot. Is she still here?"

Kit considered the young man. He seemed concerned, but he could be one of Martinez's stooges, a guard who knew Alma from Martinez's factory. Maybe he was trying to get a closer look at the ranch. *My brother will stop at nothing to take what's not his.* "Why do you want to know?"

"Because me and my family, we're going to those bunkers she told us about in the Huachuca Mountains. If Alma wants to come, we'll take all of them." He shrugged. "We'll take anyone you vouch for who wants to come."

There were more innocent people out there, as they were going into a fight. "Simeon, you need to warn your family. This place is about to turn into a war zone. Michael Martinez, the former leader of Martinez Corporation, is north of us, and he's told us to surrender or die."

"Dude, you can't surrender." Kit could see the whites of Simeon's eyes. "That man is evil. Let me tell my Mom, and I'll come help you. Alma didn't tell me much, but she's seen some bad stuff. Em and Mati couldn't even talk about him." He pulled a radio mike from the dash of the ATV. "Mama Bear, Baby Bear One."

"Go, Baby One."

"Trouble. Big trouble; could come looking for you. If no signal in twenty-four, go long way around. Copy?"

"Copy all. Stay safe, Baby."

"Love you, Mama." He put the mike down. "Can you let me in?"

"Yeah." Convinced by the boy's sincerity and interaction with his mother, Kit helped the young man move the barriers, then hopped on behind him for the ride to the main ranch. He'd almost forgotten what a luxury it was to ride rather than walk. He directed Simeon to park behind the vehicle barn, since there was no room inside. "You know how to use that rifle?"

"Sure do. I'm a pretty good shot. I hunt a lot." He pulled it off the rack and slung it over his shoulder.

"Can you kill people who are trying to kill you?" Kit didn't want to, but he would with people like Martinez—*my half-brother, Michael Martinez*—on the other side.

"Yes. Can you take me to Alma now?" He bounced on his toes.

"Sure, if you give me your rifle." Simeon handed it to Kit without hesitation, so Kit led him into the house, the sun lighting the hills behind them. He pointed down the hallway. "Alma's in the room on the left with her brother and sister. They're going to lure some of Martinez's people into a trap using a radio." Kit walked behind him, a hand on his pistol.

Simeon glanced back at him, a wry smile twisting his lips. "Don't blame you, man. I'd be careful too. Lots of crazy people around." He peered into the room, then backed out. "I see Em and Mati, but no Alma."

"What?" That girl was going to get herself killed. Kit entered the room and gripped Em's shoulder. "Em, where is Alma?"

"I don't know. She told me and Mati to stay here and help." Her eyes widened. "Simeon! What are you doing here?" Em bounded to her feet and wrapped her arms around Simeon, Matias joining her. Em peppered him with questions. "How's your mom? The baby? What happened—"

Simeon laughed. "The update's gonna have to wait, right?" He cast a look at Kit.

Em stamped her foot.

Kit cut Em's hissy fit off. "Squirt, you've got a job to do. Reunions will wait. Besides, I want Simeon to stay right here." He pulled Simeon away and lowered his voice. "Simeon, we're short on armed people who know what they're doing, and we need to protect these kids and the rest of the people in the house." He handed the rifle back to the boy.

Simeon nodded. "You bet. I'll take a look around and find the best spot."

"Come with me, and I'll introduce you to Taylor first. She's coordinating the trap Em and Mati are helping with." He led Simeon to Taylor's command post in the barn. Stone had coordinated the construction of a sniper's perch on top and they yelled enemy movements down to Taylor. Stone reported from the hillside using the walkie-talkie radios. She perched on a bale of hay, the chore chalkboard propped next to her, with a diagram of the ranch and the surroundings on it, enemy and friendly positions annotated. He hadn't told her his news. Their night had been so perfect, almost like a second honeymoon; talk of his paternity could wait until after the war. *Until we know which Martinez brother comes out on top!*

"Base, Top, forces incoming. Begin operation talk-talk now."

Taylor brought the little radio to her mouth. "Copy, start talk-talk." She put the radio on her lap. "Cindy, ring the string that goes to the pantry." Cindy ran for the barn door and outside.

Operation talk-talk was the name of Em and Mati's radio transmissions, meant to draw the enemy into the trapped bunkhouses. "Taylor, this is Simeon. He knows Alma, Em and Matias, and he's going to protect all the kids in the house."

"Nice to meet you, Simeon. If it doesn't go well, we have multiple escape routes mapped. Get Sandra to show you. She's in the house, minding the littlest kids." He was doing a damned fine job of appearing to be Kit Walsh, when in fact he'd been altered in the space of a single conversation. He'd managed to avoid his aunt, since her reveal and he intended to keep it that way. He had to concentrate on the war *he* was fighting, rather than the one his mother had fought and lost. He shook himself and refocused.

"Sure, Taylor. We can use my ATV to get the kids away." The boy nodded.

"Thank you." Taylor put a hand over her heart. "That makes me feel so much better about this whole plan. Can you run back and tell Em to start talking, too, just in case they didn't hear the cans?"

"Sure." He spun and sprinted away.

Taylor's radio squawked. "Base, Top. Friendly non-combatant spotted, headed toward suspected enemy perch. Recommend intercept if possible."

"Who?" Taylor's brow wrinkled.

"Alma." Kit kicked the hay scattered across the ground. "She wasn't in the pantry with Em and Mati. You know how determined she's been to fight. She has no idea what she's doing. She's gonna get captured or killed and that will kill Em and Mati. Blast that stupid girl."

Taylor squeezed her eyes shut for a second. "She hasn't told us everything she knows, either. Shoot, hardly anything. What if she thinks Martinez is up on that sniper perch? Would she go after him?"

She would do anything to keep her sister and brother safe. "Maybe if she got her hands on a gun, but all ours are accounted for."

Taylor stood and hugged him. "My instincts say we need to go get her, but we have so much going on here. Can we save one girl at the cost of losing the war?"

"We have to. If we can't save the girl, we lose our future." Kit gritted his teeth. He couldn't believe Alma thought she could take on Michael Martinez, a combat veteran and CEO. They'd made progress; she should understand that he and the other adults would protect her. If she'd told them about Martinez, he could have set up an ambush with Stone; he'd already figured out the enemy would try to use those rocks as a sniper perch. If she reached Martinez without backup, she was dead or back in slavery. Stone wouldn't shoot if there was any chance he'd hit the girl. "I've got guns. I'll go after her, and I'll take out Martinez before she can try. Maybe before she even gets up the hill, if I'm lucky. I wish we could talk openly on the radio to Stone, but I'm sure the bad guys are listening." He pulled back and took Taylor's face in his hands. "I love you. Stay safe, and leave with the kids if we lose."

Taylor lunged up and kissed him passionately. "Be careful. Don't take stupid chances. And as much as I hate to say it, if it's a lost cause, back away. Don't throw your life away if Alma's already dead. Hear me?"

"I do. I love you." Kit trotted from the barn, moving from building to building, and then through the secret opening in the thorn-strewn fence around the orchard. He sprinted from tree to tree and stopped behind a massive ponderosa pine when he heard Em and Mati's voices coming from the bunkhouse trap. Cautiously moving to the east of the bunkhouses, he spotted a motley collection of heavily armed intruders creeping toward them. They stopped, and a greasy-haired man with a scar on his face gathered his crew, speaking quietly and gesturing. Kit wasn't positive, but the man might be coordinating the attack. He stayed in place, watching as the men and women split up, approaching the bunkhouse with the radio, and the one next to it.

The man in charge kicked in the door. "Now!" He ran inside, weapon pointed ahead of him, people piling in behind him.

Wood crackled, and men bellowed—probably the floorboards they'd weakened giving way. Kit smiled. Then louder snaps, and the ridgepoles of both intact bunkhouses collapsed. The yells turned to screams, but no one came out. Dunia could take it from here, and he could continue on his mission to save the ridiculously brave girl.

Near the highway, he slid through the trees, then sprinted across, hoping no one saw him. He spotted Alma climbing the hillside, right below the outcropping of rock Stone had noted as the perfect sniper perch.

A blast rang and Kit ducked. Gunfire—the battle had started.

CHAPTER TWENTY-THREE

Alma Garcia. Harmony Ranch, Arizona

A loud sound, like a giant slapping a rock, then the air resounded with cracking noise. Gunfire! Alma jumped and ducked behind a towering pine, sweat running down her back. The fight at the ranch raged behind her, screaming at her to return. She touched her pocket and the weight of the pistol firmed her resolve. She was going to protect Em and Mati for good; the only way she could.

The stream dribbled over mud and trickled past stones at the edge of the property. The fence posts, tarnished with lichen and barely holding the rusted wire, marked the corner with the bunkhouses where Emelia's voice should be broadcasting over the radio. Alma was too far away to hear anything more distinct than the frantic drumming of her heart.

She turned her back to the ranch boundary, retreated deeper into the forest and clambered up the rocks and the gentle incline starting the climb up the steep bluff. Helen had warned her about being spotted from above. Traveling the longer route at the far end of the bluff, well off the ranch, should hide her from the battle lines. The ridge of rocks was unchanged. Twiggy branches offered shelter and their canopy hid the community under attack, but they couldn't stop the drifting sounds of violence.

The pool where she'd bathed was full of water and the surface still except where the stream dribbled into it. She leaned over the mirror-like surface. Dark patches framed her eyes and there was no hint of childlike happiness on her face. She shuddered at the likeness of her mother looking back at her; serious with a harsh, stubborn scowl. Bending low, she scooped up the cool water and splashed it over her face. The cold water made her stagger back. If Mama was tough enough to escape Phoenix, Alma was tough enough to end her family's pain. She had to be.

Her stomach tightened, and she retched, emptying whatever she'd eaten over the rocks. She swished out her mouth with water from the pool and wiped her face. Her foot slipped on the smooth stones coated with vomit and she stumbled forward. She caught her balance. Meeting Martinez would not go to plan unless she calmed down. Holding out her hand, her fingers trembled. That wouldn't do. She forced her hunched shoulders back and down, lifted her face to the sky and concentrated on relaxing her muscles. She eased the tension out of her neck, allowed the stillness to flow down her arms and through her body. Her fear couldn't master her; she must master it.

The grove of towering Ponderosa pines at the edge of the forest made way for tougher, gnarled versions with roots spilling over the rocky ground and clinging to the sheer faces, searching for a firm anchor. She weaved through the trunks and under boughs, considering each step, and avoiding loose stones, dried sticks or anything else that might give her away. The ground rose and she sank back into the shadows cast by the mountainside far from the perch of rocks overlooking the ranch. The shouts and screams from Harmony carried and rippled through the undergrowth, louder, more urgent and nearer with each creeping step. As she'd climbed, she'd also circled closer to the ranch and the battle.

She wiped her slick palms over her sweatpants and pulled out the pistol. The skateboard type texture made the grip secure, but it was oddly rough against her skin. She kept her finger off the trigger, instead holding it more like a rock in her fist.

A harsh beep and a crackling voice drifted through the trees directly to her right, stopping her in her tracks. "That guy we delivered your demand to said the old woman wants to talk to you, boss. Over."

"She meets my demands. Get prisoners. Let them do the talking. Over."

His voice had a soft drawl at odds with the evil and destruction he'd caused and forced her to survive, in the factory and then on the road, fighting for her life and the lives of Emelia and Matias. Alma's skin prickled. Despite his tone, the aura of control and command rang loud. She reached up into her hair, to the wound from the factory. The scab was gone, but the scar was smooth and hairless. She'd experienced his momentary loss of control. Martinez was dangerous.

Hearing him controlling the battle, commanding his troops and demanding everyone to bow under his rule made Alma's mouth dry, her courage blowing away like dust on the wind. She tried to swallow, but she had no moisture or bravery left. All Nora had done was report the truth about his family and he'd stalked her through a shaking world, found her and stabbed her. Out of control or in control, Martinez was deadly. Helen warned her to avoid the overlook but Alma had ignored her, taking on a killer, alone. Pushing a branch aside, she crept forward.

Shouts rose in the distance. Bangs and booms drifted and echoed off the rocks. The voices of angry men and women flooded disembodied through the sparse trees. She gripped the pistol tight and ducked below a twisted limb snaked with rough green growth like an old man's scraggly beard. She crept behind a cluster of several boulders at the outer rim of the peninsula of rock. Adjusting the pistol, she placed her finger on the trigger.

The convex rock overlook rose steeply and then dropped out of sight. It was flatter out where she'd once stood and watched the ranch, out where Martinez ruled. She edged around the boulders, her free hand gripping the sharp facets, helping her balance despite her trembling legs. The red-dusted sole of a boot, a muscled leg in cargo pants, the prone form of a man came into view; her mark, was lying on the ground, on his stomach, facing the ranch, just out of reach. She crept another step onto the rock, letting go of every crutch except her convictions.

Martinez, dressed in his camo gear, right down to a mottled cap, made the hair stand up on her neck. His elbows rested on a folded army jacket and the rifle was steady. His head was so low and still that he must have been studying the action in the ranch below through the scope. To his right a sleeker version of Kit's radio was propped against a stone and next to that, a handgun.

A mere fifteen feet separated her from the monster. Alma didn't want to get any closer. She planted her dominant foot forward—just as Helen Martinez had instructed her to do—and raised the pistol higher. Although she had plenty to say to him, she couldn't alert him to her position. She had one shot and she had to take it. Martinez had stabbed Nora from behind; he deserved to die that way, too. She lined up the sights, but they wavered and jumped in her trembling grip. She aimed at his torso and squeezed the trigger. Stiffer than she expected, the trigger resisted. The pistol fired, kicking her hand back and up and jarring through her arm and into her shoulder. The crack bounced off the rocks behind her.

Martinez's right arm jolted forward and blood splattered on the rock. He roared, rolled to the left and grabbed his elbow, knocking the rifle butt, twisting the barrel away from the ranch. A line of blood smeared across his chest. He bared his teeth and narrowed his dark eyes, flicking a glance at his handgun, far out of reach. He twisted his injured arm toward the weapon and flinched.

"Leave it." Alma's voice was hoarse and weak.

Martinez shifted his fingers, gripping his elbow, blood seeping between them. His breath hissed through his teeth. "Finish the job."

Alma raised her other hand to steady the shaking weapon. Her pounding heartbeat thrumming in her ears muffled the sounds of the battle on the ranch below. A lone, tiny figure darted from tree to tree and she smiled. Martinez probably would have shot at them. She'd done some good.

"Well?" Martinez growled.

Her hands trembled, and the pistol slipped in her fingers despite the grip's heavy texture. She tightened her hold. He tilted his head, then let go of his elbow. He reached over his body, yelling, and stretched toward the handgun.

She pulled the trigger. Martinez brushed the grip of his handgun with the tips of his fingers. Sparks flared across the rock and flashed across his skin, accompanying the bang from her pistol. He flicked his hand away, escaping the stray bullet but shoving his weapon in the sudden movement. It spun over the rock and clattered out of reach.

He rolled back and glared at her. "Now look what you made me do."

"Don't move." She aimed the pistol again and cleared her throat. "I mean it."

"If you meant it, I'd be dead by now."

She couldn't hate anyone more than she hated him in that moment. "I will kill you."

He laughed, but he didn't take his gaze from her pistol or his hand from his bleeding arm. "You'll run out of ammo before then. Of course, I don't need a gun to kill you."

She scanned his belt and it was free from other weapons. "Slowly, throw your knife over the cliff."

He gritted his teeth, bent his left leg, and reached around his ankle and into his boot, pulling out a hunting knife with a lethal, glistening blade. He must have cleaned Nora's blood from it. He cut a notch into his shirt and tossed his weapon over the rock toward her. It landed, spinning frantically out of her reach and just beyond his foot. "You think I was referring to weapons. Little girl, I can kill you with my bare hands. Even one that's bleeding." He jerked forward.

Alma fired the pistol. Sparks flew and a shard of rock sliced off the surface and scuttled to a halt at his hip. He'd killed Nora in cold blood and she needed to free her family, but even his arrogance couldn't make her aim any better. Her wrist ached and a spasm of pain ran up her arm into her shoulder.

He settled back, sitting on the folded jacket, and tugged at his shirt with both hands and hissed. A strip of fabric came away. "Easy! I'm just stopping the bleeding."

She couldn't stop her hands from shaking. The pistol sights

jumped from him to the open space around him.

He turned away from her, not the least bit concerned that she held him at gunpoint, wadded up half the fabric and wrapped the rest around his arm. He pulled it tight between his hand and teeth. "They must be desperate if they're arming kids." His coarse laugh lilted with scorn.

Alma squeezed her lips tight and shook her head. "This was a gift."

Martinez's brown eyes widened then narrowed, aimed at her weapon. "Helen?" He scratched his chin. "Figures. You have Helen's Ruger." He flexed his fingers, but tucked his injured hand close to his body. "It was indeed a gift. From me."

"I'll be sure to thank her." Alma hoped Helen had escaped.

"No, you won't." Martinez's drawl mocked. "You won't be around to thank anyone."

"I'm the one with the gun." Her voice shook more than the weapon did.

"Which you've pointed at me for several minutes, and yet I'm still alive."

Shouts and shots echoed over the ranch below. Martinez's men, clambered over the fence and wove through the trees near the old buildings. The surprised screams, rumble of stones and shaking of foliage meant that the traps were triggered. She couldn't hear Matias and Emelia's voices over the radio, but perhaps the plan was working and they were drawing them into the bunkhouses. She tightened her grip and her hand steadied. For them, she would do anything.

"I hate you."

"Join the list." Martinez raised a brow and snorted.

Heat rose; temper and anger burned in her body. "You took my parents."

"So, it's personal." He shrugged.

He wasn't taking her seriously. She ventured another step, her pistol still raised and pointed securely at his torso. He tilted his head and shifted his feet, the grit scratching at the rocky plateau. The tightness in her chest vanished, and a giggle bubbled up. She was going to kill him.

Martinez tore his eyes from her and showed his teeth in a grimace. Stones clattered and heavy footsteps pounded behind her. She kept the pistol pointed at him and turned slightly.

"No, Alma!" Kit strode forward, panting, with a revolver in his unbandaged hand. "Stop."

She turned back to Martinez. His smugness was swiped clean and a sheen glistened on his forehead. Kit stood next to her. Martinez eyed Kit up and down with a sneer, but sat up straighter, jostling the rifle on its stand with his back.

Kit took a step closer to Martinez blocking the view of the old buildings and the ranch below. "You don't need to do this."

"He has to die. He killed my parents." She wanted Kit's concern to flare into the rage-driven revenge she'd carried since her mother's death. Since they locked her in the disgusting room at the prison house. Since Martinez had forced her into adulthood. Kit's concern for her was nothing compared to the boiling need to end Martinez. "He murdered Nora."

"He's not worth it, Alma. Don't be like him." Kit held his hand out for her weapon, but she held it tight. This was her moment and she wasn't about to give it up. She wasn't who he thought she was. Tougher and more resilient, she had Martinez's death in the palm of her hand. All she had to do was breath, find her equilibrium, and shoot.

"They've polluted the whole world, Alma." Kit was talking to her, but had his eyes fixed on the man on the ground. "But we need to stay true to ourselves. We need to be everything they're not. Don't do it."

Martinez snorted and smiled. "Hey, brother." He tried to straighten his injured arm, flinched, and tucked it back against his body. He stretched his left arm out beside himself and leaned on it. Even with two guns pointed at him, arrogance rolled off him.

"You're no brother of mine." Kit turned back to Alma and gestured with his bandaged hand for her to lower her weapon. "I'm going to say it again, Alma. Please, don't be like him." He reached toward her, and she sidestepped. "Alma. Listen to me, please."

Alma let the silence stretch out between them, the noises of battle on the ranch oddly distant. "I won't let him walk away."

"I'm not saying we do that." Kit had taken his gaze from Martinez and focused on her. "Em said that you were brave and courageous. That you would do everything to save them. You deliberately came here to face him. You planned it. I understand why. He deserves to be punished."

"He deserves to die." Her words spilled out, the venom unmistakable.

Kit lowered his revolver. "You want to save us all. I get it. Trust me. But you don't need to do this alone in cold blood. Let us help. You aren't alone now." He extended his hand to her again. She stood her ground. "Don't let him change you. He doesn't deserve that right. You're not a killer."

"That's what I said." Martinez flashed a wide smile, as if he'd won an argument. "She's not ruthless. She's weak. You both are."

"Shut up, you belly-crawling, slow worm!" Kit didn't take his gaze from her.

Alma tasted the word, and it didn't fit. Weakness hadn't brought Em and Mati through storms and attacks, her strength had. Martinez knew nothing of her and cared even less. He couldn't see her clearly. He was blind to what his company had done to the world, and what his slave trade had done to families. Kit was right. Martinez didn't deserve to even comment. He'd stolen too much and wouldn't steal her innocence, too. She loosened her grip on the pistol; the tension draining from her fingers, and lowered her arm. Justice, even in the broken world, wouldn't make her carry around guilt for the rest of her life.

The radio beeped. "We're in position, boss. Over."

Kit and Alma turned in unison to the message. Martinez reached behind him and snapped up the rifle in his uninjured hand. He spun the gaping black bore toward her, a wicked smile spreading over his lips. Kit raised his revolver. Alma lifted the pistol, reaching for the trigger. Martinez's fingers found the trigger with ease. The gunshot ricocheted across the rock face.

CHAPTER TWENTY-FOUR

Catherine "Cat" Murphy. En route to the bunkers.

By the time Tom stumbled through Van Zant's front door, Cat had about lost her mind. The beer bottles weren't just talking to her, they were chanting her name and making all manner of promises to her. "We're your friends. We'll help you pass the time of day. We've never done you no harm. You were still the Queen of your Hill, even when you were chugging our friend Mr. Whiskey," but she'd held off and kept her mind busy and her heart strong with thoughts that Tom was better than anything the damn fool world could throw at them. Definitely worth more than a drink!

Belle slipped in behind him, her tail down and her ears flat, but there was no Van Zant in sight.

"Where's Andy?" She pushed herself out of her chair and hopped to the door.

Tom shoved his hat off, stamping the mud off his boots. "Best not ask."

Couldn't be a worse answer than that. She leaned against the sink, taking the measure of the man. He'd been there for as long as she remembered, but who he was and what he was had only started coming into focus. "There's some stew left." She'd turned the stove off long since, but there was wood and flame and she could get that going again. Maybe. Being a one-legged anything wasn't what she'd planned on, but she had no choice in the matter. Might as well be a one-legged best friend than anything else.

Tom slumped into the easy chair she'd just vacated. "Guess we should. Like the man said, no refrigeration but nature." That sealed it. Andy Van Zant was dead. She hopped to the wood pile next to the stove, steadying herself against the wall. The oven door was a heavy, cast iron affair that she'd have loved in her old life. Now, though? It required her to assess where, exactly, her center of gravity was located so she didn't faceplant and add to Tom's woes, while she was trying to lift his spirits.

Belle circled a couple of times, a slight limp in her forepaw, before settling at Tom's feet. She knew enough about dog injuries to know she was going to have to dig out a First Aid kit and do what she could for the pup.

The stove door finally yielded and she eased a hunk of wood into the belly of the blackened beast right as she realized it needed raking. She swore under her breath, gently, but Tom was up and by her side in an instant. "What are you thinking, woman? You can't do this."

She elbowed him away. "Best be finding something I can before we get to this underground paradise they've promised us. Don't imagine they want a whole flock of one-legged smart alecs."

Tom backed away, hands in the air. "Knock yourself out!" He busied himself at the sink, washing bowls in the already-bleak water and stacking them on the mesquite table in the center of the room.

Cat did her best not to watch him, keeping her eyes on her own task, but he was downhearted, the weight he was carrying something she ought to share. He was no more a talker than she was, but she'd never spent much time learning how to take the burdens of others as her own. *Hear me, Lord.* She laughed at her own daring. How many prayers had she sent up, after a lifetime of silence? Too many! *It ain't for me I ask, but for Tom here. Give me strength to carry my own burdens, that he might not.* She raked the ashes from the bottom of the stove, shoveling them into the bucket Andy had at the ready. The place, rustic as it was, had been kitted out for basic human comfort.

"We can use those." Tom had taken to the chair again. Twice in one day! Prayers really were answered! "Clean up the silverware." He folded his hands over his stomach and let his head dip toward his chest.

She'd never seen the man so tired, and certainly never to a point he let it show. She turned back, even more determined to serve him a hot meal. His snores filled the room while she hopped and leaned, hefted and rested, lit and blew and begged the flame to take. When the fire was finally going, she patted her way down the wall and took a moment on the three legged stool that sat between the wood burning stove and the rainwater sink. *We could stay here. There's land. There's livestock. A roof over our heads.* The pail of ashes stared up at her, black chunks nestled in the grey. *We feed the land, it feeds us. Feed the cattle, they feed us. Feed the...* There was so much feeding to do, but if they were right—if the sun was taking itself away for a while—there was no use feeding everything. There was a clock, ticking heavily in the sky, and she needed to heed it.

She was low to the ground and her good leg wasn't strong enough for her to stand unaided. She peeked at Tom, waited for three long, slow breaths and bumped herself onto the floor. Her coccyx screamed, but she bit her tongue and didn't make a peep.

Belle trotted to her side, snout interested in what the strange lady was doing on the floor. "Don't tell your pa, girl, you hear me? He's got enough going on." The dog lost interest in her maneuvers and took her place at Tom's feet once more.

Cat rolled onto all fours, laughing. "All threes and a stump, I think you'll find!" Her knees were scraped up, and the heels of her hands protested, but she found her way to the towel rack and prayed that it'd hold her weight. "And my arms are up to the task, Lord!" She pulled, sweat breaking out across her shoulders and forehead, but no sound leaking from her mouth. "I can do it. I can. I must!" By the time she was upright, she was fully drenched, but the smell of that stew covered her stench and called her forward. The chair was her crutch, the wall her cane, and with three-thousand different micro-motions she scooped a steaming bowl of leftovers into an almost-clean bowl and slid it onto the table. "Grub's up," she whispered.

"Thought you'd never call me to the table." Damn clown had been awake that whole time and not said a thing. Her blush rose against her irritation. He knew her better than she knew herself. She had to find a way to be in the world and he was letting her. He took his place at the table. "For friendship, food, and foolhardy folk who won't ask for a helping hand, when they're half a leg short, we give you thanks, oh Lord. In Jesus' name we pray."

Before she had a chance to protest he had his spoon in the stew and was shoveling it down his gullet. She could've sworn he batted away a tear, but she kept her eyes on Belle and her mind on all the what nexts. If someone was bold enough—wily enough, lucky enough, it didn't matter which—to take Andy Van Zant down, they couldn't stay. She knew that, he knew that, heck probably Belle knew it.

"Best get the pot off the stove." He didn't look up and she was glad of it. Getting up was every bit as inelegant as before and hopping to and from the table to the stove was about the least sophisticated she'd ever been in her life. She'd never set much stock in how she looked, leaning on the fact that she had a healthy body and a good head of hair. Weird how losing half a leg threw all that into question. She removed the pot to the trivet, then the table. "Best finish it off."

He pushed her bowl across the table. "If you don't start taking care of yourself, the hyenas will take care of you."

Cat shuddered. Van Zant had mentioned the zebra and the hyenas, but she'd never thought they could take a grown man down. In any case, if there'd been that kind of bloodshed, it would have been all over. Oh! "Where's your coat?"

Tom shrugged. "Covered Andy before I dug his grave, then I didn't have the heart to take it off him. They tore him up..." He stopped, pushing his bowl away. "Got to go see to the livestock." He grabbed his hat on the way out, Belle trotting behind him, and she was left to imagine what might have happened when Tom and Andy met up with the wild animals that were left to roam the land.

The silence settled in, layering itself over the dying embers in the stove and cooling pot on the table. Tom's words lingered, "Best be taking care of yourself." It stung, but not in the old way. He was right. She couldn't piggy-back her way to the underground bunkers. She cast her eye over Van Zant's scant belongings. He was a hat maker, but she couldn't see much evidence of his trade. "Like as not he had a place aways from here."

Like a workshop? Yup, like a workshop. Question was, could she get there without bothering Tom? Because if he saw her out and about, he'd have strong words to say about it. There was no back door to the shack, but there was a long-way around to his outbuildings. She collected a broom from the corner and stood in the door, calculating what might be where, geographically. The cowshed was easy to pick out, but there were a couple more little lean-tos that might have been something and might have been nothing.

She tucked the broom, brush side up, under her arm and took a right, determined to investigate without interruption. The grasses were high, the terrain so lumpy-bumpy she might as well have been facing Everest. "Here goes." She did an about face, held her head up and hobble-swung her way toward the first hut.

The door screamed on its hinges, a call to everyone and anyone who was on the hunt for easy pickings. Tools, tools, and more tools lined the walls and work bench. He kept them oiled and clean, ready for work, but the kind of work that involved engines and generators, rather than hats and boots and leatherworking and such. She closed the door, careful to let the latch down as quietly as she could.

She turned and swung right into Tom.

"What's this?" His face was drawn, his eyes all over the property, but always coming back to rest on hers.

"Investigating." She shoved her elbow into his chest. "Still a free country."

He relented, stepping out of her way. "So long as you're not investigating a way to get dead, Cat. They're not messing out there. They're..."

Animals never messed. They did what they did because they must. "If they come for me, Tom, they'll get short shrifted." She forced a smile. "More meat on your bones than mine!"

He turned his back on her, muttering and disappeared back into the cowshed. Something had rattled his cage and she didn't like it one bit. She wanted her Tom back. *My Tom! Who could credit he would ever be MY Tom?*

The third shed was the workroom she was hoping to find, complete with leather punches and scraps of leftover material. She was no designer and it was a shame to take his beautiful supplies—supple leather, molded felt, a tin of shining punch buttons—but she was going to put them to good use.

Four trips between the workshop and his kitchen table and Cat was done. The beers, though, hadn't given up on her. They were still chatting away about all the things they could do, if she'd just give them a chance.

"Fine." She pushed herself up onto her only leg and stumped to the line of home brew that was high on the shelf. "You want me so bad?" She leaned against the brush and smacked the head of the beer bottle on the side of the kitchen sink, so expertly the cap twirled high before it landed at her feet.

Tom was at the door, his face as long as a wet weekend in July.

She turned the bottle upside down and let it pour into the sink. "One day, I'll be as strong as you." She balanced the empty on the draining board. "But today isn't that day." She reached for a second bottle. "As long as they're in the house, I'm going to know where they are." She smacked the lid off, just as before, the cap doing somersaults before Tom clasped it in his hand. She upturned the bottle, the hoppy loveliness filling her nostrils. "The answer is clear to me. Don't have them in the house."

Tom took to her side, wrapping an arm around her shoulders and kissing the top of her head. "It was the same for most of us. Had to keep it out of sight while it was still in mind." He pulled her close and she wondered at the fact that—in spite of everything he'd been through—he still had that starch-sweat smell that reminded her of a time when she was safe from everything. "But one day you'll wake up and you won't wonder when it's time for your next drink; if it's too early; if the boss will smell it on you; if you can break early and not have anyone notice. One day, you won't be waiting on Friday, because you can spend the whole damn night at some honky tonk you never heard of and never will again. One day, you won't even wonder what time the liquor store closes..." His heart was beating fit to bust out of his shirt. "One day, you'll wake up and something else will fill that place." He kissed her hair a second time. "And, God willing, that something else will be you."

She hadn't expected him to end where he ended. The twelve steppers she'd heard talk were full of God taking the place of everything else.

"I can use these in the barn." She knew without asking that he didn't mean for him. "I want to bolster some of the smaller cattle before we go." He made sure she was upright before he left, the last three bottles snug in his arms, and made no mention of what she had laid out on the dining room table.

The felt she'd snagged from Andy's studio was soft to the touch, but too big to wrap around her stump and a seam would chafe. Once again, she cast an eye around the room, coming to rest on the comfy chair where she and Tom had taken their rest. "Well, if we're going, we might as well use everything we can..."

Andy's pinking shears were sharp, but the work was still a strain. Her shoulders ached and her gritty eyes strained against her sloppy handiwork. Measure, measure, measure, cut. Over and over. Measure, measure, measure, cut. It wasn't perfect, but eventually she had a kind of cushion that fit over her stump, lined with foam from the chair and secured with felt, then leather. "No seams means no blisters!" She knew that wasn't strictly true, but the place where her leg had once lived was toughening up, and what was true and what was wishful thinking didn't much matter. She had to be able to carry her own weight if she was going to be a lick of use once they got where they were going.

"The cradle's the easy part." She'd already decided that one of the dining room chairs was going to be sacrificed, but she'd vastly under-estimated how difficult it was to break a leg to make a leg. She sat on the floor, chair on its side, and placed her good foot in the center of the underside of the seat, grunting as she pushed with her leg and pulled with both arms.

She couldn't see a single nail, but Van Zant had glue aplenty and knew how to make something strong enough to carry the weight of a full grown man.

A shadow darkened the door. Tom had added 'barn' to his signa-ture smell, but he wasn't much the worse for it. "What you doing down there?"

"Fixing to make myself a peg leg." She smiled. For the first time since he'd sawed it off, she understood that it wasn't truly the end of the world. She wasn't made of half a missing leg, but far sterner stuff. "Don't suppose you'd like to help me?"

"I thought you'd never ask." He took the wooden chair from her and pulled it to pieces as if it were little more than a fresh roasted chicken. "Have you measured?"

Kind of? I stood near it, I guess? "If I stand next to it and balance my stump on the seat of the chair, it pushes my hips out of align-ment, so I figure once we take that off, the leg's going to be about right."

Tom nodded. "I'm impressed." He yanked again, removing each of the spindles from the uprights. "Don't want to interfere with the maestro's design, but if you'll let me, I figure we can be centimeter-precise."

Cat took her place on the stool by the stove, turning pieces of leather and holding them up to the cup she'd fashioned. "I need to fix them to this and that..."

The two of them glued, hammered, and squeezed the punch

pliers until they'd made the ugliest, most comfortable dang peg leg anyone had ever seen.

Cat tried it for size, leaning against Tom more than the wall, and let him take measurements.

"Could be wrong, but there's some interesting terrain in our future."

She waited, unsure of where he was going next.

"If this was your inside leg, and you were only using it for trucking around the house, I'd say we take a couple of centimeters off the bottom, but as it's your outside leg, you're going to wear it down soon enough."

Cat closed her eyes against the memory of all the legs that she'd failed so far, starting with her *actual* leg and running through the good and decent things people had done to get her back on her feet again.

"I'll pack the rest of the supports, some leather and Andy's punch, so we can make a new one when we need to?"

Cat leaned forward to the cowman, who was on his knees beside her and landed a light kiss. "How did I miss you all this time, Tom Callahan?"

Tom tsked. "You're asking the wrong man. I sure as sugar didn't miss who you were."

Cat blushed, amazed at her luck and grateful for a tenth chance not to mess it up.

Tom took her hand in his and raised his face. "Catherine Murphy, will you marry me?"

He was a surprise a minute, but she wouldn't have it any other way. She steeled her will and her heavy-beating heart. "Tom Callahan, I will. I shall. I do."

CHAPTER TWENTY-FIVE

Kit Walsh. Harmony Ranch, Arizona

Kit pulled his revolver, aimed, and fired again. Martinez collapsed. *I killed my brother.*

To Kit's left, the rumbling grew to thunder—Stone's group released more of the rolling log traps. He wanted to watch, but kept his eyes on Martinez, ready to shoot again. As he slid closer, it was clear the man was dead. His eyes stared at the sky, his hands were lax, the hole in his chest right over his heart. Vivid red blood pooled under the body and dripped off the rocky perch.

"Is he dead?" Alma tiptoed closer, her pistol pointed at the body as if Martinez would jump to his feet. Moss and sticks littered her hair. Behind them, a widow maker had fallen—Martinez must have got a shot off and hit the branch just right. When Kit turned back, Alma had Martinez's rifle and knife; she could keep the spoils of war, along with her intact soul.

I have no regret. He was a wicked man, bent on destruction. I acted in self defense.

"Kit? Is he?" Her voice was small, the words trembling out of her.

"Yes, he's definitely dead. And now we have a chance to win."

With any luck at all, announcing his death to Martinez's forces would slow them down, even if it didn't stop them. Kit fastened Martinez's radio on his backpack strap, turning the sound down to zero. He grabbed the body's wrists, and hauled him up on to his shoulder and stood, staggering a bit under the dead weight. Another shirt ruined by bloodstains, but he didn't mind. His half-brother was dead for all the right reasons.

Gunfire and screams rang out, and it seemed the log rollers were more successful than they had any right to expect from the number of enemies crushed on the ground far below. "We've got to be careful on the way down. They've got snipers." At her look of puzzlement, Kit pointed at the rifle over her shoulder. "Shooters, very accurate. We need to move fast, from rock to rock, and tree to tree. Stay out of sight. Got it?"

Alma nodded, eyes wide.

"Stay behind me." Kit staggered a little under the load—Martinez was a lot heavier than Nora, but he was much happier carrying the scumbag. They skittered from rock to rock and at the bottom, tree to tree. At the highway, Kit looked both ways, trotted to the middle of the road and dropped his grisly load in an inglorious heap. Then he and Alma ran to the bunkhouses. The area was eerily silent compared to the barrage to the north, nothing but dust rising from the collapsed structures. A single gunshot rang. Kit pushed Alma behind a tree and skulked through the clearing.

Dunia aimed a smoking pistol at a man on the ground, a hole in the middle of his forehead. She spat something in a foreign language and kicked the body. The other members of her team pulled bodies from the wreckage. "Dunia!"

She jumped. "Kit! It worked perfectly, except we can't get the radio back."

"That's okay, I've got something better." He pulled Martinez's radio off his fire pack and turned the volume up. Yelling voices asked for reinforcements, and calmer voices denied it. Men and one woman asked for orders from the boss, presumably Martinez. Stone said some of their leadership was clearly military, and just like firefighting, the action didn't stop if the leader fell; a new leader took over. They might pause the battle temporarily, but the war for resources would continue. They had too many mouths to feed, and too few workers. They had to find a better solution.

"He is dead?" Dunia stalked to him, pistol still gripped in both hands, aimed at the ground.

At a pause in the radio traffic, Kit clicked the push-to-talk button twice, and the channel fell quiet. "Attention, Martinez forces. Your leader, Michael Martinez, is dead. His body is in the middle of Highway 77, near the south end of the ranch. Break off your attack now, before you lose more people. Everyone you sent to the south is dead. Many more are dead in the log and rockfalls." Kit paused, but the next step was clear. He took a deep breath and continued. "Stop now, and in three days, you can have the ranch. We're leaving. Nuclear winter is coming. If you're smart, you'll leave too. There are caverns all around this area. Find one and hunker down. If you attack us again, or if you follow us, we will kill you just like we killed Martinez. Leave now, and you can walk right in here in three days. Keep fighting, and we'll kill all of you. Understood?"

"Standby," a man snapped. "South One, confirm Martinez."

After a long pause, a voice replied. "Confirmed. Martinez deceased. Orders?"

"All forces, regroup at command. I repeat, regroup at command. Break, break. You have three days, rancher."

Kit turned the sound down, but not off. "We've got to be gone in two, because they won't keep their word. Done here, Dunia?"

"Done." She aimed a final kick at the body in front of her.

A girl wailed behind the bunkhouse and they both ran. Alma pointed at a body with a trembling hand, her other over her mouth.

"What's wrong?" Perhaps Alma finally realized how close she'd come to dying. Even injured, Martinez was strong and smart. He could have easily killed her. She was lucky he'd been an arrogant jerk who enjoyed toying with others before taking the kill shot.

"That's Eric." She pointed at a man hanging out of the collapsed mess of stone and timber. "That's Mason. Are they really dead?"

Dunia toed Eric's body. "He is dead. What were they to you?"

"They were guards at our factory. They were evil."

"Well, good thing they're dead." Kit put an arm around her trembling shoulders and led her away. "Let's go. Martinez's remaining people can clean up the bodies."

Alma pulled away from him before they left the clearing around the structures, but she walked next to him. That seemed like a win. They entered the orchard, waving at the guards hiding behind the sheds. "It's over," Kit yelled.

Ranch residents emerged from their hiding spots. "Really?"

"Really. But we've got three days to leave, and we need to do it in two."

"What!" The accusations started, people throwing up their arms and getting in Kit's face. He ignored them all and entered the barn, sprinting to Taylor, pulling her up off the hay and twirling her around. "We won! They're backing off."

"Oh, Kit! That's wonderful." Taylor kissed him.

A tap on his shoulder broke them apart. "What's this about leaving in three days?" Cindy glared at him.

Kit growled at the interruption. Simply because he'd stepped up and taken charge, everyone thought they could interrupt him at any time.

"Kit? What did you tell them?" Taylor raised her brows.

He scowled at the crowd. "Okay, gather around. Taylor, tell our folks up on the hill to not fire, but stay there and watch. Make sure the Martinez forces retreat and stay in their campground."

She turned away and grabbed the FRS radio. Kit hopped up on her hay bale and waited for Stone's acknowledgement. Then he turned to the growing crowd. "Look, how many of you knew Aunt Jen talked to a group of scientists who came through? Dr. Kumar and Dr. James?" The crowd shook heads, shooting inquisitive looks at each other. "Their group was going to some old military bunkers in the Huachuca Mountains, where they claim they're able to live underground. Aunt Jen thought they were crazy because of the earthquakes, and I agreed with her." Heads nodded again and people murmured. "But the earthquakes are lessening and getting weaker while the sky darkens with ash; we've all noticed it. I think those scientists were right. And even if they aren't, military bunkers will be defendable. Harmony Ranch isn't. Not over the long run. We got lucky this time. Through sheer determination of a few people, we won." He met Alma's eyes and nodded to her. She'd been foolish, but her love for her family carried her through. Their real luck was Stone coming forward—his resolve to fight and his military knowledge was the critical piece.

"I don't think we can do it again. If they kept fighting, eventually, we'd lose. They have too many guns, too many desperate people. So, pack up what you can carry. We'll bring all the food that's left, probably in backpacks and pull carts. We'll bring small hand tools, and books on engineering, like the one Matias used to build the bike generator. Bring only things you can carry, things that will be useful in the future underground. It's a long walk, but not impossible. Get ready. If you want to stay here, you can." Kit pointed to the north. "But those people up there, they're just the first who will attack us. There will be more, I guarantee it. Get ready. We leave in two days or preferably less. They won't give us the full three. They keep slaves, and they'll want us, too. They'll eventually remember that. We'll keep people at those sniper positions at the top of the hill and listen to their radio until we leave."

Kit jumped off the hay bale and put his arm around Taylor's shoulders, leading her out of the barn, ignoring the questions and shouts. "Alma, go see your sister and brother. There's a surprise for you." He grinned as the girl ran. Kit pushed through the crowd, even though they grabbed at him, trying to get his attention. When Mr. H blocked his way, he stopped. "Look, I told you. You want to stay here, go ahead. It's a free country. But I did what I did to save your lives. You've got two days to figure out if you want to waste that gift. Taylor and me? We're leaving. We're not just surviving, we're going to thrive. Got it?" He pushed through the now-silent crowd to the house. Inside, Jaya hugged him, Faris squeezed his shoulder, and Doc shook his hand. Children reunited with their parents with cries of joy.

Aaron clapped a hand on his shoulder. "You're right. It's the smart thing to do. We'll leave and start over someplace safer, someplace defendable, someplace where the rule of law means something."

Kit took Taylor's hand. "I need to relieve Stone and his guys. Will you be okay here? Talk to Simeon, Alma's friend, and see if they can help us get some of our less-mobile folks to the bunkers?"

"I got it. Don't worry, Kit, people will come around." She squeezed his hand and let go.

At the front porch, Mr. and Mrs. H waited for him, and he tried to smile, but gave up. He was tired of dealing with obstinate, uncooperative people. To his surprise, they smiled at him. "Kit, my boy. Excellent job. You've brought us from sheer disaster to success." They were only the first to congratulate him. Even some of those who had just been yelling at him said "thank you" with shamed faces. To his left, Aaron talked with a small group of people, gesturing and speaking urgently. He must be advocating for Kit's decision; doing something positive with his overwhelming grief.

Cindy stopped him. "Look, I'm sorry Kit. I don't deal with change very well, and I overreacted. You did the right thing for all of us. And you killed that awful man. You're a real hero."

Kit grimaced, his gut churning and mind reeling. He'd barely come to terms with the idea that he *had* a brother, let alone one who wished him dead. *And who I killed.* The gorge rose and he turned his head away from Mr. H's frank adoration. "Thanks. I've got to go." Killing a man wasn't heroic. *I killed my half-brother.* If he'd been able to walk Martinez down that hill and into the barn with his hands behind his back, and held him to account, that would have been heroic. Michael Martinez was a world killer, who should have stood trial. And yet... Alma had been there, trembling with rage and willing to stain her soul. When it had come down to it, he'd fired back; not first. He'd had no choice. It didn't taste good, but it was what it was. He'd made the best out of a bad situation. He climbed up the hill, knowing Stone's people were watching his back.

Stone stood from his perch on a rock. "Good job, Kit. You made the right call."

"You were the one who won the war for us, Stone." Kit held out his hand and shook Stone's. "You told us about Alma heading up the hill. I followed her and got there when she was confronting Martinez. He tried to kill us, I killed him."

Stone slugged Kit's upper arm. "Good job on that, too. But, it's gonna bother you, so make sure you talk to someone when it does."

"Yeah." Stone was right, but there was too much to do to worry about it. "Just to be clear, I said we'd leave for the Apache bunkers in three days, but we're doing it in two. So, go get your stuff organized, and get some sleep. I got the watch."

Stone nodded. "Best you could do with the hand you were dealt." He gave Kit the little radio and his rifle. "I was thinking about heading that way, anyway. We weren't gonna make it through the winter alive. It's just too harsh an environment and there are too many people. So, yeah, good job. And don't forget—when you wake up in the middle of the night, shaking, come talk to me." He slugged Kit's shoulder again and walked away, his spotter following, wide eyed.

Kit rubbed his arm; he'd have a bruise. He sat on the spotter's rock and brought his binoculars up, scanning the enemy campsite. They burned bonfires, people standing around like they were at a party, drinking something. Probably some sort of bathtub hooch. He didn't want to know what they'd made it from. He'd rather eat than drink. At the fancy RV, three men emerged, all wearing para-military clothing. Two of them joined the drinkers at the nearest fire, the last taking a long look at his people, then sweeping the bluff with binoculars. Kit raised the rifle to his shoulder and stared back at the man through the scope. The man waved a careless salute at him, then lowered the binoculars and walked deeper into the campsite. So, most likely, these people wouldn't be a threat for the next twelve to forty-eight hours. But he'd keep watching. Enemies could act in surprising ways.

He put the rifle down and picked up the binoculars again, settling in for a long night. The darkness gave him a chance to collect his thoughts, which crowded in as soon as he relaxed. He hadn't seen his Aunt, didn't know what she was going to say about leaving Harmony Ranch, or about him killing Michael, but they were going to have to talk eventually. He had a million questions, none of them easy, but then Jen McCreedy wasn't built for easy. She'd taken him in when his mother had folded into her addiction. The lie his Aunt Stickler had told—and it was a big one—was a lie he'd have told a child, too. What a terrible burden, knowing that your mother was forced into pregnancy, the kid a constant reminder of her abuser. No, she'd done the right thing.

They both had.

All that remained was to get square with the facts and build a better tomorrow.

CHAPTER TWENTY-SIX

Evelyn Parker. Anil Kumar Sanctuary, Arizona

After a light knock on the door, Evelyn used a key to let herself into Dev and Sandy's apartment. Dev reclined on the sofa in the living room, his right leg elevated. Alec may have been the smartest person from School of Mines, but luckily, his marksmanship wasn't equal to his intelligence. He'd wounded Dev, Sandy and Floyd, but so far, all three had survived.

A one-page letter scribbled on a sheet of yellow legal paper lay on the coffee table in front of him; Evelyn's letter of resignation from the sanctuary council. She'd pushed harder than anyone else in the group to permit Alec to remain, despite warning signs he was unstable. Her bias affected her decision, and resulted in serious damage, nearly costing all of their lives. She didn't belong on anything as important as a governing council, and she wanted to spare Dev the trouble of casting her out.

He lifted his head when she entered, groaning as he struggled to sit upright.

"Please stay where you are, Dev." She took a seat on a plaid armchair. Books covering topics from agriculture to electrical circuits were stacked across the coffee table. The professor must've brought them.

Dev fluttered a hand toward the yellow paper on the table. "I read your letter, Evelyn, but I'm afraid I must deny your request to resign."

"But, Dev. I. You ... Sandy." She straightened her back. "I'm not qualified to make decisions about who can stay and who has to go."

He waved off her objections. "If you're not, then none of us is. Ultimately, it was my decision, and I chose to allow Alec to stay here. So really, all of us getting shot is on me. You, on the other hand, put him down, and saved Floyd's life. You're a hero."

Evelyn should've known better than to try to discuss this with Dev. He was far smarter than she was and had the verbal skills of a debate team champion, which Sandy said he'd been. "I allowed my own feelings to get in the way of logic."

"Welcome to the way most decisions are made. Even if I wanted to remove you from the council, which emphatically, I do not, I couldn't. You're our only founding member who's physically able to move around the facility." He half-smiled, then grimaced.

"The professor wasn't hurt, Dev." She spread her arms. "He could oversee everything until you're well enough."

"The professor's not on the council." Dev cocked an eyebrow. "And by your logic, he can't be trusted at all. It was he who brought Alec here, and he assured us Alec was fine."

"Well, perhaps he was as taken in by Alec as we all were." She raised her hands slightly.

"Ah!" Dev lifted his index finger. "So, you admit that we were *all* taken in by Alec. You're no more at fault that any of us."

Her shoulders sagged with defeat. He'd bested her argument again.

"I'm not going to let you resign, and neither is Sandy, so please, no more talk of it. I need you coordinating with Professor Benson."

She nodded, crossed to the open-air kitchen, and opened a couple cans of soup. Earlier that morning, she'd gone downstairs and fetched provisions from the food storage area, taking some items to her and Floyd's place, and delivering some to Dev and Sandy's apartment. Her injuries prevented her from carrying much, but she'd made trip after trip to get them properly stocked. She poured the soup into a small pan, set the soup on the electric burner and watched as it warmed, steam rising from the golden liquid. She poured it into a heavy, white ceramic bowl, carried it to where Dev lay on the couch and set it on her resignation letter. She tucked a pillow behind him and fed him until he refused more. "Thank you, Evelyn. What's on your schedule today?"

"Infirmary first, to check on Sandy and Floyd. Then a meeting with the Professor to look at what can be done to salvage the agricultural area."

"Alec was sane enough to know where to inflict the most damage." Dev pursed his lips. "Let's hope we can make repairs. This could alter how many people we can ultimately allow to live here. Let's hope some show up with livestock. In all likelihood, we'll need to slaughter anything people bring with them, and store it in the freezer."

Evelyn's spirit faltered as she imagined the prospects: slaughtering animals en masse, facing starvation, or turning people away. She cleared Dev's dishes, and returned to the kitchen, pouring the remaining soup into a thermos, holding it against her body to screw on the lid. She'd grown better at functioning without the use of her left arm, a lucky thing since the doctor told her recovery would take weeks.

Dev hunkered over a gridded notebook, scribbling equations.

"Is that Dr. Goode's work?" She hadn't broached the subject with him or Sandy, but she was done holding back her opinions. She needed to be in-the-know, if she was going to be an effective leader.

"Maybe?" Dev sat back and gnawed on his pencil. "She said there was a contaminant, so we have to reverse engineer what we know of her work and rebuild from scratch."

Evelyn nodded, though she wasn't sure what he'd just said.

"Problem is, we don't know when her experiments went wrong, so we're juggling fire." He waved a hand, laughing. "Not literally. This is all on paper. We're not going to *do* anything in the lab until we're all in agreement. This has to work, or we shelve it and make the best of underground living."

Sounded pretty dang complicated, but she was proud of the work the young people were doing. One way or the other, it was all going to work out fine. "I'll come by later, Dev."

Dev waved as she left, head back down in his papers. "Please give my love to your daughter."

She carried the thermos out with her, nodding at Professor Benson on his way to meet with Dev. "See you soon."

The elevators hadn't been repaired from fire damage, so she was forced to take the stairs. Fortunately, the infirmary was on the second floor, not far from Dev's place on the third. Evelyn tapped lightly and pushed open the door. Dr. Fulknier snoozed on a cot near Sandy and Floyd. She jerked awake with a gasp, rubbing her face and standing. "Evelyn, I hope you're taking care of yourself during all this."

"I'm fine, doctor." A bit of a stretch. Her shoulder ached, her hip oozed. She'd have Dr. Fulknier examine her before she left. She set down the thermos. "Some chicken soup."

Dr. Fulknier removed the lid and drank directly from the container, barely stopping to breathe. "Thanks."

"How are they?" Evelyn had been afraid to ask about their condition during her first visit, certain Floyd would die. The doc had warned her to prepare for the worst. He was gut-shot and had lost a lot of blood, and was ashy and shrunken under the white hospital sheet. That he was alive at all was a miracle. Professor Benton had stumbled into the stairwell looking for Alec, and Evelyn screamed at him to bring help. She'd begged Floyd not to die and applied pressure to his wound until Dr. Fulknier arrived.

"Improving." Dr. Fulknier tipped back the thermos. She crossed to a paper towel holder, snatching a rough brown towel and wiping her mouth. "Floyd's blood pressure has stabilized, and we like that." With her straightforward style and medical background, the doc should be part of the governing council, and Ev would recommend it to Dev. If he was going to keep her on the council, she'd at least have some say about its other members.

"I can sit here for a while if you want to take a break." They desperately needed more people with medical training; the doc needed back-up. Maybe Evelyn could take another person or two and drive back to Rancho Seco and try again to convince her uncle to join them at the sanctuary. Her uncle had amputated his girlfriend Cat's leg with the most rudimentary of equipment, and she was alive and well. She pressed her lips to Floyd's forehead. "He's still real warm."

"That's normal. His body's fighting infection. I've got him on IV antibiotics. Good thing Dev's father stocked this place well before he died."

Evelyn moved to Sandy's bed. Both her daughter's eyes were swollen and purple. Evelyn squeezed the metal bed rail until her fingers whitened. If she hadn't already killed Alec, she'd have beaten him senseless for hurting her daughter. Sandy mumbled and her eyelids fluttered. Evelyn leaned close. "Sandy? Can you hear me?"

Sandy opened her eyes, one of them clotted with blood. The knot in Evelyn's gut loosened and relief flooded through her. Finally, her daughter was awake.

Dr. Fulknier walked to the bed, pressing her fingers to Sandy's wrist and checking her watch. She placed her stethoscope to Sandy's chest. "Heartbeat is strong and regular." She lifted her index finger. "Sandy, can you follow this?"

Sandy's eyes widened, tracking the path of Dr. Fulknier's digit. "Where's Dev? I want to see him." She struggled to rise.

"Sandy." Dr. Fulknier placed her hand where her stethoscope had been. "You're in the infirmary. Your vitals are good, and Dev is fine. He's recuperating in your apartment."

Evelyn patted her daughter's hand. "Dev's fine, I promise. He told me to send his love."

"Is he mad at me because I won't marry him?" Sandy's eyes grew wet. "Is that why he's not here?"

"No, sweetie." Evelyn poured a cup of water, holding a straw to Sandy's mouth. It had been years since her daughter allowed her to behave like an actual mother. For Evelyn, there was no surer sign of reconciliation. Despite all the recent woe, her heart expanded with gratitude. "Dev has to keep his leg stable, but he needs to meet with people and the doctor won't allow him to do it in here."

"Scout's honor." Dr. Fulknier held up three fingers. "Evelyn, I'd like to take you up on your offer, go grab a shower. I'll be back in fifteen minutes." The doctor left, her rubber soles squeaking on the vinyl floor.

"I'm so thirsty." Sandy smacked her lips together. "I don't really remember anything after we left the council meeting."

Evelyn gave her another sip of water. "Alec knocked you unconscious and set fire to the electrical and agricultural rooms. He shot Dev and Floyd and came for me."

"But not the lab?"

Evelyn knew nothing about a physical lab. "Not the lab," she lied.

Sandy rubbed her temples. "Dev was right about Alec. I guess that'll teach us to listen to him next time. What happened to the freak?"

There was no point sugar-coating her actions. Sandy would find out soon enough. Hopefully, she wouldn't judge too harshly. "He aimed a gun at Floyd, and I killed him."

Sandy roused herself and looked her mom dead in the eye. "Good. I hope you don't feel bad about it, the way you always do, Mother. Sounds like you didn't have a choice."

"I didn't and I don't." She hadn't thought about it at all. At the critical moment, her body had taken over and did what needed doing. She'd sunk a knife into Alec's belly, and when that hadn't done the trick, she'd picked up the gun he'd dropped and shot him. She wasn't going to second guess her actions, now or in the future. It didn't matter that he was seventeen and traumatized, or perhaps mentally ill. Floyd's life was in danger, and if she had to kill a dozen teenagers to protect him, she'd do it again in a second.

"That's progress, Mother." Sandy sniffed. "Dev asked me to marry him. Maybe I should've said yes."

"Not if you don't want to, Sandy. You've never done that in your life. Why start now?"

"I do love him. Maybe it's more important now with the world falling apart to hold onto certain traditions."

"Or maybe it's important to get rid of the old ways. Find the things that truly make you happy in this new world."

Sandy yawned. "Ouch." She touched fingertips to her bruised face. "I'm a damn mess, aren't I?"

"You're definitely catching up with the rest of us. The good news is you'll heal. The first week of the disaster, I fell into a pit at Floyd's house, and got into a fight with a teenaged girl who bit me in the face." She traced the oval on her cheek where Raven had chomped her.

Sandy grimaced. "Ew. She bit your face?" Sandy sputtered a small giggle then stopped. "Oh, don't make me laugh. It hurts. I can't believe she bit your face."

Evelyn gripped her middle. "It sure wasn't at the time, but it's a little funny now."

When Dr. Fulknier returned, she checked Evelyn's wounds. The shoulder was healing but her hip wasn't. The doc gave her an antibiotic shot and changed her bandages. "I know you can't really stay off it but try to take rest breaks throughout the day."

"I'll do my best. Please let me know if anything changes with Floyd. I'm off to meet Professor Benson in the ag area." The descent down to the tenth floor took forever. Evelyn trembled as images from her fateful time in the stairwell with Alec flashed.

She stopped on the ninth floor, where the classrooms were located and found the art studio. It was rudimentary in terms of supplies—a variety of paper, charcoals, pastels, watercolors and acrylic paints. The lighting was good. She could teach drawing and perhaps a few tactile arts. There was plasticine clay but eventually, they'd run out of it, as well as the paints. She'd add art supplies to the list to give to scouting groups, though they weren't top priority. There was plenty of granite everywhere around them, so in theory, they'd never run out of surfaces for sculpting, but tools were another matter. The granite would wear them down and eventually render them unusable. And of course, sculpting wouldn't be appropriate for the younger students. In the meantime, she sketched a few ideas on construction paper.

She imagined a memorial to the people they'd lost along the way: Dana, Dr. Goode, Jack, and so many others. There were areas around the complex of rough granite that could be carved with names and dates, perhaps even images. She was in the early stages of planning and hadn't decided on anything yet. She'd need to heal first and every new arrival meant more people who'd want their loved ones memorialized. She left her drawings on the table and headed downstairs.

The professor waited for her near the stairwell, holding a clipboard similar to Dev's. He brushed a lock of dark hair back from his forehead. "Evelyn, how are you holding up? How's Sandy?"

"Awake, thank goodness." She clapped a hand over her heart. "Dr. Fulknier says she can go home tomorrow. I'm so relieved."

"That's great news." He looked down at his brown leather boots. "I feel just awful about everything. I had no idea Alec was capable of that."

"None of us did. He screamed at my daughter, and she advocated for him to stay. Said he was a brilliant biochemist." Evelyn didn't want to discuss Alec anymore. "What's the damage down here?" She walked toward the fishery area.

The remaining fish tank resembled an above-ground swimming pool. The other two lay in a melted, blackened mess on the floor, scenting the room with a gagging, burned-rubber aroma. "I've been searching the various storage areas for spare parts. Filters, hoses, et cetera." He ran his hand over his beard. "Right now, what we need more than a biochemist are a couple of skilled handymen."

"Dev mentioned he invited folks from the maintenance crew at the college." She toed the melted plastic, stuck to the concrete floor.

"Let's hope they start arriving. The damage to the greenhouse area isn't as bad." He led her into the next room. Hoses had been severed, and Alec had smashed much of the hydroponic equipment to bits, but the metal garden beds were unharmed.

"Do we have enough equipment to grow food for all the people who might live here?" Fatigue dragged at her limbs.

The professor removed his glasses, wiping them on his shirt tail.

Circles bagged around his eyes. "Honestly, I can't say. Dev and I have been reviewing his father's plans, but we don't know yet."

Evelyn sighed. "We need an acquisition committee." She missed Dana every day, and now more than ever. The former soldier would've been the perfect person to lead a group out to gather supplies.

"Yes, and for that we need more people, and then we'll have to figure out how to feed them." He put his glasses back on.

"We do have a huge stockroom of food." Alec hadn't damaged too much of the canned goods. She touched the key in her pocket. Until Sandy was back on her feet, Evelyn was in charge of controlling distribution. "And we'll have to set limits as to how much people can eat."

They finished their tour of the ag area and climbed the stairs back to the first floor and the main conference room. Frank, Dr. Fulknier's sixteen-year-old-son jumped to his feet when they entered, pointing at the computer screen in front of him. "We've got visitors."

A line of vehicles waited behind the stone barricade at the end of the dirt road that led to the bunker; a van towing a small trailer, a pick-up truck, and three SUVs. "Faculty and students from the School of Mines. They've got a parking sticker on the windshield." Frank focused the security camera closer on the lead vehicle.

The professor leaned closer to the computer screen. "Definitely from School of Mines. That's Dr. Meyer driving the van, with his wife, son and daughter and, I'm guessing three students. That's Chester Raymond, facilities engineer, in the pick-up. Not sure about the others, but they've all got parking decals."

"Facilities engineer? As in maintenance? Finally, some good news." She limped toward the bunker entrance, where the professor helped her strap on Kevlar and another pistol, easing a rifle onto her good shoulder while the Professor geared up.

Frank had followed them. "Can I come?" He was six feet, two inches, all lank, with bushy black hair and three struggling chin whiskers. He'd gotten some of the computers back on-line, allowing them to monitor the entrance.

"We need you to stay here, keep an eye on Mission Control." The Professor had renamed the main conference room.

"The Professor's right. You're our computer whiz. We need you to keep working to get everything back up and operational. Keep an eye on the monitors. If things go sideways outside, shut down the entrance. Leave us out there if it means protecting the bunker. Page Fred, will you?"

Fred Scott had been part of Dr. Fulknier's group. A former Army Reservist and logistics analyst, he understood the importance of discipline, systems, and order. He joined them a few minutes later. He smelled of Ivory soap, his mahogany skin moist from a shower. He wore full battle regalia: camouflage vest with a module that extended up to protect his neck, and shoulders. He'd shaved a lighting bolt into the gray hairs of his Afro.

Evelyn clicked her tongue. "Looking sharp, Fred."

He cocked his head. "One likes to put on their Sunday best when the day calls for it."

Evelyn, the Professor, and Fred headed to Dev's pickup, Evelyn and the professor climbing into the cab, Fred hopping in back. The professor drove to the tunnel, the security gate rising with a clang.

Evelyn strapped the seatbelt over herself. "More people will be arriving soon. We need to get a crew together for intake. I'm thinking of putting Fred in charge of that."

"Good choice. He's mature and experienced. Won't lose his head if ... something goes wrong."

Evelyn had assumed that once they arrived at the bunker, they'd all be safe. She'd been careless, and it nearly cost her everything. In the future, each plan they made, every system they set in place would have a back-up plan to protect the people she loved. "Soon, I'll be taking more of an overseer position, less hands on. Same for you."

"Aye, aye, Cap'n." The professor gripped the steering wheel as they bounced down the pitted dirt road to meet the new arrivals.

CHAPTER TWENTY-SEVEN

Alma Garcia. Harmony Ranch, Arizona

Emelia burst out from the house with Matias, and Alma pulled them into a tight hug. "I'm never going to let you go ever again."

"I was so frightened." Mati clung to her.

"I had to tell him. I'm sorry I broke my promise." Em pulled her closer.

"I'm sorry I made you promise it." Alma kissed Emelia's cheek. "You saved me. If you hadn't... If Kit hadn't found me, everything would be so different."

Emelia clung so tight that it squeezed the air from her, but Alma basked in her affection and love. Her family had survived. "I guess He heard our prayers then."

"Of course. And He brought reinforcements, too." Emelia pointed to the side of the workshop. Simeon was speaking with Doc.

Matias danced through the crowd milling around the main yard. He flung himself at their friend. Simeon jerked back, looked down at Matias, then searched the crowd. A wide smile brightened his grime-smeared face when he saw her, and he ran over, Matias at his heels.

Alma rushed forward and met him at the destroyed chicken coop.

"How?" It was a reasonable question, but nowhere near all that she wanted to know.

Simeon scooped her up, hugging her tight. "Thank goodness you're safe."

He smelled of sweat and desert. Heat flushed her cheeks. "How did you find us?"

He set her back on her feet. "You said you were north of Flagstaff at a ranch." He frowned at her. "You got us, well, me, all worried when you cut me off and then didn't answer when I rang back. We avoided all the towns, just like you said, and took the back routes toward Flagstaff. Thank goodness, Mom remembered the news when a white woman was able to buy the ranch out from under the tribe who was supposed to get it. She thought the new name, Harmony Ranch, was terribly ironic."

"I told you to go to the bunkers." He should have saved his family.

"That's where we're heading. This was a tiny diversion. You didn't expect me to just leave, did you?" Simeon brushed her cheek, leaving a trail of warmth burning her skin. "Mom already had the family half packed. Dad's death and the fiery water set us in motion. She wasn't planning on staying, but didn't know where to go. Your call gave her the answer. When I told her about the bunkers, she said she knew the place. Mom and Dad took us on a tour as part of that vacation when I was a kid. She said it was a brilliant solution, big enough to house hundreds of people. Alma, the world has gone crazy, and you call me to tell me where to find a refuge. Did you really think I would go there without you?"

"Did you bring everything?" Matias tugged at his sleeve.

Emelia pulled Matias away from Simeon and held him close to her by his shoulders. "What about your animals?"

Simeon stepped closer and lowered his voice. "Gramps' truck was all we needed. It's hooked up with the trailer and most of the goats and sheep. Ruth is following behind with the horses and Jude on his ATV keeping them safe. The back roads and tracks are rough. I would've got here sooner if I stuck to the highway, maybe, but I took what you said seriously. You were right. There were plenty of fires lighting up the rural areas. Traveling through the night probably worked in our favor, though. Those beacons told us the places to avoid. We only saw a few people and steered clear."

"I guess having a big family worked for you." Alma had wanted to run when Simeon's family had surrounded her and the van. "Your lot are intimidating."

"I wouldn't mess with you." He touched the strap of the hanging rifle. "I figured we'd be a target because of the livestock and gas. We drained the fuel tank on the farm into as many cans as we could carry, loaded the truck with food, tools and anything we thought might be useful, then locked up and left." He lowered his hand. "I don't think we'll see the place again."

People milled around the yard, but Chrissy and her baby weren't among them. "Where's your mom? Did they get hurt?"

"When I got here at dawn, I saw way too many armed people skulking around. I scouted on foot and found the back trail into your place, then relied on speed and luck to fly down it on the ATV. I told Mom to get away before the battle, but now that you've sort of won, she came back." He pointed at the back gate. "She's at the truck with Malachi, Martha, and the others, hidden near Highway 89. Ruth thought she should come and help, but I made her stay behind too. I don't want to leave them for too long. Let's go."

A crowd of Harmony Ranchers had formed by the barn door and Kit had climbed up on a hay bale. He lifted his arms and the people hushed. His voice was stronger than it had ever been, and the people listened and shuffled when he told them about leaving the ranch. Kit seemed to think Martinez's crew wouldn't wait three days, and Alma was inclined to agree. They'd been kicked out by a bunch of locals and when once they'd licked their wounds and realized how scrawny the Harmony Ranch crew was, they'd be back.

Alma gripped Simeon's arm. "Martinez is dead, but his men are out there. You've got to get your family out of their way."

Simeon nodded and trotted to his ATV tucked down the side of the barn. Alma, Emelia, and Matias followed. He pulled out the radio mike from the dash and turned away from Alma. "Mama Bear, Baby Bear One."

Emelia laughed, and Alma nudged her in the ribs. Chrissy was in danger.

"Go, Baby One." Chrissy's voice trembled with an edge of concern.

"All's good, but you've got to get here. Avoid armed folk heading out of the ranch. Should be going north mostly, but they won't be happy. Don't let them mess with you. Copy?"

"Copy all. Are you safe?"

"For now. Alma, Emelia, and Matias are safe too. Come up if you can. I think we can help."

"Copy that. I'll be there as soon as I can. Out."

Simeon turned back to her and she couldn't help but beam at him. "You'll help us all leave?"

"Mom said the bunkers are big enough for all of us. I'm not going to leave without you. And, there's strength in numbers. I think we'll be safer if everyone travels together." He pulled her in for a hug. "Besides, if you folks can stop a militia, I reckon my family is safer with you."

Alma laughed; the sound strange in a yard full of death and uncertainty, and one she hadn't made for an age. She could grab joy with Martinez and Eric unable to chase them. The world around her was crumbling, but that piece of safety made all the difference.

Chrissy arrived at the gate almost an hour later, baby swaddled and strapped close to her body. Matias spotted her first from his perch on the fence. Alma and Simeon vouched for her with the gate guard, and he let her in. She scanned the yard littered with the remnants of battle and stained with blood and scowled at the battered ranchers moving slowly, almost aimlessly, from house to barn and into the pastures.

"Alma!" Chrissy gave her a one-armed embrace and a small wave to Emelia and Matais. "Are you coming with us?"

"If you'll have us." Having a responsible adult to lean on was a dream come true.

Chrissy laughed and nudged Simeon, who was shaking his head at his mother. "We didn't come all this way to leave without you." She smoothed her hand over the downy hair of her baby. "This little one will want to know why we named her Alma-Ruth after all." The tiny baby squirmed. "She's already a bit of a rebel, just like her dad."

Alma leaned close to the little bundle, and her cheeks burned. She offered a prayer that the little mite would grow up more like Ruth than be anything like herself. Alma stepped away and bowed her head. "I'm sorry for your loss."

"And yours too." Chrissy tugged Alma back and squeezed her hand.

Death colored the earth in the yard. Darker patches stained the dirt where Harmony ranchers or invaders fell. A team moved the Rancher bodies to a shady spot beside the barn for burial while others gathered the bodies of Martinez's army into a pile near the front gate. Some deaths she welcomed. Eric and Martinez couldn't chase her to the bunkers. It was time to live.

Simeon rubbed his bristled chin. "Change of plan, Mom."

Chrissy twisted and frowned at Alma. "Why? The bunkers you told Simeon about are a great idea."

"I'm coming with you. But it won't just be my family." Alma tightened her ponytail. "It won't just be me, Emelia and Matias." Her throat prickled with her correction. "Kit, who leads the ranch, he wants as many of us as possible to go, too."

Chrissy rubbed Alma's arm and gazed around the open space again. "How many of you are there?"

Alma had never taken the time to count and since she had always been the outsider, hadn't noted how many mouths Taylor had fed or chores Kit had dished out. "Maybe 25 or 30." There were children around too. It could be closer to 40. "I don't know. Will that matter?"

"It might." Chrissy stroked her baby's fist. "The bunkers will hold a few hundred, maybe, but we won't be the only ones heading that way."

Alma wondered how many others the scientists had told of the safe place underground and a stab of anxiety twisted Alma's gut. "Do you think we are too late? Will it be full?"

"I wasn't asking because there wouldn't be space, but I guess you're right. We might be too late."

Simeon tutted at Chrissy. "Mom wanted to know how many to see if we had enough space for people to travel with us."

Alma turned to Chrissy. "Do you?"

Chrissy shook her head. "Not really. We've got the old truck packed with our things and the remaining fuel, pulling the horse trailer. But we're almost out of diesel. We might have enough to reach the bunkers, but there's no guarantee. And we've barely got enough gas for the ATVs."

Simeon scratched his chin. "We can't share the gasoline. We'll need to send scouts out ahead of the group for safety. We're going to attract attention for sure."

Emelia picked up a hen scratching the dirt by her toes. "There's a difference in fuel?"

"Oh yeah! You don't want to use the wrong type. It damages the engine." Simeon nodded.

Emelia leaned close to Alma and lowered her voice. "Do you think we put the wrong fuel in the van?"

Alma raised her brows. The transit van engine had smoked, forcing them to abandon it while they were being chased. Em had found the fuel. It made sense of the sudden breakdown. Emelia's eyes widened, and the hen squirmed in her arms.

It didn't matter; the van was long gone, and Em needed confidence. Alma smoothed the bird's ruffled feathers. "I don't think so. We bashed the van up. It wasn't anything you did."

"If we have to, we can leave some animals and use the livestock trailer. The horses can pull it." Simeon was talking to his mother.

Chrissy frowned. "No. If the bunker is filling up, they'll need a reason to let us in." She reached over to the hen, too. "If we have food, or means to make food, We'll be in a better position to barter our way in."

"So we should take goats, hens, cows and people?" Emelia huffed. "Like that won't be difficult! Even if Miss Jen agrees, it'll be a tough journey with all those beaks and claws and hooves."

Animals cooped up underground didn't seem like a brilliant idea, but until they had to descend into the bunker to escape the threatened winter, perhaps the beasts could provide for them. Milk, cheese and eggs were a luxury they couldn't afford to squander or abandon. Those already at the bunker might think the same. Who knew, perhaps even after they buried themselves, they would be able to care for the animals. Either way, she wouldn't want to leave them for Martinez's people.

Matias lifted his chin to Simeon. "Can we make trailers for the people out of another vehicle and get the horses to pull it?"

Simeon shrugged. "Maybe. Take out the engine and lighten the load, figure out a way to attach harnesses."

Matias pointed to the pitted feed shed which was still in one piece. "There are chicken crates in there and food for the goats."

"It's probably not going to be comfortable for the livestock, but we could squeeze a few more in the trailer." Chrissy shrugged. "We'll let them out in the pen if we need to stop."

"It's not going to be comfortable for the humans either." Simeon laughed. "But we'll manage."

"And we have tents." Emelia turned toward the pasture where their tents were previously pitched. "They're packed up already."

Chrissy nodded. "It's not forever after all."

"I think we have the beginnings of a plan. Let's see what Kit and Taylor think." Alma walked toward the house and beckoned the others to follow.

CHAPTER TWENTY-EIGHT

Catherine "Cat" Murphy. Heading toward the bunker

"I hate to do this." Cat leaned up against the wood-pole fence as Tom opened all the stall doors and switched the horses, then the cattle out into the yard.

"Yup." They'd come at the problem five ways from Sunday, but they couldn't both defend themselves from road pirates and create a critter wagon train. Something had to give and that something turned out to be the animals Van Zant had been so careful to keep alive along with the stock they'd been hauling in the back of their trailer. Tom circled the property one last time, making sure there were no gates left locked and no doors unopened. "God protect and keep them."

"Amen to that." It was a gut punch to watch the horses take off over the field, knowing what was out there. They weren't wild creatures who knew how to fend for themselves and the world was offering less and less in the way of God's bounty.

Tom helped her position her new leg, offered her the broom—its brush wrapped in some of Van Zant's gorgeous felt, and grunted as he fixed a massive backpack onto his shoulders.

"I feel kinda wimpy, just carrying this sack." Tom had given her a couple of bottles of water and some dried fruit they'd found in the back of a cupboard, but insisted that she needed to keep her eyes on the road and nothing more.

"Yeah, real wimpy to cross uneven terrain on one leg. I'd say you were up for Slacker of the Year!" He tipped his hat to the property as they left, an old-fashioned gesture that warmed her heart clean through. Belle stayed close, even as the livestock took off, her nose to the ground, with the occasional check in with her main man. That dog loved him more than butter!

With no maps and only the word of Tom's Great Niece to go by, they navigated on two parts sun position and one part trust. He insisted they stick to the road, insofar as that was possible, arguing that "Someone has already done the thinking for us. They don't build roads for their own amusement. This is going to be the fastest way."

Yeah, fastest way if you're in a vehicle, but not if you had a hale and healthy companion who could hike the way the crow flies.

"Given any thought to what you want to do when we get there?" They'd spent the night searching Andy's place for anything they could carry, all the while chatting about what they could barter with, once they had no cattle or provisions. "We come empty handed..."

"I'm going to apply for the position of camp astrologer." That at least got her a snort-laugh. But what else was she good for? She could stir a pot, but she'd die of boredom if they stuck her in the kitchen.

"Depends on whose there, but I'm ready to do whatever needs to be done." There was so much he could turn his hand to, they'd snap him right up. She had to find something she was half-way good at that could be done from a perch or a stool. The idea that she might be deadweight for others to fetch and carry for was more than she could bear.

Cat gulped down her horror. "Can we pause a second?"

"Nope." Tom took his rucksack off and perched it against the nearest tree. "Two seconds or more, but not less." He wasn't going to let her get away with being maudlin or self-pitying, but wasn't about to ruin his chance of making it to the bunkers before they closed the doors. Neither of them had said it out loud, but she knew he'd heard that bit loud and clear, too. Time wasn't on their side and no matter what the road—or her leg—put in their way, they had to soldier on.

Belle had gone on a few steps, but she circled back as soon as they stepped off the path and made her way to Tom's side, folding her forepaws and leaning her head on his lap.

"Dang! I forgot to treat her!" They had a tiny First Aid kit, but she wasn't sure there was anything to treat a dog with.

"Belle? She's good. I gave her a massage and a hot-cloth press before we left."

"Water?" She unscrewed the lid and handed him a bottle. "D'you think the horses found the creek?"

He took a long draught of his water. "Not thinking on that."

She turned her head away. Their lives had been so rich, so full of all the things she loved—the ranch, the market-to-table business, him running things so smoothly she barely knew they needed running—that she'd taken it all for granted, numbing herself with liquor rather than face the fact that she had deep, deep feelings. For the land, for the livestock, for her life, and for him.

She hiked her butt over the gnarled roots of the tree and leaned herself against him, lacing her fingers through his. "Sorry."

"You ain't got nothing to be sorry about, hon." If anyone else had said it, she'd have thought it a brush off, but his heart was big enough to forgive her for years of what amounted to emotional neglect. He'd been there, loving her all along, and she'd let that time slip by.

"This marriage thing?"

He turned to face her, eyes smiling. "Yup?"

"What does it mean?"

Tom burst out laughing, a hand to his ribs until the episode ended in a coughing spasm. "Well, when a man loves a woman very much..."

She batted him with her hand. "I mean, you've already had the worst of me. I figure you'd best not sign up for more than that."

"There ain't nothing you can bring that's worse than what I done, Cat Murphy. You're safe with me." He didn't talk about his drinking days, but she was starting to get the picture. He'd been where she'd lived—the bottom of a bottle—and come out the other side, smelling of leather and starch. She let the twin aromas twist into her brain, glad that she hadn't been fool enough to stay in her own way until it was too late.

She took a couple of sips of water. Not so much that she'd regret it later, but enough to wet her tongue and remind her throat that there were better days ahead. At least, that was her hope. The dried fruit was sweeter than any fruit had call to be, but that was because they'd been living on scraps and leftovers, with rice and eggs and beans to keep them going.

In the meadow below, a horse galloped at full tilt, its mane flapping and flowing and its tail almost a straight line out back of its haunches. "I might never see that again."

Tom took hold of her hand and flattened her palm. "I never figured you for the diamonds and gold type of gal." Her heart fluttered in her chest. He opened his fist and let a ring of woven grasses fall into her hand. "It won't last, but it'll have to do until we make it to the bunkers."

It was a delicate piece of whimsy, stronger than a daisy chain, but more fragile than a woven basket. She slid it onto her finger and kissed it. "I love it."

"I'll make you a real one."

She didn't need a ring to be wed to this man. She was already there, she'd just been blind to it. She dug in her pack and pulled out a D-ring which she'd snagged when she was stumping behind him in Andy's stables. "It's the height of fashion." She slid it onto his ring finger. "I hear all the cool kids are wearing them these days."

Again with that laugh. It rumbled from a place so deep in him, it had to be pure. "I've never been called 'cool' before." He turned his hand over, admiring the piece of nonsense she'd given him. "That's not a bad idea, Cat."

"Huh?"

"You with the herbs and me with the metal."

"You say the nicest things!"

"No, think about it. If they've got a lick of sense, they'll have some kind of hydroponic set up, so they can grow indoors. That'd be perfect for you. You've got the greenest thumb of anyone I know."

Everything that came out of Tom's mouth made her glad and his vision of her future was no exception. "I'd like that."

"And they're going to need stuff fixing." He hadn't stopped rolling her fingers through his. "But, like I said, if they want me to make meringues or stand by a door and keep the coyotes at bay, I'll do what needs doing."

She leaned her head on his shoulder, this time closer than before. "You've always done the needful, haven't you?"

"If it's got to get done, hon, someone's got to do it."

She'd never thought of her foreman as someone who did things he didn't want to, but running her property wasn't all wine and roses. *Come to think of it, there was none of that!* Cat was shot through with a pang of guilt. She'd thought herself a good boss—strong, independent, and respectful—but she'd been fooling herself. She was self-centered, aloof, and willfully ignorant.

He touched her chin and steered her face to his. "Where's that brain of yours taking you now?"

She shrugged. *No place new. And no place useful!* She found a smile and offered it up. "I'm thinking about my herb garden."

"If I had words, I'd make the savory sweet and the sweets a delight."

She frowned. It wasn't like Tom to come on all poetic. "Is that from a play?"

He blushed. "I want this moment to be the moment we remember forever."

"But..." She didn't need him any way but the way he was. He was right, she was no diamond girl and she never would be.

"I don't forget anything you say." It was true. She remembered his patience, his temper, his kindness, his insistence that she shape up and stop drowning herself. She tapped her temple. "It's all up here."

"Good." He kissed her, gently at first, but then with a measure of passion she hadn't known since she was a young woman. "Then remember this; I love you, Cat Murphy and whether you're a Murphy still or a Callahan, now, you're mine."

Her heart, which had already been in a state of riot, rose to her throat. "Are you saying we're wed, Tom Callahan?"

Belle nosed between them, wiggling to get Cat's hand away from Tom's.

"She seems to think so. Never had to share me before, but she's going to now."

Cat reached for the dog's head and ruffled her ears. "Don't you worry, little one, he's yours as much as he's mine. We're all Callahans, now."

Tom stood and pulled her to her feet. "Bunkers or bust?"

"You betcha." She tucked the broom under her arm, let Tom help her on with her miniature backpack, and made an oath. *I'm going to make this man proud of me, if it's the last thing I do.*

The road would have been hard for an able-bodied person, but it was hell on wheels for a chair-legged broad. She didn't cuss or complain, but she didn't talk either. He made them stop at regular intervals, checking her stump and slathering it with balm, but he was as quiet as she was sore and together, they trudged on.

"Figure we head up this way." How he knew where to go wasn't something she questioned, but the rise looked awful steep. "Get on." He turned and offered her his back.

She wanted, more than anything, to say she could manage on her own, but she couldn't. She sidestepped Belle and wrapped her arms around Tom's neck, letting him hike her up his back until she was halfway comfortable.

"Sorry." He bent at the knees, lowering her to the ground. "We're going to have to take your leg off."

"You say the most romantic things, Mr. Callahan." She unbuckled the ridiculous contraption that had served her so well, tucking it across the top of her pack while she leaned on him.

"Arms around my neck and hold tight."

Belle barked a couple of times and ran on ahead, circling back every few hundred yards to make sure they were still behind her.

"She's picked up a scent."

Cat couldn't see much over Tom's shoulder, but she didn't need to; she was in the best hands.

"Halt!" It was the moment they'd known was coming, but it was still a shock to the system. Whoever barked at them was out of sight, but loud enough that they had to be close by.

"Just lowering my load. I can't raise my hands." Tom bent at the knees and waited while Cat got her balance. He took the time to help her reattach her leg before turning to the trail and raising his hands. "My great-niece, Sandy, told me about this place."

"Sandy?" A man crept from behind a tree, rifle in hand but not pointed in their general direction. "You're family?"

"Yup." Tom took his Stetson off, slow as you like, and held it out to one side. "Take a good look. Tell her Thomas Callahan made it."

The static of walkie-talkies filled the space between them, but even Belle held her tongue while they waited.

"Uncle Tom!" The shout from the thick of the trees was ear shattering.

Cat laughed as Evelyn hobbled across the space between them.

"You're here! I didn't think you'd come." There was a young man behind her; he'd been introduced back at Rancho Seco, but she couldn't remember his name. "Dev! Take his pack. Oh, wow! Where are the little ones?"

A lump rose in Cat's throat. They'd allowed themselves to be talked into leaving those poor kids behind.

"They're sticking with the land." Tom inched his hat back on and helped Cat up the rise. "We tried to tell them they were welcome here, but some people ain't cut out for change."

The entrance to the bunkers was well hidden. No one who didn't already know about the place could stumble on it, except by a fluke of luck.

Evelyn, who Cat had taken a shine to when they met, was at the door to the underground home. "Hey there!" She embraced Tom and opened her arms to Cat. "Are you a hugger?"

Not before, but I guess I am now? She let the woman take her in her arms and was surprised at the ferocity of the hug.

"I'm glad you came. We need another rancher. Getting things to grow is going to be one of our major challenges." She waved into the gloom of the tunnel beyond. "I hope you don't mind?"

A man, a few years younger than Evelyn, wheeled out what could only be described as a joke. It was an office chair, or at least it had been once, fitted with what looked like bicycle wheels. "We've tried to make it as smooth a ride as possible, but there are some kinks to work out."

Tom stepped up, inspecting her new ride. "That's an easy fix! Needs some shocks and a brake. Give me an afternoon and I'll have it done." He scooped her off her feet and deposited her in the chair. "Not bad for a first iteration."

The guy laughed. "That's my fourth try!" He held out his hand. "But you're welcome all the same!"

There was little enough sun to say goodbye to, but Cat knew she wasn't going to make it topside much—if ever again. *To the trees, that I've loved without knowing how much. The earth that rumbles but still sustains. To the water, the air, and the beasts that roam, thank you.* The outdoors life, which in some sense she'd squandered, was closing down and in its place, winding corridors, dimly lit, but people full of welcome and joy.

"This is for you, Ms. Murphy." Evelyn threw open a door into a modest, but clean room.

Tom reached around her, closing the steel door. "Married quarters, now, thank you." He held up his left hand, the D-ring still firmly on his wedding finger.

Cat held hers up, the grasses fluttering into her lap.

"Just have to marry you all over again!" he whispered, wheeling her toward their joint quarters.

"This calls for a celebration! We've got a bottle of bubbly somewhere!" Evelyn grinned, broadly.

"Not for me." Cat muttered.

Tom kneaded her shoulder.

"But if you've got any coffee left? I'd give my other leg for a decent cup of joe."

The doors opened on their room. It was similar to the one Evelyn had shown them, but housed a queen-sized bed, rather than a single.

"Need some time to freshen up?" Evelyn hovered in the doorway. "There's running water, but don't complain to management if it isn't hot. We're working on it."

"I'm your man." Tom shook Evelyn's hand.

No. You're MY man, Tom Callahan.

Sandy stuck her head in the door. "I'm off to help prepare the feast, but I just wanted to say, it's perfect that you came. I mean it. We've been talking about what's missing and who does what, and the two of you..." She pressed her fingers to her lips and blew them a kiss.

The door closed on the chatter and Cat was alone with Tom. This time, as his wife.

"I couldn't agree more." He sat on the edge of the bed. "Perfect."

Cat rolled her eyes. She was many things, but perfect wasn't one of them. "You exaggerate, Mr. Callahan. I'm doing better, but I—"

He was over the room and scooping her from the chair in an instant. "Stop. I'm not listening. You agreed to be my wife, and that makes you perfect in my eyes."

She buried her head in his shoulder. "But..." *You waited so long. And I was such a butthead about it all. You deserve better.*

"Everything comes to he who waits, Mrs. Callahan. Remember that. I waited for the best, and that's what I got. The best."

Dang. He wasn't going to let up. "Okay. Well, here's the best I can do. I'm more than glad, Tom. More than. I never thought I'd deserve another go at life and I couldn't have imagined anyone would roll the dice on a broke down broad like me, but seeing as it's you, I'm going to take you at your word, and give it all I've got."

She held on to him, willing the moment to last forever. She'd made it home, finally, and was glad.

CHAPTER TWENTY-NINE

Kit Walsh. Harmony Ranch, Arizona

In the early morning hours, two of Stone's team took Kit's watch at the top of the bluff overlooking Harmony Ranch. He slept a couple of hours, wrangled disputes, and made hard decisions on what to take and what to leave, and consulted with Mati and Simeon on how to make the most of their remaining vehicles and animals. But a lot of his time was spent reminding people that they'd have to carry what they brought, and water was the most important, followed by food.

Robin stepped forward, Ladybug at her heels. The girl had been a shadow, skulking at the edges of his consciousness, barely leaving Aunt Jen's side. Her face was smudged and puffy, her eyes rimmed in red. "She talks in animal, clicks and clacks. I didn't understand at first, but then I did." Smoke nudged her hand, eager for a pet. "You have to listen to what she does, not what she says."

"Sorry?"

"She's in the barn. Crying." Robin took him by the hand. "I think she needs you."

Kit allowed himself to be led, turning over how he was going to say what had to be said. 'You should have told me.' Or 'That wasn't

239

your secret to keep.' And 'He killed my mother just as sure as if he'd pulled the trigger.' Along with,'Harmony Ranch is soaked in her blood.'

"She doesn't say 'I love you,' but she let me stay in her bed, when I was scared. And she doesn't say things like, 'You're special to me,' but she tried to find my family, even though it was dangerous. She never said, 'You're safe, now, this is your home,' but she gave me jobs and let me name the dogs and made sure I had enough to eat and held my hand when she was sad."

Kit hadn't been with his aunt much, but it warmed his heart to know Robin had comforted her.

"She told me to love the land and it would love me back." Ladybug nudged her leg and she bent to scrubble the dog's ears. "She loved by doing, not by saying. That's all." She let go of him and turned toward the orchard. Ladybug hovered, torn between tending to Aunt Jen, who was her comfort, and going with the little girl, who was all sweetness and adventure.

Kit scratched the dog's ears. "Give me ten minutes alone with her, then you can have her back." Ladybug took off after Robin, woofing gently.

"Aunt Jen?" Kit stepped into the gloom of the barn. It the far corner, his aunt rose from a bale of hay, wiping her cheeks.

"Hey." Her eyes were twice as puffy as Robin's and the lines of her face had deepened overnight.

Kit's chest tightened. *She's afraid.* He reached for her and she collapsed into his hug, sobbing onto his shirt front. Whatever words were coming out of her weren't English, as far as he could tell. He stroked her hair. "It's fine... No, really. It's all going to be fine."

"I hated that secret, Christopher. Hated it. I hated what it did to your mother. To us. But most of all to you."

He shrugged. "I didn't know. And what you don't know can't hurt you."

Jen shook her head. "Not true. You thought your mother didn't love you." She paused, but he couldn't answer through the sudden frog that had set up residence in his throat. "And you thought I didn't love you, though nothing could be further from the truth." Two frogs. "But she made me promise, because she didn't want the sins of the father to be visited on the son."

Everything he'd heard about Mr. Martinez was vile. The thought of the old man putting hands on his mother made him violently ill.

"She stayed away so you'd never see that hurt in her eyes, never take that on as your burden."

Pretty much what I thought. He couldn't get the words out. What horrors his mother had endured. She'd stayed away because she was *for* him, not *against* him. It made all the difference.

Jen slipped her hand into his. "But we never get exactly what we want, do we?"

"I don't know, Aunt Jen." *I have Taylor. And you. That's pretty damned sweet.* "Will you come to the bunker with us?"

Her smile was thin and brief, the sorrow etched around her eyes.

"Think about it?" They stepped into the yard where the people of Jackrabbit Bluff raced to pack their belongings.

Jen squeezed his hand and heaved herself up the steps and into the house without another word.

Taylor was waiting for him, a frown creasing her forehead. "What was all that about?"

Kit's chest was hopping with sad-and-sorry frogs and he still couldn't talk. He wrapped an arm around her shoulders and managed to eke out a single word. "Later."

She leaned against him, leading him to their tent. "Dunia, Jaya, and Faris have organized the remaining food and useful household items for the trip. They and the factory children will travel with us, then break off south of Sedona for Page Springs. We've given them hand-copied maps of how to get to the bunkers if they can convince the other workers to come. I've talked to Simeon; we'll take turns riding in his family's vehicles; they'll probably run out of gas before we get to the bunker, but we'll get close. I think you and I will be walking most of the way, but that's okay. We'll be fine."

Kit hugged her close. "Yeah, we'll be fine. So will everyone else."

"I know you're probably going to be sad, mad, happy, and everywhere in between in the future," Taylor leaned back, looking up at him, "but I need you to know this: you are a hero. You're my hero, saving me time after time. You saved Alma's life. And you saved the lives of everyone here by taking out Martinez and giving his people a reasonable option. I love you and I'm not the only one." She snuggled in close and held him tight.

Kit reveled in the security, safety, and love of Taylor's hold. He was so lucky to have her. And even though the days to come would be hard, he'd have her light to lead the way. He kissed her and led her into the tent.

The next morning, Dunia and Doc discussed routes and alternates with Simeon's mom, while Kit and Taylor organized the wagon train. In their case, literally a wagon train. Mati had worked with some of the more mechanically inclined residents, removing the engine and transmission from a minivan and gutting one of the smaller travel trailers and hitching it to another makeshift trailer. They'd removed almost everything from the interior, taken out the windows and pulled off the top half of the siding to lighten the load, then put the mattress and seat cushions on the floor. Then they rigged up harnesses for Jen and Chrissy's horses. They filled the vehicles with water, food and horse feed, along with some makeshift seats for the children and elderly. Ruth and Jude would drive the cows at the back of the train. Simeon and Malachi would scout ahead with members of Stone's group on the ATVs to avoid Hutchinson Security, if they were still a factor, and any other problems along the way. Their route took them to the east of Flagstaff and Sedona; water would be more difficult to find, but they'd avoid major population centers.

Kit strolled through Aunt Jen's house. She was in the living room, a dog either side of her, a stack of papers in her hand. "Do you want them?" She folded one and slid it back into an envelope.

"What are they?"

"Letters from your mother. She kept in touch, though the return addresses were all dummies. She didn't want to be found, but she wanted me to know she thought about you every day."

Just when he thought it was safe to talk, his aunt landed him with another gut punch. He took the letters and tucked them into his shirt. "So, you're not coming."

Jen pushed herself off the couch. "Oh, I'm coming."

Kit's heart leaped with the force of a million grief frogs, all jumping at the same time and without warning, the two of them were babbling like a couple of babies.

"Now that I've got you back, I'm not letting you out of my sight." She pulled a backpack from behind the couch and dragged it toward the front door.

Kit took a last turn around the house. He wanted to burn it down rather than give it to the slavers, but he wouldn't. He'd honor his word. They weren't leaving a bit of food, or any other useful, light-weight items, but they were leaving a mess. It seemed fitting.

At the door, he looked back. They had to move forward and leave everything behind, including regrets. Swallowing hard, he closed the door on their old life, to march forward into a new reality. Pushing past the long line of Harmony Ranch residents lined up between the summer and back pastures, he joined Taylor, holding the reins of one of Jen's prized horses, his aunt grinning like the cat that got the cream.

Robin danced between the two women, chattering to the dogs.

Taylor raised the small radio. "Top, are we clear?"

"Base, you're clear." Stone, his spotter, and another sniper team perched on the bluffs to the south, protecting their train from raiders on the way out. Two of Simeon's ATVs waited for the sniper teams at the base of the east end of the bluff, so they could rejoin the group once the train cleared the area.

Kit stepped up on the side of the truck bed wagon. "Everybody ready?" Arms raised and whoops sounded. "Harmony Wagon Train, ho! Let's go!" Kit jumped down to the sound of cheering and children laughing.

He led them into the rising sun and a new start on life. Like every other journey, it wouldn't be easy, but with Taylor by his side, he'd not just survive, but thrive, and he'd make sure everyone else did, too. Kit took Taylor's free hand in his, and she smiled up at him. With Taylor's love, and his aunt's backing, he could do anything. He wasn't a Martinez. Not in his heart. He was a McCreedy and he planned to tell Jen just as soon as he had the chance.

CHAPTER THIRTY

Alma Garcia. Arizona

The caravan of people and makeshift wagons slogged along the fractured highway. Alma walked just ahead of Jen, Kit, and Taylor who led Jen's horses, pulling the modified minivan full of small children and the elderly, with food, water, and gear shoved between them. The gutted travel trailer followed, pulled by two more horses.

Chrissy drove their old truck, towing their livestock trailer filled with the remaining fuel, plus the goats, chickens, the animal feed and all the water containers they could find. She rolled ahead at the most efficient speed, then turned off the truck and waited for the rest of the train, striding at a brisk three miles per hour. Some of the less-mobile members of Harmony Ranch took turns riding in the back of her truck.

Ruth and Pete rode two of their horses, helping Smoke and Ladybug drive the cows and Jen's third horse behind Kit's wagons. The ATVs, driven by Simeon and Malachi, scouted ahead and watched behind them.

The walkers quickly learned to stay in front of the wagons, or end up walking through endless stinky cow patties and batting away flies.

Only a few days into their trek the hours and days passed in an unending dull slog. Get up at dawn's first light, walk until the sun was high or they found water, rest through the hottest part of the day, have a too-small meal, then walk until just before sundown or they found water. The only differences were how much Alma's feet hurt, and whether they'd find water. Where Harmony Ranch had been greens and pines, the desert was all reds and prickly pears. She could imagine that some had found the area beautiful, but at walking speed, it was both deadly hot and horribly boring. Before they left, Taylor had given her a pair of Jen's trainers, making the walking a little more bearable. Still, she was incredibly grateful for the hour of riding she was allotted. Mati and Em rode most of the time, but walked during the early hours when it was cooler. To pass the time, sometimes she spoke with the children walking near her who had escaped the Martinez slave lines with Nora's help. They should have been kindred spirits, but there was one big difference; those kids still had a glimmer of hope. Their parents might still be alive.

"We don't have the fuel for a detour." Mr. H repeated his point that evening after they gathered around the map to plan the next day's travel. He gestured to Simeon's mother. "She told us that."

Chrissy and Simeon had measured the red diesel and gasoline they had brought with them from the farm while the rest of their family dug up vegetable plants and transplanted them into pots, found water containers and helped strip the ranch bare of anything useful. Simeon's family had brought enough fuel to get their family convoy to the bunkers and perhaps a little farther, if it turned out there was no room for them. But they didn't have enough to return home.

"Then we all walk when it runs out." Taylor crossed her arms and stared Mr. H down. "These children were stolen from their families. I'm not going to tell them we drove away from their parents because you wouldn't share what we have been given." She gestured to Simeon's mother. "Chrissy didn't need to share her precious fuel or help us in anyway. She has every right to drive straight to the mountain bunker and save her family. But Chrissy agrees with us. We will reunite those children with their parents."

"We travel together and keep as many of us alive as we can." Chrissy sat on a rock, nursing her baby. "There has been too much death and I will not be responsible for more."

Dunia stepped forward and tapped a tiny spot on the map called Happy Jack. "What if we stop near here, and let the caravan rest, hunt and gather? Then the ATVs could go to Page Springs with the news. I would go with them. The ATVs will come back to you. If my Page Spring friends decide the bunkers are the right decision, then I'll lead them back here. If they decide to stay, I'll come back with the ATVs and Jaya, Faris and I will lead the children on foot to Page Springs, using the route markers we will leave on the way back. If the Page Springs people decide to go, then we will pack everything and join you. Either way, you continue south after the ATVs return. You can leave a marking of some sort to show me your path."

Simeon traced the route Dunia pointed out. "That's only forty miles or so. Depending on the terrain, the two ATVs would use ten or eleven gallons of gas for the round trip and take a little under two hours. That's not much, really. Do you think Page Springs might have some fuel?"

Dunia shrugged. "I've been gone too long, so I don't know. I hope so, because it will take too long to bring everyone here on foot. You'll have to move on."

Stone pushed into the group. "A day or two of rest is an excellent idea. The horses and the people need it. The deciding factor will be water and food. We'll have to stop where there is water. But if we can't find additional food, we'll have to keep moving." He crouched and stacked rocks in three piles. "We'll leave these little cairns along the way, whenever we stop. They will point the direction we're going, which will usually be south so just two stacks of rocks will do, but if we need to turn, we'll leave three or four cairns showing the new direction. If we have to turn around, we'll push the cairns over, leading in the new direction. Of course, someone or an animal could knock these down, so don't blindly follow them. Keep your head on a swivel and watch for trouble."

Dunia nodded. "Always."

Doc placed a second map on top of the first. "There are two

water tanks near Happy Jack, and the Lowell Telescope. If there's no one there, there might be food."

"It should be on high ground, which is defendable." Stone raised his arms like he was holding a rifle. Alma shivered at the reminder. "Might be a good place to hunt from, if we can see the water tanks from there." He pointed at her. "Martinez's rifle would be handy for that kind of hunting. I'd teach you to use it, but we don't have enough ammo."

She'd been letting the ATV guards use it anyway; it was too heavy to carry. "You may have it." She'd keep the little pistol, though.

It hadn't reached midday, but the sun was hot through the hazy skies when the group came upon the road leading to the strange looking building to their right. Tall and covered with shiny blue solar arrays, it stood out. The Harmony wagon train stopped, and everyone riding piled out to stretch their legs. Kit hopped on Simeon's ATV for the ride to the observatory. The other ATV, with Stone on the back, rolled onward down the bumpy highway, looking for the road to the water tanks. Ruth and Jude drove the cows to an open area on the other side of the damaged highway.

Alma stood over Em, laid out in the shade of a tree while Matias and Robin poked around in the dirt near a boulder with sticks. "Do you think they'll find scorpions or snakes?"

Em chuckled and sat up. "Unlikely with the amount of noise our lot is making. There won't be any wildlife around here."

Scraggly dry grass stood in clumps to the side of the highway. She pulled bunches and poked them through the gaps in the livestock trailer. Mr. H had bent some of the metal back to give the animals more airflow, but it must have been stifling in the cramped space. The goats tugged hard on the offered food and soft muzzles mouthed the slits for more. She flicked the chicken water dropper. It was already nearly empty. She shoved a few more fronds through. Several of the other children copied Alma, giggling and screeching with delight.

Alma stepped away, and her foot sunk into a soft mound of stinking animal dung. Scat. She scraped her sneaker on the ground, then spun around and away from the thicker plants. Wild animals, like the mountain lion that had come after Emelia, could be around any corner, behind every tree, lurking and watching. The goats in the smelly trailer would be a tasty, tasty treat.

She walked to Chrissy sitting on the shady side of her truck. "How long are we waiting?"

Chrissy squinted along the road Kit and Taylor had disappeared down. "Not long, by the looks of it."

Simeon and Kit flew toward them, a plume of dust in their wake, and stopped at the front of Chrissy's truck. Kit hopped off, while Simeon turned his machine off. "There are people there, but since I told them about the bunkers, they've offered to share the water at the Happy Jack tanks. There's even a bit of a pond for the livestock. They'll also charge any devices we have, like radios." He turned to Stone. "They've been hunting in the area already, so maybe the ATVs going to Page Springs can hunt a little on their way back."

Stone's lips flattened. "Might be a good time to slaughter a cow. We can feed everyone a good meal and smoke the rest into jerky."

Kit grimaced while Taylor laughed. "Our last try at that didn't work so well."

Chrissy stood. "We know how to do that. And I think you're right. If we don't find a deer in the next day, we should take one of the steers or a goat." She had lowered her voice so the younger children couldn't hear her.

"Okay then, let's load up!" Kit waved his arms over his head. "Just a short walk down the road."

Alma made sure Emelia and Matias got back in the travel trailer. She and the rest of the train followed Malachi's ATV down the highway, then turned on to a paved road, passing three houses, and continuing when pavement turned to dirt, winding through the trees. They turned into an open field and set up their vehicles in a circle. Ruth and Jude pushed the cattle past them, continuing along the dirt road. Smoke returned with muddy paws, so Chrissy released the goats from the trailer and he herded the bleating mass in the wake of the cows.

Alma retrieved their tent from the travel trailer. "Em, Mati, come help me." They set up the tent in the shade of one of the large pines.

She could hear Kit directing some of the residents to dig latrine trenches while Jaya organized meal cooking. "Em, it's your day to brush the horses, right?" Kit and Taylor had set chore rotations the first day. Only the very youngest or oldest rested until camp was set up.

"Oh, yes." She ran off to the trailer, Mati in her wake. Alma joined Jaya and Jen, fetching endless buckets of water and armfuls of dried branches. Pots of rice and beans simmered, making her stomach rumble.

Simeon took a plate of rice and beans from her. "Thanks, Alma. Come eat with me before I go?"

She smiled at him. "Of course." But Jaya and Taylor kept her late, preparing a meat processing station. She shoveled down bites between running errands for the workers cobbling together drying racks and finding enough large knives to cut up an entire cow.

As she dug through another box of kitchen utensils, a hand touched her shoulder. Simeon smiled. "Got to go now. Wish me luck." He winked and strode away to his ATV.

"Good luck," she called. He waved, and drove away, Dunia clinging to his back, bedrolls, water and food strapped to his ATV. They'd be staying the night at Page Springs. A pair of hunters with packs clung rather precariously to the back of Malachi's ATV; he'd drop them a few miles away where the people at the telescope said they might find game, then follow his brother.

That night, Alma settled Em and Mati into bed, and they all prayed for Simeon and Malachi's safety. She dropped into sleep, remembering the warmth of his hand on her shoulder.

The next day, they had a small portion of eggs with their rice and beans. The rest had not only been good for the people, but for the chickens as well. At mid-morning, hunters carried a large deer into the kitchen area. By the end of the day, Alma's fingers ached from slicing meat into thin strips. At least there was enough water to wash away the sticky blood. Chrissy took charge of the smoking rigs; the scent of smoky meat made Alma's mouth water.

After a delicious meal of rice and beans with venison, Alma relaxed. She sat with the rest of the Harmony Ranchers around the small cooking fire, burning down into coals. Em, Mati, Robin and the children Nora had rescued played near the goat pen, Ladybug and Smoke keeping the cows, horses, goats and children from straying, herding them back to Jen each time they made it more than a few hundred feet from the fire.

Em pointed. "I hear ATVs!" Alma followed her gaze. On the road a crowd of adults, led by a smiling Dunia, followed Simeon and Malachi's ATVs, both pulling small trailers. Kit and Taylor rose and walked toward the group. Two of the newcomers ran forward, calling a name. A boy, no more than ten, turned away from the goats and dashed toward them, arms raised. The remaining Page Springs children sprinted across the field. Some jumped into open arms while others searched the faces of every adult. Alma's chest ached. The scene flowed with tears of both ecstatic joy and painful sorrow from parents and children alike.

Kit and Taylor shook Dunia's hands, and she introduced them to the rest of the adults with her. What had looked like a huge crowd was only fifteen or so people, their backs bent under heavy packs.

"All those people are joining us?" Mr. H swigged a large gulp of water from his bottle. "They can't be serious. We'll never feed them all. We can't fit everyone inside the vehicles as it is." He wiped the sweat from his forehead.

Alma squinted. "I think they're carrying a lot of food, Mr. H. Besides, the number of seats inside a vehicle doesn't determine how many people can ride. Riding on top of a vehicle is the norm in most of the world." She should have remembered that earlier.

Chrissy laughed. "It was never going to be easy, but Alma's right. They may be helping us as much as we're helping them."

Kit patted the back of Chrissy's truck. "Let's get the gear as organized as possible and consolidate everything we can. It will give us more space for water and food. We can attach the ATV trailers to the back of the livestock trailer. At the speeds we're traveling it should be safe."

Mr. H patted Alma's shoulder. "You're right. I'm thinking like an American, instead of a refugee. It's time to change my mindset." He strode to the livestock trailer and with an oof, climbed to the top, a coil of rope across his shoulders.

The man tottered along the roof, his heavy footsteps making the metal clang, and wove cord across the top. He sat down and tucked his legs under the restraint and pulled against it. He nodded, and a smile crept over his lips.

That evening, they retrieved the remainder of the Page Spring residents' belongings from their vehicles, which ran out of fuel about a mile away. The reunited families cobbled together larger tents, while Dunia and Jaya cared for the remaining three kids without parents. Alma helped rearrange the gutted travel trailer, while others organized the pickup and minivan.

In the end, they successfully stored the Page Springs citizen's belongings, including the canned food and large, industrial sized water barrels. The additional trailers attached to the livestock trailer looked odd, but seemed workable. The Harmony Ranch wagon train got stranger with every passing day, but it was worth it to see the smiles on the faces of the formerly separated families.

The next morning, they loaded up. If the vehicles could groan, they would have. Children sat on parents' laps inside the horse-drawn minivan. People perched on the larger, boxed items on the small trailers. Mr. H's harness on the livestock roof held another six, but Chrissy wouldn't allow more; the roof was built to hold hay and saddles, not people. An earthquake shook them during the morning, and further disturbed the ground, so the ride would be rougher.

Alma insisted that Emelia and Matias ride inside the gutted travel trailer, but she gave her seat to an older woman with her arm in a sling who had joined the group from Page Springs. As the day wore on, the adults in the horse-drawn wagons would join the walkers to avoid stressing the animals. But since they'd all rested, Kit was determined they'd make good time. Even he and Taylor rode on the makeshift transports, while Ruth and Pete had hitched their horses to the front of the wagons, too. The three-horse hitch would provide more power and speed. The cows had learned to follow, and required only the occasional reminder from Smoke and Ladybug, who'd eaten well on the remains of the processed deer.

When, at last, she had ensured Em and Mati were safely inside the trailer with Jen, Doc and Robin, the back was already fully loaded. She couldn't find a space on the small trailers and there was no room for her to stand, let alone sit behind her family. The crumpled, burning transit van at the gas station filled her vision. Alma swallowed the panic and let her racing heart slow. Even if she fell behind, Em and Mati were with friends.

Assorted plant pots crammed into three plastic crates on her side dangled from the minivan back windows hooked in place with coils of wire. The drooping leaves of the freshly dug up specimens almost distracted her from the bullet ridden shell. The back of the van was wide open, and people spilled from the back with bags and belongings stacked around them.

She dashed to Chrissy's truck. "Any space in there?" Chrissy's children crammed into the cab, the baby cradled in Martha's arms. "Oh." She turned. Simeon had dropped back to take the rear, but his ATV carried an armed escort.

"Alma, ride the bumper." Chrissy smiled. "You'll stay cooler out there, and you have the strength to hang on."

Alma trotted to the back of Chrissy's truck. Strapped to the front of the livestock trailer above the triangular hitch were the two familiar bikes and several bird crates full of clucking hens. Kit had moved much of the bulky gear and used the bike generator stand and a roll of plastic fencing to hold everything in place. It appeared secure, but not neat. She stepped up on the wide bumper and gripped the back of the truck. Chrissy started the engine, and it rumbled through the soles of her feet.

The wagon train rolled on without stopping for the first half of the day. The fresh horses pulled them quicker than usual. Alma's stomach ached from lack of food and arguments broke out about when they would stop to eat. For the afternoon rest period, Kit chose a sandy wash skirting the shade of trees on the slowly changing landscape, but the food was meager. Thin flatbreads baked over the fire the previous day using the last of the flour and a ration of venison jerky were distributed, but the people still complained, especially with the unexpected bounty from Page Springs. Too many of them didn't comprehend how long their journey would take.

Neither Em nor Mati made any comment. Alma pinched tiny morsels from her portion and savored every crumb. With the swelling crowd traveling together, her next meal might be the following day. The buzz of the ATVs creating a perimeter kept them safe. Simeon, Malachi and Stone's security forces also searched abandoned homes for food, water, and gasoline. By punching holes in abandoned vehicle fuel tanks, they'd found enough gas and diesel to keep Chrissy's truck and the ATVs rolling.

Chrissy, and Mr. H's wife, Sharon fussed over the exposure to the muted sun. The haze broke the terrifying glare, reducing it to stuffy brightness, but despite that, the outside riders and walkers were red-faced. They tied tent flies and tarps to cut branches to provide some shade.

"It's not as if we are traveling fast enough to rip them away." Ruth tugged on a taut string. "Fuel is running low. We can't keep this up. We'll never get there."

"Enough." Chrissy shot her an angry glare. "We'll get there together, however long it takes."

The new shade flapped mostly and roared when a stretch of road allowed the train to speed up, which wasn't often. Their journey from water source to water source continued with very little to break up the monotony of lurching bumps, gritty dust and the lack of other humans. There were no signs of life in the tiny towns they passed through. Perhaps anyone surviving in the towns was keeping well hidden from the large company trundling along their roads. Her skin prickled. There must be eyes on the wagon train; they couldn't travel unnoticed.

A few days later, around the time they'd usually stop, Simeon returned at high speed, waving his Mom onward. "Armed people, a big crew. Big signs saying keep out for the next mile. We'll have to keep moving."

Adults with weapons drew them, and the group fell silent. They stayed on the bumpy asphalt road, watching the armed guards, many perched in trees. Ruth and Pete resisted the horses' attempts to leave the road for the small, muddy lake a few hundred feet away. Three small sheds near the pond thrummed and a pipe gushed into the pond; they must have power for water wells. They turned west on to a new highway, and left the settlement and their silent sentinels behind. Taking a dirt road, they stopped for the night at a former Forest Service campground. Pit toilets and hand pumps for water were a welcome change.

The highway rolled south and the land became drier. The tall pines disappeared, twisted, stunted trees taking their place. Grass was thin and scarce and finding water became more difficult. At a high bluff, they stopped above a large city. Swaths of the city were tumbled, blackened ruins. Where green existed, thin tendrils of smoke rose.

Kit called a meeting, and they decided to take a rough trail along the bluff above the city, rather than descend into a potential trap. Even so, three times they skirted the edges of developments. The huge houses had been homes of the wealthy, but the rich were long gone. Windows had been shattered and doors broken in. No food, water, or fuel remained. Hands stayed close to weapons, and Simeon, Malachi and Stone's group were grim. Simeon wouldn't tell Alma what they'd found, just that she was better off not knowing.

After the city, the land dried more, the twisted trees turning to brush and rock and then just dull beige rock. Despite the too-frequent breaks and the sometimes-irritated exchanges about swapping seats and too-little food, the Harmony ranchers made good progress. A few complained about feeling dizzy, but the rations of water were the same for everyone. They passed a large dusty sign pointing to Phoenix and took the fork leading away; the highway taking them through a wide valley. Alma turned, hoping to get a glimpse of the city she had been heading toward a lifetime ago, but it was too distant, hidden behind hills and the rippling heat rising from the damaged asphalt.

They traveled along a dry riverbed, through an abandoned town that stretched for more than a mile. Their security crew found little to scavenge. Several stops later and the next to last can of fuel was emptied into the pickup's tank. The dry riverbed turned a muddy green from algae. Far in front of Chrissy's truck, bright, shimmering light glared off an enormous body of water. The highway took the train closer to the dry, cracked rim of a vast, depleted lake. The water sat undisturbed in the basin far from the high water mark and the road.

A fresh breeze lifted from the water and blew across Alma's face. Flocks of birds waded in the shallows, lifting into the air in a stunning aerobatic dance display. The Harmony ranchers quieted. Perhaps they thought it was as beautiful and as untouched by the mess of mangled land they'd bounced through all day, just like her. The water turned from blue gray to orange and she drank in the slowly setting sun reflecting from the surface. They camped for the night in an abandoned campground. The water faucets didn't work, so they used the ATVs to collect water from where the pool glimmered at the bottom of the dry lake bed, almost a mile away.

The next morning, they left the campground and continued on the rim of the lake. Alma looked wistfully at the water so close, and yet so far. Splashing in the water, washing her clothes; it was a dream destined to be a mirage. But the water lapped closer and closer to the shoreline; perhaps her dream could become reality yet.

The train pulled to a stop, and a prickle of panic ran up her arms. In the relatively narrow canyon in front of them, whitewater from the still-draining lake crashed over the remains of a collapsed bridge at the bottom of a long, rocky slope. Farther to her right, a cable strung with bright orange blocks hung in the air above the rapidly-flowing water. Beyond that, a massive concrete wall had once retained the lake.

Water rushed through a long fissure in the middle of the thick dam wall as if a monster had taken a huge, sideways bite. An earthquake must have rippled through the area and hit the dam at some point, and the middle of the structure must have been weaker. She shivered and turned away. Thousands of gallons would've thundered through the damaged wall and swelled along the valley below, washing away everything in its path. To remain on the crippled highway to the bunker, they had to cross the ravine without a bridge or a boat.

CHAPTER THIRTY-ONE

Kit Walsh. Arizona

The top of the Theodore Roosevelt dam appeared to be intact, but the gaping hole in the middle didn't instill confidence. Plus, they had to get to the dam before they could cross it, and there wasn't an obvious road on their side of the outflow channel. Kit walked down the long dirt track that had run under the fallen bridge. Fishermen probably used it to launch boats; fishing was usually pretty good near a dam. Behind him, Taylor and Aaron directed people to take the animals to the water away from the dam. She had the wagon train under control, so he could afford the time to survey the most obvious way across and see if they had any chance of making it.

"Kit!" Mr. H caught up with him, huffing a little. They'd all gotten thinner and leaner, taking turns walking without enough food, but Mr. H and his wife, Sandra, had made the biggest transformations. They'd walked more with every day, and both of them complained less and made themselves more useful. Cindy, on the other hand, tried to ride more than her share, did her chores poorly, and led the complaints. After they crossed, Kit was holding a meeting. He'd had enough. The whiners could stay here—with water and fish available, it wasn't an automatic death sentence, and the road was only getting harder.

"Kit, did I tell you what I used to do for a living?" Mr. H walked next to him, along with Dunia, Stone and Faris.

"No, I don't think you did." Kit figured most people's experience wasn't terribly relevant in their new world.

"I was an architect."

Kit stopped, but Mr. H kept going. He ran a few steps to catch up. "So you know a bit about structures."

"A little." Mr. H shrugged. "I'm not a structural engineer, but since we don't have any of those, I'm the next best thing."

Kit grimaced. If he'd had a Mr. H at Marble Canyon, maybe Sean would be alive. The missing piece of his soul throbbed; he still turned to say something to Sean several times a day. "Well, I'm definitely not, so your advice would be greatly appreciated."

"You know more than you think. As a structure firefighter, you're used to sizing up buildings for stability."

Kit nodded. "That's true, but I was a line firefighter, not an assessment expert. Still, between the two of us, maybe we can make this work." But as they got closer, Kit was less and less sure. Boulders fell from the tall, narrow gash in the middle of the dam continuously.

Mr. H pointed. "This dam is deceptive. The original rubble and masonry dam is encased in more modern concrete. So, I'm guessing that when the earthquakes started, the less-stable interior of the dam shifted and slid, bulging the exterior concrete in the middle and cracking it. Once the crack started, and water poured through, it would be impossible to stop. The question is, did the concrete shell stay intact enough to hold the roadway?"

"Plus, we have to get there." They'd descended to the lower part of the road. Stone pointed along the channel's edge. "I don't see the road continuing. And we can't cross the water; it's still too deep."

They passed the cable holding the big foam blocks that normally kept boaters from getting too close to the dam. The orange blocks hung at least fifty feet above the rapidly flowing water. As they drew closer, the rush of water and tumble of boulders grew louder. Where the rough road ended, rocks piled into a small cove between them and the dam, brush sticking up between the huge monoliths.

Mr. H carefully stepped on to a gigantic slab of beige rock. "It's been a long time since I visited this dam, but I think they destroyed this part of the road after they encased the dam. They didn't want vehicles driving over it. But, there was an outcropping of rocks here." He pointed up. "I think the earthquakes collapsed it, and filled this little cove. But who knows how stable it is? That channel is steep and deep." He pointed down.

Stone hopped up next to Mr. H, and a few rocks beyond. "We can't get vehicles or wagons through here, but people probably. But, there's a hiking trail above this. I sent a couple of my folks to check it out and see if we can get to the dam from there. Or if the land near the dam is stable at all. We might have to backtrack and go around the other side."

"There's no road there." Mr. H accepted Kit's help climbing off the rocks. "There's a marina on the other side. We might be able to get one of those foam blocks off the cable and use it to swim a couple of folks over there. Maybe there's an intact boat or two. Can I use your binoculars, Kit?"

Kit pulled them off. He'd gotten so used to them hanging around his neck, he forgot about them. "Of course."

Mr. H put the binoculars to his eyes. "I think the top of the dam might be intact. Maybe. Need to look at it from above." He handed the binoculars back to Kit and walked back up the road.

Kit raised the binoculars. The gash was ominous. Big rectangular blocks of stone and boulders dropped from the interior, while thick concrete slabs along the exterior dangled from rebar. At the top of the hole, the concrete appeared intact. Kit handed his binoculars to Dunia, and followed Mr. H back up the hill. "I think you're right. The top might be crossable."

Back up with the wagon train, they had a small lunch of dried meat and soupy rice. Kit was grateful they had plenty of water to go with it for once. Briggs and Jonesy, two of Stone's security and hunting force, reported to the group. "The trail is narrow and rocky. I'm not sure even the ATVs can take the trail. Especially down the slope to the dam's top. We already cut the fences, but getting there will be difficult. I hope the brakes on those vehicle trailers still work, because it's steep."

Kit turned to Mati, who shook his head. Of course they'd removed them as unnecessary weight.

"If we can find some wood fence posts, we could go old school, and use those as brakes, levering them against the tires." Taylor mimed pushing a lever away. "Like a real wagon. Plus, we could run ropes to the back of the trailers, loop the rope around a rock at the top of the slope, and use people to hold the ropes, slowing the trailers."

Kit smiled at Taylor. "Great ideas." He scanned the group; they seemed worn, but energized by the possibilities. Adequate hydration probably helped, too. "Okay. We'll split into groups after siesta. One group will lighten the bigger trailers, except Chrissy's." She nodded. "With a working truck, we ought to be able to get her across if we can find a wide enough path. We'll use the ATVs to take the smaller trailers across."

Simeon raised his hand. "We'll probably be out of gas on the other side. We're on fumes."

"Same with the truck," Chrissy added.

Kit shrugged. "I'm amazed we've had them this long. There's a marina on the other side, but chances are, everything's been taken, including the fuel. Anyway, a second group will widen the trail. While most of you rest, I'm taking a small team to the dam to see if we can safely cross before we do too much. If we can't, we have another idea, but it's not preferable, because we can't bring any vehicles or trailers."

Taylor stood. "If we can get across, we'll use the ATV trailers to ferry our things, then reload the horse wagons on the other side. Now is the time to look at your personal gear. If there's dead weight, leave it here, because you'll be carrying more and more of your own things. The desert gets hotter and drier the farther south we go, so the horses will have a harder and harder time. We'll be taking longer rests in the middle of the day, and traveling longer into the night if the moon allows. It will be difficult, so don't make it harder on yourself by hanging on to useless pieces of the past. I know it hurts to give up any possibility of seeing the pictures on your phones again, but that's several more ounces of water you can carry."

The people surrounding Cindy grumbled, but Kit didn't give them time. "I need Simeon, Malachi, Stone, Jonesy, Briggs, Dunia, and Mr. H. The rest of you can do your usual midday chores, then rest. We'll plan on staying here tonight and crossing in the morning."

"Did you want the ATVs, boss?" Simeon asked.

Kit chuckled at the title and turned. "No, let's save the fuel." They gathered water bottles and sun hats, then set off on the Arizona Trail. They climbed through the rocks, dry brush, and tall saguaro cactus. The trail was narrow and rocky, barely carved into the hillside. Kit stopped and turned back to ask what their ATV experts thought.

Simeon kicked a rock and it skittered down the slope. "Driving an ATV will be extremely difficult on this trail. No way we can tow a trailer."

Kit nodded. "Let's not waste our energy. We'll go back, and use the ATVs to get to the end of the road along the channel to the dam. Our team will find a stable route across the rocks. Then we'll bring the wagons down to the end of the road and leave them there. We'll set up a bucket brigade to get our things across the rocks to the dam's surface. Another team will lead the horses and herd the cows and goats along the Arizona Trail, then down to the dam. Sound like a plan?"

"Yep." Simeon turned, and Malachi led them back to the camp, then they unhooked the small ATV trailers from Chrissy's livestock trailer, and attached them to the ATVs, answering questions while they made the switch. Kit perched precariously on the end of a trailer, Dunia next to him, while Briggs and Jonesy rode the other one. Mr. H rode behind Malachi, while Stone got on with Simeon. They made the quick trip to the end of the road, stopping well before the jumbled stones of the former rock outcropping, before the orange warning float line.

Kit walked to the end of the road and climbed the pile of rocks, pulling his seatbelt cutter. He tested every rock before committing his weight, marking the unstable ones with an X. His team followed, while Simeon, Malachi and Mr. H unhooked the ATV trailers. The boulders and slabs were rough, tilted at uncomfortably steep angles, and some rocked precariously. As Kit climbed to the next rock, the slab beneath him moved.

"Earthquake!" Simeon yelled from below, the rest echoing.

Kit bounded upward and toward the lake, off the boulders sliding beneath him, then kept going, fairly certain there was nothing above him ready to come down. Rocks grumbled and rumbled around him but he kept moving, eventually making it to seemingly solid ground near a saguaro. Stone and Dunia stood on the slope below him, safe. Simeon, Malachi and Mr. H. gathered near the ATVs. Jonesy sprinted off the rocks toward the edge, Mr. H catching him.

Jonesy tore out of Mr. H's grip and bounded back to the landslide. "Briggs! Where are you?"

Kit scanned the jumbled rockslide below. He didn't see Briggs' hunter orange ball cap. He scrambled down the precarious slope, careful to stay away from Stone and Dunia so his footsteps wouldn't send rocks tumbling down on them. Clambering on, hopping from unsteady rock to rock, he stopped after twenty steps and searched for the orange cap again.

"No!" Jonesy ran toward the steep edge of the channel, Malachi catching his arm to hold him back. "Briggs!"

An orange ball cap floated away, drawn to the middle of the churning water below. Kit sped, his feet surfing the loose surface of the smaller rocks and sand near the group, and finally landed on the road's level surface. He ran to the edge and peered over. A hundred feet below him, a man's body sprawled face down, impaled on a pyramid of rock, red trickling down to join the roiling blue waters below. He dropped to his knees, his heart shredded in his chest.

Jonesy plopped next to him, reaching his hand out over the abyss. "Briggs." He sobbed.

Kit pulled him into a hug. "I'm so sorry. So, so sorry." He held Jonesy until his tears ebbed, then they both stood. The rest of the group expressed their sorrow, too, with Stone hugging Jonesy hard, whispering in his ear. Then they returned to the temporary camp.

The tone was somber, people going about their business with the weight of that death on their hearts. But no tragedy—not even the loss of a friend—could stem the tide of work. They might cry, or not; clutch at memories, tell stories, share what they knew of Briggs' life; but they couldn't let up on their chores if they wanted to survive.

Taylor suggested that everyone wash their clothes and themselves while they had water. Clothing lay strewn across the twisted metal of the bridge, the guardrails, the tops of tents, and the vehicles. The livestock roamed, eating whatever dry grass remained. Smoke and Ladybug remained near the water, panting, eyes on Jen. They knew the horses, goats and chickens wouldn't go far from the lake which freed them up to guard the one they loved the best, his Aunt Stickler, who'd turned out to be a thoroughly decent human being. He was glad she'd had her dogs to keep her company. And Robin, whose bubbly personality seemed to be rubbing off on Jen. Smoke nudged Kit's hand, licking his fingers. Hopefully they'd find something to hunt tonight, because there was little food to spare, except the offal and bones they'd dried along with the meat. If the desert was hard on the humans, it was doubly hard on Jen's dogs, whose thick coats were going to be a challenge in the coming days.

Kit ducked into their tent, set away from everyone else's, and curled up near a snoozing Taylor, pulling her hand into his. His heart ached, but he fell into sleep despite the pain; living required practicality.

That evening, they had a solemn, small meal of soupy meat and rice, then Doc held a short memorial service.

Kit stood. "Tomorrow will be extremely difficult. We'll take everything we need, nothing more, to the road that used to run under the bridge. Stone's group and I will find the most stable way across the rocks. We'll line up, and hand our necessary belongings hand to hand and get them to the dam's surface. Then we'll go across, one by one above the gap. We'll again transfer our belongings hand to hand. Meanwhile, Ruth and Pete will herd the horses, cows and goats along the Apache Trail. Then they will cross. Hopefully we can find vehicles to gut and make new wagons. But be prepared to carry everything you own. I'm going to say it again: leave unnecessary items behind. Remember, the desert will only get harsher from here. Aaron, your turn."

Aaron stood. "The horses and cows will need a lot of water to survive. The horses will not be able to tow the same weight they have been. All of us will need to walk a lot more. But, there is some good news. I know a lot about the native plant life here. Watch for prickly pear, mesquite pods, jojoba plants, and ironwood. Agave, cholla and palo verde can also supply food, so if you spot those plants, let me know. I'll show all of you what they look like and how to harvest them."

"I hate those Palo Verde trees." Cindy sneezed. "I'm allergic."

"Well, that may be, but their pods are good to eat, particularly after a monsoon." Aaron forced a smile. "Some taste like snap peas. Those of you who have lived here fulltime, show the others what to look for." He plopped down.

Kit took the speaker's position. "Everyone, take another look at what you need versus what you want and get a good night's sleep. We'll rise at first light." He held out a hand to Taylor, pulling her up and walking away. He was in no mood to listen to useless complaints tonight. Not after a good man lost his life.

After washing up in the lake, he pulled Taylor close to him in the tent, and slept, grateful for her love.

The next morning after a breakfast of beans and corncakes, Kit led Stone's group plus a few others to the rock fall. Together, they found the most stable way across. Kit took the hardest spot—the next person in line stood at his shoulders, so he had to lift each item to his head. Then the work began, hauling their gear from person to person. They started with the heaviest items, like the large cookpots full of rice and beans and water jugs, then the rest. Once they had gathered on top of the dam, Kit walked to the middle, Stone's group along with Simeon, Alma, and Malachi joining him.

While the idea of a fifteen-year-old girl exploring the dangers of a crumbling dam terrified the old Kit, he'd changed. The Harmony Ranchers had become useful, non-useful, and obstructive; mostly related to their willingness to adapt. Alma had adapted better than any of them and was useful, so she stayed, despite her unwillingness to trust them. After her experiences, Kit couldn't blame her.

Just before the gash in the dam below them, Kit stopped the group. He leaned over both sides, using his binoculars to inspect the extent of the damage, inside and out. Water whirled inside the gash on both sides—the masonry and rubble interior was wearing away faster than the concrete poured over it. But water hammered at the concrete, too, and the downstream hole was larger than the lake side of the dam. The structure vibrated under their feet, and beneath the sound of rushing water, the rock and concrete rasped and groaned. He handed his binoculars to Mr. H, who also looked at both sides.

"Kit, we need to go now. The erosion on the downstream side is increasing. If the top sags at all, then the whole thing will collapse quickly."

"Mr. H, choose a spotter and give the binoculars to them to watch the middle of the dam." Kit cupped his hands around his mouth and filled his lungs. "Elderly and children to the far side, now! Everyone, line up, let's get the gear across." He ran back to the piled gear, taking the spot closest to the pile so he'd be last across.

Grabbing the largest pot, he handed it to Taylor, who gave it to the next in line. After picking up the fifth item, he noticed Mr. H, just on the far side of the gap, grab Cindy and shove her into line. That woman was nothing but trouble. They moved everything, then moved the line down the dam, over the middle and started again. As they handed the last items across, the rumble of rock on rock increased and a yell went up from the far side. "Run, now!" The whole line of people turned and sprinted.

The middle of the dam was sagging, the overhanging concrete railings at the top falling with tremendous bangs, the cable railings above stretching with loud twangs. Kit reached the center. Hooves clopped on concrete and a whoop sounded behind him. Kit jumped to stand against the lakeside, precariously close to the crumbling edge.

The cows and goats, herded by Ruth and Pete, thundered along the top of the dam. As they crossed, the top eroded, starting from the downstream side, the cable railings on that side pulling free, the cables and metal pillars pulling tight, then dropping behind the dam before they snapped. The last horse, ridden by Ruth, jumped a foot-wide gap on the top of the dam, leaving nothing intact but a narrow stretch of concrete and the sagging cable rails.

Kit sprinted for the gap and jumped, Taylor's terrified face on the other side of the chasm and Sean's last moments flashing before his eyes. His foot caught the edge and slipped. Desperate, he grasped the cable and pulled himself hand over hand, even though it was about to pull loose, undoubtedly flinging him into the air above the waterway so far below.

The metal cable sliced his still-tender hands, but he climbed. Pulling himself up, hands grasped his shirt, then under his arms and his belt, yanking him on to solid ground.

"Run!" Stone bellowed.

Kit ran for the pile of belongings, desperate people flinging them from hand to hand. He picked up the next, bumping the line farther across the concrete. Gasping for breath, he hurled the bundles to Stone, who threw to Taylor, then he picked up the last and ran. The line of people did the same, running with the items in their hands to the pile and starting again. Finally, they reached the seemingly solid ground on the far side. But it wasn't safe, either.

The road was cut into a tall hill, and large boulders had fallen across the road already. Ruth and Pete herded the livestock onward, both of them carrying bundles of belongings, and a child clung to each of them. Chrissy rode another horse, her baby strapped to her chest, a child clinging to her back. Martha rode the fourth.

With a final whoosh and deafening bang, the dam collapsed. The cables on the lakeside snapped, recoiling. "Down!" Kit flattened to the ground, the cables whipping overhead into the hill above them, flinging rocks around them, while the ground vibrated below them with the tumbling of the dam.

When the clatter of rocks stopped, he climbed to his feet, still blowing like a racehorse. The middle of the dam was gone, the remaining walls a jagged V shape. He helped Taylor up, and hugged her hard. Breaking away, he hauled Aunt Jen to her feet, then he treated cuts with torn bits of cloth, all they had left. The dazed group gathered, hanging on to each other.

Kit hated to say anything, but they still weren't safe. "Alright, everyone. I know you're tired and scared, but we still have a long ways to go. We've got to get us and our stuff to the lake, so we'll have water. From there, we'll reassess. Line up, and we'll go back to transferring our belongings." Hopefully, they'd find vehicles they could gut for horse wagons, but there was no guarantee.

The Harmony Ranchers stumbled into line, and set to work. Some grumbled, of course, but they were shut down immediately—Kit didn't have to say a word. After an hour, they'd gotten their gear and themselves across a ravine where a shorter bridge had collapsed, and they rested. The clop of hooves on concrete drew his attention.

Ruth waved from the back of a team of horses hitched to a trailer. As they drew near, the reason for the oval, bowl-shaped trailer became clear—they'd taken a boat trailer, and draped a sail over it.

He trotted down the road to meet them, ignoring his aches and pains. "Great idea, Ruth."

She nodded. "Mom thought of it. She felt bad, riding away, but she has a baby to care for."

With a little effort, they got the trailer turned and piled belongings inside, the smallest and eldest riding, the rest of them hanging on to ropes to slow the trailer if it rolled too fast down the long slope to the lake below.

As the lake came into view, Kit considered the loss of a single person a miracle, but a huge loss nonetheless. That death would have long-term effects on every person in their group; some good, some bad. Unfortunately, the bad would be much louder than the good.

CHAPTER THIRTY-TWO

Alma Garcia. Lake Roosevelt, Arizona

As they trudged into the beached marina, the hazy light turned the sky yellow in what could have been pre-sunset. Alma rubbed and flexed her fingers, aching from transferring their belongings and the sail lines slowing the horse wagon on the long slope back to Lake Roosevelt. She would happily endure the pain for working vehicles.

Ahead, boats rested on trailers in front of two flat-roofed sheds with more boats inside, and a third, open to the air, with boats in dry dock, shaken free from their stands, by the quakes. The hulls of the pleasure cruisers were crumpled or smashed on the cracked concrete, and the vessels rested on their sides. Out on the lake, wooden jetties sat in baked mud instead of water and the crafts moored hung like limp puppets on strings, some tilted nose up while others dangled sideways. The weight of the boats dragged the flimsier walkways crooked and crumpled the flat roofs on top of the largest boats. A large, heavily scorched building near the highway may have been a restaurant, while another metal building below was a ransacked store. A larger building, now rubble, had been a visitors' center. Above the highway, a trailer park was seemingly deserted, but they couldn't trust that to be true.

Kit must not have thought so either, because he kept them moving to the next peninsula of land above the dry lakebed. Stone and his group stayed between the Ranchers and trailers, holding their rifles in their hands, rather than strapped over their shoulders. "There's a horse camp over there, and we'll stop there for the night. Stay together and I'll assign watches."

Taylor pointed at the crumpled marina. "The boats out there might have cushions or bedding. We should go out in threes and fours, gather what we can before it gets dark."

Simeon stepped up on their new horse trailer. "Don't fill your water bottles anywhere near the boats. The water is full of fuel. But there are ponds of water closer to the camp. We'll take the larger bottles to the lake itself with the animals."

"Thank you, Simeon." Kit scanned the crowd. "You all heard that. Check the water before you drink it." He pulled Stone aside. "Can your folks check if there are any running vehicles, and if so, do any of the boats still have fuel we can use?"

Stone nodded. "Sure."

The Harmony ranchers split into groups and spread out among the horse sites with their still-standing metal roofs above picnic tables. Alma kept Emelia and Matias close to Taylor, not allowing anyone to split them up. Chrissy's brood herded the animals to the remaining lake, far across the dried and cracked mud.

Simeon stopped. "I'm checking out the store. Want to come?"

She smiled at him even though her feet ached. "Sure. Maybe we'll find something." Em and Matias followed the two of them to the store. The glass window was smashed and no one was inside.

"We should check it out." Alma leaned in, although the shelving was broken and most anything useful was likely to already be gone.

Emelia followed her inside without hesitation and strolled over to the dark refrigerators on the back wall. Matias picked up a reel of fishing line and a packet of hooks from under a toppled shelving unit. Simeon joined him, reaching underneath the metal shelves at Matias' feet and occasionally passing something up to him.

T-shirts emblazoned with the marina logo were stapled to the wall next to a collapsed, empty clothing display. Alma climbed up and pulled them down. They'd be baggy, but they were clean and new. Another shirt and two pairs of shorts were stuffed into the back of a cabinet. She grabbed them too, flinging them over her arm. Souvenir pens stamped with advertising were scattered across the tiles. She pocketed a handful. Perhaps, if they made it to the bunker, there would be time to teach some of the kids how to read and write. She stood up and stabbed her head on a hanging rail. She winced, tentatively wiped her hand over the spot and shone the torch on her fingers, inspecting for blood. There was none.

She turned to the culprit, adult sized rain ponchos swayed from her collision with the stand. They hadn't seen rain for days, but she'd experienced the monsoon type weather and, with all the changes from the disaster, who knew what weather would hit next. She cleared the rack and found another handful below. She stuffed them in with the T-shirts. They might not have found food, but at least they could be clean and dry.

When they arrived back at the shelters, every unit was decorated with colorful cushions and thin boat mattresses. A few mangled energy snack bars, a crushed tub of crackers and a packet of vegetarian sausages sat on a picnic table in front of Taylor along with an array of canned goods; tinned tomatoes, peas and peaches, but her stomach rumbled at the highly prized pack of pasta. Jaya and Dunia were doing their best to sort what little they had into some resemblance of a meal, but with so many mouths, it wouldn't go far. Still, it would be different and that was a blessing not to be overlooked.

The night was long and noisy. Mr. H's snores echoed off the metal shade above them, and Alma was relieved when it was his turn to get up and take his turn at watch. The animals shifted quietly, tied to a long line behind them, but their calm presence made her feel safer. She finally fell asleep nestled close to Em and Mati, and in the same shelter with Simeon and his family.

She woke early the next morning to the smell of fried fish. Several of the parents they'd picked up at Page Springs had taken fishing rods and lures to the water, snagging a dozen largemouth bass and three trout for breakfast.

"We saw a fish jump in that pool when we hooked it out of the water." Simeon scooped up the mushy white flesh from one of the pilfered boat plates with his fingers. "They caught the trout at that spot."

The group didn't break camp all day. The assured water and abundant fish supply were a small comfort. The opportunity to wash themselves and their clothes again was welcome, too. They'd found a smaller pool left after the lake had drained; it had warmed in the sun to a comfortable temperature.

That evening, after a second meal of fish stew, Kit stood on a picnic table. "Stone and Doc have looked at the maps. We have a very long, very dry trek ahead to the bunker." Murmurs hummed around the group and Cindy scowled.

Matias frowned and jutted out his lower lip. "We can walk it. We walked farther than that." He kicked the dirt at his feet. "I don't know what they are complaining about."

"The hunger." Emelia crossed her arms. "The heat. The thirst."

Alma prodded her. "Enough." She didn't know how far they had walked to get back to the prison house and then from the broken-down van to Harmony ranch, but the ranch group was different. Children as small as Robin right through to older people like Doc or unfit adults like Mr. H were part of the circle. Their progress would be slow.

Kit waved a torn section of paper. "I've assigned you all duties according to your strengths. We're leaving just after dawn tomorrow." He lifted the paper. "Group one, which is most of you, will find and fill water containers." He looked up. "Anything clean and portable, fill it and bring it here. If we're lucky enough to find something really big, we'll use the horse trailer to fill it. Check the dry dock or the smashed boats for a clean water tank." He returned to his list. "Group two: Food for dinner tonight." He looked at the parents who had caught the feast for the morning. "More fishing, most likely. I don't think there's much left to scavenge. Avoid the trailer park. The guards saw people there last night." He scanned the paper and scratched his head. "Group three: Create another horse cart. They can take the water. Group four: care for the livestock. Get them out to feed and water." He taped the list to a beam. "Let's make the most of what we've got and not waste any of it."

Emelia stayed with Chrissy and the livestock while Matias joined the horse cart creation along with a mixture of ranchers and Stone's patrol. They walked to the boat storage area, where dozens of boats on trailers and empty trailers waited. Alma and Simeon joined them as assigned.

Searching among the lightweight aluminum trailers shaped like simple boat hulls, they finally found one with an easy-to-break lock. The low rails had blue rollers which must have aided in the moving of the boat.

"For hauling water, we'll need something stronger than a sail." Simeon made a scooping motion.

Matias pointed to the metal cladding on the nearby storage units. "That's not too heavy if we can cut it down and bend it."

"Great idea." Jonesy ruffled Matias' hair. "Let's find some tools and get to work. Most of the time, these metal building are bolted and screwed together, so we shouldn't need cutting torches."

At the other end of the long storage building, Alma shoved a wooden door and it gave way. Floats and rolls of fencing had fallen into a jumbled pile, but a red metal cabinet on wheels was promising. Beyond the assorted maintenance items, a second door stood in a wood partition splitting the space. She opened the door. Light reflected from foil-lined tents and two desk fans sat in the middle of the small room. Four larger plant containers with bare branched specimens sat on the floor inside both the first and second tent while shelves in the others held a mix of half emptied seedling trays and pots spilled from tubs that would have held them in place. Inside the tents, suspended above the would-be plants on stands were industrial flat lamps.

"Woah!" Simeon slid past her. "Someone's been busy. A little more than legally allowed, but all the better for us. This is perfect."

Alma bent to the dead plants. "Nothing is alive. We can't eat it."

Simeon laughed. "You wouldn't eat these plants if they were still growing." He stacked up the trays. "Let's get this lot out of here so we can see what we've got."

She frowned at his eagerness. They had a trailer to build and nothing in the room would be useful for that. "Oh! If this set up helped to grow plants in the dark, do you think we could use them in the bunker?"

"That's exactly what I was thinking." He carried them out of the inner room.

They unplugged the lights and fans, dragging them and the tents through the door into the open. One bulb was cracked, but the rest were intact. The tents folded down, and the poles unclipped into manageable sizes that easily fitted inside a large bag they found under the desk. The stands retracted, but the lights were bulky.

"We don't have enough space to carry them. We can't waste energy on something that won't help us." Alma lifted the holdall to her shoulder and bent to grab an armful of the stands.

"We need to think outside the immediate. If we are going to survive underground, this will be worth more than gold." Simeon threw open the garage door and rolled the red metal box outside. "Hey! Here's a bunch of tools!" Jonesy jogged over to roll the cabinet away. Alma helped Simeon pack the fragile bulbs as carefully as they could, then helped the others with the trailer.

They helped place the long sections of thin metal siding along the trailer's cradle, then used the screws they'd removed to attach the sheets. Her wrists and fingers ached when they were done, but they had a solid surface to hold water buckets. They pulled a sail from another boat to cover the water and hopefully keep it cooler, then attached ropes to the tongue and pulled it to the horse camp with the lights resting in the bottom.

Taylor couldn't contain her excitement about the trailer or the lamps. She hugged Alma tightly, squeezing harder than any other woman ever had. Kit agreed and set them covering the first trailer in metal as well.

Every team had been productive and they all ate well that evening. Most of the gathering were excited, knowing they were as ready as they'd ever be to leave the temporary resting place. But a few continued to grumble. Alma wasn't one of them. She was useful, trusted, but best of all, she was safe. Chrissy was as kind as kind could be, and Simeon looked out for her at every turn. Loathe as she was to admit it, she felt safe and with safety came happiness. She looked for Em and Mati, flashing them a smile, but dodging away when Em returned with a frown. *Eventually, dear sister, you'll meet the old me; the one who used to smile; the one who had a future. I'll make sure of it.*

CHAPTER THIRTY-THREE

Evelyn Parker. Anil Kumar Sanctuary, Arizona

Evelyn sprinkled a teaspoon full of dried basil into the simmering minestrone soup. Steam lifted from its surface, scenting the small kitchen. She added another pinch of salt and tasted. Perfect; enough for her guests, and plenty left over to eat throughout the week. She lowered the temperature of the burner.

Tonight, they were celebrating. Floyd had been released from the infirmary the day before and that morning, announced he felt like having company. A knock sounded at the front door, signaling their guests had arrived. Evelyn passed from the kitchen, through the living room, and into the foyer, peering out of the peephole before swinging open the front door.

Sandy and Dev stood on the threshold, Dev cradling two bottles of wine, Sandy holding wine glasses. Dev stepped forward, inhaling. "My goodness. What are you cooking? Smells delicious."

Sandy gasped. "Minestrone soup?" She hugged Evelyn, and the three of them proceeded into the apartment. "Dev, wait till you taste it. Mom used to make it all the time. In summer, she put in veggies fresh from the garden–zucchini, green beans, fresh oregano. It's legendary."

Floyd waited in the living room, leaning on a cane. Dr. Fulknier insisted he use one for the next couple weeks, whether he felt he needed it or not. "I vote we stop talking about it and go eat some." The little group moved into the kitchen, redolent with the scent of dinner. Sandy set a wineglass at each place setting, except the one Evelyn had laid out in memory of Dana.

Dev placed his wine on the kitchen counter, shaking hands with Floyd. "Great to see you up and around, Floyd." He embraced Evelyn. "Thank you for inviting us."

"I'm thrilled to have you." She lifted one of the bottles of wine. "That's a lovely offering, Dev, but I don't think I have a corkscrew."

"No worries. I came prepared." He reached into his front pocket, extracting a restaurant-style wine opener. He unfolded a small blade, slicing open the seal, and tearing it off. Drawing out a corkscrew, he turned it into the cork. "Leave it to Dad to stock wine in his doomsday shelter." He eased the cork out.

Evelyn lifted the pot of minestrone from the stove top, resting it on a trivet at the center of the table, next to the loaf of unleavened bread she'd baked earlier. "Everyone, sit."

They took their places, and Evelyn passed the ladle to Dev, who dipped into the steaming, fragrant vegetable stew, filling Sandy's bowl then his own. Evelyn served Floyd, then herself.

Floyd's hand trembled when he lifted his spoon to his mouth. "Tastes delicious, Ev."

She took up a knife, reaching for the bread. She sliced the serrated blade across the crust, its edge buzzing like a saw, barely making a dent in the rock hard surface. "Wish I could say the same for the bread. I'd say that's inedible."

Floyd shrugged. "Maybe you could try sculpting something from it."

The group chuckled. Evelyn rested her head against Floyd's shoulder. "I think it's even too hard for that." Baking had never been her strong suit.

Dev poured the wine into glasses, the splash and gurgle of the burgundy liquid making a happy noise. "A toast. Thank you to my dad, for having the foresight to buy this place, and to stock some good wine. And, to the chef. Evelyn, this is legendary."

A chorus of, "the chef," echoed as they clinked their wineglasses. Evelyn's heart expanded in her chest, grateful for Dev's compliment, and even more grateful for the moment. It was the first time since Alec had attempted to kill them and destroy the bunker that they'd all been together outside the infirmary. There was just one person missing. "To Dana, our sister and friend." Evelyn raised her glass, and her toast was echoed. Floyd's eyes brimmed with tears.

"That's tasty vino, Dev." Evelyn didn't know enough about wine to discuss its characteristics, but she loved the slightly fruity flavor and smooth finish. She hadn't imbibed any alcohol since the earliest days of the disaster when she'd had a beer at Floyd's house. The effect was quick, her limbs becoming light and loose. She had another sip, savoring the taste and sensation. It helped soften the things she didn't want to remember. The destruction, the death, the loss of loved ones. The on-going struggle to keep the bunker safe.

The day before, three teen-agers had arrived at the boulder barricade, claiming to be from School of Mines. They had a student parking sticker on their vehicle, but they resembled druggies more than college students. The female reminded her of April, the hitch-hiker they'd picked up who was part of Nate Lewis's gang, with the same watchful eyes and hard smile that fell away as soon as it wasn't useful. One of the young men had the scabby face of a meth addict. Evelyn signaled Fred Scott with a curt shake of her head, and he raised his automatic rifle. Evelyn drew her gun, aiming it at the meth head's chest. "What'd you kids do to the students you stole this car from?"

The kid skittered backward, raising his hands. "Whoa. What the heck? I don't know what you're talking about. That's totally my car."

"Really? You went to School of Mines? What's the circumference of Earth?" Sandy was no longer allowed down at the boulder barricade where they'd been attacked by Nate Lewis, but she'd supplied the guards with screening questions that any student from School of Minds could answer.

The shortest guy of the group scowled, his greasy face folding into deep lines. "That's easy. It's a million miles."

Evelyn held in a laugh. "Nice try. You three get back in your vehicle, and leave. If you come back, you'll be shot on sight. Got that, Fred?"

He cocked his weapon. "Oh, I got it. You heard her. Move out, young'uns."

The scrawny threesome scrambled back into their car, muttering curses, screaming and saluting with their middle fingers as they roared back down the mountain road. Evelyn trembled for ten minutes after they'd driven away. She remained at the boulders for two hours in case they returned, but they hadn't. Evelyn dreaded new arrivals, but Dev had pointed out they needed more people to keep the facility maintained and the science lab properly staffed, but more people meant—

"Evelyn?" Floyd touched her shoulder. "You doing okay?"

"Sorry. Just spacing out." She slurped her soup, enjoying its warmth and salty, tomato flavor, forcing herself to stay present and count her blessings. She had her family, their pantry was stocked with canned goods, they had shelter. Hopefully, they'd have the agricultural area repaired soon and begin producing vegetables, herbs, and fish.

She would soon start limiting her visits to the front barricade but wanted to be sure Fred was ready to take charge, and so stopped down once a day. They continued to improve screening practices for arriving groups. The questions started with "Where are you from? How'd you hear about the place? What can you contribute? Any history of mental illness?" and got harder from there.

Evelyn rose from the dinner table, grabbing a notepad and pencil from the counter to make a note for herself.

"Mom, really?" Sandy tapped her spoon against her bowl. "Do you have to do that now? It's a party."

Evelyn halted. It still tickled her to be called "mom," rather than "her," or "that person." She pushed away the pad. "Sorry. There's still so much to do. I worry I'll forget something if I don't write it down as soon as it occurs to me."

"You've done a great job while the rest of us were slacking in the infirmary." Dev smiled, and everyone laughed. "But we're all okayed by the doc to be up and around and working now. You can relax a bit."

She couldn't, though. Not while the bunker was still open and accepting more refugees. Maybe in a couple weeks, when the doors were closed and sealed. Maybe not even then, but definitely not before.

Dev and the Professor had been interviewing the refuges about land and weather conditions, which were worsening quickly in the outside world. They'd lost radio contact with School of Mines two days prior, and Dev figured it was the last they'd hear from them but, hopefully, more students and teachers were caravanning down. But then, once they were ensconced in the bunker, and there were fifty, sixty, or seventy-five people living there, who would ensure order? What would be the consequence of criminal acts?

Evelyn pushed away her soup. "We need to decide about what to do with people who become a danger to themselves or others."

"Mom. Really?"

Dev squeezed Sandy's hand. "My dear, your mother carried the load while the rest of us were incapacitated. Let's hash this out for her." Dev finished his soup, setting aside his spoon. "My father intended a much longer, and more thorough, vetting process for residents. His original plan for the place was for everyone here to be family or close friends. There was also to be a sizable financial buy-in. He never considered a possible criminal element. He thought the worst we'd have to face would be one or two people who wouldn't do well in extended confinement. He made certain provisions for that, but they weren't extensive."

Evelyn found herself nodding along with him.

"After what Alec attempted, I've had to rethink our approach. If someone is severely mentally ill, without a psychiatrist—even with one—we're going to be limited as far as the help we can provide. There's an isolated wing on the western side of the facility. There are rooms that could be used as cells. The question remains, though, do we want that? Should we house them, or should they be exiled? What about people who flout the rules of the sanctuary? Should we bother with a jail, or should they be exiled? I haven't yet decided and would like all your thoughts over the next day or two." He glanced around the table.

"Repeat offenders, or those who become dangerous will have to be removed. At the far end of the wing, there's an exit. It's vacuum locked. Offenders would be taken to a chamber and conveyed outside. Once the door shuts behind them, there's no way back inside. I realize it may seem barbaric to some."

"No." Evelyn folded her napkin. "It's fair. You've offered sanctuary, and safety. There have to be consequences for disrupting that."

Dev steepled his fingers. "It's going to be a shock for some people. Surrendering their weapons, and to some degree, their self-determination, but that's the price of sheltering here. I'm open to suggestions, but ultimately, this isn't a democracy. This is my home, and you're all my family." He took Sandy's hand in his. "I'll do whatever I must to keep us safe."

Evelyn's tense shoulders relaxed. As usual, she'd been worried for nothing. While she'd been busy fretting, Dev was thinking and planning. He'd do whatever it took to protect Sandy.

"But, you know..." Sandy leaned her elbows on the table, her grin infectious. "We're making progress."

Evelyn's heart ticked up again. Her kid was about to let her into the most important part of her life; her science.

"It's not going to be easy and I'm not saying we're one-hundred percent there, but my best guess is that we're looking at a year, two max, to get the fracking under control."

That sounded like a fairy tale or, at best, wishful thinking. The disaster was so far reaching, so utterly unending, that Evelyn couldn't see how they could end it with a couple of squiggles on a piece of paper.

"I know what you're thinking." Sandy took Evelyn's hand across the table. "But have a little faith, Mom. We talked to Dr. Goode for days before things went south. We're confident this can work."

Evelyn didn't ask, because she wasn't going to understand the logistics or chemistry/biology/whatever. What matters was that

Sandy understood she was on her side. "I'm a worrier by nature, my dear, but I trust you. Absolutely. If you say we're going to be out of here within two years, I believe you."

In a flash, Sandy leaned across the table and pecked her on the cheek. "Thanks, Ma."

Evelyn stood, the better to hide her tears, stacking dishes as she went.

Sandy and Dev said good night—chatting at the door as if they were old friends who did this regularly and gifting the second bottle of wine to Evelyn and Floyd.

Floyd leaned against the door, pulling Evelyn to him. "Feel better now that you've talked to him?"

She leaned into him, more relaxed than she'd been in months. "I do. I trust Dev. He's a good man."

"I agree. You ready for bed, my love?"

"So ready." She straightened, groaning from the effort. She had her share of battle scars; her body pained her where she'd been shot, but she was healing, and so was Floyd. It would take time, but they'd all recover from their injuries; the process had begun already. One step at a time, they were rebuilding: starting with the agricultural center, but every area Alec had tried to destroy would be repaired, possibly improved.

Evelyn was stepping into new challenges. She'd spent years backing away from life, but that wasn't an option anymore. Whether life was above or below ground, or a mixture of both for the foreseeable future, her work going into the future was to take care of her family and community. Perhaps she'd create some art again and teach others to do the same. She could start by gifting Floyd with a replacement of the sculpture he'd kept in his bedroom. His birthday was in a few months. It was good to have something to look forward to.

CHAPTER THIRTY-FOUR

Alma Garcia. Roosevelt Lake Marina, Arizona

The following morning meant more fish, but Alma savored it all the same. It was likely to be the last fully satisfying meal for a long time. They kept the fishing gear since the road would pass other stretches of water, and it had served them well.

The horse trailers worked better than they appeared. Jen's horses had jittered, but Ruth got them under control with a slap of the reins. She sat bareback on the lead mare and Malachi sat on the other pair, following her.

They loaded the horse trailers with their gear, the priority being water and food. Sails had been cut and personal belongings bundled, and rope harnesses created, so every adult could carry their own gear. Only the oldest and youngest rode the trailers. Everyone plodded on, the flock mostly keeping to the highway hemmed in by the straggling group and pushed forward by the attentive dogs. Competent riders, mostly Chrissy's brood, took turns guiding the horses. They traveled away from the lake, smelling cleaner and feeling hopeful.

By the midday rest time, the group was flagging and the long lake still glimmered in the distance. Thankfully, someone had found and pulled water containers from a couple of the boats. The large containers nestled safely on the horse trailers, but after the group's personal water bottles were empty, the water supply wouldn't last more than a day or two, especially with the livestock. Little bugs, nothing more than dots through the opaque plastic tub, darted up to the surface and sloshed around in their drinking water supply.

They stopped just off the cracked and crazed highway, still miles and days from their destination. The water containers were already low. The ground wasn't as hot as it had been weeks earlier, but they sought the cooler shade beside a clump of thin, dusty bushes. Taylor sent one of the wagons to the lakeshore to fill the largest containers. The cows and goats followed, lowing and baaing.

"Em, let's set some traps to see if we can catch a rabbit or, if we're really lucky, a deer?" Kit held out a set of strings and triggers he'd packed from the ranch. "I think I saw a herd earlier on the distant lake shore. They weren't nervous about us."

"You should've shot one." Jude sneered and raised his arms like he was holding a rifle.

"We need the ammo to get us to the bunker." Kit raised his brows. "Em and I can show you how to set a trap if you like."

Emelia got up and followed him and Jude into the bush. Alma snorted. Jude had been extremely quiet around the larger group, but hunting was probably perfect for him.

Dunia and Faris didn't sit down on the baking ground. They each dug a hole out in the sunlight, dragging the dry soil into a pile. When the hole was as deep as her forearm, Dunia dropped a flat container to the bottom. She cut a few leafy branches from the dull greenish-gray bushes and placed them around the pot. Next, she laid a plastic bag over the hole, with the pot and plants below and scooped the soil on top of the edges of the plastic to hold it in place. She selected a stone from the ground, rubbed it clean, and placed it in the middle. The plastic collapsed into the pot. She tried a second time, stretching the bag, and it collapsed again. "I need a bigger piece of plastic. Does anyone have some?"

Alma pulled one of the rain ponchos from her blanket pack. "Will this do?"

Dunia took it and pulled it from the wrapper. "That will more than do."

She tossed aside the smaller bag and a breeze carried it away. She laid the poncho over the hole and spread the soil from the hole around the edge, then placed the stone in the middle. The plastic sagged.

Whatever Dunia was doing, the plastic wouldn't hold the weight of the stone. "Oh sorry. I have nothing else."

Duni laughed. "It is meant to look like that. Do you have more of the raincoats?"

"Plenty."

"Let's dig some more then."

"Why?"

Taylor wandered over and bent over the hole. "Brilliant idea, Dunia!"

Dunia beamed at Taylor, then turned back to Alma. "We need water. The ground has water. This will draw it out."

Alma helped Dunia dig a second hole. By the time she was finished, the first plastic raincoat had misted over with a light sheen of droplets. It worked.

Day after day, the routine was the same. Check the traps and take them down, collect the water from the solar stills, pack up and break camp. Drive the herd and keep walking until the sun was high. Watch for birds, vegetation and insects as signs for a ready supply of water and potential food or prepare to dig holes for new solar stills when they rested. Then, if the traps had yielded any meat or fishing was available, prepare whatever was at hand. They often went hungry. Twice they had no choice but to slaughter a cow and they celebrated those lives, taking an extra day of rest. They set new traps the next day and slept the best they could on empty stomachs. Nomadic life was repetitive.

One day, they crossed through a small town. They'd gone through others, but for some reason, the trek was terrifying. The windows were empty of residents, but it didn't stop Alma from searching for them. The sense that they were being watched made her skin prickle and all the alarm bells go off in her head. The group bunched together with no word from any of the leaders. Sticking together, united against any force was the best way to survive. Stone guarded from the front with his rifle, his men positioned themselves at the flanks and roamed through the adjoining streets. Kit and a couple of the other rancher shooters remained at the back. No one complained about the faster pace. When they were clear, the group gave a collective sigh. They'd seen no one and faced no trial, but Alma was sure that every step they'd taken had been closely monitored.

A few days later, Robin chatted with Matias while they cradled a jam jar with fry they'd caught in a pool at the lake. The children had found the large shoal glistening silver at the water's edge, away from where the fishermen and women had been attempting to catch a meal. They secured their find with a torn plastic bag at the rim. Matias had picked some weed from the shallows and plonked it in with the baby fish. The water inside was cloudy, but Alma refused to let them add any of their drinking water. She hadn't had the heart to tell them to put the fish back and the new pets kept them entertained during the miles of walking. Robin chatted away near constantly, referring to Kit as the alpha wolf, even though he marched at the back of the group during the day.

"Why do you say that?" Alma finally relented, pouring a tiny amount of her water into the jar.

"The pack leader walks at the back to protect everyone." Robin pointed at Kit at the rear of the train.

"Not at the front?"

Robin giggled. "No silly. The one in charge has to make sure everyone is safe and staying together."

The small girl was right. Kit had taken the tail end for several days. Even walking at the back, he maintained his leadership role.

Their feet ached and their bodies were weary when Doc and Stone turned the group from the highway toward the mountains. But she felt the tingle of anticipation run down her spine. After hours of steady marching, Stone turned them on to a dirt road that was soon shrouded by pines. It zigzagged up the mountain, the fresher temperature chilling in her sweaty clothes. The horses protested at the climb and the goats nibbled whatever they could get to, which was easier as the group slowed. The shadows and half-light played tricks, but she didn't hear howling or growls from the trees.

An hour after turning on to the dirt road, a line of huge boulders blocked the path ahead. Repeated gouge marks in the dirt showed they had been dragged there deliberately. Stone raised his hand in a fist and the group stopped, then he waved Kit forward. The herd bustled out of Kit's way and a woman screamed.

Three armed men stepped out from the trees. The one with a heavy dark jacket had his weapon pointed at Stone's back. "Put your weapons down."

Stone's eyes widened, and he moved slowly. He lifted the rifle from his shoulder and laid it on the ground. Kit copied, removing his pistol and rifle. All the others placed their open weapons on the ground, but those who carried concealed weapons were tense and shifted uneasily, searching the mountain above them.

Kit rose, hands outstretched. "We're from Harmony Ranch, north of Flagstaff. Evelyn and Sandy came to us. We are seeking sanctuary."

The man on the gunman's left lifted his radio. "Check with the boss. Harmony Ranch. Over."

Kit took a step forward, and the men raised their weapons higher. "They spoke to my aunt, Jen McCreedy. She owns Harmony Ranch. They told us to come."

The man with the radio lifted his hand and scowled. Alma pulled Matias behind her and searched for Em. She stood with Taylor, who blocked her in a similar fashion.

A woman's voice came over the radio. "I don't see the woman from the ranch. Over."

Alma searched the trees for any signs of cameras, but she couldn't make any out.

Kit turned and beckoned to his aunt, who stumbled forward. "This is her."

The radio man pressed the talk button. "Got a woman here says she's Jen McCreedy. Over."

"Bring two to the gate. Over."

Kit put his hand on Stone's chest and shook his head. "You wait here. Keep them safe." He beckoned into the group, and Taylor handed Emelia to Alma on her way to join Kit. "Hopefully that's Evelyn on the radio. But whoever is in charge here, we'll do our best to convince them to let us stay and tell them what we know."

Aunt Jen lowered her voice. "We don't tell them what happened at the ranch. They don't need to know about the battle. They'll think we're a threat."

"Yep, I know." Kit grabbed Taylor's hand. "That's why Taylor is doing the talking."

Taylor turned away from Stone and her gaze met Jen's. "Woman to woman. I'll get her to listen. Our new family needs this break."

"I think I should come—" Jen's face folded in worry.

Kit gave his aunt a quick peck on the cheek. "Trust me, my wife's a pro when it comes to handling people. She's better than all of us put together. No offense."

"None taken." Jen stepped back, taking Robin's hand in hers. "I trust you."

Kit and Taylor joined the third man, walking past the boulder barricade, and disappeared around a bend in the road.

Under constant scrutiny from the two guards that remained, Stone pushed the ranchers back from the line of rocks. He strolled through the group, bending to speak to random adults Alma hadn't seen him interact with much before, then he paused at his friends, whispering urgently.

She'd recovered from the climb, but her heart raced. The promise of another life away from the ranch had driven her, and no doubt the others, to press for the bunker. They couldn't return to Harmony Ranch. If they were turned away from the bunker, perhaps they could set up at the marina, where they had fresh water and an abundance of fish, but with the coming winter, they wouldn't survive for long.

With the tree cover and the hazy sky masking the sun's position, it was difficult to mark the passage of time. Her water bottle was almost empty and if they wanted to refill their supply, they should head back to the highway. The road snaked downhill, dotted with the grazing goats. It would be easier and quicker than the climb.

Stone jumped up and rushed to the head of the group. Kit, Taylor, the guard and another woman hurried around the bend. Taylor's wide smile broke Alma's anxiety.

A woman, her hair ponytailed, and graying at her temples, limped into view, heavy boots scuffing the dirt. She wore a Kevlar vest over a plaid shirt and jeans. Her left arm was in a sling. A pistol hung at her waist, and a rifle was slung over her right shoulder. She nodded to the guards, who kept their guns at the ready.

"Welcome." The woman rested her hands on her hips. "I'm Evelyn Parker." Her face neutral, she scanned the crowd. "You must be tired, but gather your things, there's a short trek yet. Make your way up to the gate where you will be given water and prepared for check-in." She turned away, then twisted slightly back. "All weapons must be surrendered at check-in. If you become a real part of our community and have skills, you may be chosen for the security team. You'll be able to use your own weapons for those duties, but they will remain part of the bunker's property."

"Unhitch the horses." Kit pointed to Ruth. Stone whispered urgently in Kit's ear. They stepped aside with most of Stone's team.

Taylor jumped on one of the blocking rocks. "We'll lift the trailers over. I want the adult men and women, now. Chrissy, can you take the children and our older folks up with Evelyn, please?"

Chrissy joined Evelyn, who pointed up the hill. Chrissy turned to them, meeting Alma's gaze with a smile, and beckoned. "Come on. You're nearly there."

Young and old plodded up to the rocks and through to the other side. The guards helped lift the trailers. The dogs funneled the herd through a gap in the stones no wider than one animal. Jen's horses wouldn't like that.

Evelyn's hand rested near her pistol, her fingers tapping the gunbelt. "You've been creative."

"We didn't know what to bring, but we weren't going to leave anything of worth to those..." Taylor shook her head. "Well, we brought what we could. We didn't want to come empty-handed. Our group are hard workers and will contribute, not take." She gestured to the herd. "Nannies and one billy goat. There are four cows left. If we need meat, they'll do, but we figured milk would be just as welcome. We'd need to find a bull."

Alma pushed the blanket pack to her back and picked up one of the growing lights wrapped in cloth before someone tripped over it. "Em, grab the plants. Mati, make sure you have the bike generator." She hurried them and Robin after the animals through the gap after Chrissy.

"Cabbages." Evelyn reached out, touching the leaves of the plants. "And tomatoes." She turned to Taylor. "These are great. They'll add some variety to what we've got in the ag area."

Taylor grimaced. "Alma and Simeon found an illegal cannabis farm a while ago. We've got heated lamp lights if you have power. And I picked up some seed packets along the way, too. I don't know if we can grow underground, but with a good setup, and a bit of imagination, maybe." Taylor ruffled Matias' hair. "We have a chance to raise something good."

Evelyn released the plant leaves, stepping back. A ghost of something dark slitted her eyes. "We have a hydroponic set up. This will definitely add some variety." She rubbed her hand over her throat. "I hope we all get to sample them."

"The water is safe and enough?"

"We had tanks for fish, but they were damaged."

Matias pulled Robin closer. "Are there any small ones left? For our fish?"

Robin held up her jar. "They're only little. They won't take up too much space, I promise."

Evelyn bent down and inspected the murky water. "What type of fish are they?"

"I don't know, but I don't think they like my jar that much." Robin bit her lip. "Mati and me got them out of the lake and the water has gone a bit yucky."

Taylor pushed the jar in Robin's hand down. "If there is enough water, perhaps we'll see about it."

Evelyn adjusted her sling. "Yours will need to be quarantined to ensure they don't bring in any disease. As for fresh water, we have an underground source. Testing is ongoing but the fracking mess didn't poison the supply." She winced. "I've seen my share of what it did on my way here. Water on fire, explosions. Millions dead because of greed."

Alma pushed Emelia away from the bunker's leader and her chatter that evoked bloodied memories, fear and desperate plans. They had a new life to begin. A hopeful life.

Evelyn raised her voice, and Alma turned. "Tell them you have fish when you get to the entrance. All animals and livestock must be declared."

After the days of walking through a broken land and the final climb up the dirt track, the tall tunnel honed into the mountainside was strong and stable. Warm orange lights faded into the depths. Water, electricity and safety. It gave the impression that nothing could reach them inside. The helpful bunker staff ushered the group to a large cafeteria, made note of names and family sizes (she added Robin to their family registration) then assigned them rooms and escorted them with a small box of toiletries.

Their room was more than she could've wished for. Two sets of bunk beds with clean mattresses, and a small desk with a wheely chair. Matias jumped on it and spun around. Robin pushed him faster. A three drawer chest sat against the wall with a shelf above it. It was an extravagance. They'd never fill all the storage, but she could try. She gasped at the little restroom for their use. She twisted the tap and clear water flowed into the basin. It was perfect.

Showered and dressed in their freshest clothes, she used the map she'd been given to lead them to the cafeteria. If the room held everyone housed at the bunker, the rancher's arrival had easily tripled the numbers, but plates steamed with food and every mug was full. Alma collected her food on a tray and hesitated. There were plenty of places to sit, but it didn't feel right to sit by themselves anymore, not after what they had been through. She could join the parents laughing together while their children ran up and down the gaps between the tables. Or Stone and his friends sitting with Mr. H and Sharon playing cards. Jen, Kit, and Taylor sat with several others she'd not seen before. Taylor turned and waved them over. Alma, Em, Mati and Robin sat down in a long line next to her.

An older man, tanned and muscular, who sat across from the younger two leaned over and filled their mugs from the jug. He winked at Matias, then pushed the water to the woman with him sitting at the end of the table. Alma turned away and noticed the woman with him only had one leg.

The woman offered her hand. "Cat." She shook Alma's hand firmly, then let go. Thrusting a thumb at the older man, she flashed a smile at him. "This is Tom. My husband."

Kit put his hand on Alma's shoulder, but she didn't shake it off. "This is Alma. If you think your tale was hair-raising, ask about hers."

Alma shook her head. "I'd rather write a new story together. The past is gone."

CHAPTER THIRTY-FIVE

Evelyn Parker. Anil Kumar Sanctuary, Arizona

Evelyn yawned, glancing at the other council members convened round the table in the conference room. Floyd, ruddy-cheeked, his health slowly returning three weeks after being attacked and nearly killed. Dev, the picture of calm as he made his case to leave the bunker open for a while longer. Sandy scribbled notes, her blonde ponytail bobbing as she nodded agreement. "Dev makes a good point. While technically, we have enough people to maintain the facility, we can accommodate more, and morally speaking, we should try."

Evelyn's gut twisted with stress. Other people be damned. "More people, more problems. The longer we remain open, the more we're all at risk." Ultimately, the bunker was Dev's property, the decision was his, but he'd shown again and again he was open to being swayed by his council's advice. But it wasn't likely on this issue. He'd pressed again and again to remain open just a short time longer.

Dev rolled his chair back. "We have – people. I think we can still expect more from School of Mines, and the Boulder area. If we can bolster the ranks of the science team, we should." He shot a look at

Sandy, who smiled up at him. "Conditions are worsening out there, slowing travel. I'd like to remain open for another week, possibly two, with the caveat that if we reach capacity, we'll close."

Evelyn had expected as much. Dev and Sandy hadn't spent as much time on the road as she and Floyd and hadn't witnessed what they had. Despite the havoc Nate Lewis and Alec had wrought, Sandy considered them outliers in terms of violence. In fact, they were the new normal. All hell had broken loose, and Evelyn had passed through a lot of it. There was the entire Lewis gang, dozens of people, many of them teenagers, who'd slaughtered the sheriff and killed Dana's friends; April, who planned to sell them out to Nate Lewis; the mountain man Wade, who'd nearly raped her. She'd kept those incidents to herself to spare her daughter worry, but maybe that was a mistake.

"If there's nothing else, I'm quite ready for something to eat." Dev tapped his pen on the tabletop.

"Sounds good, Dev." Floyd stood, leaning on his cane. He complained about it every chance he got but he wasn't so prideful that he'd risk trying to get around without it.

Ev rose with Floyd, letting Dev and Sandy leave ahead of them. When they were out of earshot, Floyd took her hand. "I know you're not happy."

"No, but Dev's been right so far. There's nothing to do but go along with his plan. And be extra vigilant."

They walked to their apartment without saying much. Floyd unlocked the door. "You're going down to the barricade, aren't you?"

"Just a drop in. I won't be long." She had her Kevlar vest on, but she reached into the closet by the door for the helmet Fred Scott had given her.

"Wish I could go." Floyd sank onto the couch, setting aside his cane. He missed being able to help defend the place, but it was out of the question for him to go. He moved slowly, and limped, and would be a liability in the field.

"Me, too." Evelyn strapped her knife to her calf and slung a gun holster around her waist. As a council member, she was allowed to keep her own sidearm, but the higher power weapons were secured in the armory near the bunker entrance. She'd pick up a rifle on her way out of the building. She crossed to Floyd, leaning down to kiss him. "See you soon."

She bypassed the elevator, opting for the stairs. The members of the council had been discussing energy conservation earlier. Dev and Sandy expected gloomy weather conditions soon, which would affect the amount of energy their solar panels could generate, but they were optimistic about their long-term chances of survival. Within a day or two, they'd announce new conservation measures at a community meeting. Elevator use would be reserved for moving large cargo. She might just as well get used to taking the stairs.

As she hit the second-floor landing, the door pushed open, a man stepping into the stairwell. He started. "I wasn't expecting to bump into anyone."

"Sorry to startle you. Kit, is it?" She offered her hand. "Evelyn Parker."

He shook firmly, then let go. He was tall, fairly young, and good-looking. "Yes. Glad to meet you in person finally. I've heard good things."

"Likewise. You were a firefighter, yes? And an EMT?"

"I was. Still am, though I hope my days of fighting fires are finished." He shrugged.

"We could've used you a bit sooner. As I'm sure you've heard, someone tried to burn the place down not long after we arrived. But I'm grateful we've got a person with your skill set going forward. Doc Fulknier can use all the help she can get."

He frowned. "I heard rumors about a fire. I'm glad he wasn't successful."

"He was successful, to a certain degree, but we're still here." She forced a smile. "It's lucky I ran into you, actually. I wanted to invite you to a council meeting to discuss our emergency preparedness."

"Tell me where and when, and I'll be there." He stopped on a stair, allowing her to catch up to him.

"How about right now? Our council meeting just ended, but I'm heading down to the boulder barricade. If you have a few minutes to spare, you could join me." The area continued to spook her, and she preferred to make the jaunt with someone else. "Sorry for being presumptuous. As if you have nothing else to do."

He smiled. "I don't. I was on my way out for some fresh air. I'd love to go with you."

"Great." They reached the ground floor, exiting the stairwell near the entryway. "We'll stop at the armory for gear."

To ensure the safety of everyone at the bunker, as well as the facility itself, only council members had keys to the armory, situated near the entry behind a reinforced door. Evelyn checked the surrounding area before inserting her key into the lock. She allowed Kit inside, locking the door behind them. There were caches of weapons hidden in other places; Dev and Sandy had one in their apartment, as did Evelyn and Floyd, and Uncle Thomas and Cat. In the event of an emergency, trusted allies would be armed.

Kit wore a Kevlar vest under a flannel shirt. Evelyn passed him a helmet, and shoulder guards provided by Fred Scott. She assigned him a .45 automatic handgun, and a rifle, taking one for herself. She noted everything on a sign-out sheet before locking up, then stopped by Mission Control to let Frank Fulknier know she'd be out of the building. "Heading down to the barricade with Kit. Will you open the gate, and close it behind us?"

Frank was young but he'd made himself indispensable, manning the security cameras and repairing the computer network. "You got it. Be safe."

They headed out to Dev's pick-up truck in the garage. Kit reached for the passenger door handle, then stopped, straightening and looking toward the gate. "Do you smell smoke?"

Evelyn inhaled. The slightest whiff of smoke carried into the parking area. "I don't know, maybe."

She climbed into the driver's seat, starting the engine. The security gate rose, and she drove outside.

"Over there." Kit pointed northwest. Dark smoke billowed into the gray sky above the mountains and Evelyn put on the brakes. "Not too close yet. When your group drove through the mountains, did you notice how dry everything was? This late in summer, the woods are a tinderbox. Let's wait a few minutes and see how it's moving."

Kit got out of the truck and climbed on the bed. They both watched for the next five minutes, then Kit returned to the passenger seat. "From the looks of things, the fire's heading right this way, and it's moving fast."

"Let's get down to the barricade, and warn our folks." Evelyn pressed the gas pedal, driving as quickly as she could down the rutted dirt road. They passed the guard's truck parked on the side of the road. Ahead, Fred Scott, along with a pair of guards Evelyn didn't know, were hunkered behind boulders at the barricade. Two more emerged from the woods as she pulled to a stop. Evelyn and Kit hopped from the truck. "You all smell the smoke?"

Fred shrugged. "A little bit. I figured it's par for the course this time of the year in a western state."

Kit stepped forward. "Yes, and no. Yes, it's fire season, so fires are typical this time of the year. But given what we know about our changed atmosphere—the explosions, the chemicals that have saturated the ground—it won't be like previous forest fires. We're talking massive, unstoppable conflagrations." His words hung in the air, heavy and unanswered. In the quiet, something mechanical sounded in the distance.

Fred raised his index finger. "Hear that? Car. Nope, more than one." He signaled the guards back into the woods. "You two should take cover, too, just in case."

Evelyn and Kit followed the guards into the woods where Nate Lewis and his remnant crew had hidden before attacking her, Sandy, and Dana. Evelyn's stomach tightened. She looked forward to the day she didn't have to visit this place anymore. The moan of engines struggling up the steep mountain road penetrated the trees. As they drew closer, Evelyn trembled, lifting her rifle. A car rumbled into view, pulling up to the boulders, and stopping. As instructed by a sign Fred had posted, they turned off their engine. Hands thrust from the windows; fingers splayed.

Fred held his position behind the boulder as another car rolled to a stop behind the first, followed by a third vehicle. Evelyn couldn't perform a head count from her place behind a tree, but the refugees likely outnumbered the guards. "Kit, how many are there?"

"At least a dozen. Could be more in trunks, or on the floor."

Fred raised his head above the boulder, automatic weapon poised. "Everyone, remain in your vehicles and keep your hands where we can see them." He waved the guards forward from the woods, Kit and Evelyn easing through the trees, their boots crunching leaves.

A woman's voice cut through the air. "Please, let us stay. You have no idea what it's like out there." She sobbed.

Someone shushed her. "You're okay, Linda. We're safe now. Take a deep breath. Shh. We'll be fine."

Evelyn *did* know what it was like out there and didn't fault Linda one bit for crying. Cresting the incline, she and Kit stood behind the last car, an old jeep, stuffed with people. The two guards flanking Fred rose from behind boulders as Fred walked toward the front vehicle. "Where are you from? How'd you hear about the place?"

A woman answered. She held a card between her fingers that Fred took and examined. "Here's my driver's license, and school ID. I'm Judy Sanwood, from School of Mines. Most of us are from the college, though we picked up some refugees along the way, people who claim they were held hostage by Martinez Corporation."

Fred handed her IDs back to her. "Please be aware we have a screening process. You'll be here a while, and you'll need to surrender your weapons."

"I understand you have your procedure, but are you aware there's fire coming this way? We've barely kept ahead of it since we left Flagstaff. Also, we've got a pregnant woman on board. Can she get out and stretch her legs?"

"Where is she?" Fred's head swiveled as he scanned the line of vehicles.

"The very last car. The jeep." Judy thrust her head out her car window. "Linda? You doing okay?"

"No, I'm not. Please let me out, sir." It was the same woman who'd been crying earlier. "I need to use the bathroom."

"I'll see to her, Fred." Evelyn shouldered her rifle and opened the front passenger door of the jeep. Linda was enormous, most of it a belly that stretched the limits of the green floral muumuu she wore. She scooched to the edge of the car seat, using the door handle to lower herself to the ground, moaning she set her feet on the road. They were swollen beyond the bounds of her hiking sandals. "Hello, Linda. I'm Evelyn. I need to search you, okay? Raise your arms to the side please." Linda complied, and Evelyn patted her down. "She's clear, Fred. I'll take her into the brush to do her business." She held out an arm. "There's a little path off the road there, down the hill. Lean on me if you need to." She led Linda to the path, down an embankment, and into the woods, stopping when they reached a flat piece of ground. "I'll wait here."

Linda waddled behind the bushes. No wonder she'd been crying. Being pregnant was difficult enough but being pregnant in the midst of all this destruction had to be a nightmare. After a few minutes, Linda emerged wiping her eyes. "How long is the screening process? There's fire everywhere, and it's moving fast. I'm scared for my baby."

Evelyn offered her arm again. "Hopefully, not long. Watch your step." She grabbed the teetering woman. "You got it?"

"Yes. Thank you." She grunted, panting as the hill steepened. "Maybe I shouldn't ask, but do you have children?"

"It's fine." Evelyn pulled her along, helping her up the incline. "I have a daughter, Sandy. She's inside."

"That's good. You can't imagine it out there. Fires, and smoke, and that horrid chemical smell, and random explosions on top of that."

"Yes, I remember. But you made it here, and we have a top notch doc. You can start to breathe easy." They reached the top of the incline.

Kit approached, hand extended. Flecks of white and gray dotted his palm. "Ashes. Evelyn, that fire is really moving. We need to get these folks back to the bunker. We can process everyone inside."

The scent of heavy burning reached Evelyn before the words were out of his mouth. She checked the sky—darker, and full of smoke. She cupped her mouth, raising her voice. "Listen up, everyone. We need to head for the bunker ASAP. Fred, you and the other guards check the vehicles for weapons while Kit and I move the barricade. And radio HQ, let them know we need an intake team to meet us in the garage, and to leave the security door open."

Fred gave a thumbs up. "You got it."

Evelyn and Kit ran to the pick-up truck. Ashes speckled the windshield and hood. Evelyn turned the truck around, backing toward the barricade. Kit lifted the chains from the back bed, strapping them around a boulder, and affixing the load to the trailer hitch. "Go for it."

Evelyn went easy on the gas, worried if she applied power suddenly the chain would snap. She dragged the boulder from its sentry position, off to the side of the road. Kit unhooked the chains, carrying them to the next rock, and they repeated the process two more times, clearing a passageway wide enough for the refugee cars. Evelyn parked the pick-up, taking the keys from the ignition, and stepping out.

Finished with his weapon check, Fred banged on the hood of the front car. "You're clear. Drive through slowly and pull to the side of the road." He spoke into a handheld radio he unhooked from his belt. The other guards processed the second car, sending it through. A cache of weapons taken from the refugees lay on the ground near Fred's feet.

Linda gripped Evelyn's hand. "Can I stay with you? I can't get back in that jeep. The smell in there is making me sick."

Evelyn had also been sensitive to odors when she was pregnant. "Sure. Wait here while Kit and I finish, and you can ride back with us." The third vehicle eased through, idling on the side of the narrow dirt road. Evelyn hurried to Kit. "I say we leave the boulders where they are."

"Agree." Evelyn tossed him the keys. Kit hopped into the driver's seat, while Evelyn opened the back door, helping Linda climb inside. "Fasten your seatbelt." She closed the door, turning to Fred and the other guards. "Grab those weapons, and head to the bunker, right now." Fred saluted as she hopped into the front passenger seat.

Kit maneuvered the pick-up past the other cars, taking the lead back to the bunker. "Check out the sky."

Angry, orange flames flared above the distant treetops, black smoke filling the air. Evelyn gasped. "It's moving so fast."

"Yep. It's gonna get faster, too. And who knows what kind of toxic chemicals are mixed in at this point. We should close the bunker."

Evelyn's heart thudded. She'd been counting the minutes until the bunker was sealed, longing to have a locked door between her loved ones and outside forces, but after meeting the newest arrivals, the finality of closing it hit her like a fist. Anyone else traveling to the promised sanctuary of the bunker would find the place locked. They'd be doomed.

Dev had explained that once the place was closed, it wouldn't be reopened; not until they were ready to roll out "the solution that ends it all." He couldn't risk the entire bunker and everyone in it by bringing late arrivals into the garage for processing. "A crazy person with a bomb in their trunk could cost us everything." The specter of another crazy person bent on destruction had become a part of their every decision. She hoped Fred had searched every nook and cranny of the vehicles joining them.

They reached the bunker, and the door lifted to admit them. Evelyn had taken her last trip outside. She turned in her seat. "Linda, were there any other refugees coming behind you?"

Linda pressed one hand against her belly, while the other gripped the overhead handle. "No. We started on the road with five cars, but we three are all that's left."

"Got it. You'll need to stay with your group until you're processed, but I'll see you soon. Kit, come with me." She rushed from the pick-up truck, Kit hustling to catch up to her. They stopped at the armory, shelving their weapons, and stripping off their gear. Evelyn locked the heavy door, running down the hallway to Mission Control. "Frank, page Dev and Sandy, Floyd too, and ask them to meet us here."

"Sure thing." Brushing dark hair from his eyes, Frank picked up a handset, his page echoing through the room and nearby hallway. "Everything okay?"

"No." Evelyn moved close to him. "Can you pull up a full-screen, northwest view?"

Rather than running a bunch of different computer screens, each with a separate view, Frank ran two, toggling between views. He pulled up the northwest view, choking with black smoke and towering flames. "Whoa. What the heck?"

Dev hurried in. "I hope this is important. The Professor and I–" He stopped, his mouth open, then rushed forward. "Where is that?"

Evelyn crossed to him. "Northwest view and coming our way. It's time, Dev. We've got to seal the bunker."

Kit stood next to her. "Evelyn's right. That's the fastest moving fire I've ever seen."

Dev remained poised in front of the computer screen. "Do you know that every morning I get up very early, to take a walk outside? I breathe in the mountain air, and listen to the birds sing and I think, just another week or two, then we'll shut the door." He turned to Evelyn with a bitter half-laugh. "But today, of all days, I skipped my walk because I wanted to get a jump on some work down in the agri-cultural area."

Evelyn stroked his arm. "I'm sorry, Dev. Take comfort in knowing you've done everything you can. Sixty-some refugees, plus three carloads that just arrived."

"Wise words, Evelyn, as usual." He sighed. "Frank, prepare to seal the exterior. Kit, will you stay here with Frank in case he needs assistance?"

"Of course." Kit rolled a chair next to Frank. "We haven't been formally introduced. I'm Kit."

"Hi, Kit. Welcome to Mission Control."

Sandy and Floyd entered, Sandy rushing to Dev. "What's going on?"

Dev lifted his hands. "Everything's fine, but we're sealing the facility. Evelyn, you said a new group just arrived?"

"Yes. With the fire coming at us, we secured their vehicles and brought them up here for processing. They're in the garage."

Dev took Sandy's hand. "Shall we go welcome them, my dear? Evelyn? Floyd? Join us, please. Frank, give us a couple minutes, then close the garage door."

Together, they headed down the hall, past the armory and into the garage. Fred and the other guards stood watch as the new refugees were processed. A couple card tables had been set up, and were being manned by Cat and Tom. Linda, the pregnant woman, was seated at a table across from Dr. Fulknier, who referenced a checklist in front of her. The other refugees waited nearby, standing or seated on folding chairs. Their meager belongings were piled on the floor where a guard sifted through them, checking for hidden weapons they might have overlooked earlier.

"Evelyn?" Cat waved a card over her head. "D'you have a minute?"

Ev made her way to the small table. Cat handed her the intake card. "What am I looking at?" She scanned the name, checked the women seated opposite Cat, whose eyes were downcast, and checked the card again. "Does this mean what I think it means?"

The newcomer shrugged. "What do you think it means?"

Evelyn didn't want to say the name out loud for fear of inciting a riot. "I..."

"I'm not one of them." The woman squared her shoulders. "Truly. I care for the common man. The worker. The ordinary Joe on the street."

A million thoughts raced through Evelyn's mind. She was face to face with none other than Helen Martinez and no amount of sugar-coating that name could make it any less bitter. "I'm going to recommend we quarantine you, for your own safety."

"Did Alma make it? She was headed this way with her kid sister and little brother." Helen stood. "Alma Garcia?"

Evelyn's eyebrows rose into her hairline. "You know Alma?"

Helen smiled. "Sure. She'll vouch for me. As will the guys I rode in with."

A clutch of half-dressed, grimy, smelly refugees had massed behind Ms. Martinez. "It's true, Señora. Miss Helen isn't like her brother..."

The rush of voices all told the same story—Helen was one of the good guys, could be trusted, had helped bring Michael Martinez down—but it was too much for Evelyn to process on the spot. She had to remove Helen to another room, for her own safety. "I won't leave you there. I promise, but we need to process the incomers. You understand?"

Helen shrugged. "I'm here as a private citizen. I've come to do my part to heal the breach." She allowed herself to be escorted out of the intake center without so much as a peep of protest.

"Well, I'll be." Cat wiped her forehead on her sleeve. "Didn't see that coming."

"Mom?" Sandy hailed her from the far side of the room. Evelyn made her way past the desks, checking in with people as she went, and joined Sandy and Dev as they prepared to address the masses.

Dev froze when he reached the loading dock. His face was drained of color. "Evelyn, would you mind saying a few words? I... I can't do it."

Evelyn cringed. The idea of speaking to all of these people made her tremble.

Sandy pushed her mother forward. "Seriously, Mom. He has a phobia."

Evelyn stepped to the edge of the loading dock, clearing her throat and firming her resolve. "Hello everyone, I'm Evelyn Parker. On behalf of the council members, welcome to the Anil Kumar Memorial Sanctuary."

The refugees quieted, turning to face her. "We're glad you made it, and appreciate your patience with the intake process, which is necessary for everyone's safety. As you know, the atmosphere outside is deteriorating quickly. We've decided to lock down immediately. If you'd like a last look at the outside world, now's the time." She lifted her arms, indicating the massive garage entrance behind them. Heads swiveled.

Explosions erupted in the distance, sending a collective gasp through the group. Hot wind carried the smell of char and flames racing across the land, burning everything in their path. Evelyn lifted her T-shirt to mask her nose and mouth. Her throat burned, bitterness coating her tongue. Ash flew into the garage entrance like snow flurries, dirtying the cement floor. All this destruction, wrought by greed and hubris. When—or if—they emerged from the bunker, the world would be unrecognizable. Tears wet her cheeks.

The security door chugged to life and began to lower. The dark sky vanished from view, then the trees, and finally the dirt road disappeared as the door thudded closed. A hush fell over the group. Floyd wrapped an arm across Evelyn's shoulder, pulling her close to him. "Who would've thought Dev was scared of public speaking?"

Evelyn wiped her eyes. "Who would've thought I wasn't?" Her fears still crowded her brain, and tensed her body, but she no longer gave in to her urges to escape them. She channeled her anxiety, pushing through it, using it as a guide to comfort others. She offered solutions when she could or asked other people for help when she couldn't.

The pregnant refugee Linda, rose from her seat across from Dr. Fulknier, smiled and waved. Evelyn returned the gesture. The isolation she once craved had no place here. She, and everyone else at the sanctuary, were interdependent, smaller pieces of a whole entity, each person needing everyone else to survive. Whatever came her way in this changed world, Evelyn Parker was ready.

Made in the USA
Middletown, DE
14 October 2023

40780469R00186